More than FAMOUS

FAMOUS NOVEL-TWO

Kahlen Aymes

Cover designed by Sarah Hansen, Okay Creations

Cover photography: © ASJack

Interior Design by Cassy Roop, pink Ink Designs

Published by Kahlen Aymes Books, Inc.

Visit the author's website: http://www.KahlenAymes.com

ISBN: 978-0-9967344-0-0

Version: Sample: 2015.8.30

More Than
FAMOUS

Famous Novel-Two

Chapter 1
Whirlwind

Caden

THE WHIRRING OF the airplane engines surrounding me was the only sound in the quiet darkness of the first class cabin. Most of the cabin lights were off and there was little movement of others to disturb the silence.

The last three months passed by in a blur. Up to now, Brook, Martin and I had many promotional appearances around the U.S., as well as some around the world, but the real juice was starting now as I made my way from London to Rome for our first premiere.

I was meeting Brook and Martin there; it would only be the three of us this time. Well, almost. I sighed in frustration as I thought about Brook on a plane with David, traveling from L.A. at the same time I made my way from London.

With David. Fuck.

I couldn't wait for the time when we could stop all of this pretending. I knew it was necessary to uphold the contracts, but that didn't mean I had to like it. To give David credit, he'd been decent to me whenever we were at events together, but I still felt uneasy around him. I could sense the same tension in him. It was to be expected; we were both in love with the same woman. I still had guilt and jealousy to deal with, but the heart wants what it wants, and it was impossible to deny my feelings for his benefit.

Brook said he'd become a good friend through all this, and even though I trusted her, I wasn't sure I trusted him. There had been many times over the past months I'd been stuck in London when he'd been near her, going to her house to hang out with Nathan. The problem was I didn't believe Nate was the draw. I could see he still wanted her. His eyes tracked her every move in a hungry, predatory sort of way, and he was extremely guarded when he was around me.

But what did I expect? Who could blame him, really? As far as he was concerned I'd stolen his girl.

As far as I was concerned... she was *always* mine. Even before we'd met. Before we were even born.

I felt her in my soul. She was part of me in a way no one else ever would be and I doubted would ever be again. She wasn't a choice I'd made... she just *was*. This was another echo of the book series turned into movies that we were filming.

I closed my eyes and tried to let sleep overtake me, but visions of the recent months flashed behind my closed lids and wouldn't let me sleep. So much had happened with the photo shoots and the many interviews that had been pre-recorded. There were countless airplane trips across Europe and North America; so many that it was beginning to make my head spin. I lost track of time, and where the schedule would take me next, mixed in with more auditions and filming of other work, I was exhausted.

I'd just been home to London, spending ten days with my family for what would be the last real break I'd get until all of the premieres for *The Future of Our Past* ended in Tokyo the coming February.

Holy Hell. It was an endless array of cities, paparazzi and screaming women. It was completely insane. I still couldn't get my head around it all even though I'd dealt with it for the past six years. This seemed worse and more invasive because now my privacy and the need to be able to be open with Brook, was my foremost priority. I never liked crowds and well, these were more like mobs. I'd never bloody get used to it.

I would've been a nervous wreck if Brook wasn't with me for the majority of it. When I'd signed for this movie, I had no idea it would be this much madness. The fans were more adamant than on my other movies, and younger fans turned out in bigger numbers. All I knew was that Brook had become my focus and despite the craziness, I was glad I'd taken this job. She was my reason for everything since her audition.

Brook had a way of grounding me and putting a smile on my face even in the most frantic moments. Her inexperience should make her the uncertain one, but she was solid and confident, less jaded than I. We'd gotten into trouble a few times due to our comments about each other, and our expressions when we looked at each other. Our managers, Jeanne and Denise, literally read us the riot act on several occasions. Hell, it was impossible. I loved her too much to hide it completely, and I didn't want to. Brook just shrugged it off with a small laugh.

I smirked to myself as I thought back to our weekend in San Diego.

It was beyond incredible.

Being surrounded with her very essence had been complete and utter joy. I wanted it to last forever; I wanted it every day, every morning, every night. She was so soft and loving in the way she took care of me. We couldn't get enough of each other, and since then, we hadn't had any time like that alone.

I'd been able to sneak into her house a few times when I'd been in L.A., but it was never like the complete satisfaction of getting to spend day and night with her. I missed her every second she wasn't with me. The loss was like a tangible thing, and it made my heart ache. I thought time would lessen the pain of being apart, but the reverse was true.

I leaned back in my seat and let the memories rush over me, thinking back to the last day of our weekend...

I caught her popping the tab off of my Starbucks iced coffee can while I lay by the pool. The sound made me open my eyes to see what she was up to. The sight of her stunned me as always, but the look on her face was priceless.

Her eyebrow raised and her mouth smirked as she tried to hide the fact that she'd taken it, shoving it into the pocket of her shorts.

"Brook what are you doing?" I had to ask. "Are you trying to make me cut my lip so you can suck my blood?" The corners of my mouth lifted in the start of a grin.

"What?" She tried to brush it off as she lay down on the chaise next to me. "Nope," she said and emphasized the word. She'd been all too good at giving me what I wanted over the weekend and I felt a rush of desire flood me at her teasing remark. She reached over and pulled the tab from her own can, too.

"What are you doing with those?" I laughed as she blushed. "Are you going to auction it off on eBay?" I reached for her hand.

"Hmmph! Give me a break, Cade." She laughed. "If I were going to do the ebay thing, I'd steal a pair of your underwear. I'd get so much more for that. Give me some credit, please." Her mouth twitched as

she bit her lip and cocked her head to one side.

"What then?" I wouldn't let it go, pressing her to answer.

She sighed. "I wanted it to be a surprise..." Her lips pursed and her brow wrinkled.

"You're going to surprise me with a collection of bloody can tabs?" Her brows shot up and her eyes popped up to meet mine. "Don't think I haven't noticed you stealing them all weekend. I watch you like a hawk, in case you hadn't noticed."

"Oh, I notice, but it's usually not can tabs you're watching." Her eyes flashed at me and her lips lifted in a smirk. She was so damn sexy when she flirted with me. I wanted more and more.

"Brook, you're killing me. Are you going to tell me or not?" My fingers traced up and down her arm.

She turned on her side and propped her head on her hand. She had a serious look on her face, but her fingers trailed down my chest to my stomach making me catch my breath.

I thought this was a joke, but maybe it wasn't.

"I'm going to give a little clue to the world about us... to see if anyone can pick up on it." She shrugged.

"What do you mean?" I was intrigued.

"Well, don't you think it's bullshit that we have to hide our relationship and sneak around like we have? Frankly, it pisses me off."

Her expression was hilarious as her face set in a stern line and she tried not to laugh. I felt my eyebrows raise and a grin settled on my face as I watched her.

"Yeah? And?" I asked impatiently.

"Cade, remember in the book with the pad locks? And the coffee Sunday thing?"

"Yeah... of course." I shrugged. "What does that have to do with can tabs?" I laughed at her as she nodded. "Well?"

She moved up to straddle my lap and began to kiss my lips softly as her hands ran down my chest.

"That feels nice, babe, but I'm not going to let you distract me, not until you tell me what you're up to." My hands ran up her waist to her ribs and squeezed lightly.

She threw her head back as she laughed out loud.

"Cade, see? I'm going to put my little collection on a bracelet and wear it in some of the photos and interviews." My eyebrows raised in confusion.

"Brook, I'll buy you more bracelets, you don't have to resort to making them out of rubbish." I was teasing her now. "I think we've both quite risen above that, don't you?"

She pushed my shoulders and sat back on my legs. "God! You're so exasperating." She shook her head at me. "You're Ryan; I'm Julia... so I'm telling the world we're together by giving them a hint. I'm going to connect these with tiny pad locks. Get it now?"

"So you're going to wear them to see if people can pick up the parallel?"

"Yes, exactly. The real diehard fans will get it." Her eyes were sparkling as she looked down at me." I guess it's the rebel in me. It›s a small, insignificant bit of revenge. At least it will make me feel better.

I shook my head at her and she snorted. "They won't know the tabs came from Starbucks."

"We'll know. They'll get the lock part, but the tabs are for us. It's me telling the suits to fuck off. Happy now?" She let out another throaty laugh.

"Delirious!" I smiled as I reached for her. She bent to kiss me *again, sucking my lower lip into her mouth and biting it with her teeth. My heart and my body started to respond.*

My eyes were closed, but I felt her hands come into my hair as she moved up higher on my lap. I slid my hands around her to pull her tighter against me. Her skin was so soft, like silk and she smelled so good.

Her voice lowered as her mouth hovered over mine. "And at least you'll know that it's a connection to you when you see it in some of my pictures." My right hand moved up to the back of her neck to bring her closer. "I'll wear it with my other bracelet."

My mouth split into a wide smile. "That's bloody brilliant, babe. I love it. Thank you." I pulled her down for a series of kisses. Her arms tightened around my neck as our breathing sped up. I knew where this was headed and I couldn't have been happier about it. The weekend had been filled with incredible moments and breathtaking lovemaking sessions. My body and my heart couldn't seem to get enough.

She pulled her mouth from mine and kissed lower across my jaw and throat. Her hot breath scorched along the trail she followed. I felt my dick tighten and grow beneath her.

"I can't wear my ring in public yet, but I'll be damned if they're gonna stop me from wearing something to connect us, okay?"

My heart swelled at her words as I took her mouth hungrily again. She was so amazing in every way. "Yes, I want to tell the world. Now," I'd whispered against her lips.

I took a deep breath and let it out in a sigh as I heard the pilot's announcement that we'd be landing in Rome in thirty minutes. The flight attendant came over to check on me. She was blonde, attractive and she looked at me intently.

"Mr. Carlisle, would you care for anything else?"

"Just some water, thank you."

The last thing I'd done in L.A. before going back to London had been the Movie Phone interview with Brook, Martin and Noah. It wasn't scheduled to air for two weeks yet, in Mid-November, but our frantic schedule demanded we tape it in advance.

There it was; her can tab and padlock bracelet, for all the entire world to see. It was a beautiful thing, considering the meaning behind it. I was so elated about her wearing it that I wasn't able to keep the giddy smile off of my face even though I'd wanted to. Each time I looked at it, I had to renew my effort. I knew I probably looked like a bloody git, but something as simple as having some form of public claim on her, made me so damn happy, I was just beside myself and had teased her mercilessly during that interview. Denise, Joel, Ken and Jeanne had all called to bitch about it, but I was beyond caring.

I leaned back in my seat and prepared myself for the scene on the red carpet. I'd face a huge, horrific mob of screaming fans no doubt. Martin and Brook were going to arrive shortly before me, and I knew I'd be faced with seeing her there with David. I felt she should arrive after me, but the managers insisted I was the A-lister, so I had to be the last to arrive.

I hadn't seen her in ten days, and I missed her so much I could barely stand it.

I would get a few hours at the hotel before I'd have to face the crowds, but I wouldn't see Brook until the red carpet right before the premiere. Her flight schedule didn't allow her any time in Rome in advance and she'd have to come straight from the airport.

My chest tightened and my fists clenched in my lap, wondering how they'd dress and primp her.

Would she be wearing the same clothes all the way from L.A. or would she have to change in the limo with *him* there? I felt so jealous and possessive, even after all of these months of being with her. She'd assured me a hundred times that she and David had made a smooth transition to being friends, but something in my gut told me to be on guard.

I fucking hated that feeling.

I tried to tell myself to be fair. After all, it was a lot to ask of David. Would I have been able to be her friend and stand aside while another man staked his claim on her? After loving her like I did? The answer was clear.

No way in hell.

The flight attendant brought my water and lingered a few seconds. I smiled and ran my hand through my hair and turned away. Looking out the window into the dark night sky, all I could think about was that soon, very soon... Brook would be in my arms again, and the thought made my heart beat a little faster.

Brooklyn

AS DAVID AND I made our way through the Rome airport, we were bombarded with flashing cameras and screaming fans chasing us out to the cars. The bodyguards did their best to keep them at bay, but inevitably, there were some that got too close to us and we were jostled about a few times as we kept moving. Our pace was as fast as we could manage through the crowds.

The Future of Our Past premiere in Rome was the first of several, and I didn't think it'd be this crazy yet. I mean, yeah, the girls were all screaming at Cade during our many mall appearances and book signings, and of course at the MTV awards, but I'd figured it'd be mostly about him and I wouldn't have to deal with that much of it. Apparently, I was wrong.

The schedule was nuts. I'd taken my dress for the red carpet with me in my carry on and changed in the airplane bathroom just before landing. Due to timing, we were going straight there without a chance to check in at the hotel.

Even though David held my hand as we made our way through the throng of fans, he'd been distant during the entire flight.

He and I had transitioned back into friendship, even being able to hang out and joke around without him making snarky comments about Cade, but he was withdrawn now. If I were honest with myself, we didn't really talk about Cade that much and it made it easier. I tried not to rub either one of them in the other's face. It was an unspoken thing that David didn't want to hear it, and I respected that wish. I could understand it totally.

When we got in the car that would take us to the Fiesta del Cinema, I looked over at David as he looked out the car window. His arm up by the window and his chin resting in his hand, his brow dropped over his eyes; he looked lost in unhappy thoughts.

"David, is something bothering you? You've been so quiet."

I wasn't sure if I should have asked the question, but the silence inside the car was killing me. That, combined with the nervousness of this first premiere, I needed to find out what was up.

He turned to look at me without speaking for a moment.

I shrugged. "Well?"

"I just don't think I can do this anymore, Brook. I've tried to be your friend, but I'm still in love with you," he said flatly.

My breath rushed out. I should have just kept my mouth shut.

This isn't the conversation I wanted to have right before stepping out for a premiere, and anyway, I wasn't exactly sure what to say in response. I'd already apologized over and over.

"I don't like fading into the background while you hook up with that British—"

"Please don't start," I interrupted. "I'm sorry this has hurt you and I've told you a hundred times that I never meant for this to happen. I thought we were past all of this." I reached out to take his hand but he pulled his back from me.

His mouth quirked, "I guess you are. Obviously, I'm *not*." His tone was sardonic.

"What brought this on now? Why right before one of the biggest moments of my life?"

He was getting agitated and angry. "I fucking *told you*, Brook! I don't want to do this anymore! I mean what happens now? I deliver you to his arms again and then pretend it isn't killing me while you go off and fuck him in his hotel room, right?"

I felt the heat rise under my skin at his words and felt my cheeks burn.

"You've destroyed me with all of this. I've loved you for years and trusted you when you said you loved me... and yet, you dump me for the first bastard that happens your way."

My face flushed and angry tears pricked the back of my eyes as I looked at him.

"Why *the fuck* are you doing this to me now? You know how I feel, David. You're *still* important to me! I've told you that again and again."

David cut me off. "Yeah? Is that what you tell *him?* That you still love *me*?"

I didn't know what to say. What words would make a difference? I shook my head. "I don't want us to end up hating each other, I never did, but I don't love you like that."

I put my hand over my eyes and swallowed hard as I tried not to let tears fall. I had to get out and face the crowd in only a few minutes and I didn't need this shit now.

And worse, Cade would see me struggling with my emotions. He wouldn't know exactly what was up, but he could read me like a book, so I wouldn't be able to keep the turmoil from him.

The last thing I need is for Cade to believe I'm crying over David.

Suddenly I felt David's arms go around me as he pulled me close. I tried to push against his chest but his hand was on the back of my head, roughly forcing my face closer to his. His mouth was hot as he brought it roughly down on mine. His tongue snaked out and tried to gain entrance to my mouth. I was shocked, but I finally found the strength to push against him again. He was crushing me to him and I couldn't breathe.

I tried to twist my face away, but his hand only gripped tighter at the back of my head. He was hurting me, his other hand digging into my thigh as he pulled my body closer, and then moving to grip my breast. I cried out in pain.

Holy shit! This is a nightmare.

"Does he make you feel the way I did? Does he? Remember what it was like between us?"

Oh, Jesus God. Not even close.

His mouth was wet and ragged as he dragged it from my lips, then across my face. I was petrified, and disgusted that he would force himself on me like that.

My body went limp hoping he would stop; I didn't move a muscle as I waited for him to stop. David brought his mouth back to mine and kissed me again, but softer this time. Without my resistance, he didn't need to force me.

I felt the anger drain out of him, as tears dripped from my eyes. I felt sad that he was so hurt, sad that it had come to this and angry as hell that he would do what he just did.

"Brooklyn, please come back to me. I'll forgive you for being unfaithful to me with him. Just please come back to me and we'll forget any of this ever happened."

We were arriving at the theater and the crowds were screaming everywhere around. I shoved him from me roughly after his grip on my flesh lessened.

My eyes flashed at him and I lowered my voice to almost a whisper. "Don't you *ever fucking touch me* again! Do you *hear* me?" I rasped out.

I angrily moved to the other side of the car as far away from him as possible.

I struggled to wipe the tears from my face. I was so upset my body was shaking and my voice trembled.

"You bastard! I was never unfaithful to you, David! I wasn't with Cade until after we broke up!"

"You fucking expect me to believe that? I saw how he mooned over you!"

I tried to calm down and get control of my emotions. The crowds screaming outside the car reminded me that I had to go out there and act like a star, despite my inner turmoil.

"Look, I never wanted to throw it in your face, but you leave me no choice now. I *love him*, okay? More than I've *ever* loved anyone!

Nothing you say or do will ever change it! Now, I have to step out of this car and put on a happy face in front of thousands of people. I fucking *hate* you for doing this right now!"

He sat back in his seat like I had slapped him, and I ran a trembling hand through my hair, trying to take some calming breaths.

Jesus... what was Cade going to think? It wasn't like I was going to get a chance to talk to him about it before all of the bullshit started. David hurting me didn't even matter compared to what Cade's reaction to it would be.

I took out a mirror and wiped the smudges of mascara from under my eyes and retouched my lip gloss, but my face was pale as hell. Martin was already waiting beside the car for me to join him, along with Ruth, my publicist, but thank God, Cade hadn't arrived yet.

David tried to reach for me again, but gentler this time. He'd seen this side of me before and he knew I was dead serious. I flinched away from him, my eyes glaring.

"I want you off of the red carpet. I want you as far away from me as possible, so the fucking minute I get out of this car and join Martin, you will exit and the guys will escort you out. You wanted this to stop, well, it's stopping. I'm done!" I took another shaky breath.

"Brook, I'm sorry...," he began and I put up my hand to stop him.

"Fucking save it," I said. "I'm so over this bullshit."

His expression hardened as he stared at me, dead calm replacing his desperation. "You know, I could totally fuck you up. I could tell the media everything I know about you and Cade, blow this shit wide open. That's what I *should* do. What will the world think of their golden boy, then? They'll think you're a two-timing whore." His face was livid.

"You know what? Go ahead, David. You'd probably be doing Cade and me a huge favor." Deep down I was scared shitless, but I couldn't let him see that. "Do your fucking worst."

I was shaking as I grabbed the door handle and pushed open the car door. As I stepped out onto the red carpet, I ran my hand through my hair and tried to steady my legs all the while the fans were screaming around me. It took effort not to fall apart.

I felt myself literally crumbling, not ready for any of this; especially after the scene in the car.

Martin came to me and put his arm around me. "Are you okay, sweetheart?" He could see the stress on my face as I struggled not to cry. I bit my lip and nodded, feeling tears threaten again, and shoved my hands in the pockets of the black leather jacket I wore over my dress.

I inhaled deeply, blowing it out as Cade's car pulled up on one side of me, while David was being escorted out on the other.

Talk about fucking irony.

The minute Cade opened his door the screams increased by a hundred decibels, and my hungry eyes sought him out. He was as gorgeous as ever, and my aching heart screamed for me to run into his arms. *God, I need him right now.*

I stepped back with Martin to wait as he cleared the car and tried to get control of my emotions.

I hadn't seen him in ten days. It felt like ten years, especially when I was feeling so fragile. I wanted to feel his strong arms around me, and his passionate kisses on my mouth, but knew that couldn't happen for several more hours. At least I'd have him standing beside me.

We had to get through the movie and the interviews before we'd be allowed to retreat to the hotel, when we could finally be alone and I could tell him about what happened with David. My stomach lurched as I worried over his reaction. He would be outraged.

His eyes searched for me and he smiled when he saw me, but it quickly faded when he saw the look on my face. I knew he could see the angst in my features and he visibly tensed.

Cade's hand ran through his golden hair again and again as he talked to some of the press on the carpet lined up to interview him, a sure sign that he was agitated as well. He walked a few feet toward me, and put his arm around my waist. *Finally.*

He pulled me closer to his side and leaned down to speak in my ear as the cameras began to flash all over again, and the fans increased their din of screams and chants.

"Brook, are you okay?

We were both trying to smile for the cameras and I was extremely shaken.

"Not really. I just had a big fight with David in the car. He threatened to out our relationship to the press. We are *so fucked*!"

I smiled stiffly as his arm tightened around my waist as the cameras flashed a million times a second.

Chapter 2

Seeing Red

Caden

AFTER ALL OF the screaming fans on the carpet and the film had run, we were then ushered into a huge auditorium for the interview session of the premiere. Brooklyn was still visibly shaken and I was worried about her. I'd never seen her so upset, other than the times we'd had to say goodbye. I knew crowds made her uneasy. Maybe as much as they did me, but this... well, I knew this was something else. This had to do with the way David disappeared. When I'd gotten out of the car, I saw Brook's bodyguards walking away with him, but that was all I knew of what had happened.

During the photo calls, I wasn't near her alone and couldn't ask questions. I was going crazy not knowing what happened. Being unable to talk to her was maddening and then the interviews created the same problems. I was very happy to see her, but the look on her beautiful face scared the hell out of me.

She'd been crying and was struggling to calm her breathing for the first twenty minutes on the carpet. I felt her mood as if it were my own.

When she told me she'd had a fight with David and he was planning on going to the press, I felt a mixture of relief and trepidation. Maybe it would be a good thing if we didn't have to hide anymore. I was very private by nature, and didn't feel the need to parade the truth around, but I was sick of the lie. We needed the chance to be together quietly, without having to sneak around, yet not being overly anxious to expose the details.

Now, I had this new worry.

Was she more upset about us being exposed or was she more upset about her fight with David? Given the fact that she'd devised the little bracelet ploy to let out little hints about us, I doubted it was the former. *Shit, maybe it was both.* Damn it, I wouldn't be able to find out until after the interviews were finished.

I glanced at Brook as they sat us down on some black leather chairs in front of thousands of screaming girls. I should be flattered by the attention, but really it struck me as annoying. These women didn't even know me and I was the same person that I was when I was in my other films, so what was all the fuss about?

Brook was shrinking in her chair, visibly cowering from the crowds and the noise. Maybe she was sick. She put on a good front, but it wasn't impenetrable and I could see she was crumbling in the way her shoulders slumped, the paleness of her pained features, and the way she kept running her hands through her hair.

They had us put on some headphones so that the translators could give us the questions as the crowd asked them. It all became sort of surreal, a blur of sorts as the questions passed between the three of us and the crowd's roars rising and falling. The standard questions were always asked, you know, "What's it like to work with Brook?", "Have you read the books?", "Will you do the other movies in the series?" For Brook they were "What's it like to kiss the hottest doctor in the world?", "What's it like working with Caden?", and the same sort of mindless inquiries. It wasn't fair really, how most of the questions were about me, even if they were directed at her. Her contribution to the film was equal to mine, for God's sake.

I caught her glancing my way several times, and I longed to reach out and take her hand in mine, to give her reassurance, to take the pain off of her face. I didn't think she was really listening to the girl asking the next question, because her chin was bent down and she was playing with her hair.

"Cade are you anything like Ryan? Are you romantic to the girls in your life? Is there one special one?"

Yes, she says I'm incredibly romantic, and that's all that matters.

I took a breath and smiled as I considered how to answer the girl without giving too much away.

"Uh... sure, I can be romantic if I'm properly motivated." I smiled as another blast of screams hit me. "I kind of have the, you know the whole attitude which Ryan has that..." I was stumbling a little bit, but I realized how true the words were that I was about to say. "If you're gonna make an effort with someone, then it has to be with that *one* person, and that's it. There's only one true love."

Brook's head snapped up to look at me and I saw something like fear in her eyes. "What?" Her eyes probed mine for the meaning behind my words.

The host of the event spoke and broke our little bubble. "The next question will be for you Brooklyn."

Another girl from the audience stepped up to the microphone; "Brooklyn, what is it like to act?"

I saw her face twist as she searched for the answer. The question was so obscure there could be any number of answers, and surely it was a very personal question. She threaded her fingers through her hair and I heard the emotion rise up in her voice when she spoke.

"Um... it's natural. It came easy, sort of like breathing, I guess." She turned it into a question. Her face went down and she swallowed back the tears I knew were so close to the surface. "Sometimes... it hurts a lot. I mean if you really immerse yourself and become the characters, you can't help it, and I think that's how we made it work so well." She made a gesture in the air with her hand to indicate she really didn't know what type of answer they were looking for.

Sometimes it hurts a lot. Was she talking about the movie, the current situation or both?

Brook didn't look at me for the rest of the interview, which lasted another thirty minutes. I was agonizing over what could be going through her mind; was she sad because she's realizing that she wants to go back to David?

What the fuck happened in that car between the airport and the cinema? I was going completely *bonkers*.

As they finally ushered us down the corridor to the waiting limos, I watched her closely as she walked in front of me. Her resolve was shot, and I guessed the minute we got into the car she'd lose hold of the delicate control she'd maintained for the last four hours of this ordeal.

Martin was with us and I silently prayed that he'd be taking a separate car.

"Cade, Pinnacle wants Brook to ride with me, and we'll meet you back at the hotel, okay?"

This wouldn't do at all. Screw the rules; I desperately needed to talk to Brook, and *now*.

"Um, actually, Martin, I'm going with Brooklyn. Please don't ask any questions, it's personal."

Brook's head came up and Martin shot a look to see what she wanted. Brook bit her lip, and nodded as she looked at the ground.

"Okay. Can we meet for dinner later, then?" Martin's eyes narrowed as he watched the pair of us. "Discuss the itinerary for the rest of the tour?"

"Um, sure, maybe. Whatever Brook wants to do is fine with me," I said softly as I put my arm around her waist to lead her out to the car. I felt her body tremble as we whisked past the curb and I held the door as she entered ahead of me.

Once the car started to move, I reached for her hand and she drew it away from me. My heart stopped. What did this mean?

"Brook, I don't know what happened in the car with David, but I'm here now. Do you want to talk about it?"

She completely disregarded what I said.

"Cade, what was that answer in there?" Her eyes filled with tears and my heart started to ache within my chest.

"What? I don't understand. Which answer?" My voice was low, so the driver couldn't hear my words.

"The one about being with one person and that's it! Were you trying to tell me you thought I was two-timing you with David?"

My eyes widened at her words. I never dreamed she'd interpret it that way, but given all that had happened earlier, I should have considered it. Fuck, I still didn't even know what had happened. Her lips were trembling and her brow crinkled as the tears threatened to overflow.

I took her by the shoulders and turned her to me. "No, love. I said the words because I meant them. You are the one person, *my* one person. I wasn't accusing you of anything... " She let out a sigh and melted into my arms as the tears fell from her eyes.

"I'm so sorry if I'm being a bitch, Cade. This trip has just been awful, but it isn't your fault. I've missed you so much."

I pulled her across my lap and wrapped my arms around her, and she leaned into me.

Jesus, she felt so good.

It had been too long since I'd held her last. I turned my face into the hair at her neck and breathed her in. I wanted to kiss her so badly, but knew that would be too much in front of these drivers.

"I've missed you, too. I couldn't wait to get back to you. I love you," I whispered near her ear and she nodded.

Her fingers curled into my arm, clutching the fabric of my suit jacket. "Me, too."

"Do you want to tell me what happened with David?"

She sniffed against me and slid her arm up around my neck as I traced circles on her back to soothe her.

"Maybe we should wait until we get up to our rooms?" she suggested.

I nodded against her head that was tucked under my chin. I was anxious to know what the hell was going on, but I realized the logic behind her words. I settled back in the seat and held her the rest of the way without talking.

Brooklyn

I FELT BETTER with Cade's arms around me. As always, he was what I needed to get some perspective on things. Our handlers had gotten us checked in and handed us our room keys as we stepped out of the car and made our way into the hotel. Still more screaming fans and we had to stop and autograph a number of pictures and some of the books.

Cade was more in demand than me, so I went in a little ahead of him and made my way up to my suite. It was nice and furnished with cherry wood furniture with plush cushions on the sofa in dark navy blue and ivory stripes. The bed was large and covered in a huge white duvet. I yearned to sink into it.

Martin was going to be disappointed about dinner. I didn't know how he did it, but he was like the Energizer Bunny. He never fucking got tired. Personally, I was exhausted. The time difference wiped me out in combination with the tears and the anxiety I felt.

My eyes were so tired. Crying always did make me sleepy and my eyelids felt like they were lined with sand paper.

There was a large whirlpool bathtub encased in beautiful Italian marble. I looked at it longingly as I took off my jacket and high black heels. Knowing the fan girls, Cade wouldn't get up here for several minutes, so I decided to take a swim in the tub.

Sadness engulfed my heart as I thought back on my fight with David. I really did care about him and it hurt me that he was in pain. I wasn't sure if Cade was going to understand my feelings, and his reaction worried me. I didn't want to hurt him either. I hated that I'd hurt either one of them. But Cade... he was my priority, and I needed to make sure he knew that.

I could read him so well. He watched David exit and then glanced back at my face. He knew I was in turmoil and probably due to something that happened with David. Still, he reached out and pulled me to his side, wrapping his arm around me, no questions asked.

Well, other than if I was okay. He was so beautiful, and good.

I turned the lights out and lit one of the candles on the bathroom counter, before going to the tub to start the water. The sound of the water falling into the tub was soothing to my nerves and I found one of those little hotel shampoos and dumped it in the tub to make bubbles. I smiled to myself. My mother would admonish me for not using some expensive moisturizing bath salts. *Whatever. I wasn't that finicky.*

I pulled the dress over my head and let it fall to the floor, the gauzy material splaying all over the tile. I didn't care if I ever wore the damn thing again anyway. Ruth would have my hide if I ever wore it twice anyway.

As I stepped into the tub, the hot water made me gasp as I eased down into it slowly. My body was strangely aching and I hoped the heat would ease the muscles and relax me. I leaned my head back and closed my eyes as I let the sensations seep into me. It felt so wonderful.

I wasn't sure how long I lay like that before I heard the card in the door and then someone walk into the room. I smiled thinking of finally being alone with him.

I kept my eyes closed but raised my arm so Cade could take my hand. Mmmm... He brought my fingers to his lips, then brushed them back and forth a couple of times.

"You better be who I think you are," I said softly.

He didn't say anything, but came down on his haunches behind the back of the tub and his warm mouth found the chord in my neck; his hand coming up to cup my opposite cheek, his fingers like warm velvet on my skin. Chills ran through me at the touch of his lips on my skin, his husky scent surrounding me. It was heavenly.

"Mmmmm. You taste so delicious." That sexy voice could make any woman drop her panties, and his thumb brushed across my lower lip. He kissed the corner of my mouth and then moved his lips over mine in a deep searching kiss. I loved the way he tasted, too.

I sighed in contentment. "I've missed you so much. Did you have a good time in London?" My eyes opened to stare into his blue depths only inches from my face. He was so close I could feel his breath.

"Brook, there is plenty of time to tell you all of that. Tell me about *tonight*." His eyes were serious as he looked at me. I would never get enough of looking at his face as my hand came up to cover his.

"Why don't you jump in here with me?" My eyes danced into his. He smirked and placed another small kiss on my lips.

"I thought you'd never ask, my love." He stood and started stripping off his clothes. I was mesmerized watching him shed each and every piece before he was standing naked before me. I felt like I was starving; I couldn't stop looking at him in the glow of the candlelight.

I moved up a little as he stepped in behind me and sat down. He pulled me back against his chest, his legs on the outside of mine as we both leaned back and slid deeper into the tub.

"This is my idea of paradise," he murmured in my ear as his hands started to roam over my flesh beneath the water, my skin slippery from the shampoo in the water. He kissed the side of my neck and continued the loving touches all over my skin. I felt the stirrings of desire deep within me and arched my neck back into him as I let out a soft moan.

"Tell me what happened, Brook." His voice was low and sexy, but insistent.

I sighed. I didn't want to ruin the moment, but knew I had to tell him. We'd promised never to have any secrets between us, and I wasn't going back on that.

"Well... David was distant the whole plane ride over here and stupidly, I asked him what was wrong." I paused, but Cade didn't say anything, just kept running his hands up and down my arms, gently soothing me as he waited for me to continue. "I should have just left him be. He told me he didn't want to pretend he and I were together any more, and wanted me to come back to him for real."

I felt Cade's sharp intake of breath as he tensed. "Hey you. You're the one here with me right now. No tensing up necessary. I love *you*." I turned my head and placed an open mouth kiss at the base of his neck and sucked on the skin as I raised my mouth away.

"I know. It's just... I can't help being a little agitated. I'm jealous of every minute he spends with you that I can't." His arms tightened around my torso after sliding over my stomach, and mine slid over them.

"There's more," he stated matter-of-factly.

"There is?" I cringed as I hoped he'd let it lie. I didn't want to tell him about David's trying to kiss me, and what came after.

"Brook, this is me. I hope I know you better than anyone, so you can't ask me to believe you were that upset over a simple statement like that."

He was right, of course.

"Yeah, there was more, but it's really irrelevant. I don't want to ruin our time together tonight, okay?" Cade didn't say anything, which meant he wasn't going to let me get away this easy.

"Okay, the gist of it is that I told him point blank that I'm in love with you, and that he and I will never get back together." I took a deep breath as Cade's arms tightened around me again.

"That's when he threatened to tell the press that you and I are together. I yelled at him and told him to go ahead and that I wanted him as far away from me as possible. And he left. End of story."

I closed my eyes hoping Cade would believe me and let it be. His hands paused on my body for a few seconds and I knew he was fighting with the fact that there might be more.

"This feels so good to be with you... all I want to think about is your hands on my body." My voice was low and sultry and I knew he was as aroused as I was. I could feel the evidence of it behind me, pressing on my lower back. I wrapped my arms around his knees and pulled myself tighter against him, making him groan.

One hand moved to my breast and the other slid lower across my stomach to reach between my legs, his fingers seeking and parting the flesh.

"Oh, God... " I arched my body into him.

"I'll always give you everything you want, love. You know that, right?" His lips burned a trail of kisses down my neck and onto my shoulder and his fingers teased my body to life.

"I'm counting on it," my mouth opened as I gasped. "I love the way you touch me."

His hand became more urgent as he rubbed little circles on the sensitive flesh between my legs, pulling and tweaking my right nipple with his other hand. I could feel my body start to writhe and tighten under his skilled touches.

"Brook, come on, honey. So many nights when I'm away from you, I dream about you like this. I want to see it. I want to hear you come. I need it, love."

"Jesus, Cade. I love you." I leaned back against him as he continued to play my body like an instrument. I wanted to touch him, but the only place I could reach were his legs and up around his shoulders to the back of his head as I tried to arch up to kiss him.

His mouth closed over mine in a hot kiss; his tongue dove into my mouth the way his fingers found their way into my body, his other hand following the same path to take up rubbing where his other left off.

"Uhhh... mmmm... Cade. Oh, God. I'm close." I panted his name over and over.

"That's right my love. I'm doing this to you. You're mine, babe. I love you, so much." I felt my body clench and pulse around his fingers as I came, my body convulsing and twitching as the spasms washed over me. I was breathing hard as Cade's hands lightened their pressure, slowing their movement, and then sliding them up my body around my ribs to cup my breasts.

His face buried in my neck, he kissed me and told me over and over how much he loved me.

As my breathing slowed back down, I turned in his arms and took his mouth with mine. I was starving for his kisses and I wanted his tongue in my mouth, as I fisted my hands in his hair to bring him closer, deeper. We kissed over and over again, wanting more and more of each other.

God, I loved this man so much. I couldn't even breathe without him.

He pulled his mouth from mine to suck on my lower lip and I felt his hot breath fan out on my face. "I want you, Brook. I want you, now. Right now." His sexy voice filled me with new rush of desire, as his arms slid around my body and he went to lift me up on to his lap so we could make love. He was flushed and urgent, almost frantic in his movements.

"Uuuhhhh." I flinched against him, and he stilled instantly.

"Brook, what is it? Did I hurt you, honey?" His eyes searched my face; his pupils were dilated, his lips swollen from our passionate kisses, and a slight flush to his cheeks. His hands moved to both sides of my face as he brushed my wet hair back.

I felt a sharp pain when he lifted me, and I had no idea what it was from. My eyes were half-lidded with desire as I bent to take his mouth with mine again. His arms went around my hips to pull me to him, and I winced again.

"Brooklyn, what the hell? What's wrong?"

"Nothing." I shook my head. "Just hold me, Cade. Love me, please."

He drew back to look at me his eyes skating across my breasts and then like lightning he leaned forward to look over my body. Before I knew what he was doing he was standing up, lifting me out of the tub to stand me up in front of him. I shivered from the removal of the hot water and his body from mine as he turned me to look over the left side of my body.

His face turned to stone, the color draining from his features, then flushing red.

"*What the fuck?* How did you get these bruises, Brook? Tell me, fucking *now!*"

I saw my reflection in the mirror and was shocked to see that I had a bruise on my rib cage and one on my thigh, but I wasn't sure how they got there. Maybe during the rush through the airport, but I couldn't say for sure.

Cade's breathing was coming in short bursts as he grabbed his pants and threw them on.

"Brook, I'm not going to ask you again. Tell me or I'll draw my own bloody conclusions. *Tell me!*" he yelled at me.

He saw me flinch, and his face softened slightly as he brought a towel around me. His hands were so gentle but he was so upset that he was visibly shaking.

I put my hand on his bare chest. "Cade. Look at me," his hand came up to cover mine and I saw there were tears in his eyes that began to spill softly to his cheeks.

"Did that motherfucker do this to you? I will *fucking kill him* for touching you!" His voice was fierce, and I could see the muscle in his jaw working as he struggled to get a hold of himself.

I felt my own tears overflow as I tried to put my arms around him… I started to sob. "Cade, please listen to me. Don't. Don't shut me out right now." Suddenly his arms closed around me and he cried into my shoulder. My eyes closed as we quietly held each other for a few minutes.

"Brooklyn. You need to tell me what happened. Now. I mean it. Everything." He pulled back and looked in my face; my heart exploded into a million pieces at his hurt expression.

I took his hand, and pulled him into the other room, to the sofa to sit beside me. I reached up to touch the side of his face as I looked in his eyes. I let my thumb brush back and forth on his jaw.

"I told you what happened." He stiffened before I could continue. "Wait," I tried to control my emotions but my voice trembled as I held him. "Please, let me finish. I don't know how I got these bruises. Honestly. I mean, maybe rushing through the airport. Things happened so fast, that I honestly didn't even feel sore until tonight."

I took both of his hands in mine as we sat there, both of us crying silently. The tears on his cheeks broke my heart. The fact that he would get so upset so fast worried me.

"Did he *touch* you?" Cade asked quietly.

"After I told him I loved you, he tried to kiss me." Cade's hands tightened on mine and I knew I had to try to put it in perspective before he blew it out of proportion. "It was only a kiss, babe. Yes, he clutched at my body, and tried to pull me to him, but I didn't respond. I-I turned my face away."

"Brook! You should have told me the minute I got out of that fucking car." His eyes were tortured as they looked into mine.

"I... I didn't want to hurt you like this. It meant nothing to me, and it's over. You are what matters." My eyes begged for his understanding. I tried to smile through my tears. "Besides, how would we have kept our secret with you beating the shit out of David at our first premiere, hmmm?"

His mouth quirked a little at the corner as he listened to my words, but his eyes were full of sadness. He nodded softly.

"Well, I'm still going to bloody kill that little bastard." He raised my hand to his mouth to place a soft kiss on the back of it. "No one kisses you but me... and for sure as hell manhandle you like that... at least while I'm breathing."

My heart swelled in my chest at the tenderness in those words.

"He apologized, afterward. And Cade, I feel sorry for him. He really does love me. In his way."

Cade's head snapped up and he shook his head. "Fuck no, he doesn't. Don't make excuses for him, Brook. There is no excuse for hurting you or touching you against your will. And, I'm going to make bloody well sure he knows it."

His arms went around me and as his fingers wound in my hair to bring my mouth to his in a gentle kiss, a sharp contrast to how David had been.

"Will you stay with me tonight? We can deal with David tomorrow. Please?" I whispered against his mouth.

Chapter 3

Brooklyn

I WOKE UP to the sound of my phone ringing and Cade stirred slightly at the sound as well, flinging his arm over me and pulling me close to his body. Even in sleep he was gentle, subconsciously aware of my bruises. I was stiff and sore as I snuggled into him, pressing my lips to his chest and snaking my arm around him. I took a deep breath enjoying the scent of his skin and faint remnants of his cologne all around me. The warmth from his body seeped into mine as our legs tangled together.

That song really was annoying. I really needed to change it. I had used 'Flash' by Queen because of David's role in a Marvel flick he'd been in. I was young and idiotic, and he thought the superhero theme was cool. It was clear it grated on Cade's nerves like nails down a chalkboard.

I pushed the hair from my eyes and looked at the clock and it said Noon, which would make it 4 AM in L.A. I hated the jet lag involved in traveling the world. It was exhausting. I didn't want to move and

I sure as hell didn't want to answer that phone call. After the scene yesterday, what could David want? He'd made his position perfectly clear.

My brow wrinkled as I considered the possibilities. I suppose I should find out. My phone tinged as the message was left.

Ugh! I closed my eyes.

I'd never seen Cade as pissed as he was last night when he'd discovered what David had done. An involuntary shiver ran through me at the memory. He'd been so furious, I wasn't sure what he would have done to David had he been anywhere in the vicinity. Lucky for everyone involved, he hadn't been.

Cade definitely wasn't a violent person, so this side of him took me by surprise. I knew he still would want to confront David at some point, but I didn't know what good it would do. Cade's feelings had been a mixture of anger, frustration and pain at knowing that David had touched me at all, and worse, tried to kiss me.

My heart ached when I saw the tears on his cheeks. He had been so tender with me later, touching me with kid gloves... making sure I knew he would always treat me with respect, love and reverence.

My face flushed with color as I remembered the several hours that followed and the passionate, yet gentle, lovemaking he'd lavished on me, always careful not to hurt me.

He just wanted to hold me so there would be no chance of any further pain, but I'd begged him to finish what we started, and then we couldn't stop for hours. We were both full of want from the separation and the out-of control emotions from earlier in the evening.

I smiled to myself. He'd turned me into an insatiable wanton woman whenever he touched me... sometimes with only a look or even a memory. I couldn't get enough of his body and hands, and his beautiful voice always making love to me with his words; and, his perfect mouth. I blushed at the knowledge of how easily he could make me want him and with such amazing intensity.

"What are you thinking about with that sexy smirk on your face?" Cade's hand came up to brush my cheek gently, then raising my chin so he could place a kiss on my mouth.

"Last night. You. Always, you..." His hold on me tightened slightly as did mine on him. "I never want to move. You feel so good. I love being with you. Will you forgive me for losing it last night? When I found out what he'd said to you... that he touched you, I just went crazy. I'm sorry, my love. I never meant to yell at you." He kissed the top of my head that rested on his shoulder.

"I know. I understand. I love that you care about me that much. Having Cade Carlisle jealous over me is sorta hot." I smiled.

"Hmmph!" He snorted. "Are you kidding, Brooklyn? I'm so furious I can't even put it into words. I still want to beat him to a bloody pulp." He tensed as he said it.

"Cade." I said gently, and placed my folded hands on top of his chest to rest my chin on them as I looked in his face. Moving made me wince a little and his brow dropped over his eyes and he drew in his breath.

"That bastard, Brook. My blood is still fucking boiling."

"Babe, I know and I love you for it. It's so sweet." I smiled up at him.

"Sweet?" His brow raised and his mouth quirked. "It's bloody sweet?"

"Yep. There's no need to go after David or for you to get hurt in the process."

"You think I'd get hurt? Pffft! Fuck that." He was agitated as he moved from beneath me to sit up on the side of the bed.

"I didn't mean he could hurt you, physically, babe. He could do damage in other ways. We don't need the wrong type of publicity right now." I moved up behind him and wrapped my arms around him and snuggled up close to his back. I nuzzled into his neck and his hand came up to cover mine in front of his body.

"I know, but I can't let this go without saying something, Brook."

My phone went off again, and I started. Cade knew the ring tone and stiffened in my arms.

"He's got a lot of nerve calling you after yesterday." He stood up and walked into the bathroom, leaving my empty arms wanting.

"Cade, please don't pull away from me. I know you're upset, but don't let this come between us, okay? It's over." I waited in silence and my mind pictured him in the bathroom with both hands resting on the vanity before he decided how to answer me.

"Cade?"

He came back out with a towel around his waist. "I don't know. How do you want me to feel, Brooklyn? The thought of him trying to kiss you is bloody bad enough, but to put his hands on you against your will... Bloody hell!" I could see the color rush into his face as he spoke. "I can't stand the fucking thought of it, let alone the reality that he could bloody well convince you to leave me." His hands went to his hips, and his head dropped as he rubbed the back of his neck.

Still on my knees, I reached out a hand to him.

I watched the conflict cross his features until finally he took my outstretched hand. I tugged him to me until he sat on the bed and then I crawled into his lap. His arms circled around me immediately as I settled in close to him.

"That isn't going to happen, so what can I do to make you feel better? What do you need to happen?" My hand traced patterns on his chest as he held me, and he sighed, but he didn't say anything right away.

"I don't understand you, Brook. You should want me to pound the shit out of him."

"The truth is he does care about me, and I can understand his feelings to a point. You've got me, he lost me to you and he has to be hurting. I thought he was over it, but he was only pretending to be my friend because he thought he'd be able to win me back." I reached up to kiss the underside of his jaw. The stubble rough against my mouth, but I liked it. He was oozing sexuality without even trying.

"I knew it."

"David knows now that there is no chance I'll ever leave you, Cade. I told him flat out, okay?"

He took my hand off of his chest and took it to his lips where he placed a wet kiss to the palm, his eyes never leaving mine. He took a deep breath and smiled.

"Okay, babe. So I won't kill him then, but he and I are going to have a few choice words between men, yeah?"

I let out my breath. "Yeah, okay." I smiled and set my forehead against his cheek. "I love you."

"So, I *guess* I love you too." He laughed before his mouth descended on mine in a hard kiss. My mouth opened to his and our tongues slid on and around each other's as we deepened the kiss. My hands slid around his waist as he held me on his lap when the phone went off again.

*Flash! Ahh ahh!"*My phone lit up. Cade stiffened and pulled away from my mouth.

"Brook, bloody hell, *please* change that fucking ring tone. It drives me up the wall! I'm begging you."

I wound my arms around Cade's neck and buried my face in his shoulder trying to stifle a laugh.

"Um…" I bit my lip as I looked at his face with amused eyes, "what would you suggest I change it to, then?" My shoulders were still shaking with laughter as my brows rose.

"Well… 'Beat it' might be more appropriate."

We both burst out laughing and Cade tightened his arms around me. I threw my head back and giggled. "Oh my God! That's hilarious!"

"Yeah, probably that wanker's favorite activity of late. That's bloody brilliant."

We both laughed so hard we cried.

Several minutes later after our laughter had died down we lay on the bed facing each other. I could've stared into his face forever and never tire of the sight.

Cade took my arms gently, and pulled me closer to him, before brushing the hair off of my face.

"You're so beautiful, honey." He placed a soft kiss on my mouth.

"Mmmm… I want more." I moved closer and moved my mouth up to his.

The phone rang again and Cade rolled away from me onto his back to stare at the ceiling. "Fuck! Just take the call, Brook!"

I gathered the sheet around me and went to find my phone in my purse.

"Yeah?"

"Hey Brook. It's David."

"Um, I know."

"Can we talk? They have us on the same flight later, and I thought we should talk first."

I bit my lip and glanced at Cade. *Shit. I forgot about the flight with him.*

Cade rolled to his side and propped up on his elbow as he listened intently to my side of the conversation.

"Maybe, David. I'm not happy about what happened and um, I'll need to talk to Cade."

"Oh, I see." I could hear the sadness in his voice. "I really need to speak with you before we leave, so can you just call me when it's okay to come down there?"

"Yeah. Okay."

"I'd like to talk to you alone. Without Cade there."

I sighed. "I'm sure you would, David, but unfortunately after that scene in the car, you've put me in a difficult position. He's very upset, but I'll ask him."

"What, is he your fucking dad now?" His tone took on a sneer.

"David, enough. You did this, not Cade. He cares for me and is feeling a tad protective right now. Deal with it."

Cade's eyebrows shot up sarcastically, then he angrily pushed off the bed, going into the bathroom and slamming the door behind him.

Crap!

David sighed on the other end of the line, but didn't say anything.

"Okay, I'll call you back. Bye." I closed the phone and threw it back in my purse before going to the bathroom door and knocking.

"Cade, can I come in?"

He flung open the door to let me in. The water was running and he walked toward the shower, pulling his towel off as he went and giving me a good view of his gorgeous ass.

Steam filled the room as he went about his shower without saying a word to me.

"Why are you mad at me? If you want to talk to David, he's going to come down here when I call him back. He said he wants to talk to me."

"I'll bet he does. Are you going to ask me to leave before he gets here?"

"No. He doesn't want you here, but I do." Cade turned his head to look in my face and I bit my lip. "Babe, what did I say that upset you?"

"I'm a *tad protective* of you, am I? I *care* about you, is that it? Jesus, Brook, I care about my next door neighbor's dog, for Christ's sake, but not even close to adequately describing what I feel for you."

I smiled despite myself. His possessiveness sent a rush of love right through me. It was sweet and kind of cute.

"What should I have said? I figured you'd have some things you'd want to say to him yourself. Don't you?"

He was shampooing his hair and he stopped and leaned his head against the side of the tile. "Yeah, I'm sorry. I'm just wound really tight, I guess. I didn't expect the feelings that would rush through me at the sight of those bruises, love."

I threw down the sheet and opened the shower door. When he raised his head and turned to me, his eyes raked across the bluish marks and the pain flashed across his features.

"Hey, I'm here to make you feel good; not cause you pain." I looked into his eyes and raised his hand to my breast. "I know these hands will never hurt me," I whispered against his mouth as his arms slid around me and his mouth opened over mine in an earthshaking kiss, his tongue sliding into my mouth to play with mine.

"Uhhh... " I moaned against his mouth and then dragged my lips down to his shoulder as he bent to lift me, taking all of my weight in his arms and pinning me up against the shower wall. I sank my teeth into his neck and Cade groaned.

"Oh God, Brook," he breathed against my skin as he slid inside my body, filling me with every inch of him. Making love with him was amazing every time; to feel his body connected so intimately with mine, knowing he wanted me as much as I wanted him was everything I needed and more.

He was everywhere. Over me, under me, all around me, and inside of me; yet it wasn't enough.

I couldn't touch him enough, get close enough to his body, or taste enough of his kisses. I wanted more. Always more. I needed to ease the ache in his heart caused by the events of the last twenty-four hours, wanted to show him how much I loved him, and that I'd always be his.

As our bodies moved together in the heat of the shower, we needed no words between us.

In the total silence, except for the sounds of the water rushing and our panting breaths, our bodies communicated our love better than words could.

The desperation we felt to be together, the pain we'd gone through to get to this place, the overwhelming love between us... It was all screaming in the silence, as he brought my body, heart and soul to places only he could take me. He pushed into me over and over, our hips grinding together, our mouths hungry as he made love to me.

When it was over, he held me in place for several minutes, placing soft kisses all over my face and then on my mouth, his body still connected to mine as we regained control of our breathing.

Finally, he spoke as he rested his head on the tile beside my head and turned his mouth toward my ear.

"Dear God, I love you, Brook. If I could never touch you again, having you like this for even a moment is worth an eternity of pain."

I wrapped my arms and legs around him and held on for dear life as my heart squeezed within my chest.

Caden

AS I SAT in the living area of the suite waiting for David to arrive, I heard Brook fidgeting in the loo. She was nervous about what I was going to say to him. He'd be left in no uncertain terms of where we both stood in regard to Brook. I'd make sure of it.

I was dressed casually in black jeans and a white button down with the long sleeves rolled halfway up my forearms and both Brook's and my bags were waiting by the door. I had called Jeanne and asked her to book me on the same flight as Brook and David and to make sure she and I were seated together.

"Cade, you know we're supposed to keep you and Brooklyn traveling separately."

"For God's sake, Jeanne, can you just do it this time? Something's happened and she needs me with her. I'll explain everything when we get back to L.A. Martin and David are both on that flight, so what's the bloody difference? We won't be seen at the airport alone, and you can send different cars for us, okay?"

There was a knock on the door and Brook came out of the bathroom. Pausing to look my way, she started toward the door when I indicated that I'd be right there.

"Okay, Cade. I'll take care of it."

"Thanks, Jeanne, I love you, you know, but don't tell Denise, she'll get jealous." I smiled into the phone.

"Okay," she laughed. "Me, too. See you both when you get back."

I rang off and waited as I listened for a moment to the exchange in the other room.

I hovered back from the doorway and waited.

"David, what did you need to say to me?"

"Just that I'm so sorry about yesterday in the car, but I love you and the thought of you with him, makes me nuts."

"I accept your apology, but um, nothing is going to change between us. I'm in love with Cade. I'm sorry. I never meant to hurt you. Some things just happen." My heart filled up as I finally heard her say the words to him.

Brook was dressed for traveling too, in jeans and black leather jacket she wore on the red carpet over a white T-shirt. I could see her running her hands through her hair in the mirrors reflection across from me.

He took a few steps toward her, reaching out toward her. It was my cue to casually turn the corner and lean on the doorframe.

"After yesterday, I'd think twice before you ever fucking touch her again." My voice was low, but menacing. He stopped and his hands dropped to his sides as he looked back at Brook.

"So what? You hide him in the bedroom to ambush me?"

Brook started to speak but I moved forward and took her arm, pulling her slightly behind me to my right side.

"I'd reconsider your tone when you talk to her. I haven't quite figured it out in light of current events, but she seems to really care for you, and her feelings are my first priority, which is where you get lucky."

My eyes narrowed as I looked at him, the anger simmering just below the surface, I could feel my muscles tighten and my skin began to burn.

It wasn't really my style to rub salt in the wound but he'd hurt her, so I would make my point, and make it well.

"Brook told me what happened in the back of that bloody limousine. I was fucking livid, to put it mildly. If it were up to me, I'd rip your bloody head off; however, she seems to think you'll behave from now on." I took her hand and brought it to my mouth, looking at him from over her hand. "Is she right?"

"I care about her. I love her."

Brook put her hand around my arm above my elbow.

That's my girl, I thought, *show him you're mine.*

"We both know that if you really loved her, you'd respect her wishes and let her go." I sighed as I looked at him and shook my head. "You certainly wouldn't be trying to man handle her."

Seeing the defeated flash across his features, I suddenly found myself feeling sorry for the bloke.

Jesus, get a grip, Cade. This wanker tortured you for months.

"I've learned to accept that the two of you have become friends, even though it's against my better judgment. It's what she wants, so I'll deal with it. For *Brook.*"

My gaze never wavering from his flushed face as I felt her hand tighten on my arm. I kept my voice even as I continued.

"What I *won't accept or allow* is a repeat of last night. You're very lucky you weren't around last night when I found out, because I would have beaten you to a bloody pulp. I swear to Christ, if I *ever* hear of anything like that again, I will not be responsible for my actions. Am I clear?"

"You're overreacting. It's nothing I haven't done a hundred times," David stammered.

I put my hand up to stop his words. "Am I? For a fucking year I wanted her, but I didn't try to kiss her or seduce her against her will.

I respected her bloody choice and I expect no less from you now that she's with me." I knew my mouth quirked at the corners when I said it.

Damn it, I couldn't help it, the little bastard!

He glanced at Brooklyn who stayed by my side with my hand in front of her, still holding her behind me.

"You know Cade; you don't have to be such a prick. You got what you wanted. What you worked *so hard* to steal from me."

"I don't see it that way, at all." I shrugged. "This thing between Brook and I is bigger than the both of us. I'm sure you're a decent guy otherwise she wouldn't care for you like she does, but she means everything to me, and I will do whatever is necessary to protect her. Even from you."

The silence hung over us like a cloud and I ran my hand through my hair as my eyes narrowed; watching him.

Brook finally spoke. "David, I'm sorry you've been hurt. Truly. I... I meant it when I said I'd like to be friends, but I'll understand if you can't do that."

"Yeah. I don't know. I've tried to do that, and it hasn't worked. I'm sorry, Brook."

"I know." She smiled weakly. "I hope we can work past this and forgive each other, someday."

She went to him and put her arms around him in a short hug. His eyes were wary as I watched him put his arms around her to hug her back, before she moved out of his arms and came back to my side

"Are we finished then? It's almost time to go," I said when she moved toward me.

David's eyes narrowed as he turned to go and slammed out the door.

Brook flinched and I went over and took her in my arms and

placed a kiss in the curve of her neck.

"Okay, love?"

"Yeah. Just don't let go of me."

"Not in ten lifetimes." I pulled her tighter against my chest and bent my face into her hair.

Chapter 4

Premiere Mania

Brooklyn

IT WAS FINALLY here. What we'd worked for the entire past year, and now, one short year later, my life was completely different. I'd watched the news and there was a report about our premiere at Mann's Chinese Theater showing the fans lining up outside more than forty-eight hours in advance. *Jesus, that was completely unbelievable!* I knew it was due to the book series and the fact Cade had top billing. I was lucky to have him on a film with me so early in my career. No way would I have had this kind of visibility without him.

Cade's family was in town, and they, along with my parents and brother, would be attending with us. He was staying with them at the Beverly Wilshire, but our families were going to arrive apart from each of us. For once, Pinnacle was letting us arrive together due to the mass amounts of fans and traffic jams that would be involved. Thankfully, Noah, Jennifer, Wendy, Gavin, and the rest of the cast would arrive before us, which would limit our time at the press stations and with the fans before the movie began.

This was a weird experience for me. My publicist, Ruth, hired a stylist, and they'd flown dresses in for me from New York, Paris and London, as well as shoes and accessories.

Okay, seriously? They are making way too much out of this; especially since most of the fans would be clamoring to get a glimpse of Cade, and they wouldn't give a *rat's ass* what I'd be wearing.

Frankly, the only reason it mattered to me was because Cade would be looking at me so I always wanted to be as beautiful as possible.

Ruth and I picked out a midnight blue, strapless gown in silk chiffon that was fitted through the bodice with a flowing skirt that had been tailored so the hem fell perfectly to the floor to brush the top of the strappy high heels. I knew that a little skin would tantalize and tease Cade, so I'd give him a little taste. There would be women throwing themselves at him throughout the evening and I wanted to look my best.

For the past month, he'd been getting thousands of letters from fans begging to meet him, stating their undying love. He'd teased me, mocking that he didn't find even one love letter from me within the many piles. I just laughed it off.

"Even if I did send one, how would you find it in there? That's Mount Everest!" I'd shoved him down amongst the piles, and he pulled me with him and we'd ended up making out in the middle of them all. *Take that, fan girls.* I laughed to myself at the memory.

What worried me more were the half a dozen or so personal notes sent to him through his manager from actresses asking to meet up with him at the after party at the Armand Hammer Museum. Pinnacle made it plain that Cade was to socialize at that damn thing, and make sure he appeared *unattached.* Well, he damn well was attached.

For the first time, David wasn't going with me, but as far as the world was concerned, he and I were still together. This wasn't going to be so much fun watching Cade talk and flirt with a lot of the women there, even though I knew it was part of the job.

His job. That's what he called it. To me it was more.

The only consolation was Cade had a radio interview pretty early the following morning, so hopefully, he'd have an excuse to leave early before too much socializing with actresses like Roxanne Mason.

She'd sent him *two* notes. *Please.* I couldn't help huffing and rolling my eyes at the thought. *Could she be more obvious?*

They particularly pushed Roxanne at Cade because she had a movie coming out from the studio shortly after our movie released. What a mega-media machine; to have the two leads from two of their movies hook up? There were plans to have Cade meet her out for coffee and a couple of other 'dates' as well.

I wanted to throw up, and it wasn't nerves over the premiere either. It was particularly grating because the studio was working the "relationship" angle for Roxanne's movie, but Cade and I had to lie about ours.

Ruth had the hair stylist put my hair up which was unusual for me but I liked it. There were little wisps trailing down on either side of my face and my jewelry was simple. That was me; simple, easy, no bullshit and no pretenses.

After this premiere we'd have the Western European circuit, which would include Munich, France, Berlin, and London, all the first week of December. That was going to kill us, but at least I'd get some alone time with him then.

Ruth was fiddling with my hair and shoving a black clutch in my hand as she went over the designers I was wearing. I rolled my eyes as I checked my make-up one last time.

"What is that? What who do you have on?" Her face was stern, insistent as she looked at me.

"Ruth, come on. Is this really necessary? These girls care more about what brand of hair gel Cade uses than whom or what I'm wearing."

"Brook," she said; her irritation clear. I sighed.

"Okay, the dress is Balenciaga, the shoes and purse, are Christiana… Er, somebody or other, and the necklace is Chanel."

"Don't be flippant. This shit is important, especially if we think this movie is going to explode as projected. Your career could take off and you could be the next Angelina Jolie! We don't need these gossip shows dumping on you before you even get out of the gate. So who did your shoes?"

I laughed out loud. "Why would I want to be the next Angelina Jolie? She's strange. First she's wearing some dude's blood around her neck, then she's a home wrecker and she's adopting and popping out so many kids, she can't even remember all of their names. Not to mention all those tattoos. What a nightmare. Jesus." I shook my head. "Cade would flip if I got any tattoos, or you know, wore a vial of his blood around my neck," I said and smirked at her. Really, I didn't think the actress was weird at all, I mean, to each their own, but playing with Ruth was fun.

I was making fun of her and she was getting frustrated. I bit my lip to keep from smiling as I peered at her reflection in the mirror. She was getting hot.

"Brook! Your *shoes*?" Her eyes widened and her mouth set as she glared at me.

"Ugh! Ruth!" I stood up and picked up the shoes to put them on, glancing at the label in the bottom as I did so.

"Um... *Christian* La-boo-tin, okay?" I read it off and looked at her with a shrug.

"No. Not okay. That's pronounced loo-bow-tawn! Got it?"

I was laughing again as I shoved my bare feet into the shoes.

"What the fuck am I doing here if you're just going to make fun of me, huh?" she huffed at me.

I sobered up and went to give her a hug. "I'm sorry, Ruth. You're right. I'm just nervous and am trying to have a little fun. I knew the shoes and purse were Louboutin." I made sure to pronounce it correctly this time. "I was only playing with you, okay?"

Ruth cocked her head to one side and I could see her tongue in her cheek.

"You *know* you love me." I was smiling at her again.

She let out a huge sigh and relaxed. "Yeah, I *love* you, all right."

"I know." I moved toward the door when my mother called from downstairs to tell me the limo was outside. Cade would already be in the car.

"Relax, Ruth. I got this, I promise. I won't embarrass you."

Downstairs, I hugged my parents and brother goodbye as Cade's driver, Shane, waited in the foyer. They were all dressed to kill and looked very stylish.

"Wow, you guys look amazing."

"We're very proud of you, Brooklyn. Tonight is your night and you look beautiful." My dad hugged me again, and my mom handed me my wrap as the driver waited for me in the hall. The fans camped outside my house prevented Cade from coming in.

"Good evening." The driver said, nodding at my parents and then my brother and me. "Mr. Carlisle offers his regrets at not being able to come inside to collect Miss Brooklyn, and begs your pardon. He said he would like to spend some time with you at the after party so he can introduce you all to his family. Would that be acceptable?"

My mom's face glowed at the English formality and respect Cade was exhibiting, even if he couldn't do as he wished. My heart thumped in my chest at the look on her face. My father's lips lifted in a smile and I breathed a sigh of relief. Cade had met my mother, but had yet to spend any time with my father.

"Why, yes, thank you. Tell Cade that's just fine, Shane."

He bowed his head to her, and then ushered me to the door. "Shall we go, miss?"

"Yes, thank you," I answered and preceded him through, as he held the door open for me.

This was it; the big U.S. premiere. It was finally here, and I was nervous. From our phone conversations earlier in the day, it was clear Cade was a little out of sorts as well. Neither one of us knew what to expect. If Rome had given us a taste, this would be madness.

Shane opened the door for me and I slid in next to Cade. He was impeccable in all black, his shirt, suit and tie all the same tone. His hair was perfectly messy as usual, and his eyes were bright as he looked at me, with a beautiful smile on his face.

The minute Shane closed the door; he took me in his arms and placed a hot kiss on my mouth.

"You look gorgeous, love. I missed you." His blue eyes devoured me.

"You just saw me this morning." I poked him in the ribs with my index finger.

"Yeah. I missed you." He reached out to cup my face as our eyes met.

"Are you ready for this?"

We both leaned back in the seats and faced each other. "As ready as I'll ever be, I guess." I searched his face for reassurance. He had done this numerous times. "Can you believe it's been an entire year? It's weird, isn't it?" I didn't really know how to put my thoughts into words.

"Yes. Only a year since we met, and this all started, but so much has happened in that year. The best part is us, Brook. Kahlen writing the books; the movie being made... I see all of it as fate's way of making sure you and I find each other. We were meant to be."

Thud. My heart was beating so fast at his words. How in the hell did he do that all of the time? His words melted me and lifted my heart right out of my chest.

My eyes began to sting and well with tears as I looked at the beautiful man who had changed my life.

"You're amazing. Thank you for being in my life, and for loving me so much."

His eyes and smile softened. "Like I have a choice in the matter. You're everything to me," he said words that echoed Ryan's, but I realized they were his words and he meant them.

He pulled me into his arms and his mouth brushed mine. "I'd like to make love to you right here, but I know Ruth would kill me. Literally." The corners of his mouth quirked in the adorable way I loved.

"Yeah, I already yanked her chain enough tonight."

"What?" He took my hand between both of his and laughed.

"Oh, I teased her about not knowing the designers I'm wearing. She thinks that crap is *so* important."

We arrived at Mann's where the u-shaped red carpet awaited us with the thousands of screaming fans. I could hear the din from several blocks away through the closed windows of the limousine. The skylights sweeping back and forth across the sky guided us to our destination. This was really happening. With the rest of the cast already there, we'd be the last to go into the theater, where our families would be ushered through a back door to meet up with us.

"Did your sister and brother come with your parents?" I'd met his younger sister Layla, but had yet to meet his older brother, Oliver or his parents. I was a little nervous at the thought of meeting them. Cade read my mind.

"They'll love you, Brook. We won't have much time to talk with them tonight, but I'd like to arrange something for tomorrow evening, okay?"

"Jeanne told me that we can't have our parents socializing beyond the premiere because it screams that you and I have a relationship outside of the film, but maybe I can sneak over there and have breakfast or something while you're at your radio thing."

"Yeah, I'd like to be there with all of you, but I guess that would work. Are you sure?"

"Sure. I want to know them, Cade. Don't worry, I won't ask any embarrassing things about you, I promise." I grinned at him and he smiled in return.

The screams got louder as we inched closer to where we'd disembark from the limo. He brought my hand to his mouth and placed a soft, open-mouthed kiss on the top.

"Here we go. I won't be able to kiss you all night, so I need one for the road." He smiled as he tilted my chin up with his hand and covered my mouth with his. I opened to him and put my hands at the back of his head, pulling him closer, but careful not to make a mess of it. Our tongues slid deliciously into each other's mouths as we sucked and pulled on each other's lips in what turned into several kisses.

"Ugh!" He pulled his mouth from mine for the last time, and I clung to his lips, not wanting to let him go.

"You make it hard to stop. I love you, Brook. Tonight while we're talking to all these other people, my mind will only be on you. Remember, this is my fucking job, and that's it."

I knew what he was saying, but my heart fell slightly, despite my conviction to steel myself against it. "I know." I placed another small kiss on his mouth and inhaled deeply. "I know."

"Are you scared?"

"A little, I guess."

"We're going to do this together, just like we've done all along, right?"

I nodded. Cade squeezed my hand one last time before letting go as the driver opened the door. The screams flooded our senses as they increased in volume. Cade got out first, paused, and then offered me his hand.

We waved at the crowd, and each of us went to opposite sides of the carpet to begin signing autographs and talking to fans. It seemed like hours later when we stepped off to our individual photo calls and were able to talk to some of the other cast members.

Wendy and Jennifer were there along with Martin, our director. We had photos taken with all of them. Wendy and I weren't hanging out as much, so when she came over and hugged me to her for a photo, I was surprised.

"Hi, Brook! It's great to see you. *Love* your dress!"

"You look good too, Wendy. Let's catch up at the party, huh?" I smiled warmly at her and hoped the strain between us would be in the past.

"Sure thing. See you later!" She walked off into the theater, but I still had some photos to do.

When they called for Cade and I to pose together, I was thankful to have his arm around me again as he pressed his fingers into the side of my waist.   His hand went around my body so naturally and as I gazed up at him, I felt calmed by his presence next to me. Peace within the madness. I watched him talk to his fans and do the interviews with me, and when his hand ran through his gorgeous mane again and again, I figured he was a little flustered, too.

I felt like we were shouting our answers to the television hosts and news media, and I could barely hear myself talk above the roar of the crowds.

"I think I'm going deaf!" Cade murmured down to me at one point. "But I'm not going blind. You're so beautiful; I can't keep my eyes off of you, Brook. I'll be watching you all night, babe. I love you."

"Me too." I smiled as the cameras flashed again and again.

***

CADE AND I sat next to each other in the middle of the theater with our families on both sides. He'd introduced me to his parents, and his brother, Oliver, briefly, but I hadn't really had a chance to speak to them. Oliver had Cade's coloring and was very handsome, though, my biased mind argued, not as handsome as his brother. Layla, who I'd met during the filming, was slender and elegant, dressed head to toe in Versace, her dress glimmering softly as the cameras flashed. Cade's parents were a lot like him, down-to-earth and normal people. It was apparent that they were extremely proud of his success by the way his mom couldn't stop smiling and touching his hair, and his dad's chest was all puffed up.

Rightfully so, I thought. He's amazing. I took a deep breath as the movie started and my voiceover came over the speakers. Cade grabbed my hand and held on tight. I glanced up at him and smiled to myself.

The looks on the faces of our mothers were priceless. There were times during the movie when I felt Cade tense and sensed he wanted to flee the theater. He was especially uneasy during the scene when his character, Ryan, touched Julia as a lover for the first time.

It was so emotional, and he played it so realistically. I did too, but I'd been in such awe of him, and I was secretly living it in real life. I could watch him for hours on end. I of all people knew it was acting, but it seemed so real. I watched the reaction of some of the people around us, and people were completely drawn in.

I scratched the inside of his palm and he glanced at me with a secret smile, and then rubbed the top of my hand with his thumb.

Hopefully, everyone was so caught up in the movie that they didn't notice our entwined hands, but somehow, we just *had* to touch each other.

Memories flooded my mind as the movie played, of times that we shared during the shoot; so many memories. Being in the car mock-up against the green screen for hours and hours while we did the scenes of the drive from San Francisco to Boston, the closeness we felt while we worked on Ryan's bedroom scene, totally lost in each other as we rehearsed, and the full day of filming that first make-out scene.

I felt my pulse speed up as his hand moved on mine again.

Wow, that was quite a day. Reality was so intense, it made the film that much hotter.

I'd allowed myself to give in to all of the want I'd been feeling; the longing caused by being near him and not being able to touch him. He had too. I'd felt his arousal pressing against me several times during that day, and I wanted him so badly, I ached with it. He wanted me to feel it as he moved against me, needed me to know that he really did want me. There had been many times when we'd been alone that I'd wanted him to touch me like that, but we both held back, so when we finally had the chance to get our hands on each other, we really let ourselves fall in to it. The thoughts made my blood flush my skin as my body quickened.

Martin used the close up shots instead of the full screen ones. He'd said the full body shots were too hot. That was an understatement. In interviews, he continually made fun of Cade because he fell off the bed during one of the takes. Hell, I would have too, if he hadn't caught me. We'd forgotten anyone was on the set with us and had gotten so lost in each other. I was shaken when it was over. Obviously, the studio hadn't reined Martin in the way they had Cade and me.

Remembering, I'd been stunned as Cade picked himself up and sat down next to me on the bed sheepishly, running his hand through his hair. He'd taken my hand in his other one and looked into my face as we waited for the crew to reset the cameras and the set for the next take. Something passed between us in that moment that changed our relationship. Any time we spent alone after that lost the light, carefree feeling and something unspoken hung between us from that moment on; the sexual tension thick.

I sometimes wondered at Martin's mental maturity. I was young, but he was so completely juvenile, always ramming that slip up in Cade's face.

I could feel the sweat starting between our palms and his breathing increase, sensing he was sharing the same thoughts as the scene played out in front of us. *Oh, God.*

I wanted so badly to lay my head on his shoulder, to communicate with him how this was affecting me. He leaned his head closer to me and whispered in my ear.

"I know, Brook. Me, too. Watching us like this together... it's stunning."

Of course, he knew. He always knew. His hand tightened on mine.

Caden

THE ROOFTOP TERRACE of Armand Hammer Museum was decorated with lots of twinkling lights and a mural of the Boston skyline in the background was lit from behind, making it appear realistic. It was cool and insanely crowded. The theater held thirteen hundred people and while all of them weren't invited to the after party, there must have been somewhere around a thousand people in attendance.

The crowds outside the theater had been maddening. I was thankful that Brook was there with me. Even though I'd attended loads of these things, her presence gave me a center. Unconsciously, my eyes were always searching for her when she wasn't near me, even as I was talking to other people, or doing interviews. It was hard to keep track of her with so many people in attendance, but I would find her and meet her gaze every now and then.

Roxanne Mason tracked me down and basically followed me around most of the evening. She was pretty, in a hard sort of way. She seemed so much older than her age, and I wasn't sure why.

"You know, Cade, the studio has plans for us." She smiled and put her hand on my forearm. I took a drink from my glass and looked at her blandly. I hoped I wasn't being rude, but I wasn't interested in this conversation at all, as my eyes landed on Brook across the room.

She was talking to Noah and Gavin, laughing with them until her eyes landed on me with Roxanne's hand on me. She visibly stiffened, and I had to tear my eyes away from hers. *Fuck.*

"Yeah? Like what?"

"Oh, they didn't tell you? We're supposed to hang out, plant speculation that we may be dating."

"Yes, my manager mentioned something of it to me, but I'm not particularly into lying to my fans or anyone else." My voice was flat and bored.

Her lips pouted as she looked at me. "Maybe it wouldn't be a lie. You might like me, you know."

I moved away from her slightly so her hand fell away from my arm. "I'm sure you're a wonderful person, Roxanne, and very talented as well, but I thought you were dating that Eli Dominic."

Bloody hell. Brook was gone from where I'd last seen her.

"Well... yes, and no. So, you've been checking up on me, have you?" Her blue eyes flashed over my face. "I'm flattered."

I raised my eyebrows at her and wanted to kick myself for mentioning it. "Um, not really. My manager keeps me informed of things she thinks I need to know. Will you excuse me for a minute?" I nodded to her and moved off to see if I could find Brook. I hadn't spoken to her since we'd arrived at the party, and I just wanted to make sure she was okay.

As I made my way through the crowd, I didn't see her anywhere. Her parents were gone as well, so maybe she'd left. My sister and brother, along with Nathan, were along one of the walls talking, so I made my way over to them.

"Hey, are you all enjoying yourselves?" I leaned in and gave my sister a kiss on the cheek.

"Yes, excellent, Caden. This is a big one," Layla teased. "Mum and Dad are so proud of you. We all are."

I smiled at her. "Thanks, sis. Have any of you seen Brooklyn? I was going to leave soon because I've got an early call tomorrow for a radio program and wanted to say goodbye."

"I think she left a little while ago, Cade. Crowds aren't her thing." Nate put his hand on my shoulder.

"Yeah, I know. Okay. Listen, Oliver, Layla, I'd like Brook to have brunch with you at the hotel tomorrow morning with Mum and Dad. Can you arrange to have it brought into the suite? I'll have Denise figure out how to get her over there, yeah?"

"You won't be there?" Layla asked.

"Um, not sure, but definitely not at the beginning of it. I'd like her to have some time with all of you. She's fine with being there without me; we discussed it tonight."

"Sure, sure. I'll take care of everything. I've got her number. "

I hugged her, and shook hands with the two other men, before setting off to find my parents. I wanted to get out of there before someone else hooked into me and forced me to extend my time there. I found my parents on my way out of the venue.

"Thank you both for being here with me. It's meant the world to me." I hugged my mum and shook my dad's hand.

"We couldn't be prouder of you, son." My dad never was one to show his emotions on his sleeve, so this was a lot coming from him.

"Thank you, both. I've got an early morning, so I'm going to go back to the hotel now. I've asked Brook to come to brunch tomorrow, if that's alright? I want you to get to know her."

My mother's arms came around me again. "It's obvious how much she means to you, Cade. Of course, we'd love to have her."

"Good. I know you'll love her as much as I do." My dad's brows shot up at me as I turned to leave but I just smiled brightly at him.

A few minutes later in the car, I took out my phone to text Brook.

I wish I could have you in my arms tonight. I'm on my way back to my lonely bed with only thoughts of you to fill my dreams until morning.

I leaned my head back and closed my eyes. We had a couple of weeks of interviews and appearances here in the United States and then one more intense week of European premieres before a break for the holidays. Brook and I hadn't discussed holiday plans, but I knew I didn't want to spend them without her.

My phone buzzed in my pocket and I smiled as I pulled it out.

You looked hot tonight, babe. Wish you were here to warm me up.
I miss your body. XOXO

My body stirred as I read the words. She had so much fucking control over me, and she didn't even realize it. Control I was only too willing to hand over.

I'd love to be there with you, to bring your body to life under mine. I wish... I'm hard just thinking about it, my love.

Mmmmm... I closed my eyes and let the visions over take me. Her white skin, soft under my fingers and the soft moans that I brought out of her as I made love to her, drove me wild.

I love what you do to me... every touch is paradise.

Bloody hell, this was going to be one fucking long night.

Chapter 5

Perusing with the Parents

Brooklyn

CADE'S INTERVIEW WAS early this morning and I'd set my alarm so I could get up in time to listen to it. There were so many screaming fans in the background, obviously camped outside the radio station, that sometimes it was hard to hear his answers. When the girls would call in, they were all so giddy and gushing.

God. I rolled my eyes because I couldn't help myself.

That voice. I could listen to him talk forever.

Hearing it over the radio caused so many memories to flood my brain; The first time he said my name when we were introduced at the audition, all the times running lines, the breathless way he panted my name when we made love, or the way he made my heart race when he said he loved me.

Uuuugggggghhhhh! I wondered if he made every woman he met feel the same way I felt. Maybe even some who'd never met him, and only seen him on screen. It was crazy.

I got out of bed so I could take a shower and get ready to go over to his hotel to meet with his family. I cranked up the volume so I wouldn't miss any of it as I went about getting dressed.

I was a little nervous, but anxious to know them better. I knew some of the background Cade had shared about each of them, but it would really be intriguing to see if they saw him as extraordinary or was he just "Cade" to them; simply their brother or son... and nothing special?

I could hardly believe that was the case, but I knew my family didn't make a big deal out of my career, so maybe his didn't either, even though it was gargantuan. Hell, he didn't make a big deal out of it, so I assumed he'd prefer they didn't either.

I knew I'd never make it to the hotel before the interview was over, but Oliver called and asked if I could be there around 10:30 or if I needed a ride. They were bringing in brunch and my mom was going to take me over so my car wouldn't be parked in the garage. The damn paparazzi would be stalking us more than ever after last night's Hollywood premiere. I was going in through the garage, the same way I'd gotten out the night Cade pulled me into the shower after the Entertainment Weekly photo shoot. Mmmmm... Those were some delicious memories.

My stomach was caught in a knot. What if they didn't like me?

Suddenly, it became imperative that they did. Usually, other people's opinions didn't' matter to me, but Cade's family was another story entirely.

I showered quickly, and put on some jeans and a button down shirt, wondering if I should dress up more. What do you wear to English brunch with the parents of your boyfriend?

I stopped.

My boyfriend? Did I really just think about Cade in those terms?

"Hmmph." Was that what he was? *I couldn't go around calling him my "universe", so boyfriend it is.* I shook my head at myself. Shit.

I glanced at the clock. I needed to get going. The interview was winding down and the DJ was asking Cade the last few questions.

I wasn't paying that much attention because, let's face it, we'd been asked the same damn questions multiple times already and I knew all of his answers by heart.

"Could you fall in love with Brook? I saw the film and the chemistry is strong on screen. What's it like in real life?" The question slipped out, immediately after a caller had just finished asking about doing the stunts in the film, so given the change of subject he was taken off guard.

Okay, what?

"Yes. She's amazing," Cade replied and then the people in the studio broke out in laughter behind him.

My heart leapt in my chest. *Holy shit. He did* not *just say that, did he?*

"There's that quote!" The DJ shot back.

I sank down on the edge of my bed with my toothbrush in my hand.

Cade, my mind implored, *Try to save it, or Jeanne and Denise will have your ass.*

"Uh, I just like making her life really difficult." He laughed some more. "You know, she's got a bloke."

"But help us understand it, Cade. You said earlier that you really felt this film and it's gotta be *bizarre* to sit with this girl... a beautiful girl... who you've spent a lot of time with..." The DJ's voice drifted off.

"Yes."

"And develop this type of instant chemistry, which we all sort of look for in real life, have it play out on film and then not develop feelings for her?"

Okay... here we go, I thought. I couldn't breathe; my heart was pounding so fast I could feel the blood rushing through my ears.

"Yeah, it's really quite strange. Well, you do though. Sometimes. You do because that's the type of damage you undergo when trying to do anything real in acting. Like, you know, you kind of leave jobs with both people feeling like we have no idea who the other person is, so it's just like this horrible experience afterwards."

He was laughing it off, but I knew the pain behind the words he'd stammered around. He wanted to admit how closes we'd become, but instead had to make it seem like we'd left the set as strangers.

But for us, the horrible part being left with very real feelings you have to deal with when you try to go back to your regular life.

He told me it wasn't always like that on previous jobs; taking a very real chunk out of you, but it was for *this* job... for Cade and me. Remembering the agony at the wrap party and the morning after... I'd never experienced anything that painful ever before.

My heart seized and my mind screamed with love for him. I needed to get to him as fast as I could. I rushed around and got my stuff together so I could get over to the Beverly Wilshire before he made it back from the station. "Mom, are you ready?" I ran down the stairs with my purse in hand.

"Yes, Brook. Let's go." She followed me out.

An hour later, as I sat on the couch in the hotel room laughing with Cade's parents, his brother and sister, I wondered what I'd had to feel nervous about.

His mother was generous and giving, and his dad had a wicked sense of humor. He told me how he practically had to force Cade to try his hand at acting, but his son had insisted it was for sissies.

"He was only fifteen and he'd had aspirations of being in a rock band, but what kid doesn't at that age? He was wise to listen to his old dad. Look at him now."

"Carter, I'm sure Cade won't like you telling all of those old stories to Brook," Lillian Carlisle admonished her husband.

"Cade's already told me the story, but it seems funnier when you tell it, Mr. Carlisle."

"Oh, sweetheart, how many times do I need to tell you to call me Carter?" he smiled at me warmly.

"Thank you. If you're sure." I smiled back. "You must be very proud of your son. He seems to excel at everything he does."

"Well, he wasn't always like that. He hated his studies. Not that he did poorly, but he always had better things to spend his time on, at least that's how he tells it."

"Dear, did you get a chance to hear Caden's interview today?" Layla moved into the room with a plate of food from the buffet set up on the bar in residence on one side of the suite.

"Most of it. We get asked the same questions over and over. It's hard to sound fresh in those things, but he always does a much better job than I do. I get so flustered."

Oliver was quieter than Layla, but both of them were so beautiful. Blonde and tall and very regal in their movements, the gene pool was kind. I felt like an ugly duckling beside two swans.

Layla's eyes sparkled at me. "So, what dirt do you want to know about Cade, Brooklyn?" She laughed as she asked me. "I'm only too happy to spill."

"Well... "

"Layla. I doubt Cade will appreciate your enthusiasm," Oliver said pointedly, but he laughed as well... He was the oldest, four years older than Cade and six years older than Layla.

"He's pretty much told me everything, I think. We've spent quite a bit of time together while we were filming."

"Did he tell you about that hag, Tina?"

"Layla!" Lillian spoke up sternly.

"What, Mum? You know you agree with me." Layla rolled her eyes.

"Well, whether I agree or not, it's not appropriate for you to bring that up to Brooklyn."

I glanced between Cade's mom and his sister on the other sofa. I bit my lip to stifle a smile.

"I know who she is, and that she was Cade's longest relationship, but he doesn't talk that much about her."

"Probably because he's so embarrassed that he was ever with her, she's that horrible. Sure she's tall and leggy, model-ish, but her personality is that of a cold fish." She leaned forward in her seat, eager to share all of the sordid details. "It had to be the shagging," Oliver inserted wryly. "I shudder."

"Oliver!" Lillian reprimanded.

"What?" He looked up from his plate blandly.

"That's insensitive."

"It's the truth, Mum."

"She's an artist now, if you can call it that. All those squiggly lines can hardly be called art," Cade's dad scoffed. "She pushed enough of that rubbish off on us to start a bloody gallery."

"Not you, too Carter," Lillian said, with a sigh.

"Lil, the girl had the personality of a stone, we all know it."

Layla giggled at her father's remark, "Yeah, I swear to God, her head is literally two sizes too large, and she was so full of herself... I never understood what Cade saw in that nag. She was always trying to dictate to him who his friends were and what he should do. I mean, constantly!"

"I thought she was an incredible bore, so as I said, *shagging*." Oliver said tongue-in-cheek, his eyes widening. He was turning out to be very engaging, despite his quiet demeanor upon first meeting, and it was clear that he shared his sister's opinion. "Cade always lost his fire around her. He wasn't ever happy, I don't know why the bloody hell it took him so long to wise up."

I burst out laughing at them. "Cade was afraid you were going to tell me some nappy stories or about how he used to imitate Elton John."

"What? He told you about that, did he?" Layla looked stunned. "He's ruining all of my fun!" She chuckled under her breath. "Damn, I don't have any of those pictures with me, either. He used to rummage through mom's frocks and jewelry. It was ridiculous."

Cade's mother just shook her head. "He always was theatrical."

"So Brook, tell us about yourself."

"Come on, Dad," Oliver interrupted. "Like she isn't the only thing Cade talks about! Honestly, Brook, I think we know you as well as he does by now."

I felt my cheeks flush as color came into my face at his words.

Lillian leaned over to pat my hand. "Don't worry, darling, he thinks very highly of you."

"Pffft. Is *that* what you call it?" His father got up to get some more coffee. "That boy's done for, I'd say. Brooklyn, can I get you anything else?"

"Um, no, thank you. It was delicious." I bit my lip as pleasure filled me at his words.

"I'm so sorry for my husband's, uh, brashness, dear. Men are so indelicate, aren't they?" Lillian shot him a look that clearly told him to stop talking. I wanted to laugh. They were so cute.

"It's just that we just haven't seen our son this happy before, and we know there is much more to it than his success." She arched her brows and her mouth widened in a big smile.

"He deserves everything that is happening for him. He's very dedicated in his work." His sister and brother were both looking at me with their eyebrows raised. She and Oliver were so like their brother. "He always downplays how talented he is, but it's just so essentially... Cade."

Okay, why are they all staring at me?

I couldn't help but shrug and shake my head. "Is this the place where I say, he's gorgeous and brilliant and sexy as hell?" I smirked at them as they all burst out laughing. "Seriously," I nodded at them, "Because he is *all* of that! But, if you tell him I said so, I'll completely deny it!" We all laughed for a couple of minutes, and his mother came over to hug me wiping her eyes on the way.

"Cade is very lucky to have such a supportive family. I can see where he gets so many of the awesome things about him. You're all so great! I'm really glad to have this time with you. Thank you, for making me feel so welcome."

"Oh, it's our pleasure to finally meet you, honey," his mother put her arm around my shoulder. "It's obvious why Caden is so taken with you."

"Well, I'm very... taken, with him, too."

"Is there anything about him that you, Brook?"

"Layla!" her mother admonished, though his father just laughed. "Forgive my children their terrible manners, Brook."

"Oh, come on! Don't be such a bunch of prigs, will you? You know you're all dying to know." She would not be put off. "Well?" Her eyes sparkling as she looked at me over her coffee.

Carter chuckled again and shook his head.

I laughed. "Uh... um, not really. I basically think he's pretty perfect." They all looked at me expectantly as if they wanted me to continue, "Um, except for the fact that so many women are in love with him... I could definitely live without that." I laughed and they all laughed with me again.

"You're a good girl. You make sure to tell me if my son misbehaves, honey, and I'll have his arse," his dad winked at me.

We were all still laughing when Cade walked in, wearing black jeans, a white T-shirt and a black stocking cap. My heart stopped at the look on his face.

"Okay, enough of poisoning my girl against me! Don't believe anything they say, love." He walked in and his mom got up to put her arms around him.

"We'd never do that, would we?" His mom's eyes looked pointedly at her other two children. I had to bite my lip to keep from laughing.

I wasn't sure what to do next. *Do I hug him, just sit here, what?*

Cade let go of his mother and moved to where I was sitting on the sofa next to his dad.

"Hey, give me some love." He took my hands to bring me up from the sofa to take me in his arms and pull me close. "I haven't seen you in what? Ten or eleven hours?"

I let myself melt into him as his scent closed in all around me as he buried his face in my hair and held me tight. *Mmmmm...*

My arms slid around his shoulders to hug him back and he pulled back slightly to place a brief, hard kiss on my mouth.

"Yeah, I missed you." All eyes were on us as we greeted each other.

He sat down on the sofa and pulled me down next to him, his arm going across my knees

"So, tell me how ridiculous they've been." He gazed at me with an expectant smile on his face. "Don't leave anything out!"

"Well, they've been great. Very nice... and they only told me one or two really horrible things, I promise." I nudged his shoulder then winked at Layla who smiled wickedly.

"Yes, how dare you question our loyalty, Cade?" She added.

His parents and siblings laughed at Cade's expression when it twisted wryly.

"I'm sure," he said flatly.

"I like this girl, son. She's sassy. She's gonna kick you in the arse, boy," Carter teased his son.

Cade looked at me and then back at his family while everyone remained silent, all of them trying not to laugh. I bent my head to rest it on Cade's shoulder and put my hand over my mouth to hold back the laughter.

When his eyes returned to my face, his brows went up. "What?"

I shrugged and looked at his dad from underneath my lashes.

As the morning progressed I told them about my family, my mother's interior design company and my dad's job with Reebok, as well as my aunt who was in the business. It felt great to spend time with Cade in an atmosphere where we could be ourselves and let our feelings show. I was relaxed and calm and so was he.

Lillian was so warm and loving to everyone around her so it was easy to see how Cade would turn out to be so wonderful, too. All of them were witty, and I thoroughly enjoyed my time with them.

"Brook, what are your plans for the holidays?" Lillian asked as her husband and children went to get their bags together. They were going to the airport to take an evening flight back to London.

"Um," I looked at Cade. We hadn't talked about the holidays, but my family usually went on a trip somewhere, and up until this year, David came along. "We usually take a trip somewhere, but I'm not sure my parents have made any plans yet."

"Well, if you would like to, you're welcome to come to our home in London. We'd love to have you join us."

"Mum, I haven't had a chance to talk to her about it yet," Cade interjected. "Don't feel obligated, love." He put his arm around my shoulders and rubbed my other arm with his free hand. I could see in his face that he wanted me to make the trip.

"I'd love that, but I do need to check with my family. I know you don't celebrate the American holiday of Thanksgiving in London, but I'm hoping Cade will join us this year." His eyes lit up and his hand closed over mine.

I turned to look at him and our eyes met.

"We have several more promotional obligations up through the first week of December, so you'll still be here, right? Until we fly to London on the 5th?"

"Yes. I'd love to, thank you." He hugged me closer to his body with the arm that was wrapped around me. "Will you be making the big turkey dinner, Brook?" He was teasing me.

"Caden! You shouldn't put her on the spot like that."

"Oh, Mum. It's Brook. She *expects* me to put her on the spot... quite frequently, in fact." He grinned at the both of us and I couldn't keep the silly grin off of my face.

"Yes, like you did in your interview, today?" I shoved his shoulder with mine.

His eyes widened and his brows went up slightly as an easy smile played around his mouth.

"Oh, about that; Bloody hell! He asked that question out of nowhere, and um, I wasn't prepared, I suppose. I'm not good at lying, as you know." He rolled his eyes at me.

"Hmmmm... Well, Denise won't be happy, so get ready for a lecture." He leaned in closer to me and stopped a few inches from my mouth.

"How about you? Are you going to *give it to me good*, too?" The corners of his mouth raised in the start of devilish grin before he placed a soft kiss on my mouth, his hand and thumb brushing against my jaw as he brought my mouth to his. I blushed at his emphasis on the words.

Cade! Did you forget that we aren't alone?

I couldn't say it aloud, but he knew what I was thinking, and he shook his head, his mouth still hovering over mine.

My face burned at the blatant display in front of his mother, but I wouldn't give him the satisfaction of backing away from the challenge. He was testing me, and I knew it.

"You wish." I scoffed, laughing back and then glanced at his mother, who was smiling from ear to ear as she gathered her things.

"Yes... I do. No disputing here," he said as he once again lowered his mouth to mine.

Chapter 6

London Bridge

Caden

I WAS SITTING in first class on Virgin Atlantic with Noah, Martin and Brook on our way to London for the first of our Western European premieres. Both Brook's and my managers, Jeanne and Denise, were also accompanying us on this trip.

We had a five or six day stint in the series and while they weren't all stacked on top of each other, it would be tiring due to the jet lag and the fact that we'd have to hole up in the hotels for most of it. While we didn't expect mobs to the proportion that we did in the States, there would be more than would allow us to go out or see any of the sights.

We were on another red eye flight, designed to help us sleep in advance of the tour so we'd be as rested as possible during it, and get us in with the least amount of press coverage. The plane took off just before midnight L.A. time and we'd be arriving at about 11 AM in London, with one stop in New York to refuel.

The stellar success of the opening weekend in the United States had secured the scheduling of the second film in the series, which was slated to go into production in March. We'd gotten confirmation just three days ago. Our heads were still spinning at the seventyish million dollars that it had made in the first three days. Extraordinary and certainly passing even the studio's lofty expectations.

I had mixed emotions about it. While it would be great to work with Brook again, it would also jettison her career at breakneck speed, and it would mean more sneaking around. Before this, they hounded me incessantly, but less so Brook. Now all bets were off. *Holy Hell.* If only we didn't have to sneak around anymore, but no doubt it would be ten times worse now.

She was sitting across the aisle by herself. The light over the seat next to her was casting a soft glow on her skin and hair as she slept. She was wrapped up in one of those red, airline blankets, and I yearned to go sit next to her, to take her in my arms and hold her close to me.

I sighed loudly and Denise leaned in to speak to me. "Cade, it's only an airplane ride. She's right there in front of you."

"Jesus, am I that bad? But that's not the point, is it? I'm sorry. I just see this as a huge bloody waste. I mean, why is this necessary? We've practically got the whole of first class booked, so no one would know if we sat together," I whispered urgently.

She looked at me sardonically, but I knew that she felt my misery.

Due to all of our promotional obligations and the paparazzi hounding us night and day, Brook and I had hardly had any time alone for the past three weeks. Even when we had interviews and such together, usually Wendy, Jennifer, Ethan or Noah were in the mix as well.

I missed being alone with her.

I was in the same damn town, not halfway across the globe, and yet, we'd hardly even seen each other. The only exception had been over Thanksgiving when I'd spent a couple of days at her house with her family. Unlike the first time when I'd stayed over after the MTV awards, her father was home so we weren't able to spend the nights together in her room and I was relegated to the spare room.

Talk about aching. Knowing she was ten feet away and not be able to go to her, to touch her like I wanted was torture. *Like now.*

I glanced toward her and her eyes were open looking at me. When she met my eyes, her right arm slowly extended down, her hand reached out toward me, as she curled her fingers back toward her.

The look on her face was full of want and I knew the pain in my heart was an echo of hers. The ache in my dick didn't help either. My body was also feeling the loss.

Christ, this was the limit of my endurance.

"Denise, cancel my contracts if you must, but nothing is going to keep me in this bloody seat for even one more minute."

I got up and moved across to the seat next to her and she sat up a little to make room for me.

Martin looked up from the book he was reading and raised his eyebrow. I didn't give one damn what he thought. If he didn't know Brook and I were tight after seeing us daily on set, then he wasn't as intelligent as I'd given him credit for.

I lifted the edge of her blanket and laced my hand through hers as I stared into her blue eyes. We just sat there, gazing at each other for who knows how long. Her thumb rubbed the top of my hand and I gave hers a little squeeze. My muscles relaxed and the tightness in my chest eased.

Her hand was warm and so soft. I closed my eyes and dreamed of more extensive patches of her velvet skin beneath my hands, plastered up against my chest and beneath my body. I shifted in my seat as the stiffening in my pants became uncomfortable.

"Are you okay?" Her eyes were sleepy as she looked at me, her lids drooping over her irises.

"I am now, love. I can't stand being so close to you and not touching you. I've had bloody well enough of it." My voice was rough with pent up desire. "It's been too long," I whispered so only she could hear.

I was aching to be with her, and wondered how in the world we'd be able to pull it off with all the paps stalking us and also the hawk eyes of the studio watching every move we made.

She paused as she just continued to look at me.

"Yeah. I'm there, too," she said finally. Her mouth parted as she took a deep breath and her eyes dropped to my mouth.

"Brook, don't get me started. I'm already so worked up I can't stand it."

She nodded, smiling slightly. "I'm sorry, baby. I'm just missing you. *Bad*."

"Oh, honey. If you only knew what I want to do to you right now." I smiled at her and her mouth twitched as she drew in her breath.

"I think I have a pretty good idea." Her brows went up with her words. "You make me crazy. How are you going to get into my room, hmmm? Because, you *are* gonna get in, right?"

Her eyes sparkled in the low light and I reached above my head to shut off the overhead lamp, cloaking us in darkness, with only the small sidelights left on.

My hand in hers, resumed its rubbing on the top of her fingers and I leaned back in my seat.

"Where there is a will, there's a way... one bloody strong will, my love. Don't worry; I'll make it happen, but probably not until after tomorrow's premiere."

"Yeah, I know we won't have time for anything other than changing before we have to go to the venue for the carpet and the photo calls. See what I get for hanging out with the hottest movie star ever? Lots of sexual frustration and rampant wet dreams."

She was so beautiful when she got that teasing look in her eyes, prompted by desire. I fucking loved how she made me want her. My lips lifted in a soft smile.

"You have no idea what I go through, babe. I replay every touch over and over in my mind. It's almost too much to bear sometimes."

I couldn't stop looking at her. I was mesmerized by the emotions passing across her face. "Do you know how much I love you?" My voice vibrated with want.

She nodded and leaned her head toward me on the seat back, her eyes never leaving mine. I shook my head, emotion filling my chest. "I don't think you do..." She couldn't possibly know because there were no words to express it.

Denise reached over and nudged my shoulder. I turned to her and saw the look of stern consternation in her eyes. Even though our voices were mere whispers, she could tell by the way we were huddled together what we were talking about.

The Cade and Brook bubble, she called it. Something we'd been made all too aware of after the Comic Con event in San Diego right after our long weekend together there.

"Okay, I'll be good." I mouthed to her and Brook let out a frustrated breath.

"Hmmmph!"

I decided it might be safer to change the subject. As I turned back to her, I was again engulfed in the wonderful scent of her perfume mixed with her shampoo, and I wanted nothing more than to pull her to me and breathe her in.

"So what's up with your family this Christmas?" I really didn't want to be without her, but I knew that sometime between Christmas and New Year's she had to fly somewhere to meet up with the director of her upcoming movie to discuss scheduling now that we'd be going into production on the second film of The Remembrance Trilogy, things would need to be rearranged. She wasn't cast for sure yet, but Brook was gaining ground in popularity, and that meant they wouldn't want to lose her on their project. It was more likely they would rearrange production to accommodate Martin's production schedule.

Brook really wanted that part, and while the suits had all worked out the money, the casting wouldn't be confirmed until they met with Brook in person and had her read for the part. While I was happy for her, I was disappointed we wouldn't have the holiday together. There was always something keeping us apart.

"Um, Mom's booked us all at Veil for ten days over Christmas. Jeanne called Ken and they're working out that audition as well. I'm sorry, Cade. I don't know what my schedule looks like yet." She had turned toward me in her seat a little and leaned her head against the back of it.

"I'd ask you to come with us skiing, but it will be obvious enough that David won't be with us this year, so Jeanne said no way. I'm so sorry."

"Hmmmm." I knew the disappointment was dripping from my voice and showing in my face.

"I really wanted to share Christmas with you and I can't take a chance on losing that part, but I'll try to work it out... " Her hand still laced with mine, her other one came up to squeeze my forearm above the blanket, "Even if my mom will have a hissy at my missing Christmas with them."

I smiled at her even if it didn't quite reach my eyes.

"You'll have lots of parts to choose from, but I understand how important this is to you. If we can't be together over the holidays, I'll be okay, but I'll miss you." I lifted my other hand so that my fingers could brush her chin. "I'll just be looking forward to March all the more, love."

"Ken and Jeanne said Pinnacle will still make it hard for us during filming, too. I'm sorry, Cade, I wish... " Her brows dropped and she grimaced.

"Why are you sorry? You didn't do this. Neither one of us did. I hate it, too, but we'll deal, okay? It is what it is."

She nodded softly, and pursed her lips in a silent kiss at me.

The pilot came on the intercom and told us that we would be landing in New York for a short layover, and then this same plane was traveling on to London. That hardly ever happened where we'd get the same plane all the way, but it was good... it was one less mob to deal with.

"I'm so thankful we don't have to change planes," I sighed and settled back in my seat, moving the back into a recline position.

"Thank Jeanne. She's taking good care of us this time. I think she'll try to do that more and more now, since our movie has released. Thank God."

"Try to get some rest, sweets. You're gonna need all that you can get." I smiled at her and nudged her shoulder with mine.

"Again with the promises..." She rolled her eyes and chuckled under her breath as she leaned, ever so slightly, into my shoulder.

***

MARTIN AND NOAH were supposed to meet Brook and me in the lobby, but I wanted to have a moment alone with her first.

When she opened the door to her hotel room, I just stopped and stared at her. She was dressed in a shiny black dress that left both shoulders bare. The skirt was slightly full which accentuated the slimness of her thighs. Wow.

"Well? Don't you have anything to say to me or are you just going to stare at me all night?" She smirked as I ran my eyes over her face and hair, down her body, all the way to her feet.

"Um... yeah. Staring all night works wonderfully well for me at the moment." My mouth twitched in the start of a grin as I swept her into my arms.

"You smell delicious," I whispered, as I brought my mouth down on hers for a slow kiss. Her hands immediately went into my hair at the back of my head to pull me closer as her mouth opened fully to mine. Responding to me in the passionate way I adored, her mouth moving and sucking just as wildly as mine did on hers.

God, I love it when she does that. It's so hot.

"Mmmm.... . Oh, Cade. God, I miss you so much," she moaned her mouth coming back for more kisses as my arms around her slid down her body to her bum to pull tight against my arousal. I was so hard I thought I would burst.

"Brook, I'm starving for you, my love." My fingers gathered up the edge of her skirt so that I could touch her. I pulled my mouth from hers as my eyes widened.

"No panties? Mmm..." My hands squeezed the flesh of her bare ass.

"I have on panties, it's a thong, babe." She was breathing hard from our kisses as her mouth ghosted over mine, begging me for more.

My hands moved higher to find the lace and ribbon at the top of her butt cheeks that turned into the band around the top of her hips.

"You're so sexy. Stop it. You're killing me." I licked and nipped at her lips before she crushed her mouth to mine for another deep kiss. "I want..."

Brook let out a soft, seductive laugh. "We can't. We have to go. I don't want to, but this is your town. Everyone wants to love and adore you."

"I only want you to love and adore *you*." I smiled against her mouth as I hugged her close.

"I do, but I have to share you for just a little while. We'll get back to this later, Cade. I promise, okay?"

At that moment my phone vibrated in my pocket and I reluctantly let go of Brooklyn to pull it out of the inside breast pocket of my dark suit. It was a text from Martin.

"They're waiting downstairs."

Brook went to the mirror to check her hair, and replace the lipstick I'd just kissed off before grabbing her coat and coming back to place a hand on my chest.

"You look amazing." She opened the door to the hallway and dropped the bomb that only punctuated the erection I was trying to calm. "You make my mouth water just looking at you."

Well, it might be utter hell just getting through the next four or so hours until we could finally be alone, but one thing was certain, I was going to enjoy every second of the delicious torture up until then.

The carpet at the Vue Theater wasn't red, it was black, and there were even more screaming fans at the London premiere than there was at the one in L.A. How was that even bloody possible? The sound was deafening as we did our little song and dance, answering the same questions over and over, signing autographs and the endless photo calls. The flashes went off it was an endless succession of blinding light.

My hands itched to get a hold of Brook's as I watched her talk to fans and reporters, longing for the end to this evening. I should have been so fucking happy, all of my friends and family were here to support me, but all I could think about was that socializing with them at the after party was going to postpone the time that I would be alone with Brook.

Once I touched her for our posed photos together, I was hard pressed to let go of her for the rest of the night, my hand always on the back of her waist, guiding her into the theater and later, to the party. Martin shot me some dirty looks when he saw me touching her, but I pretended not to notice.

It was a cold evening, but the party was in the courtyard of a nearby restaurant with radiant heaters put all around to keep us warm. Brook began to shiver, so I helped her into her suit jacket as we made our way to a railing overlooking the river. The lights were low, and the scene was set with twinkling candles, almost to excess. The hundreds of fans that still lined the streets outside were still screaming, which only increased when they saw the two of us wave in their direction.

"This is crazy." Brook smiled. "They all just want a glimpse of you."

"Of us." She was so beautiful with the breeze in her hair, I longed to reach out and touch the silky strands.

She was leaning on the brick ledge that was about waist high, and I was standing behind her and off to one side so that we could watch the goings on at the party without taking direct part. The problem was, all I wanted to do was look at her.

"Brook," I groaned her name, the longing I felt pouring through my words.

She leaned back into me just slightly and glanced up into my face. "Exactly."

I gasped when I felt her left hand that was hidden from everyone's view by my body, reach behind her and rub the already erect length of my dick. Her hand was moving in sensuous rhythm up and down as my knees got week and I was helpless underneath her ministrations.

Each second; my breathing increased. It felt so amazing, to have her bold enough to do that with all these people around. All she had to do was look at me; say my name or the smallest touch and she had me on fire.

"Mmmmm. Looks like we need to get out of here, hmmm?" she said softly.

Her head fell back toward me and her mouth parted as she looked over her shoulder at me.

My hand on her waist increased in pressure as I longed to turn her into my arms. Suddenly, our obligations, the people around us, the thousands of fans clamoring below, all evaporated into thin air.

"Yeah. Let's go."

"Should I let you leave first? Martin won't want us leaving together."

"I don't give a flying fuck what anybody wants or thinks is the proper thing to do. All I want is to get you alone. And, *now*." I turned her and led her toward the entrance.

"Oh Cade, Brooklyn, I wanted to introduce you to… " Martin said as we passed right by him without stopping, his hand pointing to a woman to his left. He turned to watch us as we passed and I raised my left hand in the air to stop his words.

Not tonight. I had other plans.

Chapter 7

Midnight Snack

Caden

I HAD THE driver let me out in the garage so I could sneak in through the stairs, while he took Brook around the front of the hotel. With all of the fans and paparazzi around front, we knew it best to go in separately and better if I was able to avoid the madness all together. The fans were great, but I didn't have it in me to spend countless minutes held outside signing autographs tonight.

I hurried up the stairs and waited for her by the elevators on the fifteenth floor. It was taking a big chance that someone would see me, but I didn't want her walking to the room alone. I wasn't sure if I was breathing hard due to the fifteen flights of stairs I'd just sprinted up, or the excitement I felt at the prospect of the rest of the evening.

As I leaned up against the wall, anticipation flooded through me. The three weeks since we'd made love had me wound tighter than a drum. It had been so bloody hard keeping my hands off of her in the limo, but this driver was a transient and we couldn't have someone we weren't sure about leaking any information. If we'd been in L.A. and

Shane, my regular driver would have been there, then it would have been a different story altogether.

"Mmmm..." I said aloud at the thought. Taking her in the back of a limousine was something I would have to put on my priority list. I smiled to myself at the prospect.

I was anxious, loosening my tie and removing it, finally able to shove the damn thing in the pocket of my jacket. I hated this celebrity rubbish. I wish I could make the movies and skip the premieres and promotion. It was exhausting, but I understood the need for it. The marketing was part of the contracts. The floor indicator lights above the elevator doors flashed as the car drew closer. Each second that passed like an ache in the silence.

The elevator dinged, the doors beginning to open; there she was, my beautiful girl, smiling at me as she started to come out. Her eyes were intent as they met mine, both of our senses flooding with each other.

I longed to take her in my arms, but I could only thread my fingers through hers. She handed me the key card to the room with her other hand, as we began to walk down the hall. Her blue eyes were burning into mine as visions of what was going to transpire in a few minutes rushed through my head.

It felt right. Just perfect.

Something so simple as openly walking down a hall with her hand in mine sent an extraordinary surge of satisfaction through me. I wanted... no, I needed to be able to be open with our relationship. I wanted the world to know she was mine, and in no uncertain terms. I brought her hand to my mouth as we walked down the carpeted hallway, and she leaned her head on my shoulder.

My heart swelled in my chest, beating harder. We belonged

together. I felt it deep within my soul.

I didn't let go of her as I slid the card in and waited for the light to indicate the door was open. She entered in front of me and I immediately pulled her back to me with our entwined hands. My free hand came up to slide from the side of her face to the back of her head to draw her mouth to mine. Our mouths were urgent, but not hurried as we explored each other deeply, sucking and nipping. Our lips went from teasing and ghosting over each other's to hungry; deeper, to dive in and devour each other over and over again. Our hands explored each other's bodies as our mouths tasted and teased again and again.

"Fuck, I love kissing you, Brook."

I couldn't get enough of her luscious mouth. God, she tasted so good.

"I've missed you, so bloody much," I breathed against her mouth before I went back for more.

Brook's hands were impatient as she pushed my jacket from my shoulders and down my arms, our mouths clinging together. My hands slid around the sides of her waist and back to draw her up against my chest.

"Cade, I want you. Make love to me."

Jesus, her sultry voice was my undoing, the throbbing in my body to the point of pain as her hands frantically pulled at the buttons on my shirt. She didn't have to ask me twice.

"Just rip it, Brook. I want your skin on mine. Now."

Our mouths still clinging passionately, we were both panting, mingling our breath as passion overtook us. My hand found the zipper on the side of her dress and I slid it down as her hands hesitated for the briefest second before she pulled with all her might. The material ripped and the buttons flew in all directions as her warm hands splayed out on my chest, and slid up around my neck.

My hands followed the path of the dress down her body until it fell from her hips in a pool at her feet. I pulled her to me, my hands roaming all over her back and her bare breasts were pressed to my chest.

My skin was so sensitive, I could feel her taut nipples burn into me.

Jesus, this is paradise.

I turned her in my arms so my hands could cup her breasts from behind as I placed wet, open mouth kisses on her neck and shoulders. Her hard nipples under my palms drove me crazy and I wanted to feel every inch of her skin.

I let my hands roam and knead over every inch of exposed skin and she felt like warm silk.

Brook shuddered as I sucked on the skin of her neck again and again, and my hands moved lower over the lace that covered her center. One hand reaching lower to slide under the material and feel the heat and dewy wetness that told me she wanted me as much as I wanted her.

"Uhhh." She sighed. "That feels good, Cade." Her response drove me insane with wanting.

"Oh my God... You're so hot, baby. Brook... Jesus," I moaned against the sensitive flesh of her neck as she arched it to one side, giving me unlimited access.

Her body pressing into mine, she moved her ass on my hardened cock. She ground against me, each new groan she brought forth from me driving her on. I felt her hands moving behind me to press on my ass, bringing my body tighter against hers.

I couldn't wait anymore as I lifted her in my arms and lay her crosswise on the bed.

The room was in total darkness except for some of the city lights flickering in through the windows that cast a soft glow on her translucent skin. She raised her knees slightly and arched her back as she looked at me, her eyes drunk with love and passion.

Her mouth parted and she breathed my name as she raised her arms to me. "Cade... pleeaaassse."

Something slowed me down. As much as I wanted her, I wanted to bring her pleasure even more. Extreme pleasure.

I wanted to look at her, savor her, make every touch last. Even though we had all night, I knew it wouldn't be enough. I would never get enough of her body, or her love.

My heart thumped in my chest as I slowly reached up and hooked my fingers under the edge of her thong and pulled it down and flung it aside.

She was lying naked to my view with nothing but her black stilettos on.

It was so fucking erotic I could barely move. I felt myself start to shake with desire and it was completely out of my control.

As I fell to my knees beside the bed, I slid my hands slowly up her legs from her ankles to her legs and thighs. My fingers closed around her hips, my thumbs rubbing and caressing back and forth on her hipbones as my hungry gaze devoured her. I gripped tighter and pulled her to the side of the bed, bringing her bottom to the edge in front of me.

"Baby... I want to hold you. I need you in my arms," she beckoned and my heart surged again.

"Brook, I want to make love to you all night long. I want to savor every touch. I want to kiss you, taste you all over. Let me..." My voice was a rough whisper as I bent to place a series of kisses on her tummy, causing her muscles to contract involuntarily. My mouth was making a hot trail from her breasts to her pelvis and back again. My tongue coming out to drag along her skin, I was overwhelmed with the desire I felt for her. "Let me..." I begged.

I could feel her flesh tremble under my mouth as I moved over her and I wanted to worship this woman for the rest of my life.

She gasped as my mouth moved lower and my hands parted her thighs. I closed my eyes and rested my cheek against the delicate skin below her knee as I let myself breathe in the scent of her arousal.

The blood pounded in my ears and my dick was so engorged, the skin pulled tight like it would explode. I slid my hands up her body to cup around her breasts and my fingers teased both nipples as I kissed her perfectly flat stomach with my open mouth.

"Oh, baby... you make me so hard, just the scent of you is just... driving me mad."

"Jesus, Cade," she begged. "Stop torturing me. Uhhh... please..."

I slid my arms under her thighs and up over her stomach as my mouth came down on where she wanted it most.

It was heaven.

Her essence was the sweetest thing I'd ever tasted as I licked and sucked on the delicate flesh, flicking my tongue on the little nub and then moving down to dive inside her.

She arched against me as her breath came in short gasps. Her hips undulating under my mouth was the sexiest thing I'd ever experienced, and I wanted more. I wanted to give her everything.

My right hand moved up to tug on her left nipple as my left splayed across the skin of her belly below her navel. My dick was straining so hard against my pants, throbbing in increasing need.

"Brook," I breathed on her skin as I continued to suckle and tease her flesh. "You're incredible. Let me feel you cum in my mouth... Let go, Brook, please."

"Uh, Uh, Uh..." She was moaning and panting, her hips increasing their movements under my mouth, and I felt her start to tremble under my tongue. I brought my left hand down and inserted two fingers into her body as my tongue continued its quest. I hooked my fingers and pressed upward until I found her g-spot and I pulsed my fingers there at the same time as I pulsed my tongue on the flesh above it.

"Unnnn, Cade. Oh baby... Mmmm." I felt the convulsions begin, and seconds later her body was arching off of the bed as she came hard, her hands fisting in the sheets, her head thrown back. I lightened the pressure but continued with the pulses until I knew the waves were lessening.

She was breathing hard, her hands going into her hair as I moved up her body to take her mouth with mine.

"You're so good to me. I love you so much," she breathed into my mouth. My heart soared that I could bring her that kind of pleasure. Her body was trembling in my arms as I sucked on her lips and brushed her hair back off of her face.

Her face so flushed with desire was the most beautiful sight I'd ever seen. I could look at her forever.

I placed a deep kiss on her mouth and then pulled away to shed the rest of my clothes.

I moved over her and settled into the cradle of her gorgeous limbs.

Her arms began clutching at my back and she wrapped her arms and legs around me as I lifted her to the center of the bed and then entered her in one motion. She was swollen from her orgasm and so tight, so wet, that she drove me to distraction. I closed my eyes as her warmth engulfed me and my mouth hovered over hers.

"Bloody hell, Brook... I'm so in love with you... I can't breathe. I can't breathe..." I panted against her mouth then sucked her lower lip into my mouth. I thrust into her body again and again, wanted to be closer each time. She was clenching around my dick and her arms and legs curling around my body. It was amazing. I was drowning.

"God, Brook..." I gasped as I brushed her hair off of her face. Her eyes were closed and her breath was coming in fast pants through her parted lips, as she turned her face to one side and raked her nails down my back.

"Oh, Cade..." Her head turned back toward me and her hands went into my hair to pull and tug, bringing my mouth back to hers. "Kiss me."

Her body sucking on mine was making it harder and harder not to come. I groaned and licked at her top lip and took her mouth in a long, deep kiss. Her mouth was wild on mine, her hips matching me thrust for thrust. "Brook, you're making me come, honey... Are you there?" My mouth was hungry on hers as I kissed her again and again. "I'm gonna have to slow down if you're not."

"Uhhhhh, yes..." Her body clenched around mine and hugged tight. "You're so good, Cade."

Hearing my name in that panting voice sent me over the edge, my muscles tensing as I spilled into her body. She arched into me and her body started to convulse around me, making my orgasm even harder; each wave stronger than the last.

We were both breathless, covered in a thin sheen of perspiration as our bodies came back down.

I brushed my knuckles across her cheek and then her chin as I softly kissed her eyes, cheeks and mouth. "Oh my love... You're going to kill me." I smiled down at her as her eyes finally opened.

"What a way to die." Brook smiled lazily, her glittering eyes, a darker blue in the low light. Her arms tightened around me and she pulled my face down and nuzzled my nose with hers, before coming in for a kiss. "Cade, you're so beautiful."

My heart was still pumping, but I wasn't sure if it was due to the lovemaking or the emotions that were washing through me. "I love you so much, Brook."

I rolled her to the side and turned her toward me so we were facing each other. I couldn't keep my hands off of her as I brushed up and down her arms and torso.

"Do you get tired of me telling you I love you?" I was drowning in her beautiful eyes.

Brook was very still, contemplative as she met my eyes, then her hand came up to touch my jaw with her fingertips.

"Never. I never hear it enough. I love you, too. You know that." Her thumb brushed across my lower lip. She was so sexy, even though we had just made love, I could feel my body already tightening, ready for more.

We lay there entwined and holding each other in the dark, with only the sound of our breathing.

"I know you don't know if you can come to London yet, but what do you want for Christmas?" I wanted to get her something special.

She shook her head. "I have everything I want. You've given me so much already and I don't need expensive presents, Cade. I have you. That's enough." Her dark pink lips broke into a soft smile. "What about you?"

"Everything I want is right in this room, in this bed. I never want to leave." My hand went to the back of her head to twine in her hair, at the same time as I pulled her closer to me with my other arm wrapped around her waist.

"The only thing I could possibly want is to put my ring on your finger for good."

I shivered as her arm slid under my arm and around my body, her fingers tracing patterns on my back.

"I wear it every night when I'm at home. It's on my finger every day at some point," her soft voice vibrated on my skin, the words held so much meaning. "I sleep with it on."

I leaned down and kissed her temple then her cheek, as my heart thumped in my chest.

Her stomach growled loudly and she giggled. "Oops, sorry. I had too many people to talk to tonight, I forgot to eat." She blushed. "How embarrassing."

"Well, there is that basket of stuff that the hotel sent up. Let's see what's in it." My mouth lifted in a grin. "I can't have my girl fainting on me. How would I take advantage of you later if that happened?"

"Hmmph." Brook snorted. "I should have known you have an ulterior motive. Is that all you think about?" she teased.

"Yes." I nodded and smiled even wider.

Brook laughed out loud as she moved to the edge of the bed. I was enjoying the view of her naked body, but then she bent to pick up my discarded shirt to throw it on. Of course, the buttons were gone so she just held it closed in front of her as she went to the basket of snacks.

"There are some strawberries, grapes, cheese, crackers and of all things, Twinkies!" Her head came up as she looked at me. I pulled myself up to the head of the bed and was leaning back on some pillows, completely naked, my legs crossed at the ankles.

She smirked at me and her right eyebrow went up. "What do you want?"

"You decide, but dessert sounds good." I loved sweets, though I didn't indulge often.

"Oh, so that narrows it down to the Twinkies then." She brought the basket to the bed and took out a bottle of Perrier mineral water, some strawberries and the snack cakes.

I stared at her body through the open front of the shirt as she crawled up onto the bed and then onto my lap to straddle my legs.

My hands moved to her hips as I pulled her closer. "Mmmm. Now, this is what I call a midnight snack." I leaned in to place a soft kiss on her lips.

"I thought you already had that earlier," she said suggestively.

"Yes. It was delicious," I agreed, holding open the shirt slightly to let my eyes run over her naked form. I felt my dick getting hard underneath her.

Her eyes sparkled as she searched my features. "Hey, sustenance first." She ripped open the wrapper on the Twinkies and held one up to my mouth. I took a big bite off of the end as I watched her face.

She dipped her finger into the cream filling and licked it off with the tip of her tongue. Openly flirting with me, her eyes never left mine.

Brook picked up a large red strawberry and brought it to her lips and took a large bite. The juice ran down the edge of her mouth and I bent to kiss it off.

"That's the best strawberry I've ever tasted," I whispered against her mouth.

She pulled off the stem and then stuffed the rest of the strawberry into the Twinkie. My eyes widened as I watched her.

"Try it. I bet it tastes like strawberry shortcake." She wagged her eyebrows at me. She was so adorable.

I opened my mouth and she put it to my lips so I could bite off the end. It was delicious.

"Yeah. You're a genius," I said with my mouth full.

"Duh." She smiled and I laughed out loud.

She continued to feed me more of her invention until it was gone, and then brought another strawberry to her mouth.

Slowly she bit into it and I found myself mesmerized by her mouth moving on the fruit. She held out the rest of the berry to me and I took it in my mouth.

Suddenly the humor in the situation was lost as desire rushed through me.

"Mmmmmm." My body was coming to life under hers and my hands moved her hips to rub back and forth across my erection. She moaned against the new strawberry at her mouth, her head falling back and her lids falling to cover her eyes.

I bent my mouth to take the other half and then kept my mouth on hers in a deep, strawberry scented kiss. I picked up another one and took a bite, then pushed it against the skin of her neck, pulling down across her breasts and on to her nipples.

I bent to lick the juice from her skin as her nipple hardened under my tongue. She pulled the rest of the berry from my fingers and brought it to her mouth, her blue eyes burning into mine.

She gasped as I lifted her body onto mine, and I slid inside her, my arm around the back of her waist to guide her thrusts on me.

Her body fits mine so perfectly. I didn't think anybody I'd ever been with fit so well.

I pulled her down onto me as I again bent to share the strawberry she was eating. I sucked the juice from her lips and then thrust my tongue into her mouth as hers came into mine.

Her arms wrapped around my shoulders and her hands wove into my hair as the passion between us flared anew. So hot, intense and delicious.

That night, I gained a whole new appreciation for strawberries.

Chapter 8

Christmas Presence

Brooklyn

I CAME OUT of the bathroom, wrapped only in my towel. My hair was dripping wet as I padded across the floor to my suitcase to select something to wear on the trip back to the States. I glanced at the beautiful man sleeping in the bed and my heart became heavier in my chest.

Our series of European premieres ended last night in Paris. It was a fun day, the interview extremely so, since we couldn't speak French and no interpreters were used. They gave us questions fed live through Twitter with the hashtag #CadeNBrook.

We teased each other and joked and laughed with the host the whole time. Thank God, Cade could speak French and could translate. The host was clearly smitten with him, judging by her wide eyes and rapt expression. Some of the answers we gave were complete and utter bullshit, but seriously some of the questions were beyond intrusive, designed to unearth any secrets about your relationships.

Cade was still pressing me to answer whether I felt he was sexier than Ryan Gosling or Zac Efron, since I'd managed to evade it during the interview. That was one I had pressed to pass. He said he was *still* waiting for my answer.

Like there was any contest. He damn well knew the answer, but he just wanted to hear me say it.

So, here we were. I would be flying with Jeanne, Noah, Denise and Martin; and Cade was jetting back to London for Christmas. The past six days had been like heaven. We'd spent every night together, completely alone, always ordering breakfast from room service.

I sighed, thinking back on our time together. He was so incredible, his lovemaking so passionate and amazing. He took my breath away each and every time he touched me. I felt my throat begin to ache as I packed up my suitcase. I was going to miss him.

Don't cry, Brooklyn. Don't cry and ruin the perfection of these days. I kept talking to myself in my head.

Cade began to stir in the bed, and I went to sit next to him. My fingers itched to touch him, so I reached out and brushed his hair off of his forehead. He sighed then his eyes opened, and a soft smile came to his lips.

"Good morning, gorgeous girl." His hand came out and he took mine to his lips, kissing the inside of my wrist.

"Good morning, yourself." I leaned down to kiss his mouth and the stubble on his chin scratched a little on my face. I gripped his chin with my hand as I bent to kiss him again. "You're so yummy." I tried to keep my voice light, but the tightness in my throat was undeniable.

I got up to resume my packing, but struggled with keeping the towel in place. I'd laid out the clothes I planned to wear; typical of my casual style, especially for traveling. I had an oversized white tunic T-shirt and black leggings, with some Vans that I could slip off during the flight.

Cade turned on his side and propped up on his elbow as he watched me.

"Brook." His voice was matter-of-fact and commanding. He wanted to talk. He wanted me to look at him, but if I did I might lose it.

"Uh huh?" I glanced up from my suitcase, briefly.

"Come here, please." His tone was serious.

I did as he asked, and he lifted the covers next to his naked body to beckon me back to bed.

I felt the tears start in my eyes as I dropped my towel and crawled in beside him. His arms engulfed my body as I curled into his side, my head fitting perfectly onto his shoulder. He kissed my forehead and moved his bent fingers to lightly scratch up and down my arm, as I fought the emotions threatening to overflow. I turned closer in and buried my face in his neck as I lost my battle with the tears, the hot wetness dripping onto his skin.

His arms tightened around me.

"It won't be so long this time. Maybe we can see each other for Christmas or New Year's Eve, hmmm?"

"Mmm, huh." I didn't trust myself to speak without my voice breaking.

"Oh, babe. I hate this part, but I wouldn't trade one second of the time we have together. It's so incredible. You're my whole world, Brooklyn."

I nodded, still plastered against him, my fingers clutching into his naked skin anywhere I could touch. I brought my lips to his neck and I sucked lightly on the skin as the hand around his waist slid up to the back of his neck. I raised my chin and kissed his jaw.

"Brook, I'm going to ask Denise to get me a flat in L.A. I'm tired of not being close to you."

My heart leapt at his words as I raised my head to look into his face. He reached out to brush the line of my jaw with the tips of his fingers.

"But, you'll miss your friends and family, right?"

"I miss you more. I can't stand leaving you all the time, and I can't stand seeing you cry."

I hugged him tighter and turned my face into him again as more tears flowed from my eyes. I wanted to be stronger, but I wasn't.

"I've been thinking about it for months actually. If something happened to you and I was in London, it would be twelve or fourteen hours before I could get to you. That bloody terrifies me."

Hope leapt in my chest and my heart beat faster, but I knew it was a big sacrifice for him to make.

"I love that you want to do that, but we still have to be apart, regardless. Look at these past few weeks, you've been in L.A. and we've still barely had any time together. I'd hate for you to make those kinds of changes with no guarantees we'd be any better off. Plus, the press would go nuts. The studio wouldn't be supportive."

"I'll take my chances. If we have an opportunity come up, it's a hell of a lot easier to sneak across town than for one of us to fly bloody half way around the globe, yeah?" He smiled the beautiful smile that was uniquely him, and bent to pull my upper lip in between both of his. My mouth opened to him and he brought a groan out of me when his tongue dove into my mouth. My mouth was clinging to his when he finally pulled away.

"You are," I said.

"What?" His brows went up and his mouth twitched.

"I said you are." I smiled through my tears. "I think *you're* sexier than Ryan or Zac."

He laughed and brought his mouth down to mine again in a brief kiss. "I know." I felt his breathy smile against my lips as the words left him and I couldn't help but laugh a little.

"Of course, I'm not exactly objective. I've never made love with either of them or seen them naked. Maybe I should do some research, just to be fair." My mouth quirked at the corners and I had to bite my lip to stop from laughing.

"Um, no. That won't be possible. Ever." His fingers brushed against my cheek, wiping at the remnant wetness.

I pulled myself up so that I could prop up on his chest and look into his face. "Okay. I can live with that." I stared into his blue eyes, and his expression was a mixture of amusement and sadness.

"I'm going to miss you so much," I breathed the words against his mouth.

"I'll think about you every second, sweetheart. You know that."

"I know." I smirked at him as I echoed his earlier words, while his fingers brushed the last remnants of tears from my face. His touch was so tender, like a butterfly's wings on my cheeks.

Cade rolled on to his side and took me with him, both of us ending up lying on the pillows facing each other. He stared into my eyes and took my hand to his mouth as he kissed each of my fingers and then the palm.

"How long until your plane, my love?"

I felt my brow crinkle and I lowered my eyes, the pain in my throat beginning to throb again.

"Um, three hours." I drew a shaky breath as I raised my eyes back to his. The pain clearly visible in the liquid depths, his brow dropped lower over his eyes. His hand was shaking as he brought it to the side of my face.

"I know you've already taken a shower, but I need to make love with you one last time," he whispered against my mouth, his hot breath fanning out on my cheeks. "Just one more time." His aroused body pressed into mine, and I had no thoughts of denying him.

The tears fell from my eyes as his mouth met mine in one of the most tender kisses he'd ever given to me. His lips moved on mine so slowly, his tongue gently exploring and seeking mine. Each touch was feather light as his fingers moved on my face and then down my neck and across my shoulder.

My arms slid around him as he moved above me and he stared intently into my face. Propping himself up on his elbows, he brushed the hair back from my face as he nuzzled my nose with his and finally bent to take my mouth with his as the tenderness gave way to the desperation, hunger and need that flowed through both of us.

Every touch was exquisite, completely and utterly communicating the overwhelming love we felt between us. My heart ached, yet love made me euphoric, the entire time as we made magnificent love to each other, worshiping with each touch, kiss and thrust of our bodies.

The coming separation left a tangible and poignant veil of sadness hanging between us. So thick, it made it hard to breathe.

Cade's gorgeous eyes welled with tears after he'd once again brought my body to shivering climax. The experience left us both spent and breathless as we lay together, still entwined.

"I'm coming back to you, Julia. Soon, so very soon, so don't forget to remember me." His velvet voice was so dazzling, with his American accent firmly in place. He was Ryan once again as he smiled softly down at me. His thumbs traced delicately along both sides of my forehead as he bent to kiss me one last time. I folded my arms and legs around him as I fought the sobs building in my chest and poured everything I had into that kiss. I desperately needed to show him how much I would miss him. How much I loved him.

I knew he was hoping to ease my grief at leaving him today by reminding me that we would soon be together for three months, when we went to Vancouver in March to begin filming the second movie in the series.

We stayed in bed for several more minutes, getting control of our emotions and holding each other close, trying to stretch the time we had left. Finally, he spoke.

"I love you, baby. Always."

"Me too."

"Do you want to take another shower? You're leaving sooner, so you'll need to go first, my love."

"Uh uh. I'll shower when I get home. I want to smell you on me today, to take you with me. I don't want to wash you off of my body... not yet, Cade."

His eyes widened and darkened as he watched my face, and his arms tightened ever so slightly around me.

"Do you think that's gross?" I finally asked against his mouth.

"No. It's sexy as hell. It makes me love you all the more, if that's *even bloody possible.*"

***

AFTER I GOT back to Los Angeles, I worked on my mom to get her to let me make the trip to London for Christmas.

"Brook. We always do the family trip and this may be the last year that both you and Nathan will be available. I don't want you to miss this, and you always loved to ski."

"Mom, that's what I'm saying. I'm not really available *this* year. I want to be with Cade. Can't you understand? Please?" I flopped down on her bed as she put clothes in her closet.

"Where would you stay?" She was skeptical.

"Mom. You let Cade sleep with me in my room and you're worried where I would stay in London? With him, of course." I was feeling so exasperated by the fruitlessness of the conversation. I shook my head at her.

She sighed. "I'm not a hypocrite, baby. What will his parents think of you if you shack up with their son? They are, after all, proper English parents, right?"

I rolled my eyes at her. *Okay, seriously?*

"Well, they'll think I love their son more than anything. They pretty much know that already anyway. If you'd feel better, I can stay with his parents. Lillian already invited me when they were here for the premiere."

She sat down on the bed next to me and I turned to prop my head on my arm.

"Mom, can you *please* support me in this? I love him so much and he's so sad at not being able to be with me at Christmas. It hurts me to see him so sad."

I reached out for her hand. "Please?"

She nodded in agreement. "What are you going to get him for Christmas? Have you thought about that?"

"Yeah, but I'm struggling. He doesn't *want* anything, and he isn't into material crap. Obviously, he can buy anything he wants. I mean, he'd rather have some rare book or original sheet music than anything more traditional. I've tried to think of something spectacular, but I haven't been able to yet."

She watched my face and smiled at me.

"What?"

"Nothing. I can just see how much he means to you, honey."

I flushed. "Yes. I know it happened fast, but it's so strong, it terrifies me."

"You're lucky, Brook. Most people never have that."

"There was one other thing I thought about giving him for Christmas, but it's so personal." My fingers traced the patterns in the comforter on my parent's bed.

"What could be too personal for someone you love that much?"

"Well, you might get mad at me." I hesitated to gauge her reaction before I continued.

"Why would I do that, baby? Did you rob a bank or something?" She was openly laughing at my expression.

"No."

My mother cocked her head to the side and raised her brows.

"I know how much you loved David, but I've always been drawn to Cade... since the audition, so... "

"For God's sake, Brook! Can you just spit it out?"

"I kept some notes about the feelings I had. I even wrote him some letters sometimes when I wanted to tell him the truth. There were times I was afraid to share my feelings, either out of guilt related to David or because I was worried that it would hurt Cade even more... I couldn't tell him how I felt, so I wrote it all down."

"Why would Cade be hurt by your feelings? I'm confused."

"Because I kept running away from him, even as I felt closer and closer to him. I fought the feelings that he desperately wanted from me. By telling him that I couldn't *help* falling in love with him, yet still choosing not to be with him, it might hurt, right? Wouldn't it hurt even more than thinking I didn't love him?" My voice was getting thick as my emotions rose to the surface. "He was already struggling with his own feelings, so I couldn't bear to cause him more pain than he already had."

My mom sighed and patted my hand. "But, what does this have to do with a Christmas gift?"

"Well, I thought I might give them to him."

"Don't you think it would still hurt him, for the same reasons?"

"No, I don't think so. I think it would mean a lot to him to be able to see that I felt the same for him as he did for me, all along. I've told him so already, but to let him read my thoughts as I had them, seems extremely intimate, and something that would have a deeper meaning."

My mom's eyes were full of tears when I looked up from my hands in my lap.

"I think that's perfect, Brook. I know he loves you very much, so I'm sure you're right."

***

IT WAS CHRISTMAS Eve and I was on my way to surprise Cade in London. I'd worked it out with Lillian and Layla to keep it a secret, and I'd even shipped my gifts to his family early to solidify the illusion that I wouldn't be able to make it. I'd packed up my journal that I'd kept about Cade in an elaborately wrapped box with a note that he couldn't open it until Midnight on Christmas Eve. My plane was landing around 10 PM and Layla was going to pick me up at the airport.

All of the Carlisle children were gathering at their parent's house for dinner that evening. Cade told me their traditions included sitting around the fire, all of them singing Christmas Carols as he accompanied them on the grand piano. He said his father always made special Christmas grog of spiced wine and rum that they all drank all night long. I couldn't wait to get there and be part of the festivities.

The time difference made it impossible for me to call him before I left. It was only 4 AM and he'd never believe I was up so early just to go skiing, so I'd have to try to call him after I landed in London. It was a risk because if he heard the airport announcements in the background it would blow the surprise. Hopefully, I'd be able to call him from the car.

I couldn't wait to see the look on his face when I showed up at his door. *It would be priceless.*

My heart already beat faster as adrenaline pumped through my body while I made my way from the plane into the airport terminal. I had on dark sunglasses and a scarf over my hair as I huddled down and made my way through the terminal. It was somewhat deserted, given it was so late on Christmas Eve and most of the holiday travelers had already moved through by now.

I was only staying for two days so didn't check any bags; my carry on was sufficient. I was able to make my way straight to the curb very quickly and I saw Layla right away. She was standing outside waiting for me as I rushed to her. She took my carry on and stashed it in the back of her little BMW as I dove into the front seat. I was wearing a long brown wig and a scarf, and kept my head down as I rushed through Heathrow. Only at customs did I have to disclose my real identity. It was a risk, but I picked an older customs agent, and thankfully, she didn't even flinch at the name on the passport.

"Wow. It's great to see you, Layla! I'm so excited to be here." I threw my arms around her in a big hug and then tore off the scarf and wig, running my hands through my hair.

"It's a good thing Cade is used to seeing me travel worn. I'm sure I look like a hideous hag!" I laughed.

"Not at all. He'll be so happy to see you. You should see how he's been moping around. Pathetic." She rolled her eyes and laughed. "I told Dad to wait on the grog until you arrived. I figured you'd want to get drunk with us!"

"How far are we from your parent's house? I need to call your brother, but I wanted to be on the phone with him when I walk in." I couldn't help the huge grin that split my face. It had only been two weeks since we'd seen each other, but it felt like longer. "Oh, my God! I'm so excited!"

"Just about ten minutes now." She winked at me.

"Wow. I'm not used to things being that close together. My house is an hour and a half away from LAX." I pulled out my phone. "Okay, here goes."

The phone rang only once before Cade answered.

"Brook, where have you been?" he demanded. "I've been calling all bloody day! You've had me worried sick!"

"Merry Christmas to you, too."

"Aw hell, I'm sorry, love. What's bloody merry about it?" He was exasperated and I could just see him running his hands through his hair.

"Well, I get to talk to you. I miss you."

Layla was grinning from ear to ear as she looked at me. If she kept that up, I'd never get through this call convincing him I was as miserable as he obviously was.

"Yeah. I'm missing you too, Brook. So much it hurts. I hate not being with you tonight, love."

I sighed. *Keep acting, Brook,* I told myself.

"Me too! I'm miserable without you." I bit my lip. *Jesus, don't laugh Brooklyn. You're supposed to by wallowing.*

"Did you get the gift I sent to you?"

Shit.

"Um, no. Where did you send it?"

"To your hotel in Vail. Bloody hell!" His voice was irritated.

"I'm sure it was just the holiday mail rush. I'll get it soon. What was it?"

We were pulling into their driveway, through a front gate. The lane was about a quarter of a mile long leading up to a large brick and stone home. It was gorgeous, the outside lighting casting a soft glow on the house and the snow covered grounds.

My heart started thumping in my chest. He was so close now, I could hardly breathe.

"You said you didn't want anything expensive, so I just sent you a CD of some of my stuff, and some of the songs in the films. You know, from the piano scene?"

I gasped at his thoughtfulness. "That's perfect, babe. I can't wait to hear it. Thank you."

"I really miss you, Brook. I hate that we're apart at Christmas."

"Me, too. I hate it. I wish I didn't have to come to Colorado. I fell three times today and I'm not having a good time at all." I was lying through my teeth. I grimaced at Layla as a huge smile split her beautiful face.

"Did you hurt yourself?" I could hear the panic in his voice.

Layla got out and opened the trunk to get out my suitcase. I had to figure out a way to keep him on the phone, yet not have him hear us moving and the car doors slamming.

"Not at all. Just being me, you know. Are you playing Christmas carols for your family yet?"

"Only a little. I'm not in the mood, really."

"Cade, it's Christmas. *Get* in the mood. Will you do something for me?"

"Anything" I could hear his breath come out in a huff. "You know that."

"Play something for me? Maybe the song from that scene? Take the phone and set it on the piano so I can hear it, okay?"

"Oh, Brook." His voice lowered. "Okay. Just a moment." I listened to the sound of him walking into the other room and setting the phone on the piano. The beautiful music instantly flooded into the phone and I turned and motioned to Layla to go into the house.

We ran up the walk and quietly opened the door. Lillian was there and she gave me a quick hug and motioned to the music room where I would find Cade playing the piano.

I could hear the music flood the house as I walked in to find his back to me as his long fingers danced across the keys. He was so beautiful and I wanted to stand there and watch him, undetected.

Jesus, would I ever get used to how beautiful he was?

My heart was beating so fast I thought it would fly right out of my chest. I waited as he finished the song and picked up his phone.

"There. I love you, Brook. I wish you were here."

I didn't say anything into the phone because he would hear me behind him.

"Brook?—Brook?"

I handed Lillian my phone. His entire family was standing quietly behind me as I silently inched toward him.

"Brook!"

"Yes?" I ran my hand gently down the back of his head, the silken strands so soft to the touch.

He turned instantly to me, his face lighting up when he saw me. Less than a second later, he jumped up from the bench and enfolded me in a huge bear hug lifting me off of the ground.

"Oh my God! Oh my God, really?" He was laughing as he held me and then he drew his head back to place a kiss on my mouth and several more all over my face as his family cheered behind us. "You little liar!!"

"The song was beautiful. Thank you, Cade." His hands came to the sides of my face and his thumb traced the edge of my jaw.

"No, thank you, my love. You couldn't have given me a better Christmas. Everything is perfect now."

"Thank God. Maybe now the Grinch can go away!" Oliver murmured dryly.

Cade's eyes bore into mine and it was apparent he wanted to kiss me, but I was overly aware that we had an audience, so I decided I needed to make him aware as well.

"Layla and your mom helped me, so I'm not the only liar involved."

He wrapped his arm around me and walked to a large, over-stuffed leather sofa near the fireplace and ten-foot-tall Christmas tree, which was decorated in lots of sparkling ornaments and white lights. We sank down into it with our arms wrapped around each other. The house was gorgeous with lots of wood paneled walls, stone and tile, antique tables and big, plush furniture.

"Brook, what are you doing here?" He was smiling but incredulous. "I mean, I'm bloody elated, but I'm in shock!"

"I hope making my boy happy." I leaned into him and took his hand in mine. "I missed you, and I hated hearing you so sad."

He grinned at me. "Well, now I'm triumphantly delirious!"

"Come on you lovebirds, let's not make the rest of us nauseous!" Layla shot at us with a laugh.

We had a very nice evening with his family and when his dad got ready to make his wine concoction he asked me to help by pouring the rum over a large sugar cone. It was similar to a sugar cube, very hard and it sucked up the pint of rum I dumped onto it.

Carter then set it up in a large copper kettle by the fireplace and proceeded to pour six bottles of cabernet around it. I watched as he and Cade opened the bottles and laughed together.

"Brooklyn, thank you so much for relieving us of the sour puss we had dealt with all day. He's so much more agreeable now." He mocked his son.

Cade just laughed. "Yes, now that Santa Claus has delivered my present, I'm much happier."

I blushed as the two of them watched me. Lillian came into the room with a large bowl of sliced oranges and lemons and scattered them into the wine.

"Oliver, I forgot the spices. Can you bring me the cinnamon sticks, whole cloves and nutmeg grater?" Her son got up, grumbling that cooking was women's work, but did what he was asked.

After everything was compiled in the pot, Carter came to me with the candle lighter. "Would you like to do the honors, Brook? Caden usually does it, but I'm sure he'll be glad to acquiesce this time."

I looked at Cade who smiled and nodded toward the pot. "Yeah, get going woman. It takes a while for that thing to burn down and I'm thirsty."

"Do I just touch the flame to the sugar?" Cade's eyes followed my every move and I raised my eyebrows when he didn't answer right away.

"Yes, that's right, darling," Lillian finally spoke up.

I touched the flame to the sugar and instantly the rum fired the cone from top to bottom.

"Now, as the sugar melts it will heat the wine and after it's finished, we'll put the kettle over the fire. It's really quite good. You'll like it." Cade pulled me back down onto his lap and I rested my head in the crook of his shoulder. His scent all around me, I inhaled deeply as I felt his mouth brush the top of my head. I wasn't sure we should have such an open display of affection, but it felt too good to fight.

"Are you planning on getting me tipsy and taking advantage of me?" I whispered so only he could hear.

"Mmmmm. Naturally." He smiled widely then kissed my mouth softly, his eyes sparkling into mine. "I'm so happy you're here, love."

My arms tightened around him as I snuggled closer.

"Oh, look at them, will you? Sickening, just bloody sickening." Layla's eyes were alight as she teased us and her laughter rang through the room and we all joined in.

We opened presents and when Lillian asked Cade to play carols, he pulled me up to join him on the bench. It reminded me of the shoot when we'd spent hours at a piano together. The difference was that this time, I could touch him openly, and rest my head on his shoulder.

We had a great time singing and playing around with his family, who seemed to enjoy the gifts I brought them. I found some really nice cashmere sweaters for his father, brother and sister, but I had a bracelet made for Lillian. It was gold and smooth with three princess cut stones bevel set, each one a birthstone of one of her children.

"Oh, Brooklyn. This is just lovely. Thank you, so much. You're so thoughtful." She stood and I got up to give her a hug, before Layla and Carter gathered around her to look at it.

"You're amazing, Brook. I can't tell you how much having you with me means to me. My family simply adores you." He nuzzled my nose and touched his lips to mine. He licked my top lip with the tip of his tongue and pulled my lower lip in between his in a soft, tugging kiss.

"I've missed you so much," I whispered as my hand went up to touch his face.

We were sitting on the floor next to the fireplace with our backs up against the sofa and I noticed we were suddenly alone.

"Where did everyone go?"

"It's late and I'm sure they're giving us some privacy." His arm was around me and my hand went up to hold his, I leaned into him. "Mmmmm..."

"You see that other box under the tree? That red one, with the silver ribbon?" I pointed to it.

"Yeah?"

"That's your gift from me. Do you want to open it?" My fingers threaded through his.

It felt so good to be with him; I was so content I could sit here on the floor with him forever.

He sighed. "Love, you didn't need to get me anything. You're all I need, I told you that. And, you're here. That's a miracle in itself."

"This is a piece of me. Trust me." I looked into his blue eyes and thought I would drown in the love shining out of them.

I let go of him and crawled to the tree to retrieve the package, bringing it back and handing it to him as I returned to my place by his side.

The fire cast an orange glow on his face as his hand hesitated on the box. The smell of the wine and the wood burning in the fireplace filled the room. He turned to look at me again and his eyes searched my face.

"You're so beautiful, my love. You give me so much. You have no idea." He reached out and touched my face.

My heart thumped in my chest and he took my left hand. His thumb running over the engagement ring that I'd allowed myself to wear on this trip.

"This means everything, right here." He softly brushed his lips over the ring and the top of my hand.

"Cade. I love you, but are you going to open the damn box or not?" I was dying to see his reaction to the diary inside. I grinned at him.

He laughed out loud. He was stalling and knew full well that I couldn't stand it.

"Give me a hint."

"Just open the damn thing, okay?" I poked him hard in the ribs.

"Ow! I thought you loved and adored me." I cocked my head to the side and scowled at him.

"Oh, okay." He pulled the silver ribbon and then ripped off the paper, before lifting the lid of the box.

"I've seen this book before. Haven't I?"

"Yep. I had it with me all through filming remember? I kept my stage notes in it, as well as some of the script changes we made."

"You're giving me your *stage notes*?" His mouth twitched and curved up at the corners.

"It's also my notes about you, and some letters I wrote to you during those months." His eyes widened and he drew in his breath.

"What? You didn't give me any letters."

"I used to write everything down." I dropped my eyes to my lap and I wondered why I was so fucking nervous. "Things I thought about you, felt about you... I couldn't share with you then because of my situation. But now, I want you to see how amazed I was, mesmerized by you. And, how I really loved you all that time..."

"Brook..." He took a deep breath, and put his hand on the cover before looking at me.

I brought my eyes up to his. "So, I'm finally letting you see everything."

My eyes were blurring and I couldn't tell if it was just the tears in my eyes that made his look watery as well, but he cupped my cheek and rested his forehead on mine.

"This is perfect. I'm overwhelmed, baby." He placed a soft feather kiss on my mouth and his wine-scented breath fanned out on my face. He was so delicious, so warm and soft. "Thank you."

I closed my eyes and for a few minutes, we just sat like that; silent and touching.

"Can I read it now?"

"There's a lot in there to read so you won't be able to read it all tonight, but if you want, of course, you can look at it now. It's yours. Read it whenever you want."

"Do I get to keep it, or just borrow it?"

"I'm giving it to you, Cade. It's like my heart; yours always."

Tears welled in his dark blue eyes as his looked at me. "I love you so much, Brook. I don't know how to put it into words, but you mean more to me than anything in this world. It hurts, it's so intense."

First one tear, then another fell from my eyes as I nodded. "I know, Cade, okay?"

He tore his eyes from my face as he opened the diary.

Dec. 18

Final callbacks today for the three of us the director has narrowed down to make the final cut. I wonder if it's just the girls or if Cade Carlisle will be there to read with us. I know he's making a movie in Southern California, so I'm hoping.

My heart jumps around in my chest whenever he's around, and the chemistry between us is obvious. At the first reading he hinted he'd have input, so I hope he wants me for the part. I mean, I could seriously get lost in those blue eyes and knowing the story like I do, I know we could "be" these characters. He's been so amazing. Better than I ever could have imagined.

Cade's eyes glassed over as he read it aloud, and then turned to look at me.

"Brook... you felt everything I did."

"I know, babe. That's the point. There's so much more in there for you to discover. I hoped that sometimes when you're missing me, you could open this and know how much I love you and I always have. I wanted to take away some of the pain I know you've felt. Now you never have to wonder again." I smiled gently and reached out to cup his face with my hand. The emotions between us were tangible. Always so strong.

He set the book down and gathered me to him, holding me so tight it was difficult to breathe.

"I'll read it a million times. I want to memorize every word. It's such a beautiful gift, and I'll always treasure it. Thank you, my love." He began to laugh through his tears. "It means more to me than anything anyone has ever given me. I love you! So, much, but I must punish you for keeping it from me for so long."

I squealed as he threw me back ward on the floor, pounced on me and began to tickle me within an inch of my life. I screamed out loud and Cade burst out laughing before falling down on top of me to push my arms up over my head. I spread my legs to let him settle in closer and his face sobered, his eyes darkening.

I sighed and arched into him when his mouth settled on mine.

"Uhhh...." I breathed again, just before the kiss deepened; our tongues met, beginning an intimate dance, and all thoughts beyond how his body felt against mine, vanished.

Chapter 9

Love Letters

Caden

AS BROOKLYN LAY sleeping next to me, I perused the diary she'd given me. It was an incredible thing to see my emotions flowing through her words. My heart stopped and tears came to my eyes more than once as I read through the pages.

Jesus Christ, I thought. *She bloody amazes me.*

Feb. 10

> *Cade and I spent the entire night talking and getting to know each other. He is such an amazing person and so talented! I can't get over how he thinks about things and how much he knows about everything. He dives into the scenes and picks apart the juxtaposition within them and it's amazing to be part of it. The emotions he exudes are so similar to what I imagined between these two characters. I found myself staring at him more than once, as he talked, unable to do anything else. He's so animated... not to mention so fucking beautiful. I'm completely mesmerized.*

Feb. 26

Cade and I are spending a lot of time together. We have a great time. He's so hilarious, and makes me laugh so much. I find my eyes searching for him constantly and I look forward to seeing him every day. David is visiting next weekend, and I'm feeling weird about it. Cade and I are getting closer, and I don't want David to come. I feel guilty, but it doesn't change how I feel. The fact is, I'm scared of my feelings for Cade. He's such a huge star and I'm nobody; lucky to be in a movie with him. It's all so surreal. I'm scared my whole world will come crashing down around me. I can't breathe.

I skipped through, flipping pages and getting glimpses of her feelings through the entire time of filming, because I couldn't help myself. I planned to go back and read the entire journal later, but once I started reading, I couldn't put it down.

March 11

We filmed the scene in the kitchen today. Standing so close to Cade all day, I could feel the heat radiating from his skin. After we smeared dessert in each other's faces, we laughed until we cried. Martin was pissed and we had to do it all again. All I know is I'm in serious, serious trouble.

March 19

We worked all day today. It was just rehearsal and we were working out all of the camera angles around the coffee shop set. Touching Cade is like a drug that I can't get enough of. The electricity between us is tangible and I never wanted to let go. I get lost in his eyes and never want the moments to end. Jesus. I'm falling in love with him. What the fuck am I going to do?

My breath left my body when I read those words and looked at the date again. My heart began to hammer in my chest. If only I'd known then. I was so miserable, pining away like a lovesick teenager. I glanced at Brook sleeping next to me and tenderness washed over me. She was so beautiful and I was still stunned that she was lying beside me in my bed, in London.

March 21

We filmed the agonizing scene in the bar after Ryan gets his acceptance letter. It was all I could do not to reach out and touch Cade. Martin insisted we kiss at the end of the scene, and it was a struggle. I could sense Cade's inner battle as well. That scene in the script didn't call for a kiss, and

Cade echoed my thoughts aloud. "What's he bloody doing? This will never make the film." I can't believe how similar we think. I'm so confused and overwhelmed by all of these emotions.

March 25

Cade just left my room. We were running lines and practicing for the scene in Ryan›s bedroom. We had the whole thing memorized, never missing a line. He kissed me with that beautiful mouth and something inside me is drawn to him like a moth to a flame. I never wanted it to stop, and each time we repeated the scene it got hotter and hotter. I doubt we could perfect that scene anymore if we tried. I didn›t want him to leave. I didn't want the scene to stop... I love him so much my heart is bursting. I am SO fucked.

Again my heart felt like it was going to fly from my body. I remembered that night; every second of it. It was like some private treasure that was mine alone.

April 18

It's my birthday and it went by in sort of a blur. David was here and I could feel Cade pull back. It hurt knowing he was hurting. He sat in the corner of the table and glared at David and I all evening. Pain was written all over him and I wanted David to disappear and to go to him. I can't believe how pissed I was at David for just being here... I'm supposed to love him, and all I want to do is push him away. I picked a fight with him so that he'd leave. He wanted to make love and I can't even bear to kiss him. I don't know what to do, but I know I can't bear the pain in Cade's eyes. It fucking breaks my heart in half.

April 18 - Again

After David left, I called Cade and asked if we could talk, I needed to ease the pain. Something inside needed him to know I wasn't with David tonight. He gave me the most beautiful guitar for my birthday and said it was so that we could play together. I smiled so much, my face hurt and I asked him if he would help me learn to play better. His face lit up when I asked. He's so damn beautiful he stops my heart. It was like he was giving me a piece of himself. He is unbelievably sweet to me. My heart is so full of him it's incredible. He asked me to marry him again and I'm aching. Just... ACHING.

I was dying to know what she'd written following the filming of the scene in Ryan's bedroom so my mind searched to remember the date. It was somewhere before her birthday and so I flipped backward through the pages.

April 7

We did the bedroom scene today. It was real and Martin yelled at us for making the scene too hot, the kisses too intense. I was so hot for him that I completely forgot about everyone else on set… it was just us. I felt his hardness as he pressed into me… he wanted me too. We lost ourselves in the scene and as we waited for the crew to reset the scene, the look in his eyes burned me alive. It's all I can do not to run to his room right now, take him down and beg him to make love to me. God, I know it will be so amazing.

My heart constricted as I read those words and I reached out to touch the beautiful girl who had written them. She stirred under my hand. I knew I needed to let her sleep, but reading those words left me aching for her; my heart swelling with love and my dick swelling with desire. Her words and my memories of that day were so in sync.

I set the diary on my bedside table and turned out the lamp, then settled down under the covers, and turned on my side to face her in the darkness. I propped up on one elbow so I could touch her with my other hand. She was breathing softly, evenly, and her skin was like velvet under my fingers. Her dark lashes fanned out on her cheeks and her skin glowed translucent in the soft rays of moonlight that shone through the window. My hand moved to her temple to brush her blond tresses back from her delicate features, and my heart pounded in my chest just looking at her.

I ran my hand over her arm and up again, then gently over the swell of her breast. My hand cupped it and I brushed my thumb over the nipple softly. It hardened immediately and my mouth dropped open.

"Uhhhhhhhhhh… .." My breath whooshed out of me at the responsiveness of her body. She was so sexy and I was so turned on.

"Cade… ." Her lips parted in a breathless whisper as she arched her back to press her breast more firmly into my hand. My thumb brushed the nipple again and then slid down her body, over her rib cage and hip down to her thigh. My hand clamped down and kneaded the flesh before pulling her close and pressing my arousal into her stomach.

Her arms came up around me as she raised her mouth to mine. The instant our lips touched we were devouring each other, our hands roaming each other's bodies, our mouths sucking and wild in the exchange.

Dear God... if this is dying, let me die.

My hand pushed her T-shirt up and I bent my head to lave her nipple. She tasted so sweet as I flicked it with the tip of my tongue and then pulled it into my mouth to suckle it. She moaned my name as I moved to her other breast and her little hand found its way under my boxer briefs to knead my ass. I rolled on top of her so I could grind into her.

"Uhhhhhh... Mmmm," she sighed as she pressed back against me.

My hands held the sides of her head and her free hand slid up around my neck to fist in my hair, pulling my mouth tighter, closer into hers. She tasted so bloody good. It reminded me of a make-out session one might have in high school, only hotter than anything I'd ever experienced. I would be satisfied with kissing and petting all night if that was what she wanted from me.

"Cade... Cade..." Her mouth was reaching up for mine and she licked my top lip and then sucked my lower one into her mouth, again and again she kissed me and I was starving for more.

"Oh my love... I never want to stop kissing you, Brooklyn."

I rolled onto my back and took her with me. Her knees came to rest on the bed around my hips, and our hungry mouths continued the onslaught on each other. It was so fucking amazing... utterly incredible.

She moved her body up and down on mine, the delicious friction causing both of us to pant even more. We were both breathless as she pulled her mouth from mine.

"What do you want?" Her voice was husky with desire. She licked at my lips and then dragged her open mouth down my chin and jaw to my neck where she sucked on my skin, her open mouth sending delicious shivers racing through my body. "Tell me what you want."

"I want you, Brook." She sat up on her knees still straddling my lap, and her hands came down to rub my dick. Grasping, moving up and down, she applied pressure to the head. "Ahhh... Jesus, that feels good, love."

"Yes, but *what* do you want?" She continued to rub my member until I thought I was going to come. I was panting, my head falling back on the pillows.

Her hands slowed and she bent to kiss me, her lips clinging to mine as she spoke in a whisper. "Do you want more of this?" Her hands went back to their task and her lips continued to tease mine. "Do you want me to go down on you... or do you want to *fuck me*, Cade?"

Holy Hell... I felt my body engorge even more at her words. The air rushed from my lungs as I sat up and wrapped my arms around her, pulling her pelvis tighter, grinding her into mine.

Her brilliant blue eyes bore into mine as her lips hovered and ghosted mine. "Tell me what you want... and it's yours." Her hand was at the side of my face and her thumb drug my lower lip down before I couldn't take another second of the exquisite torture.

"Dear God, you're killing me, babe. I want... to make love with you, Brook." My mouth plowed into hers with everything I had as my hands moved her shirt up and off of her body, our mouths parting for only the seconds I needed to throw it aside.

Desire surged through my veins so hot I thought it would burn me alive, as my mouth once again found her nipples and pulled one into my mouth to gently graze it with my teeth. Her arms wrapped around my head and I felt her mouth in my hair.

"I love you, Cade. I love you, so much."

I held her around her waist and under her ass as I flipped her on the bed. I sat back and ripped her panties from her body before pushing my boxers down. Her eyes roamed over me and came to rest on my erection as I took her hand to pull her up to me again. I lifted her above me as I searched for her opening.

"You're so beautiful... so beautiful," she moaned against my neck as I slid into her body. She was so hot, slippery wet and it was heaven. Our mouths resumed the greedy kissing as our bodies moved together. For several minutes we moved together, kissing over and over again, until I could barely take anymore, yet it was never enough.

"Brooklyn. Jesus... I love you, too. You're everything. So perfect. Amazing. Tell me you belong to me. Tell me you're mine."

I felt her body clenching at mine, her legs started to tremble and she was moaning my name. I knew her body so well. I knew she was starting to climax. I felt so incredible that I could make her body quake and writhe with such incredible pleasure. I wanted to give and give and give to her.

I rolled over with her and thrust into her harder as my own orgasm started to build.

"Brook... tell me your mine. *Say it*." I needed to hear it.

"Uhhhh. Uhhh... " Her pants came in time with my thrusts into her body. "Oh, Cade, you already know. I'm always yours," she cried out against my mouth as she came. Her tremors and spasms exciting me even more. Those beautiful, sexy sounds she made drove me to distraction.

"God, Brook... I need you... so... fucking... much," I groaned against her throat as I exploded inside her. Her arms tightened around my body and I kissed the side of her face. I continued to thrust into her until I was completely spent, the last of the tremors finally subsiding.

When I opened my eyes, all I could do was stare into her face. That beautiful face, damp with perspiration, eyes heavy with desire and love, lips so luscious that I never wanted to stop kissing them... she was mine. Always mine and I felt my heart would burst at the knowledge.

I rolled off of her to her side but left my leg over hers and my arms pulled her to me. I couldn't help myself; I had to touch her, my mouth pressed to her forehead.

"Oh babe. That was incredible. As always."

We were breathing hard as we held each other, both of us softly stroking and touching each other. I didn't know how long we lay in silence, but just having her near me was enough to make me content.

"Were you reading the diary?" Her voice was full of emotion, her eyes shimmering and glassy.

"Yes. It's so beautiful. I haven't gotten all the way through it, but I treasure every word I've read so far. You're amazing."

"Have you read the last entries? At the end of the shoot?"

"Not yet, do you want me to?"

She shook her head against my chest and traced invisible patterns in my skin with her delicate touches as she began to speak.

"I don't know how I'm going to make it, how I'll get through tonight. I don't think I'll be able to breathe without him. I can't believe I've wasted so much precious time... I'm so mad at myself, just sick inside. I don't think I'll be able to say goodbye and I can't lose him... " Her voice broke on the words, and she took a shaky breath before she continued... "I don't want him to leave thinking he isn't my entire world because that's exactly what he's become. I'm dying, falling apart and I can't stop it or change it. It hurts so fucking much. Jesus, I love him." She recited off what I assume was the last entry on the night of the wrap party in Portland. I sucked in my breath and bought her closer to my chest.

"I felt the same way, my love. I didn't know how I was going to say goodbye to the one person that I needed and wanted the most in the world. I was in hell that night." My throat thickened as I remembered the pain of that evening and I felt her tears fall on my chest.

"It's silly to cry over it now, since here you are in my arms... but the pain was so unbearable. Even the memory is so real. I never want to lose you, Cade. Promise me."

"Oh baby. I promise. That can *never* happen, Brooklyn. I can't survive without you now."

I meant every single word.

Chapter 10
Goodbye Again

Brooklyn

I LEFT CADE asleep in the bed and mo ved quietly around the room to dress. He looked so peaceful with his hair falling softly across his forehead as he lay sprawled flat on his stomach, his arms stretched above his head. Last night was amazing. I felt stupid at how my mind kept using that word when thinking of him, but that's what he was. The look on his face when I surprised him filled me with indescribable happiness. This was our roller coaster; super highs, plunging to the deepest depths, and even if it was scary at times I didn't want to get off. I sighed contentedly as I threw on an old T-shirt and jeans.

The delicious smell of bacon frying permeated the air and I could hear the low sounds of a television coming down the hall as I quietly opened the door to Cade's room. He was planning on taking me to see his apartment later in the day before I had to catch my plane shortly after midnight. He called it a flat and I reminded myself that I wasn't in California anymore. Not yet. Two days, one night, then who knew when we'd be able to be together again. These redeye flights helped with the jet lag and also the mobs of fans, but it cut our time together short.

Lillian was in the kitchen making tea when I walked in." Good morning." I smiled at her and sat down at the curved marble bar that arched around the kitchen.

"Morning, darling. Did you sleep well?"

"I did, thank you. You have a very beautiful home, Lillian. Thank you for helping me with Cade's surprise."

Her face lit up in a bright smile. "Yes that was precious. He simply adores you Brooklyn. I've never seen him so besotted before." She reached out and patted my hand.

"Well, I think he's pretty special, too." I hesitated briefly before the next words burst from me. "I love him a lot." I ran my hand through my hair nervously, waiting for her reaction. Lillian nodded, her eyes filling with warm admiration as she gazed across at me.

"Would you like some tea? Or, I have coffee and juice? Caden insists on coffee since he's been spending so much time in America, so I always have it on hand for when he comes home."

I grinned. Cade did like his Starbucks. "Coffee'd be great, thank you."

Lillian had the same color hair as Cade and the same blue eyes. She was calm and genuine and had a wonderful way of making me feel welcome.

"You look sad, Brooklyn, are you alright?" she asked as she brought me the cup. "Cream?"

"No, thank you," I sighed. "I always love seeing Cade, but leaving him just always hurts so much. It's just something that we deal with, but never seems to get any easier." I shrugged and gave her a weak smile.

"Cade struggles with it as well. I hate seeing the two of you so unhappy," she reached out and took a hold of my left hand and examined the engagement ring that I wore, "but on the other hand, you're both so blissful, aren't you?"

I felt my face flush and nodded. Had Cade told his parents about the ring? I still kept it hidden from mine. Even though I was really open with my mother, she would think eighteen too young to be engaged.

"He did a nice job on that, didn't he?" She smiled again, and my breath rushed out in relief.

"Yeah. I… " I paused, "I wasn't sure if you knew. I don't usually wear it because we have all of those contract restrictions, but it makes him so happy; I thought for these few days, it would be okay."

"He told his father and I that he was going to marry you about half way through the filming." I gasped and my mouth dropped open at her statement. The shocked expression on my face made her nod gently. "It's quite beautiful, isn't it? Simple and elegant."

My eyes widened in shock. "Um… he didn't give me the ring until July. The movie wrapped at the beginning of May."

"No matter." She shrugged. "He told us in March." Her smile was so warm and reached all the way up into her eyes, so much like her son's.

"But…" I was speechless.

"He said he didn't know how long it would take, but he said you were *written on his soul.* He seemed extremely determined."

"Wow." I was speechless. "He's just…" I shrugged incredulously. "Incredible." I felt tears prick the back of my eyes and flood my eyes as I blinked them back quickly. "You must be so proud of all he's accomplished. How long has he been playing music? He sort of downplays everything, like he's only mediocre at everything. Sometimes it completely astonishes me that he doesn't get how wonderful he is. Or how beautiful." My mouth lifted in a gentle smile as I let my breath out, "Hmmph."

Lillian's face softened as she looked at me.

"Well, I'm his mum so I have to think he's fabulous. He's been playing piano since he was about four and he got a guitar as a gift from my brother when he was five and taught himself, really. He's always loved music and he has a brilliant ear. He would play for hours and hours, or go into his room and lock himself away with his records."

"Layla was always the more flamboyant of the children. Caden's more introspective, like Oliver, but he does have his sister's wit."

I nodded as a smile came to my lips, "When he talks about all of you, it's evident how close you all are. I think that's great. My family is very close, as well."

The door at the end of the hall opened and soon Cade padded his way to join us in the kitchen. He was wearing black jeans and a grey T-shirt, his hair seriously messy, but incredibly sexy.

So fucking hot. Jesus. My body quickened just looking at him and I blushed. I bent my head and scratched the back of my neck, hoping to hide my reaction from his mother.

Cade was rubbing his stubbly face as he came in and walked up behind me. He wrapped his arms around my waist, bending to kiss the side of my neck, as I remained on the stool. My eyes shot to meet Lillian's. My mind resisted the PDA in front of his mother, yet my heart and body craved even more.

He felt so good, and I closed my eyes as he rested his chin on top of my head. My arms covered his of their own volition.

"Do you want something to eat, darling?" Lillian asked him.

"Not quite yet, Mum. Thank you. What are you girls out here jabbering about?" His lips curved in a boyish grin.

"Wouldn't you like to know?" I teased. "I was just telling your mother how absolutely wonderful your family is."

He leaned in and placed a soft, open-mouthed kiss on my lips then moved to the stool next to mine, but kept my hand firmly in his the whole time.

"What are your plans today, Caden? Your father had to go in to work, but wanted to know if you and Brooklyn would be around for dinner," Lillian asked as she brought Cade his coffee.

"I wanted to take Brook to my flat, to show her what an utter slob I am." He offered a boyish grin. "But the bloody paparazzi always hounding us will prevent us from going out and doing anything else. We can't let it out that Brook's in London," he said as he added some cream to his cup.

"And I have to be at the airport later tonight, Cade," I reminded sadly.

His hand squeezed mine and he turned to face me. "Can't you stay longer? What is it you're running back to?" His brow dropped over his eyes as he searched my face.

"You know I'd stay if I could, but I have a meeting with the director of that urban flick and I don't even know when that will be. Jeanne is still trying to nail it down, but I've got to be available just in case. I guess with these temperamental directors, you never know their schedules."

"That seems bloody inconvenient and inconsiderate!" Cade huffed indignantly.

"Caden," his mother admonished him.

"What, Mum? It is, isn't it?" His expression was agitated.

I laid my free hand on his arm. "Yes, but I really want this part. More importantly, Jeanne tells me I really want it. I have to trust her, since I barely know what I'm doing. After I'm better known, maybe I'll have more leverage." My eyes pleaded with his for his understanding.

"Yes, it's just— Well, you just bloody got here and now you're leaving me already?"

I laid my head on his shoulder without saying a word as my fingers twined through his.

Suddenly Layla ran into the kitchen, flustered and frantic.

"Jesus, Cade! Tina is in the drive! How in bloody hell did she know you were home?"

Cade's eyes widened, "Uh, no idea. I didn't tell anyone." He glanced uneasily in my direction and it was clear he was wondering how we should handle it. Obviously, she couldn't know I was in London because she might leak the information to the press.

"I'll just go in your room, okay?" I pointed down the hall.

"Brook, you shouldn't have to do that." Cade said softly just as the doorbell rang.

"She has a nerve for showing her face around here after all this time, and how she dumped you," Layla huffed.

Dumped him? The girl must be on crack. "Cade, its fine. Okay?" I put a hand to his face and kissed his mouth. He nodded as I turned to walk away down the hall at the same time Lillian went to answer the door.

"Don't worry dear, we'll shoo her off, toot sweet," Lillian reassured me and I nodded and smiled at her as I left the room.

"Fuuuuuuck!" I heard Cade say behind me, and I smirked at his frustration. At least I knew he wasn't excited to see his old girlfriend.

Caden

MY HEART ACHED as I watched Brooklyn disappear into my room and close the door behind her. I didn't want to hide her or my feelings for her. I was fucking sick of this whole charade and our relationship was so new, I didn't want any chance for misunderstandings.

My mum came back into the kitchen closely followed by my ex-girlfriend, Christina Baines. We'd dated for a few years when we were both in drama school together. She wasn't as pretty as I remembered, though maybe it was my pissy mood because she'd arrived without an invitation. Was my perception clouded because Brook was a few yards away or because Tina had ended our relationship unceremoniously two years previously, before I'd made it big? It had stung when it happened, but it was probably more of a blow to my ego than actual pain at the loss.

Layla leaned up against the counter with her arms crossed, not attempting to hide her disdain. She raised one eyebrow then rolled her eyes.

"Well... Tina, to what do we owe this fascinating honor?" Layla asked sarcastically.

"Layla," Mum admonished her quietly.

"Hmmph," she said and turned to begin loading dishes into the washer, clanking the glasses so much I thought they might shatter.

"I um, heard Cade was in town for Christmas and I thought..." Tina shrugged. "That well, we might catch up. It's been such a long time." She came to me and put her arms around my waist. I brought my hands on her shoulders as she tried to place a quick kiss on my lips. I turned my head and pushed her away so it landed on my cheek, hearing her sharp intake of breath.

I quickly pulled back and separated from her. "Yes, it's nice to see you, but I'm only here for a short time and my schedule is rather full, actually."

I knew my voice was flat and dismissive, and I didn't care. I was in fact lying through my teeth. I was in London indefinitely—until I could figure out a reason to fly to L.A. to be with Brook which would also satisfy the bloody studio.

"Um, well are you going to go see Daniel's band play or anything? Maybe I can come with you. I've really missed you." She bit her lip and moved closer, her hand coming out to touch my stomach.

"More like you've decided to hitch a ride on Cades's recent blast into the stratosphere, yeah?" Layla interjected. "Well, he's done perfectly well without you up till now, and he doesn't need any dead weight. Get the picture?"

My lips twitched in an involuntary smile; it was all I could do not to burst out laughing at her remarks. I adored how Layla stepped in to protect Brook's interests, and it was hilarious as hell. I crossed my arms and raised my eyes to meet Tina's. Her steel grey eyes hardened at my sister's comment.

I cleared my throat. "Um, yes, I'm doing quite well. Things are busy and we'll be filming the sequel soon. I've also just read for another project in New York afterward, so I may not even be in London much after the end of February, Tina. What have you been up to?"

Jesus, what can I do to get her to leave? What must Brook be thinking, sitting alone in my room?

"Still working on my art. I have a friend who shows my stuff in her gallery as a matter of course, now."

"Congratulations. That's brilliant for you." My words were stilted. I didn't have anything to say to her and I was pandering.

"Can you come out for a while today, love? Maybe we can walk in the park or have tea?"

"Um...," I stuttered.

"Oh, for God's sake!" Layla threw up her hands and turned to face Tina abruptly. "What my brother is too much of a gentleman to say is that he's seeing an American girl, so there really is no point to your little attempt at weaseling back in his life." Her eyes widened dramatically as her hands spread in front of her. "He's clearly not interested! Are you bloody blind?"

I almost choked at Layal's bluntness. She'd never liked Tina and she didn't make an effort to hide the fact.

Tina looked at me with shocked eyes. "Cade, is that true?"

"Yes, I'm seeing someone." I nodded.

"Who is she? Anyone I know?" She wanted details.

"Now that my life is no longer my own with the press chasing me around everywhere, I don't share many details of my personal life, but it's... it's serious."

"That's a bloody understatement, if I ever heard one," Layla spouted. "Suffice it to say that the woman in question is in no doubt of Cade's adoration."

My eyes flashed to Layla and her face was full of mischief. She was bloody enjoying herself and my mum stood in the corner with a hand over her mouth, completely speechless.

"I see. Well, how does she feel about you? You can't have more than what we shared, right love. I mean, no one could love you more than me."

"Wrong!" Layla interjected shaking her head, her dark blonde hair moving around her shoulders.

I frowned. I had no desire to hurt Tina, but I was growing tired of this conversation and I was conscious of Brook in the bedroom.

"Look, I apologize Tina. I really didn't expect to see you and I don't want to be rude, but I did have plans today. As far as my feelings for this woman, I can assure you, that I love her more than I've ever loved anyone," I hesitated only briefly as Tina's face fell, "and I'm in no doubt that she returns my feelings."

Layla's face broke into a huge ass grin. "There! You see? Does that about do it, then? Good, have a nice day won't you, Tina? It's been so um, *annoying* of you to stop by without ringing up first." Layla was motioning her to the door. "Happy Christmas!"

"Layla, that's harsh," I said quietly.

Tina shook her head and the look in her eyes was hurt, but what did she expect, really? I hadn't talked to her in eighteen months.

"Okay. I'll go. But Cade, I do care for you so if you change your mind..." her words fell off as she walked out of the door.

"Bloody lucky she didn't bring you another one of those hideous paintings of hers. Complete rubbish! Though I did quite enjoy the bonfire we made of the last ones," Layla said dryly. "The nerve of that nag coming here like that."

We all burst out laughing. "Layla! I love you!" I hugged her close.

"What? Is it my fault that I've the bigger bullocks of the two of us, then? You can thank me later, little brother. I rather like a Mercedes or Jaguar, but not in some hideous orange or yellow," she smirked at me and I continued to chuckle as I went to my room to get my girl. I needed to get my hands on her for the fourteen hours we still had before she jetted away from me again.

***

IT'D BEEN ANOTHER tearful goodbye at Heathrow airport. I'd ridden with Layla to drop Brook off and we'd both lost it again, clinging to each other until the absolute last possible moment before she had to leave or miss her plane. Bodyguards in street clothes waited by the curb to inconspicuously escort her from the car. She put her hoodie up and pushed on a pair of sunglasses despite the lateness of the hour, bowing her head as she walked quickly through the doors and they closed in around her.

My chest hurt and I couldn't breathe as Layla and I returned to my parent's house.

"Are you doing okay, Cade?" Layla asked as I stared out the window while she drove through the streets of London.

"Yeah. I just have to get a flat in L.A. It bloody guts me to say goodbye to her, never knowing when I'll see her again. It rips my heart out."

"What did she give you for Christmas? I was there when Mum opened the box from her, so I know she sent you something. What was it?"

"Oh." I smiled, my heart swelling despite my sadness. "A journal she habitually wrote in when we were filming. She carried it with her constantly and wrote the director's notes in it and some of the scene changes we came up with. I never thought twice about it, but now I find she was also writing notes to me, even some full blown letters about the feelings and conflicts she was facing. So, she let me have access to all of those emotions that she was experiencing. It blew me away. She's shown me that she has loved me the entire time I've loved her. It's... amazing. It literally stops my heart when I read it, Layla."

"That's very special. It's obvious how gone she is about you. You know that, don't you?"

I nodded and swallowed, trying to assuage the lump rising in my throat. "Yes. It's a miracle; the biggest miracle of my life. I sometimes still have to shake myself when I'm with her. Our time together is so unbelievable. I can't even explain how she makes me feel."

I ran my hand through my hair as I watched the planes taking off, wondering which of them Brook was on. I knew in that second I wouldn't be staying away from her for very long.

"I'm calling Denise in the morning and having her arrange a flat and a car for me in L.A., and then I'm going to surprise Brook for New Year's. There's no bloody way I'm going to stay away from her until the Tokyo Premiere two and a half months from now. "

My mind was working on how I'd surprise her like she did me. It was only a week away, and it couldn't come soon enough. I'd call Ethan and have him arrange a night out on the 31st and invite the gang, including Brook then I could just show up. It would be brilliant... I couldn't wait. Only six days. Just six days. I could live through that.

Brooklyn

MY PHONE RANG as I packed my suitcase for my impromptu trip to New York to see Joan Jett after her New Year's concert. Finally, she was going to make time to meet with me, and not too soon either.

"Hey Babe." I knew I was breathless.

"Hey, yourself. What are you doing, you sound all out of breath." His voice was happy and relaxed.

"It's so good to hear that sexy voice. I miss you. I'm packing my suitcase."

Silence followed for a good three seconds. "Why?"

"Oh, I'm finally going to meet with that new director. Jeanne finally got me some time after his premiere in New York tonight. I'm in trouble because I don't even remember his flipping name."

"But... Brook, it's New Year's Eve. I thought you were going out with the gang?"

"Yeah, I wanted to, but this has to take priority. They'll get over it if I don't go."

His voice seemed stilted. "Ugh!"

"Cade, what's wrong? What is it?"

He let out his breath in a big rush.

"What happened?"

"What happened is that I'm coming to L.A. to be with you tonight, and you won't bloody be there!"

My heart stopped in my chest then plummeted to the pit of my stomach as elation rushed only to be followed close behind by sheer disappointment. "Shit, Cade, I'm *so* sorry! You know I'd love to see you, but I can't miss this. I have to go. Where are you now? "

"I'm on the plane, sitting on the runway at Heathrow right now. Fuck, Brook!" he retorted.

I took a deep breath as I sank down on my bed searching for words that would comfort him. "I'm coming right back in the morning. Can't we be together then? Do you want to meet at my parent's house?"

"No. I had Denise get me a flat. I told you I was going to do that." He was so upset and I wanted to alleviate it in any way I could.

"Babe... that's so great! I'm so excited! I never expected you to do that this soon."

He didn't answer me.

"Cade, I know you're still there, I can hear you breathing." I tried to make my voice lighthearted and teasing, but it wasn't easy. "Text me the address and I'll come straight there from the airport tomorrow, okay? I'll let you know when I leave New York and I won't stay one minute longer than necessary, I promise."

Again; the silence.

"Cade?"

"Yeah. I'm sorry! I'm just so bloody disappointed. I'm so anxious to get my hands on you, and I wanted to surprise you. Now it's ruined!"

"It was sweet and I appreciate it. I've been missing you so much, but it's only one more day and you can go out with the gang instead of me, then Ethan won't be upset I'm not there."

"Ethan is already expecting me. They're meeting me to help me load in the furniture that Denise ordered for me. We're setting everything up." He sounded so freaking annoyed.

"Cade, you know I need this part or else I'll go insane next summer while you're in New York filming without me."

"Hmmmph. " He huffed. "I'm sorry, my love. I don't mean to be selfish. I just miss you."

"Well... maybe I love it if you're selfish when it comes to me. I love you, but I have to go. I'll call you from New York, okay?

"Okay... just so you won't be shocked when you see me, I cut my hair."

"What? You mean, you trimmed it, right?"

"No. I feel bloody bald."

"Oh my God, is it that short?" I was speechless. Did he mean like a crew cut?

"No, Brook. Relax. I just wanted a change and we have two months before we begin filming, there is plenty of time to grow it back." He was amused at my astonishment.

"Is there still enough for me to pull on when you make love to me?" I lowered my voice into the phone. "I know you love that."

He audibly groaned. "No, the girl got a little carried away. There's a little. I'll pull yours instead for a while." I could finally hear the smile in his voice. "I love you."

"Love you more, but I gotta go. Don't forget to think about me at Midnight, and no kissing strange women!"

"Can I kiss the not-so-strange ones?" I knew he was teasing and I was glad he was in a better mood.

I played along, enthusiastically. "No! All your kisses belong to me. I'll miss you tonight.

"You, too. Talk to you soon, love. Bye."

***

AS I WAITED at the premiere after party with Jeanne at my side, all I could think about was Cade in L.A. and his voice on the phone earlier filled with all the fucking disappointment. I thought about how I would've felt if I'd made the trip to London for Christmas only to have him not be there when I arrived.

Fuck. What the hell am I even doing here? The movie I'd just been forced to sit through was boring, so I wondered what the hell was so great about this director, but I kept my mouth shut.

I looked around at the chaos backstage and ran my hand through my hair. I felt an overwhelming need to get on a plane back to Los Angeles to be with Cade. I'd never make Midnight at this point, but I knew I wanted to get to him. *Now.*

The music was loud and a lot of conversations were being shouted above the noise. I stuffed a finger in my ear so I could hear myself talk and then leaned into Jeanne.

"I gotta go. I'll have to come back tomorrow to see this guy… unless can we talk to him at all now?"

"No!" I could hardly hear her, even though she was shouting, but I could tell by her expression and the adamant shakes of her head that she wasn't happy with me. I didn't care.

"I said… I have to go!"

"Brook, are you nuts? He's right over there. We'll have his attention in the next couple of hours."

I inwardly groaned. *Two hours!* "He obviously doesn't care if he talks to me. He's looked over here and seen us waiting at least four times. I can't wait anymore, part or no part. I have to get back to L.A. tonight."

A stunned look crossed Jeanne's features and she shook her head. "For what?"

"Cade came to L.A. to surprise me for New Year's and I have to get back to him!"

"Brook, he'll understand. You *need* to do this. *Now!*"

I ran my hand through my hair again and looked around. I knew she was right, but fuck if I cared.

"You might lose this part, Brook! Think about what you're doing!" Jeanne's features were strained and angry. "Ken and I busted our asses to get you an audition!!"

"What audition? This is an audition for an audition, Jeanne! Please understand and let me reschedule. I'll fly right back tomorrow, or can you just go interrupt him?"

She looked taken aback and pissed off, a red flush forming under her skin. "Yeah that would be awesome and sure to endure me to him!"

"Please?" I pleaded. "This is our first New Years!"

Jeanne sighed heavily. "Okay, wait here. I'll try." Jeanne was shaking her head at me, "Shit, Brook. You're killing me!"

Ten minutes later she came back to talk to me.

"Okay, his wife is here and she's starting to rock and roll, so you can talk to him but it's short, so you'll only have a minute or two. He suggested you wait for him by the entrance and he'll meet you there. And Brook... don't fuck this up. If he doesn't agree to reschedule, you stay here. Deal?" I nodded. "And don't forget his name. Patrick Armstrong! Got it?"

My heart fell. It should sound reasonable, but I was itching to leave. I bit my lip and nodded. "Got it. I promise!"

I got my coat and then stood by the door and waited. It seemed like an eternity until he and finally the middle aged man Jeanne had pointed out finally came toward me. He was distinguished looking except for the unkempt iron-grey beard that didn't exactly go with the tux he was wearing.

"Hello Mr. Armstrong, I'm Brooklyn Halloway. Do you have second to speak to me?"

"Yeah, I know who you are kid. Your manager said you have an emergency and need to reschedule? Are you serious about this part or not?"

"Yes, sir, I am, but I've got a little problem. I have to be back in L.A. and I was wondering if you'd have time tomorrow or the next day or two. I'm really very sorry, and I will stay if you can't reschedule, but this is extremely important to me."

He paused and looked me over. "It must be important if you'd fly back to L.A. now and back to New York tomorrow. It's nuts, if you ask me. Martin Deering has great things to say about you."

I felt a rush of adrenaline at the prospect of two well-known Hollywood directors discussing me. "That's a great compliment. I'm so sorry about this!"

"Is this a relationship thing?" He smiled at me before he took a drink from the tumbler of some sort of amber liquor he was holding.

I flushed guiltily. "Um, yeah. Someone came to L.A. to surprise me from a very long distance and I just found out today that you wanted to talk to me tonight. Needless to say, it was a huge disappointment to him."

"It wouldn't be the British man who's in the film with you, would it?" His brows raised knowingly and her mouth quirked. "My daughter's about your age and she's all about the boys."

"Um..." I was taken off guard. "No one is supposed to know, but yes. I think you're so incredible and I love the script. I really, *really* want this part, but he was so upset that I just had to ask." I bit my lip as I looked urgently up at him.

He nodded toward the door. "Yeah, go ahead kid. I like your passion, but get your ass back here by tomorrow evening, okay? It's my last day off before I go to Europe for more of the premiere tour."

My face lit up and I hugged him, then stepped back when I realized what I was doing. "Oh, I'm sorry! Thank you. I promise I'll be back. I'll have my manager find out where you want to meet up with me. She'll be staying in New York tonight, so she can set it up."

"Get going." He didn't have to tell me twice as I flew out the door.

Caden

ETHAN, JENNIFER AND Dawson were all with me at Drai's, a

popular nightclub in Los Angeles where celebrities could go and not be bothered. The security was high and so it was one of the only places that I felt I could go and not get mobbed. There were still a few times when I was asked for autographs throughout the evening, but finally we found a table in the corner without any traffic around it.

The music was loud, the lights were flashing and giving me a headache. I wasn't even really *there*, and I was drinking way too much, but *fuck*, my heart was broken when my plan to surprise Brooklyn fell to shit. Jennifer and Dawson were sticking to each other like glue and I was jealous as hell because I was alone.

Ethan just made the rounds and was a total party animal. Always laughing and making jokes, he tried many times to get me into a better mood, but I just kept to myself and continued to order Crown Royal on the rocks, and downed them like they were water. I hoped that maybe eventually the boorishness of the evening would fade and even better, that the evening would come to an end and it would be tomorrow sooner.

Earlier that day, they guys came over to help me unpack all of the furniture and get it somewhat in order. Wendy stopped over, too, and I wondered how in the hell she knew I was in town or how she got my address. The furniture was delivered the day before and rather than have the delivery people set the bed up in the wrong place, I instructed Denise to have them leave it in pieces, but when we started to put it together it was discovered there were no screws. I had to go get some and Wendy hopped in the new navy blue Mercedes to tell me where to go.

I knew in my gut that it was a fucking bad idea, but I didn't give a shit about anything in that moment. She acted normal and didn't try to come on to me, so I hoped maybe she and I could get back to some sort of friendship. After all, we had to work together in two months, and I didn't want any awkwardness, especially around Brook.

Wendy was Brook's friend long before I met either of them and I didn't want to be the cause of a break in their relationship. As long as Wendy respected my boundaries and didn't antagonize Brook, I was willing to be cordial to her.

Unfortunately, there were paparazzi waiting. *How in the hell does that always happen, and, at a hardware store of all places?*

It was completely innocent but I knew I'd have to explain the pictures to Brooklyn, but that she'd understand. She knew how Wendy was always looking for a photo op and the papz always knew where she was and when. It was just too convenient to be a coincidence. Jesus… it was messed up.

Sitting at the table, my head fuzzy, I realized it was about 11:45 and I longed to be with Brook. New Year's Eve… our first one, and we weren't together.

Bloody hell!

That's when I saw Wendy. She moved through the crowd toward me with a determined look on her face and a drink in her hand.

"Hey, Cade. How are you doing? Are you having a good time?"

"Not at all. Will there be another photo op tonight, Wendy, because if so, I will fucking lose it."

"I don't know what you mean." She smiled coyly at me. Her tits were totally hanging out of her dress, the bodice so tight it was ready to burst.

"Of course not," I said in disgust. I turned away from her and took another drink from my glass.

Ethan was on the other side of me and I felt Wendy touching my thigh, rubbing her hand closer and closer to my crotch.

"Wendy, stop. I thought we could be friends, but you can't leave me the fuck alone."

I grabbed her wrist and removed her hand from my leg. "*Fucking stop!*"

She leaned into me and I pulled away again. "Cade." She leaned in closer, her voice seductive despite the din of the place, and I could feel the heat of her breath on my neck. "Brook isn't here. She's with David. She's still with David, so why are you resisting me?"

Brook was not with David. Of this I was certain.

She ran her hand down the back of my head and pressed her breasts into my arm.

I slammed my drink and turned toward her one last time. "It's Midnight Cade. Kiss me." She put her arm around my neck and tried to pull my head toward hers. I shoved her from me with more force then I meant to and she stumbled back.

"Get the fuck off me, Wendy!! I'm in love with Brook, okay?" I yelled right into her face, unconcerned with where I was or that I was in public. "How many bloody times do I have to tell you that?" I ran a hand through my hair in exasperation.

The expression on her face looked like I'd slapped her.

Good. Maybe she'll finally get a fucking clue.

I ordered another drink from the bartender and took Ethan by the shoulders, manually moving him next to Wendy.

"You and I are trading places, man. Keep that bitch off of me. I'm bloody begging you."

Ethan turned toward Wendy, but she was already storming out of the bar.

Thank you, Jesus. I sighed in relief.

I sat back in my chair and resumed my love affair with the whiskey in my glass.

Brooklyn

THE CAB PULLED up to the curb in front of Cade's new apartment in a secluded neighborhood of West Hollywood. It was inconspicuous and not very celebrity-like, which was so like Cade. I jumped out; the excitement flowing through like a river as I threw some money at the driver.

"Thanks!"

My skin was flushed and my heart was pumping. He'd sent me a text a couple of hours back and I couldn't wait to surprise him like he'd planned on surprising me.

Happy New Year, my one and only love... I miss you and wish you were here

Well, here I am, babe, I thought.

It was 2:10 AM, and so I hoped that Cade would be home from the club the gang had gone to, though he might not be. If not, I'd text him and tell him he had a surprise waiting for him.

I found the apartment and could hear soft music coming from within as I knocked. I was fidgeting and looking around the hallway, but excited because apparently he was still awake. It wasn't anything expensive or ostentatious, but that was right up Cade's alley. He would want to blend in and just be normal, which suited me as well. Maybe then we'd get some time to ourselves without the stalkers.

The door finally opened and I turned toward it with a big smile on my face, which quickly faded. My heart fell to my feet and my breath left my chest in a big whoosh.

"Well, well, well... if it isn't little Miss Halloway." Wendy was standing wrapped in Cade's comforter from his bed and nothing else. My heart began to beat so fast and I could feel the blood rush to my face as heat flooded under my skin. I felt sick to my stomach. "What are you doing here, Brook? Cade said you were in New York."

I struggled to speak; I couldn't breathe, I couldn't feel my legs. I could feel myself crumbling, and my heart exploding into a million pieces.

I stumbled back from the doorway like I'd been shoved, "I... I need to talk to Cade." Tears were welling in my eyes and I couldn't see anything but a watery blur of color. "Now, Wendy."

"Isn't it a little late for *best friends* to come calling? He can't come to the door now. He's sleeping. Poor thing, I completely wore him out, but he was so fantastic. My legs are still shaking." Her expression got hard and mean as she stared at me. She had to know by looking at me I was completely devastated. "You didn't think you'd be able to keep a man like Cade satisfied, did you? Get real, Brook."

My whole body was shaking as I struggled for breath. "But... "

"I'll tell him you were here," she laughed wickedly as she shut the door in my face.

I dropped to my knees right there as I fought for breath, I couldn't move as the silent sobs racked my chest. I don't know how long I huddled there, hunched over my knees as the pain ripped through me.

Dear God... please no. No, Cade! My mind screamed as my heart burned.

Tears poured from my eyes as the sobs continued in silence until finally I pulled in a tortured breath. This was pain unlike anything I'd ever experienced, slicing through my body like a white-hot knife.

I didn't care if I died; in fact I wanted to. Anything to stop this unbearable ache the throbbed through me like a living thing.

I couldn't see where I was going as I pulled myself up and tried to leave, each step away from him torture.

I stumbled along the wall, until I found the entrance and out into the street. The cold air hit me in the face but my body was numb; my mind racing and heart aching; I prayed for it to cease beating so the pain would stop.

I don't know how it happened, but somehow I ended up in the back of a cab telling the driver to take me back to LAX so I could catch a flight back to New York. Back to my fucking life before Wendy and Cade ripped it out from under me.

I prayed it was only a nightmare and that I'd wake up from the unbearable pain.

I didn't remember any of the flight, moving through the airports or getting back to the hotel. I didn't call Jeanne, I didn't have bodyguards... it was only me alone with the pain.

I was like a zombie until I hit my hotel room, and then it was if a dam burst and I completely lost my mind. I cried and screamed like I'd never done before, clawing at the bed, at my skin, cursing at God and at Cade... until I had no tears left, until my head ached so much I could barely stand it, and until I couldn't utter another sound.

The pain was physical, tangible... sucking my life away.

My life had ended in thirty seconds.

Over. *Just like that.*

Dear God, please let me die... because to keep on breathing hurts too fucking much.

Chapter 11
Heartache & Healing

Caden

OKAY, NOW I was getting worried. Brook told me the day before she'd call before she left New York and it was 6 PM and I hadn't heard a word from her. This day had gone completely to hell from the moment I woke up this morning. My fucking head was pounding like a jackhammer and it hadn't stopped all day. Couple that with ten bloody unanswered phone calls to Brook, and it couldn't get any worse.

I had one hell of a hangover courtesy of the multiple shots of whiskey I'd consumed the night before. So many, I couldn't even remember how in the bloody hell I got back to my flat last night. I was feeling sorry for myself because I couldn't be with Brook, and maybe I'd let it get a little out of hand. I wasn't usually one to go off the deep end but where she was concerned, my emotions ran raw.

The whole night was a bloody blur besides a few highlights, if you could call them that; Wendy annoying the shit out of me at the bar, the loud music endlessly throbbing in my head, signing a few autographs, and a ridiculous amount of drinking.

Brook, I'm getting worried now. Please call me back. I sent a text since she wasn't answering the calls.

In about thirty seconds I would be forced to call Jeanne or Diane to find out what the bloody hell was up. What if something had happened to her? My heart thumped inside my chest, and the panic I'd been fighting all damn day, rose up anew.

I tried to relax and unpack some of the boxes of books and clothes my mother had shipped over from London. Another hour pulsed by at a snail's pace. I tried to make myself a sandwich, mostly because eating was what I thought that I should do.

Fuck!

I wasn't hungry anyway. This was the longest I'd gone without some sort of contact with Brook since we met. I was going out of my mind with worry.

What the fuck was going on?

I pulled out my phone and dialed Jeanne, Brook's manager. She'd accompanied her to New York, so surely she'd know where my girl was.

"Hello? This is Jeanne." Her voice was a little frantic as she answered.

"Jeanne, its Cade."

"Oh, Cade! Have you heard from Brook?"

"What?" My heart fell. "No! That's why I'm calling, to see if *you* have. I haven't heard from her since yesterday morning, very early." I felt the bile rise up in my throat.

"Cade, she isn't answering her phone. I spoke with Pat Armstrong and apparently Brook did go to see him this morning, but she's checked out of the hotel and I don't know where she went after that. I thought she'd come home, but Diane hasn't heard from her either. I'm really worried. This isn't like her at all."

My breathing sped up and I paced back and forth across my living room.

"Why aren't you with her, Jeanne? I thought you went with her?"

"I was. I am. I'm still in New York, but Brook left, she was supposed to fly back early today. It's a long story."

"That makes no bloody sense! Someone better tell me what the hell is going on, and fast! I'm out of my mind; worried sick! She *never* does this. We generally talk several times a day and it's been thirty-six hours since the last conversation. What can I do? Should we call the police? What?"

My heart was beating so fast I felt it would fly right out of my chest and my mind was racing. Why would Brook leave and then come back. I wanted to know the details but I was more concerned with finding her.

"We can't call the police yet. It hasn't been twenty-four hours since someone's seen or heard from her. We have to wait until tonight. You might try calling some of her friends. Maybe David has heard from her." I knew she was grasping at straws, looking for any possibility, but damn it, the mention of his name made my blood boil.

I signed heavily and ran an impatient hand threw my already messy hair. "Okay, I'll call around. If you hear anything, please let me know immediately. When we find her, I'll expect full disclosure on what fuck went on and why you don't know where she is!" I felt my throat tighten and the blood rush through my ears.

Jesus Christ, this is a nightmare.

"She's an adult! She can do what she wants, and I can't tell you anything she doesn't want you to know! I'm her manager not yours,

Cade." Jeanne's voice elevated and I could hear the panic behind her words. She was right. She couldn't tell me anything Brook didn't approve.

"This is not some contract detail, it's about her safety! Find her! I don't care what it takes!"

When I rang off, I started calling everyone. I even called Wendy who was only too eager to talk to me, but I couldn't get a straight answer out of her.

"I don't know why you're calling me, Cade. Why would I know anything about Brook?"

"Wendy, bloody hell, this is serious, can you just tell me if you've talked to her?"

"I haven't, but if I do, I'll tell her you're looking for her. You really should get a clue, Cade. If the girl isn't calling you back, she doesn't want to fucking talk to you. *Hello?"* she said sarcastically. I hated that bloody American slang. "She's probably with David."

Why the hell did I even bother with this bitch, anyway? I should've known she wouldn't help me.

I slid down the wall next to my window until I was sitting on my haunches, and waited.

And waited.

I took out Brook's diary and read some of her letters. My chest tightened with emotion as I read her words and my mind raced at what could have happened to her. Was she in an accident, mugged or kidnapped for God's sake? I closed my eyes at the horrible thoughts.

Please God, keep her safe. Bring her back to me.

Three hours later I still hadn't heard a word from her, and five more unanswered calls to Brook's phone. Fuck this, I couldn't just sit here and do nothing.

I called Denise and told her I needed help getting over to Brook's parent's house.

"Cade...," she hesitated.

"What? What Denise? Do you know something? Fucking *tell me!*"

I was hyperventilating. My hand went involuntarily to my chest and started pulling on the material of my T-shirt.

"She's home. She came in about thirty minutes ago." Denise's voice was strained.

I let out a sigh of relief and covered my eyes with my hand as the tears burned behind them.

"Oh, *thank God.* What happened and why didn't Jeanne call me? Is Brook alright? Why didn't she return her calls? Did she lose her phone?" I blasted her with a barrage of questions.

"Cade, where are you? I should come talk to you." She was pensive and hesitant.

"Denise, please just bloody tell me what you want to say. I've been going out of my mind." I knew she could hear the tears in my voice.

"She's sort of... despondent."

"*What the hell does that mean*?" Why couldn't she just tell me and put me out of my misery?

"She's been crying and she won't talk to anyone. Diane said she locked the door to her room and won't answer when they knock. I'm sorry. I wish I could tell you more." She sucked in a shaky breath and waited for my response.

"Did someone hurt her? Should she go to the hospital? I need to get over there. *Now.*! Please send the car or I'll drive myself and I won't give a bloody fuck who sees me." I sat down and dropped my head in my hand over my knees. I could feel my body and my voice shaking.

"Okay, I'll send it. Maybe you should call Jeanne. She might know more now."

"Yeah, thanks." I rang off and my phone vibrated immediately.

It was a text from Brook.

Thank God! My heart leapt in my chest as I opened the message.

Cade, I need you to stop texting and calling. Please.

What? The words on the screen came out at me like a 3-D movie, screaming that my life was over. My heart constricted and I couldn't breathe. This couldn't be happening... how and why was this happening? Was it just a week ago that she came to London for Christmas? And now she didn't want to talk to me?

What the fuck?

The walls were crashing down around me and I didn't know how to save myself. I felt like I was having a heart attack. My breath was coming in rapid gasps, my heart was beating a hundred miles per hour, my chest ached and I felt every inch of my skin burn. I was on fire.

I had to get over there and talk to her. Had to find out what happened. Had to wake up from this nightmare. I sat in a daze, glancing at the time over and over until the car Denise sent arrived.

When I finally got to her house, Brook's mom answered the door and I rushed through it without waiting for her to invite me in.

"You have to let me talk to her. I don't know what's going on, but this is not happening. I'm... " I paused for less than a second as I struggled to find the words to describe the feelings inside me. "... fucking *dying*, Diane." I grabbed her shoulders as tears welled in my eyes and my throat ached. "Why is she doing this?"

Diane's arms came around me and I couldn't stop the tears from flowing. "I don't know how this is happening. Oh God... is she leaving me?" Her arms tightened around me as I completely lost it.

"Cade, we don't know what's wrong with her. I've tried to talk to her and she won't say anything. The only sound coming out of her room is her crying; sometimes sobbing. Brook is a very strong person so I've learned to leave her alone when she has something to deal with, and she eventually comes around and tells me what is bothering her. Maybe that's what we need to do now."

I had so much emotion rushing through me I barely heard what she said. I pulled back from her and she brushed the tears from my cheek.

"This can't be happening. I have to try to talk to her. Please. I love her so much." I knew my words sounded desperate and frantic, very unlike me, but I was drowning and completely out of control of myself. "Just... *please!*"

"Oh, honey. I'm sorry you're hurting, Cade. Maybe this isn't even about you."

I pulled away from her and shook my head. "No, it is. She sent a text asking me not to contact her. But I have to talk to her, Diane." Our eyes met and pain flashed across her face, her mouth opening and closing. She had no idea how to respond.

"I just have to try. I need to find out what is going on," I said again.

I walked away from her and took the stairs to Brook's room two at a time. The door was shut and I could hear her crying softly on the other side of the door. My hand hovered on the wood and I rested my forehead against it, drawing in a deep breath.

"Brook. Please let me in." Her sobbing increased on the other side of the door.

"Go away, Cade. I beg you. Just... *leave.*"

I closed my eyes against the ache in her voice. The pain her words caused in my heart was unbearable.

"No! Open the door. What is going on?"

"G-Go away, I d-don't want to t-talk to you." Her words came out breathy and broken.

"Brook! Open the fucking door! Why are you doing this?" I took a shaky breath and tried to calm down; knowing blowing up at her wouldn't get her to talk to me. "Babe... let me in. I love you and I know you love me, Brook. I can't leave, not without ripping my heart out." The tears ran silently down my cheeks as I slid down the door to the floor. "Please, Brook." I waited thirty seconds and she didn't respond but the intensity of her crying increased. "*Brook!* Jesus Christ.*"

"I'm not... strong enough to talk to you right now. I can't look at you. Please. Just go." Her voice was barely a trembling whisper that I struggled to hear.

I felt like a steel band was constricting my chest as I struggled for breath. I knew she could hear the tears in my voice as much as I could hear them in hers.

"Brook, please. Don't... don't do this. I feel like I'm literally suffocating. You have to tell me what this is about."

"*Fucking leave*, Cade, okay? I'm *already* dead. You fucking killed me. Just leave." Her sobs were louder, rougher, ripping from her chest.

I started like she'd shot me. My heart was breaking, my body shaking as I wrapped my hands around my knees and let the tears overtake me, my body racked with emotion. The helplessness I felt to stop my world from spiraling out of control, completely overwhelming me. I was lost.

What the fuck did I do? I struggled to figure out what could have happened. If I lost her, my life was over. *How can I stop this from happening?* My mind screamed.

I sat there for hours, leaning against her door until the sun came up. There were no more sounds coming from her room, and she'd stopped answering me when I tried to talk to her. I finally got up off of the floor and walked down the stairs in a daze. I felt dead inside, numb, my chest a hollow shell. My eyes were swollen and tired. I was bloody exhausted.

Diane came out of the kitchen when she heard me on the stairs and hugged me. I barely moved, my arms limp at my sides. She was crying. "I'm sorry, Diane. I don't know what for, but I'm so sorry. You have to believe me when I tell you that I love her more than my own life... The last thing I'd ever want to do is hurt her. Please call me if things change and she wants to see me." Then I walked out the door for the last time. The car was still waiting. If there were paparazzi around, if cameras were flashing, I didn't notice.

Brooklyn

IT WAS MID-FEBRUARY and I read online that Cade had been asked to present at the Academy Awards two days before our Tokyo premiere. He emailed, texted, or called every day for a month after I got back from New York, but I didn't answer any of them. I was still too fragile to even open the email and I'd finally had to block his texts. It was the hardest thing I'd ever had to do, but seeing his sweet words on the phone and then having flashbacks of Wendy's smug expression as she stood in the doorway to his apartment were just too much to bear.

Finally, he stopped trying. It was a mixed bag of emotions for me when that happened. I was relieved but I was miserable too. Every day it hurt. The minutes and seconds ticked by... each one screaming that it was taking me further and further away from Cade.

David came over a couple of times, and after I'd finally convinced him that I didn't want to talk about Wendy or Cade, it was somewhat comforting to have him around. He was familiar and I could pretend my life was normal for a while. He didn't say "I told you so", he just hung out, and sometimes, held me when I needed to cry. I didn't tell anyone why I was so sad, or what happened, not even Nathan. It made it easier to deal if I could pretend it never happened and to do that, no one could know. I put on a good front and went about my life as best I could, but I wasn't really *me*. I was hollow, a shell of myself.

My mom tried to ask me about it, but when I told her I just needed to deal with it in my own way, she never pressed me again. Jeanne, too. She was pissed at me for disappearing from New York, but after I'd secured the film with Patrick Armstrong, all I wanted was to be alone. I always did what was expected of me but after that I needed to disappear into myself for a while.

Two weeks after the night Cade came over, Jeanne told me he went back to London and as far as I knew, he hadn't been back to the States at all since.

Somewhere between then and now, I'd faced the realization that I was always going to love him. I was struggling with it, but there was nothing I could do to change it. Trying to stop was like trying to stop breathing. I couldn't live without breathing and I knew I couldn't live without loving Cade.

So how was I going to deal with it? Could I forgive the night with Wendy? Could I forget it?

I missed him. I missed him so much I ached with it, but I was scared, too. I found myself listening to songs we listened to together and remembering all of the beautiful times we'd shared. I longed for him so much I was overcome with it.

Could we go back to the way we were? Would Cade still want that now? How would I ever be able to let him touch me without thinking of him sleeping with Wendy? My skin flushed with heat at the thought of it. My heart plummeted. There had been pictures of him and Wendy a couple of times, and despite Jeanne's coaching that paparazzi pictures and the stories connected with them were false ninety-nine percent of the time, it still hurt. What happened still hurt so fucking much, but not as much as living without him. Jesus, I was so screwed up.

No, I couldn't go back to the way we were, but I desperately needed to find a way to keep him in my life. Maybe he didn't want me in his anymore. I had to face that was a possibility now after the way I'd shut him out.

I took a deep breath and put my head back on my pillows. Maybe if I wrote him a letter and tried to explain how I felt, maybe he would still want to be friends... or *something*. I decided that was the safest route; try to be friends in Tokyo. Then we'd have some time to acclimate to being around each other before *Don't Forget to Remember Me* started filming. I also had to come to terms with the fact that maybe he was with Wendy now, and I'd have to watch that shit go down. No. It hurt too much to think it, so I wouldn't believe that unless I came face to face with it on set. I'd have to see evidence of it with my own eyes... that hope kept a thread of sanity for now.

I got up and went to my laptop.

> **Dear Cade,**
> *I'm sorry it's taken me so long to be in touch. I just had a lot of stuff to figure out, but the bottom line is I miss you. You're my best friend and I'm so sad without you. I'm miserable. I don't need or want to talk about what happened, but all I know right now is that I want you back in my life in some*

way.
      I've hurt myself by shutting you out and nothing takes away the pain. Pushing you away is the most hurtful thing I can do to myself and I lose who I am because the agony of it consumes me. I need you to wrap me up... The way you always do.
      Can we start over in Tokyo?
      I love you.
      Always
            -Brook

I attached the song, *Breathe Me*, by Sia because it communicated how I felt, held my breath, and hit send.

I knew he'd get it on his blackberry and his email. I unblocked his number so his texts and calls would come through, and then I just had to wait. And hope.

The hardest part of reaching out is the waiting. I knew I'd have to forgive him because if I didn't, I'd never be free of the pain, and I'd never have him back in my life.

Within thirty minutes my phone vibrated.

The song is beautiful, perfect. I love you and missed you so much.
I need you to Breathe Me, too. I say yes to Tokyo.

I let out a sigh of relief and the ache in my heart began to ease just a bit, as the tears squeezed from my closed eyes.

We had a lot to overcome, but this was a start.

Chapter 12
Remembering Tokyo

Caden

ONCE AGAIN, I was in town before Brook, and this time as nervous as hell. That was a fucking understatement if there ever was one. I'd been so anxious to get here; I went to LAX directly from the after parties from the Oscars'. The entire night, I was dodging this woman or that one. Millie Sinclair practically stalked me. She was trying to get me to work with her on a movie and I decided to tell Denise that would never happen, I didn't care how many millions they offered me. That was one scary bitch. I sighed in exasperation. No doubt pictures of us together would circulate. *Terrific*, I thought. That was just what I needed.

I hated the fancy parties, the award shows, and appearances just for publicity... I bloody hated it all. More than once, I'd considered chucking it all and just writing music or buying a ranch in Montana and maybe raising horses. I didn't need any more money. I had enough to last a lifetime and the propaganda perpetuating Wendy and I was the tipping point to push me to it. Obviously, that bitch had fed pictures to the press, but the studio wasn't squashing the rumors. I was frustrated. I only wanted to be with Brook, but her career was just starting, so the odds were she wouldn't want to give it up for several years at least.

I was finally going to be with her after two agonizing months without her. I'd been dreading this premiere until I'd gotten the email and the song from Brook a few days ago. I was so afraid of what she'd say that my hands were shaking when I opened it. I literally dropped to my knees and cried when I read it and listened to the song she sent. *Maybe there was a God in heaven, after all.*

I was still completely in the dark as to what the separation was all about, but it didn't matter as much as getting us back to where we were before this bloody mess started. I was hoping that I'd get her to open up and finally tell me on this trip.

Brook jetted in with Noah Westin and for once we were sans Martin, which meant maybe we'd get to have a little fun this time. I wasn't sure what was going to transpire between Brook and myself, but I was so grateful to have the chance to be with her, just to talk to her would be like balm to my soul. Maybe I'd be able to find out what happened in January. Her email said she missed "her best friend" and it wasn't exactly what I'd hoped for, but I'd take what I could get.

At least she'd said she loved me, and that was like a glass of water in the desert that my life had become these past weeks. I ran my hands through my hair as I waited in the limousine for the two of them to come from the hotel and join me.

Jeanne and Denise were here to make sure we were where we needed to be and to make sure Brook had her wardrobe changes. It was raining and she probably wouldn't want to keep the same clothes on for the entire day of appearances. We had the red carpet, the movie, interviews with the press, and fan panels to do.

I was anxious. It was too much to get through before I'd get any real chance to talk to her.

I was sort of buzzed, and my hands were shaking. I was living on coffee and energy drinks, having stayed up throughout the many hours needed to get to Japan from Los Angeles. I was too nervous to try to sleep on the plane, and I wasn't sure if the shakes were from the caffeine, lack of sleep, or nerves. I leaned my head back on the seat and closed my eyes while I waited.

I heard the screams increase and I raised my head to see Brook and Noah coming out of the hotel with bodyguards in front and back of them. The incessant cameras began to flash, and as they stopped to sign some autographs I got my first real look at her. I hadn't seen her in almost two months, and hadn't talked to her either.

Jesus... she was so beautiful. Her blonde hair tumbling down around her bare shoulders and the brilliant aquamarine dress she wore was a perfect match for her eyes, clung like a second skin to her slender form, then flowed to the ground. The swells of her breasts and her hips were so beautiful, and brought up so many perfect memories of touching her and making love to her.

I felt the familiar tightening in my body as my pulse increased. Only a few more seconds and I'd be next to her. My heart rate increased and it pounded painfully in my chest.

Finally.

The driver opened the doors, and the fans all tried to get more pictures of me inside the car as well as Brook and Noah entering. When she came through the door to take the seat next to me, her blue eyes met mine and I was speechless. I wanted to take her in my arms and crush her to me as her familiar scent wafted all around me. Oh

God, it'd been so fucking long.

She settled next to me as Noah moved to the seat opposite us and I couldn't help it, my left hand entwined with her right one. I took a deep breath and looked at the ceiling as I let it out in a rush. Her hand squeezed mine, and I finally let myself look straight at her.

Noah looked out the window as the car started to move away from the curb and make its way toward the theater and convention center where the premiere would be held.

Jesus Christ! Was this the first time I'd been able to breathe in all this time? I felt my lungs expand almost to the point of pain.

We didn't talk, but I brought her hand that I was still holding to my mouth to place a kiss on the top of it.

My heart thudded in my chest as Brook leaned into my arm and I felt her head come ever so lightly down on my shoulder. There was comfort in just touching her; this small bit. She glanced up at my face and I got lost in the blue depths of her eyes.

Dear God, I love you, Brook. I've missed you so much. I can't take my eyes off of you right now.

Her eyes welled with tears and she bit her lip. I could only hope she knew what I was thinking and trying to communicate.

"Hey Cade. How have you been?" Noah started the conversation that broke our little bubble.

"I've been... okay. Thank you, Noah. How about you?"

"Stressing out about the next flick. The new director talked about recasting me, though I'm not sure why," Noah's brown eyes were smiling and warm as he looked at us. He flexed in front of us and I wanted to roll my eyes. "Maybe I need to work out more."

"Yeah, you should feel his muscles," Brook piped up.

"Hmmph," I snorted and Noah blushed.

"I saw you at the Oscars. You looked really, really good." Her hand tightened on mine as my head snapped toward her.

"You saw it?" I knew surprise showed on my face. "On the telly?"

Brook nodded. "I told you, I'd always be watching you. Of course," she said so softly it felt like a caress on my skin. I felt myself flush as we came up to the Red Carpet outside the theater and the fans began screaming in earnest.

"You'd think the screaming would sound different, but they sound the same no matter what country we're in. *Loud*," Noah laughed.

Brook smiled. "Yes. You boys have your work cut out for you. All the girls will be clamoring for you both, and you guys are looking hot." She smirked at Noah, then at me. I loved seeing the smile on her face and a blush to her cheeks. She was gorgeous.

"You look beautiful, yourself. A sight for sore eyes," I breathed near her ear, just as the door opened and the screams increased. Noah made to get out first.

"Let the games begin." He laughed out loud as he disappeared through the door just as mine opened.

They held umbrella's for us as we walked up the stairs among the screams and took our time signing autographs. I glanced at Brook a few times and smiled softly at her as we played to the crowds. She had to be freezing in that dress and I could feel her shivering when we stood together for our photo calls. Noah and I both put our arms around her to try to keep her warm, but I pulled her closer to my side. It felt so good to have my arm around her, and it was all I could do not to crush her to me and never let go.

The viewing of the film gave me almost two hours to hold on to her, both of us clinging to each other's hands in the darkness. I was ultra-sensitive to each and every breath she took and each subtle movement she made. She smelled so delicious, it was all I could do not to lean over and kiss her sweet mouth. It was agony, but blissfully so.

The fan meeting was fun and casual. We joked around quite a bit and Brook flirted outrageously with me when she answered the usual questions about being in a film with me. She turned to me and wagged her eyebrows at me, pleasure ripped through my entire being, and I wanted to reach across and pull her close. The fans laughed and squealed at her actions. I smiled and raised my eyebrows at her as the fans continued to cheer. My cheeks flushed as I laughed with her. I feared love was shining out of my expression, but the whole thing was so much fun, I didn't care that Denise and Jeanne would read us the bloody riot act for being so obvious. After that, I couldn't take my bloody eyes off of her.

We would have been taken to task in a big way if we'd acted like this in the States or in Europe. Maybe it was the fact that we'd not seen each other in so long, that made us more brazen, but whatever the reason, I loved it. It was brilliant.

Finally, it was the press panel, and Brook changed into a really sexy black dress. It was strapless but she wore a black jacket over it. She was so amazing and again, I wasn't able to keep my eyes off of her.

On our way out, I was able to finally pull her aside behind one of the sets and draw her to me. Her head settled into my chest and her arms wrapped firmly around my waist as mine closed tightly around her shoulders. I buried my face in the top of her head and breathed her in before kissing her temple.

"Jesus, Brook. I've missed you so bloody much."

Her only response was to tighten her arms around me even more and nod into my chest. I felt her hands splay out across my back to bring our bodies even closer together.

"I love you," the words tore out of my chest. I couldn't fucking help it. She just held on tighter, and it felt so good to be so close to her, I never wanted to let go.

They took us back to the hotel in separate cars to avoid suspicion. Brook went with Jeanne, and I went with Denise. I hated letting her leave without me, but I'd met Lawrence Parks, a well-known actor I'd met at the Oscars and we'd ended up on the same plane coming to Tokyo. He was here promoting his new film, and was traveling with the producer and director of the two of the musical numbers performed at the show, and he wanted to introduce me so I'd agreed to meet them for dinner.

Afterward, we arranged to meet up later at the piano bar not far from our hotel. Larry was aware of my affinity for music and thought it would be a good time after the hectic pace of the day. Deep down, I didn't really want to go, since I wanted to spend some time alone with Brook, but maybe it might be an ice breaker to invite her, Jeanne, Denise, and Noah to join. I'd been writing a new song for her and it might be a good opportunity to play it for her.

I changed out of my suit and texted her from my room.

> ***Lawrence Parks and pals invited me to go out with them later. Want to grab everyone and join?***
> ***I'd like to see you, Brook.***

It didn't take long for her to answer.

> ***Sure. I'll check to see who wants to come. Where is it?***

I texted back the address and told her what time I'd be there, and headed out.

I was there for a couple of hours before Brook walked in with Noah. No sign of Denise or Jeanne. I'd told the blokes Brook and Noah would be joining us, and he motioned for them to join our table. She was smiling and I loved seeing the joy on her face. After listening to her sobs outside of her bedroom door in early January, her smiles were a balm to my heart.

Lawrence and I stood as Brook and Noah approached and she extended her hand to my new friend. "Hi, I'm Brook Halloway."

"Of course. I'd recognize your beautiful face anywhere. It's very nice to meet you," Lawrence greeted her as he took his seat and more introductions were made around the table.

She sat down and took off her jacket. She was still wearing the strapless black dress.

I pulled my chair closer to hers so I could speak to her privately. Her shoulder nudged mine in a silent plea for contact. We fell into our easy camaraderie, with our ever-present undercurrent of desire. I ordered some wine and settled in next to her. We laughed and teased each other, as well as had a great time making fun of Lawrence and the others as they sang an old Abba song in an overly exaggerated way. Brook and I joined in because everyone in the bar was singing along to the various tunes that were being played and this one was particularly fun. Noah refused to sing but after a couple of glasses of wine, I was able to convince Brook to sing with me.

Her hand came out to cover mine and my skin burned under her hand. Incredible as always, the electricity sparked between us and I felt my heart speed up. My hand wrapped around hers and we stared into each other's eyes. I felt like I was melting into her and everyone else in the bar disappeared. Suddenly, I couldn't wait to get out of there and have some time alone. I needed to talk to her about what happened in January.

After the song ended, I took her hand and led her back to the table. "Do you want to get out of here, sweetheart? I'd really like to spend some time alone with you."

Her fingers twined with mine, tightened on my hand and she nodded.

"Gentlemen, it's been a fun evening, but Brook is tired so we're going to call it a night. Thank you for everything. Larry, I look forward to seeing you again, perhaps in L.A., soon?"

I shook their hands and patted Noah on the shoulder.

"Noah, will you be okay or do you want to come with us?" Brook asked as we got ready to leave.

He shook his head. "I'm fine. It's only two blocks. I can find my way back." He knew what we were about and I was thankful he was giving us our privacy.

It was only two blocks and it was 3 AM Tokyo time, but for us it was hours earlier. I didn't let go of her hand as I led her out of the club. It felt so good to have her by my side.

"Do you feel like walking?" I missed walking but in the States or at home, I didn't get enough of it since my career blew up.

"Sure. That sounds nice," she murmured as we left the bar. It was cool, but not overly so, and the rain had stopped.

I felt her free hand wrap around my bicep of the arm that held her hand, and her head came down on my shoulder. She let out a deep sigh, as we walked the few blocks back to the hotel.

"Are you doing okay with this, Brook? Being with me like this?" I could hear the desire in my voice as I leaned closer to whisper in her ear.

"Uh huh. I've really missed you." She raised her eyes to mine and the need in the blue depths shone like a beacon. She drew a shaky breath and let it out.

"Brook," I almost groaned. "I've missed you too. You were so beautiful today, and I loved how you flirted with me." I smiled softly as I looked down into her face as we walked. "It was all I could do not to sweep you up in my arms right there in front of everyone. These last months have been hell, love."

I felt heat radiate between us, despite the coolness of the night as we drew near the front entrance of the hotel. I glanced down at Brook's face and saw that her brow was knitted in a frown.

I didn't say anything as we walked through the hotel and took the elevator up to the 23rd floor. Both of our rooms were on this floor and I wondered if she'd want me to join her in hers. My heart thumped harder as we got closer to her room. I didn't want to be presumptuous after all that had happened, but I desperately wanted more time with her.

Exactly what had happened? I reminded myself that I still didn't know.

Outside her room, I took her shoulders and turned her toward me. I wanted to take her in my arms and kiss her breathless, but knew we needed to talk first. I raised my hand to her face and placed a whisper soft kiss on her luscious pink lips. When I drew away, her chin lifted toward my mouth for another kiss and I gave it to her. This one was longer, lingering, our lips playing with each other. My body sprung to life, but my heart still ached over the abyss we'd had between us. I needed it resolved before I could make love to her.

My God. She tastes so good, all wine and sweetness. I felt my breath leave my body and fan over her face. Her eyes were closed as she raised her mouth toward mine, again.

"Brook. I want more time with you. What do you want?" I felt her tremble in my arms and step up on tiptoe to press her mouth to mine again. I could feel desire flood through me. Jesus, it had been so long since I touched her.

"Cade." She said my name and it did something to me deep inside my soul. "I want you to come in with me." Maybe it was my imagination but she sounded like she was begging and I wouldn't be able to deny her, even if I didn't want to do as she asked.

I couldn't help myself, my mouth swooped to open hotly over hers and her arms instantly went around my neck and into my hair. *Oh, there it was.* I felt those gorgeous hands tugging in my hair, to pull my mouth even closer to hers. I pressed her up against the hotel room door as I devoured her, my tongue seeking the deepest recesses of her mouth. I couldn't get enough and my body strained against her, I pressed my hardness into her stomach and she moaned.

I drug my mouth from hers and placed my forehead on hers, both of us panting wildly. I struggled to get control of my breathing and the urges that were surging through every nerve and sinew of my body. Brook pressed her card key into my hand and I reached behind her to put it in the slot. My mouth ghosted and licked at hers as I heard the door click and I pushed it open behind her. My arm went around her waist and I lifted her with me through the door and her arms and legs went around my body.

"Oh God, Cade." My arm still around her waist, the other one went underneath her bottom as I carried her into the room. I buried my face in her hair as I kissed her neck and shoulders.

Trying to get in control of myself, I went to the bed and sat down with her still wrapped around me. I stroked her back. "Brook. I want you so much right now. So much. But baby, we should talk first."

I brought both of my hands into her hair and pulled her head back so I could look into her eyes. I nuzzled into her throat as I took a deep breath. "We need to talk," I whispered against her skin.

She shook her head as she buried her face in my shoulder, her hands stroking the back of my head. "Please, just make love to me. Just make love to me." My body surged at her words, but I wanted to get her back into my life... not just into my bed and I told her so.

I shook my head. "No Brook. Not until we talk. I want us back, every piece of us. Please talk to me. Why did you push me away? What did I do?"

She stiffened in my arms. "Please don't make me relive it, Cade. It hurts too much, and I need this. I need to be with you. I've ached so badly. In a lot of ways" Her voice cracked as emotion swelled within her.

"I've been in hell too, Brook. But I have to know why this all happened. It's all I've been able to think about." I was rubbing her back when she suddenly pushed off of my lap and walked to the window with her back to me.

Her shoulders started to shake and she dropped her head into her hands. "It's been such a beautiful day, why are you ruining it?" Her voice trembled over the words.

I walked to her and put my hands on her shoulders and she pulled away from me. "I'm not ruining it. I'm trying to fix this. Just tell me, Brook."

"Oh God. As if you don't know, Cade!" She turned her tear-streaked face toward me. "I *know*, okay? Are you happy now? You had to know why I needed time to come to terms with it, so why do you make me fucking say it now?"

The pain in her face was horrific, but still I didn't have a fucking clue what she was talking about.

"Know what, Brook? Just say it. You say I should know, but I don't!"

Her chin jutted out and she looked pissed through her tears. "I know you had sex with Wendy! And it destroyed me."

"What?" I felt like she'd slapped me. "You think I slept with Wendy? When? I can't decide whether to laugh at the ridiculousness of it, or cry because you don't trust me!"

She was crying again, her hand was covering her eyes as she stood shaking in front of me. She sank down to sit on the edge of the bed.

"Please stop denying it. You're only making it worse. I *know* it happened. I was willing to move past it. I need you. I miss you... why did you make me have to say it out loud? Couldn't we just pretend it never happened? Now it feels like it's happening all over again!"

I felt furious, broken-hearted, and just fucking devastated that she could think I would betray her. My hand went to grasp over my heart as I watched her slide off the bed and drop to her knees on the floor and cover her head with her hands.

"So you're willing to forgive me for something that I haven't even fucking done? Is that it?" I knew my voice was harsh and I felt my face flush, burn. My heart was splitting in two inside my chest, because she believed me capable of such a thing, and also because she was obviously suffering terribly. I knew that she really believed I'd been with Wendy.

Why did she think this? Because of those stupid photos when we went to the Home Depot?

How could I make her see this wasn't possible, to make her see that after her, I couldn't ever touch another woman for the rest of my bloody life. It just wasn't possible for me.

My throat ached, my eyes burned, I couldn't breathe. I ran both hands through my hair as the desperation built within me. I felt helpless and my hands were shaking.

I stalked across the room to her where she knelt on the floor and bent to lift her to her feet. I grabbed both sides of her face and took her mouth with all I had. She was crying and shocked at the onslaught, but within seconds she opened her mouth to mine and we kissed again and again. My heart was breaking, but I loved her and I had missed her more than I ever believed possible. Despite her misery, she couldn't help but fall into my arms, completely surrendering to the pain and the desire that throbbed all around us. She kissed me back with all the emotions I felt myself.

It was apparent that she was just as desperate for me as I was for her. Our hands were tearing at each other's clothes, grasping at each other's bodies... our mouths tasting, worshiping each other. My body throbbed with want as I lowered her to the bed.

Brook had somehow managed to unbutton my shirt and her hands ran up my chest and played with my nipples. After all the time apart, feeling her hands on my body was like paradise. I unzipped her dress and started to move it down her body, my mouth sliding to her breast. I could feel her chest heave beneath my mouth as she sobbed at the pain between us. I realized that I was crying too.

How in the fuck did we get to this place? Didn't she know how much I loved her?

"Brook, tell me how you feel when I touch you." I was begging against her skin, searching for a way to stop aching.

"Cade... you melt me. I never want anyone else to touch me. Oh my God..." My mouth moved up her neck to her mouth and across her cheek. I tasted her salty tears on my tongue and my arms tightened around her as I buried my face in her hair and gave way to my own tears. The pain in my chest constricted my lungs as I gasped against her skin. I knew I had to stop. I couldn't make love to her when she thought I could betray her like that.

I don't know how I found the strength to pull from her and move to the side of the bed. She rolled to her side and reached for me. My hand twined through her fingers, and my throat thickened as I struggled to find my voice. I was still fighting for breath.

"I thought we were going to talk everything through. Didn't we promise each other that? And still I sit here not knowing when or where I supposedly shagged Wendy."

She raised her face up to look at me. I could barely stand the tortured look on her face.

"I'm sorry I closed off but I wasn't strong enough to talk about it. Even now, I want to forget it ever happened. I just wanted you back. I wanted to wake up from the nightmare and... find that you... still love me." Her breaths were coming in hiccupping gasps.

I put my free hand to my head as I leaned down over my lap. I couldn't let go of her, but I couldn't take a hold of her either. The tears fell from my eyes unheeded. I knew that she loved me desperately, but in this moment, it wasn't enough.

"I'll always love you, Brook. I can't even keep breathing if I don't love you, but what is killing me is that you don't trust me. I have missed you so much I thought I would die if we didn't fix this. Literally die. And right now, I want you so bloody much, my entire body is vibrating with it... but, I can't do it."

I needed her, wanted to feel her love flood through me. I used our laced hands to pull her onto my lap and we resumed the heavy kissing, my hands moving over her body and my mind screamed at how perfect she fit under my hands, how velvet soft she was, and how desperately she was responding to every touch.

My chest was still aching as I once again pulled my mouth from hers. "This is us, Brook... this is *US*! No one else. Jesus, don't you feel me, like I feel you?"

"Cade... don't... don't pull away from me." She was trying to bring me closer to her again.

"Do you feel me Brook?" I whispered against her mouth. I let myself feel her, taste her, smell her scent. "Because I *feel* you; on my skin, in my mouth, in my heart and soul. *Only you.*"

"I feel you, Cade. I love you."

With my heart breaking, I pushed her from me and stood up from the bed. My body was shaking so bad I thought I'd fall to the floor.

"Do you? If you bloody did, you'd believe that these feelings, this intensity that we have between us, is only US. You'd trust that I can *never fucking touch* another woman again after you! It's impossible." My voice was raspy and harsh as it ripped from my chest. I put both of my fists over my eyes as I struggled with the emotions welling within me.

"I just... fucking can't." I was struggling to breathe as a sob rose in my chest. "I love you so much it's killing me. You have to know that, Brook. But I can't touch you when you think I am capable of touching someone else the way I touch you."

She was on the bed, the sobs violently racking her small frame. "Don't go, Cade. I don't think it's the same. I know... I know it was just a mistake. It's a mis—a mistake."

I was dying, but all I knew was that I had to get out of there before I gave into the want, the need and the desperation I felt for the beautiful woman begging me to stay. It would be wrong to take her when we had this bullshit looming between us.

Jesus, give me strength, I begged silently.

"I can't do this anymore. I can't love you this much anymore; not if you don't trust me. It's bloody killing me!"

I turned to leave and found myself stopping before I got to the door, the pull I felt toward her like gravity when she spoke.

"Oh God, Cade, don't do this. Don't leave me now."

I took one more breath and left the room. It was the hardest thing I'd ever done and after the door closed behind me, I leaned back against it and closed my eyes. Once again I was on the opposite side of a door from Brook and I could hear her sobbing desperately on the other side of it... but this time, I was the one who was walking away. I barely had the strength, and I felt like I was killing myself by leaving her. Maybe I was.

I knew I'd never be able to leave her for good because my heart was exploding inside my chest as I walked back to my room. I was so fucking weak where she was concerned, but I had to figure this shit out. I had to find the answers so I could ease the pain in both of our hearts.

Chapter 13

If I Can't Have You

Brooklyn

I WAS HAVING a nervous breakdown. The two weeks since my argument with Cade in Tokyo had been so hard. I knew I'd have to deal with working with him, being in love with him and also seeing him every day with all this crap between us, and it was weighing heavily on me.

The way he'd walked out on me left me devastated. I had been crying every day since, despite my resolve to move past it. I felt helpless, out of control and certainly not like myself. How did this happen? I felt disgusted with myself that I couldn't push the pain away.

I'd called my manager and lawyer and begged them to get me out of the movie, which was totally uncharacteristic of me. Normal-Brook would tell everyone to go fuck themselves, and go about my business. I'd do the film and not care one whit for any of them, none of their actions or thoughts mattering to me at all.

Normal-Brook... where was she when I needed her?

While Joel was matter of fact and business like, telling me to man up and deal, Jeanne was more understanding. She was going to fly with me up to Vancouver so that we could talk on the way and also try to make sure I wasn't in the same hotel as Cade and the rest of the cast.

I decided that this wasn't going to be like the last film. This time, I was going to keep to myself, do my job and that was it. No socializing or letting myself get so involved again.

Isolation would be my salvation during the next few weeks. My chest tightened and tears pricked at the back of my eyes.

Dear God, I'm not strong enough to do this. To see him, have to kiss him, and be with him every day on set—I didn't think I had the strength. Despite the strength I had in most aspects of my life, I had none to resist Cade's pull on my heart; that traitorous heart that thumped so painfully inside my chest.

I had one other thing that had to be done; I needed to return the engagement ring and the bracelet.

I started to shake as my hand ran lightly over the boxes. I hadn't worn either one for the past three months. Sometimes in my weaker moments I did allow myself to look at them, but not very often. My hands trembling, I took them from my drawer for what would be the last time and placed them in my purse. I had to take them with me to Vancouver so I could give them back to Cade, and then it would be over.

My heart dropped at the thought of the day we'd said goodbye after *The Future of Our Past* wrapped when he'd given me the bracelet. I sighed but it hurt as the air filled my lungs. And what about the beautiful weekend last July we spent in San Diego where he'd given me the ring? It had been so perfect. I longed for those times. They were some of the most beautiful moments of my life.

The loss I felt brought such unspeakable grief that it ripped at my chest until I couldn't breathe. Hot tears rained unchecked down my cheeks as I packed my bags and threw my script in the suitcase.

I wanted to fall to my knees, collapse, and scream at the injustice of it all. How could Cade fuck Wendy and then lie to me on top of it? How could he say it didn't happen when I'd seen her there with my own eyes? I mean, how would he have felt if David had answered my door without any clothes on? Even in the face of my willingness to forgive it, he still denied the entire fucking thing.

I felt so incredibly stupid and so angry at myself because I let myself be so open and vulnerable. I trusted myself, and my feelings. I never believed in a million years that Cade would ever do that to me.

David; yes. Not Cade.

Maybe that's what made it so brutal. I'd trusted him beyond anything, but there she was, naked on his doorstep. And now, I couldn't even trust myself.

"Hmmph…" I sucked in a shaky breath, fighting a full-blown sob from breaking from my chest.

I still missed him so much. Missed him despite everything. Needed him despite everything. Loved him despite everything. I felt so fucking weak. If I'd never known hell before, this was it.

I'd used the time since Tokyo to center myself, to resign myself to the fact that it was over, and to convince myself repeatedly that I didn't care. I'd been trying to find the strength I knew I was going to need in the next months.

Yeah, right. What a joke. *Brook is so strong*; everyone thinks I'm made of iron, and I can handle everything and anything. Yeah, I was tough most of the time, but not when it came to Cade. He was capable of taking me to heaven or sending me to hell and there is nothing I can do to stop it. I didn't like being so out of control. It wasn't me. This was just another thing resonating from the script. My head fell back and I tried to breathe for a few seconds before woodenly resuming packing.

My hands were shaking as I gathered my things. It still cut to the bone; pain worse than I had ever imagined possible. As much as I tried to hate him, I remembered everything wonderful about him; so many beautiful times that we'd spent together and they far outweighed the bad. We'd always taken such good care of each other and he was my closest friend. That's what scared the shit out of me. I still needed him so much.

After he'd texted me from the Red Carpet of the Oscar's telling me we could talk in Tokyo, I wanted to believe, needed to believe that we could at least be friends. It felt good to see him, to talk to him and when he held me close and kissed me, I swear I lost myself again. He felt so good and all I wanted was to hold him close forever, no matter what happened.

Jesus, the desire and love that overwhelmed both of us in Tokyo was amazing until it fell apart when he insisted on talking about Wendy. Everything was so bittersweet.

I threw a couple of shirts carelessly into my open suitcase. What was going to happen now? I didn't know if we were going to be able to get back to any sort of comfortable relationship like we had during the first film. Based on what had happened on New Year's Eve, and then in Tokyo, I just didn't know if I was strong enough.

I felt myself breaking. After two weeks of being stoic and burying all of my feelings deep down, the dam had finally burst.

I sat down on my bed and bent over with my head in my hands as the sobs I'd been fighting, finally overtook me.

If I cry enough now, maybe I'll be able to hold it together for the next four months.

There was a soft knock on the door.

"Brook?" My mother cracked the door. "Honey, are you okay?" She looked at me with worry on her face.

"No." My shoulders were shaking in pain as I fell over and buried my face on the pillow. "Oh, God, Mom. I'm *never* going to be okay again. I just," I gasped, "want to die!" I sobbed. "I can't go back to being his friend, I can't stop loving him, I'm so mad at him, but I can't breathe without him and it hurts *so much*. I just can't fucking make this movie now."

She lay down on the bed and gathered me in her arms as I cried and cried. "Baby, I thought some of this had passed." Her voice was soft as she stroked my hair over and over.

"I tried," I gasped. "I tried so hard." She handed me a tissue and I sat up, trying to dry my tears and to blow my nose. "In Japan last month, I tried to be his friend, telling myself that we meant more to each other than one stupid mistake, that I needed him in my life, more than I needed him to love me. That being his friend was better than being... nothing." My head pounded so bad I could feel my heart beating in my temples. My hand clutched at my hair as I looked at her.

"But then, we couldn't keep our hands off of each other and he wanted to talk about it. I wasn't ready, and all of my resolve left me. It was like reliving it all over and the love and pain was so much more than I could take. He kept insisting that it didn't happen. We ended up fighting, and screaming at each other. Even though we admitted how much we still loved each other, yet he left me anyway. It was *even worse* than finding Wendy in his room. I just don't know how I'm going to get through this, Mom."

I wiped at the tears still falling from my eyes." I fucking hate myself that - I can't stop loving him." Another sob broke from my chest and tears squeezed from beneath my closed eyelids.

She took my hands. "Brook. You are such a strong young woman. So strong. You'll get through this. You *will*, because you're you. I know it hurts right now, but that's because you allowed yourself to love so deeply. I'm so proud of the person you've become and the choices you've made."

I sat up and grabbed another tissue and mopped at my face. "A lot of people are counting on you, honey. This movie means a lot of jobs to a lot of people. It isn't just about you and Cade. It isn't just about this movie, but your future career. Jeanne told me that he probably wouldn't be on set for the first couple of weeks, so that will give you some time to get used to being there and get in the groove without dealing with him."

"I... I don't know. He always wants to be there early." I was gasping for air, trying to stop the tears. "But, even if he isn't there right away, it's going to hurt being there without him, too. Either way, I'm so screwed."

I threw the last few shirts on top of the jeans in my suitcase and added some sneakers. I didn't give a crap about what clothes I packed since I wouldn't be going out at all anyway. The doorbell rang; it was Jeanne. She was here with the limo that would take us to LAX for our flight to Vancouver. I ran a hand through my hair as my mom got up to go downstairs.

"I'll tell Jeanne you'll be down in a few minutes. Wash your face. I *know* you can do this Brook." She hugged me tight.

***

IN VANCOUVER, JEANNE arranged for me to have a different hotel from most of the others. Noah, Gavin and Sarah would be in the same one, but the others, especially Wendy and Cade wouldn't be. My heart tightened. Did I really want them to share the same hotel? I pushed the thought to the back of my head, and told myself it wouldn't matter anyway.

I could feel Jeanne's eyes following me around the room as I got ready for bed and unpacked. I hadn't talked much on the way up here because it was the easiest way to keep it together, to be how everyone expected me to be.

"What?" I finally asked her as I crawled into my bed.

She was getting ready to get into hers also. "Brook, do you want to talk about this at all? Are you *sure* Cade slept with Wendy?"

I sighed and looked down at my hands. "Yes." I knew my voice was getting thick.

"I see." I could tell it wasn't what she expected. "Have you talked to him at all?"

"No." I glanced over at her and threw my script aside. "Look, I found Wendy at his place when I went to surprise him New Year's Eve, okay? She answered the door wrapped in his blanket. It's not too difficult to figure out what she was doing there, is it?"

She gasped. I hadn't told her what went down.

"Did you go into the apartment?" she asked quietly.

I shook my head. "I left right away. I couldn't even function; seeing him in bed with her would only devastate and humiliate me more. I didn't take his calls or texts for a month and finally, he stopped trying.

I took the time until the Tokyo premiere to deal before I was able to talk to him, but yes, finally we did talk in February." My heart dropped. "He said it didn't happen."

"Then... are you sure it did?" Her voice was soothing, yet inquiring.

"I *saw* her there, Jeanne. We didn't talk about the details of it. I told him I knew he'd been with her and he denied it. Somehow it got turned around into my not trusting him, rather than his screwing Wendy. It was horrible." I wiped at the tears. "It hurts so much. I've never experienced anything so excruciating."

"Brook, Cade called me and came to my room in Tokyo. Right after he left you," she confessed. My eyes widened as I sucked in my breath. "I hope you're not mad, but he needed to talk to someone who knows you and the situation."

It was obvious she really cared for Cade and for me, so I couldn't really be mad at her.

"I'm not upset, but I really don't want to know what he said." I closed my eyes. "It's all too raw for me and I'm sorry that you've been put in the middle of all of this."

"Brook, I'm your friend, not just your manager, so I'm *going* to tell you this." She came over and sat on my bed. "He *loves you* so much, he's hurting just like you, and he's – angry because you wouldn't talk to him for months, and wouldn't tell him why. He was going out of his mind wondering what happened and was confused that you wouldn't take his calls." She put her arms around my defeated shoulders as I hung my head, the tears raining on my crossed legs. "And then when you wouldn't believe him in Tokyo, he was devastated all over again, but he loves you more than he's mad. He is suffering, Brook, as much as you are."

"But Jeanne..." I began miserably. "He doesn't know *why*? Was he there when he screwed her? How the fuck did this get to be my fault? I *can't* hear that he loves me when he did this!" My voice cracked. "He took all of my love, my heart and soul and just flushed it down the toilet. Like I was nothing!" My voice was trembling as I fought the pain. "*He* cheated, *not me*. Please don't ask me to forget that."

I started to sob, and buried my face in my hands as I lost the fight against it. "I'm so pathetic. I did everything to get over it... I even tried to have sex with David in January, but Cade has fucked me up so bad, I couldn't even kiss him. I'm so disgusted with myself. I couldn't even do it to *get even*, Jeanne. It made me physically sick."

She looked at me with sad eyes. "Okay, Brook. Wendy is a snake in the grass. You can't trust her. If you could have heard him, Brook, or seen his face," she paused and her eyes pleaded with me. "Just like you wouldn't let David touch you, Cade wouldn't touch any other woman, honey. I believe him and he wouldn't risk losing you to be with someone like her. Think about it."

"I saw his face; I heard his voice in Tokyo. Yes, he was hurting. We both were." I was getting angry now. "So I'm supposed to forget that I *saw* her there? Cade is a very hot, sensual man, and Wendy has been on the prowl for him for a year. Most men can't resist that kind of shit for very long. Maybe he was drunk, I don't know. I have considered that and I've even forgiven him, but it doesn't change that he still didn't want me in Tokyo." I drew in a painful breath. "Jeanne, can you please just try to understand how I felt when she opened that door? It was like I was punched in the gut. I couldn't breathe. I died in the moment."

I froze where I was as I relived it, and felt the tears fall from my eyes silently again. I brushed them off my cheek quickly and got up from the bed. I needed to be alone and to get a grip on myself.

She looked like she wanted to say something and was searching for the words, but I didn't want to hear it.

"I just can't talk about it anymore. I know he loves me, but I'm scared to risk my heart again." I shook my head, "Reliving it only makes me weak and I'm struggling. I'm sorry." I paused and saw the sadness in her face. "I'm going to take a bath and go over the scenes that I have to shoot with Noah and Jennifer tomorrow."

I went to run the bath and try to get lost in the script.

Chapter 14
Breaking & Breathing

Caden

WE WERE GETTING ready to film a scene in a gym when Aaron encourages Ryan to cheat on Julia. Jesus Christ, my chest hurt, but I almost laughed at the irony of it.

For once it mattered to me that we were filming out of sequence. My heart constricted as I remembered a conversation Brook and I had during pre-production of the first film about sequence. She'd been so green, she was clueless about the "hows" and "whys" of filming and was concerned she wouldn't be able to emote appropriately if the scenes were shot out of order and the story was jumbled in her mind. I understood where she was coming from. On most of my action films, it didn't matter, but this one we needed that connection, and that was the start of everything. All of those late nights running lines and reading the books together were what made us, "us". I sucked in my breath and gave my head a few quick shakes to try and get my focus back.

I was thankful I didn't have to make it through a love scene, but it would still be emotional because it was very relatable. I started to run a hand through my hair, but stopped when the make-up artist called my name sharply. My head snapped around to look at her as she was rapidly shaking her head. "You'll ruin it."

I grimaced. How could I ruin it? It was covered in crap that made it look sweaty and plastered to my head, but whatever. I let my hand fall to my side and turned away from her.

I was royally screwed, even though I'd talked to Martin during pre-production and explained the situation about Brook and me and the misunderstanding about Wendy. He'd agreed to leave the love scenes, which were more over-the-top intense in this movie, until the end of production so maybe I'd be able to mend the abyss with her, though I was hurt and angry. I'd also asked him to keep Wendy the hell away from me as much as possible.

I thought I was prepared for this scene; I'd memorized every line but something didn't feel right. It felt too real and the pain in my chest was undeniable. I was all fucked up because Brook and I hadn't met and worked on anything in pre-production. In fact, I'd avoided Vancouver until a day before my first call.

We always rehearsed together and never went to set without going over every scene, even if it wasn't one we were in together. We weren't just actors working on a film, we always wanted it to be prefect and had spent hours and hours perfecting every nuance. This time, it felt like we were strangers and it tortured me. If this were any other actress or any other movie, maybe it wouldn't have mattered. But it was Brook. It felt wrong. Horribly wrong.

I walked over to Ethan and he nodded at me as I approached. "Hey, man."

"Hello," I returned.

We were both in workout clothes, I was shirtless and the make-up people made sure I looked like I was glistening with sweat by spraying me with a mixture of water and glycerin, and I went through a series of stretches to loosen up my muscles right before the costume assistant taped up my hands and was lacing up the second boxing glove. I flexed my hands inside them because they felt uncomfortable. I would have rather hit the bag with my bare fists, but that wasn't the way the script was written, and I couldn't have my hands banged up for the rest of the filming.

I was wound really tight; my body coiled and my heart hollow. All I wanted was to get at that bag and begin working myself up before the scene started, then I'd be sweating and out of breath for real, so I turned to Ethan.

"Would you mind spotting me? I want to get started. It'll make it more realistic for filming."

"Sure. No problem." He nodded and grabbed the bag.

I immediately began attacking it. "Ugh!" I delivered the first hit with my right hand, harder than necessary, and then another with my left.

"Whoa, save it for the film, dude." The look on his face was concerned. "Is something up with Brook? I haven't seen you two together since we hit set and she's been holed up in her room and not hanging with the rest of us, like before."

It was the first chance I'd had to speak to him since I'd arrived. "Uh..." I hesitated, but continued to hit the bag over and over. My heart rate began to elevate as I beat the hell out of the bag. Ethan was solid and holding it firmly. "I haven't really talked to her yet." My chest was heaving and I was beginning to get winded. Still, I kept hitting.

Ethan's expression was incredulous. "What? Really?"

The hair on my forehead and back of my neck was plastered to my skin, but I felt a prickling sensation and something made me turn to glance behind me. Brook was walking onto the sound stage and toward the set.

Fuck! Did I want her to watch this? Probably not.

Focus! My mind was screaming at me.

"Okay, places, guys," Martin said, unnecessarily. Brook took a chair behind Martin, and although I kept my eyes down, I could feel her gaze burning into me.

I sighed, shook my arms and bounced in place even though I was already warmed up. Ethan glanced at Brook, who was talking to Martin and then back at me. His eyes were knowing as they met mine, but he didn't ask any further questions. Thank God.

The two supporting actresses in the scene took their places a few feet away. They were pretty, outfitted like those Barbie girls who make going to the gym a fashion show rather than a workout. I'd seen one of them on set of another film, but the other was unknown to me.

"Okay, roll film." I turned my attention to Ethan who crouched and grabbed the bag again, then took another deep breath. "ACTION!" Martin yelled from off side.

The scene unfolded with Ethan's character goading mine that I should take advantage of the opportunity the two girls were presenting as I worked out. The sexual tension and frustration manifesting inside me was right on, it'd been so long since I'd been with Brook, and I was able to channel it into the scene. I knew Brook was watching and it pissed me off. Each blow to the bag was harder and harder.

Remember you're Ryan, not Cade, I thought. Ethan began his lines as Ryan's brother, Aaron.

"Looks like you've got a fan club," he murmured and nodded over his shoulder toward the two actresses ogling us.

"Stupid bitches," I grunted between punches, adopting the American accent that was now second nature to me. "After four years, you'd think they'd get a damn clue."

"They *are* hot," Ethan said.

Exertion was setting in and I was sweating profusely. I stopped to wipe the sweat out of my eyes with the towel around my neck as the script dictated. It was awkward with the gloves on, but they were starting to burn.

"Hadn't noticed," I said and continued with more blows to the bag.

"Ryan, come on. Julia's been away all this time and I love her dearly, but you're a guy. Guys have needs. It doesn't have to mean anything and they're certainly willing."

I didn't say anything, but hit the bag harder, still. Ethan was jolted and readjusted his stance. *The script, the script, the script,* my mind screamed. *Don't look at Brook!*

"And now... you seem so miserable." Ethan continued with his lines. "Maybe you need to cut loose a little."

"That's what I'm doing," I said through clenched teeth while I kept pounding the bag with all my strength.

"You know what I mean."

"Don't." I ground out.

"You're leaving here in a couple of months. God knows you need it. You're ready to blow, brother. Julia doesn't remember. She wouldn't have to know."

"Aaron, I said that's *enough!*" I yelled, easily channeling my real emotions. I was so pissed I felt like my body would fly apart.

"Ryan..." he began, but I shoved the bag with such force that he stumbled back and nearly fell.

"*Shut up*! Just shut the fuck up, Aaron!" I felt Ryan's rage and pain as I felt my own. "I'll smash your Goddamn face in if you say one more word, do you hear me?"

Ethan's expression was incredulous and his voice became as elevated as mine. "I'm just looking out for you! I see you suffering, you asshole! You're killing yourself! You better think twice before you threaten me little man, because I'll take your. Ass. *Out*!" Ethan came toward me and shoved me in the chest. The fight was choreographed, but I found myself using more force than I needed to and soon Ethan fell.

He sprawled backwards onto the mats as tears welled in my eyes.

"Noooo!" I screamed at him. "Maybe it's in you to fuck around on Jenna, but I will never do that to Julia!" The two actresses moved in closer in observance of the script, their eyes wide and mouths hanging open as I thundered at Ethan. "It is *impossible* for me to even think about anyone else! You know that so just shut the hell up! It would kill us both, for God's sake! I'm in *love, damn you*!! So much I can't even fucking breathe. She's all I want! She means everything and I just want her back like we *were*!" I was yelling and my chest was heaving. I stumbled back and began to turn from him, still on the floor, staring up at me with a stunned look on his face. "*She's all I want*," I said more softly, defeat and heartbreak lacing my tone. "Brook is all I want!"

"Cut!" Martin said loudly at the same time Ethan said "Shit, Cade! That would have been perfect."

"Bloody fucking hell! Just edit the fucking thing!" I said and ripped at the laces of the gloves. My eyes were blurry and I couldn't tell if the sting was from sweat or tears, but my chest was tight and I couldn't breathe. I felt claustrophobic and I needed a break. "I'm not doing that scene again!" I ripped the gloves off and dropped them where I stood, my eyes searching for a pair of blue ones.

Her face was so pained, and I remembered that look from Tokyo and tears were raining from her eyes. Jennifer and Wendy were both standing near her, and Jennifer put a hand on her shoulder.

"Brook," I choked out, trying desperately to keep my voice even, but my throat ached and all I wanted was for all of these people to disappear so I could make things right between us. I moved toward her without thinking but she put up a hand to stop me.

"I can't..." Her voice caught on a sob.

My face twisted in pain as I recognized that tone in her voice.

My heart was squeezing within my chest, the heat burning the back of my neck as I felt my skin flush, and my heart pounded loudly in my ears.

Her face dropped and crumpled as she struggled for words, her shoulders slumped and she shook her head brokenly. "I... can't do this," she said so softly I barely heard her.

I looked at her defeated form and chastised myself. She was broken and for what? I caused this. It was my fault. I should have swallowed my pride in Japan and straightened it all out.

Brook was visibly shaking, tears running down her face. "Don't," she whispered achingly. "Please don't do this." She took a step toward me, her tortured eyes rose to mine as her arms reached for me. She'd said the same damn thing as she lay on the bed in Japan. "I can't go through it again."

Jesus, I want to take the pain away.

Her mouth opened to speak but no words came out. She looked up into my eyes and I could see Brook in those eyes. Brook's eyes, not

Julia's.

My mind flashed to the hotel room in Tokyo when I told her we were done, the worst mistake of my life.

She was lost; her eyes went blank for a moment and my face softened. I hated seeing her pain. I couldn't bloody stand it.

"Why?" she whispered, tears still falling softly from her eyes.

Dear God. My heart pounded so fast I thought it would fly from my body, and my eyes burning with unshed tears.

She was sobbing and falling to her knees, her hands came up to cover her face as she cried and cried; her sobs so intense that there was no sound, only the violent shaking of her shoulders until she gasped loudly for air and fell to her knees.

My heart was breaking as I watched. My throat ached and my heart felt like it would fly from my body.

"Cade, I ca—can't take this." She was gasping for breath; her voice was softer now, but so tortured. I knew I wasn't breathing. "I can't be near you like this."

The cast and crew stood motionless around her.

I couldn't take any more. I walked quickly to her, unbelieving she was falling apart in front of everyone. The studio suits would be furious, but they were the last thing I was worried about. My focus was on her as my arms wrapped around her and lifted her to her feet. She melted into me, her hands clutching at my shirt, still sobbing. I drew in a deep breath and despite the situation and the eyes on us, she was in my arms and that was all that mattered. It was like a weight had been lifted off of my heart.

"Brook, my love... it's over." I tried to soothe her but she was lost to me, deaf to my words as she continued to cry softly now. My hands brushed her hair back and cupped her face.

"Brook!" I said sharply.

When she didn't respond, I gathered her up in my arms and strode off the sound stage and out into the lot toward the trailers. "It's going to be okay, babe. I'm here and I've got you." Her arms crept around my neck and she snuggled against my chest as her shaking lessened slightly.

The entire cast and crew stood with mouths agape as they watched me carry her across the lot. I strode past Wendy, and Jennifer and both of their faces were stunned, Jennifer had tears in her eyes.

"I guess he really *does* love her," Wendy said astonished. I heard their conversation as I passed.

"Where *the hell* have you been for the past year and a half? You'd have to be freaking blind not to see what's between them, Wendy. You just didn't want to believe it." Jennifer sounded incredulous.

I kicked my way into Brook's trailer and settled on the couch with her in my lap. I tried to soothe her by rubbing her back and kissing her forehead. It reminded me of the time when she'd cried on the prom set of Twilight last year.

"Oh Cade..." she sobbed against me.

"Shhh, Brook. I'm here with you, love." My arms tightened around her and my heart leapt when she said my name.

"I've missed you so much. I just- I can't do this *without you*. I tried, but now that you're here, I... I can't," she cried, a new set of sobs racking her slender form.

"Oh, sweetheart, you don't have to. You never did." I kissed her sweet mouth. "I've been half alive without you," I breathed into her hair. "I love you, Brook," I whispered, "more than anything."

She pulled back and looked into my face with her teary eyes and shook her head. "No. I-I can't. I need us to be like we were last year before we... " She sniffed and pushed at my chest. She looked into my stunned face and shook her head. "Before, you... we—"

"Are you telling me to *pretend* I don't love you?" My heart hardened. "That we never..." I shook my head in disbelief and ran a frustrated hand through my hair.

"Everything that's happened has hurt so much, and I'm - I'm scared. I, I don't want to go through that again. Loving you like that, it hurts too much. I lost myself, and then I lost you. It left me empty inside but you were my best friend, and I need you back like that." She was so shaken I wondered if she even knew what she was saying.

"You're so important, and that part of our relationship was safe." She was rambling, on and on. "Maybe we can only be friends, but I can't lose you completely." Her voice broke as she brought the back of her hand to her mouth. "I-I know that now." She raised her liquid blue eyes to mine.

I felt my lips tighten into a firm line. "Brook. The point is-I don't even *know* what happened or why you've shut me out since January. Why did things change between us? We were *so* happy."

"Wendy..." she began.

 I set her on the couch and stood up, took a few steps away as anger welled up inside me, and then turned back to face her. "I was *never* with Wendy. *Never!*" I yelled at her and she flinched. It shook me out of my temper.

Oh God, what was I doing? I didn't want to hurt her more. This was not the direction I wanted this conversation to take.

I knelt in front of her and took her face between my hands, brushing her cheekbone with my thumb. "I've been in *Hell,* Brook, just... *bloody hell* these past months," I said urgently, but softly.

Her hand came up to touch my face of its own volition, the sadness pouring out of her eyes. The touch of her soft hand settled me a little, but my mind was still conflicted. She rested her forehead on my cheek.

"Love," I said, my voice rough, thick, "I know you're upset right now, so maybe it would be better if we talked tonight, where we can be alone and uninterrupted. I really, really need for you to tell me why you're so sure I was with Wendy so I can address it and get to the bottom of it, okay? I was *not* with Wendy, Brook. For you to even think I would do that to you, rips my bloody guts out. You know how much I fucking love you." My voice broke and my thumb continued to stroke her cheek as I looked deeply into her eyes. "I would *never* hurt you like that. It would be worse than hurting myself." I was so emotional, I felt my throat start to choke off and my eyes prick with unshed tears.

There was a knock on the door. "Are you guys okay? We're all getting ready to leave. The cars are waiting," Wendy called.

Leave it to Wendy to put a fucking exclamation point on what this was all about. At the sound of her voice, I could feel Brook's body stiffen in my arms. She pushed off the couch away from me and ran both hands through her hair, clutching at the scalp. Her features were pained.

I felt the fury rise within me. I never hated anyone so much in my life as I did Wendy in that moment.

"Yeah. We should still talk tonight." She nodded as she regained control of herself. "We're fine, Wendy," she called.

I took a deep breath, my hand threading through my hair. "Good. I'll come to your room around ten, then? "

"Okay. I'm just going to get myself together for a minute, change my clothes and then I'll grab a car back." Her eyes were softer and her voice was gentle as she placed her hand on my chest. "I'll see you later, then."

"Yes." I touched her chin with my thumb. "Alright." I placed a small kiss on her mouth and then moved to the door. "See you in a while, then."

I walked out of the trailer I could finally breathe. Wendy was still close by and I had to walk past her. She reached out a hand to me.

"Cade—"

"Leave her alone, Wendy. Stay away from both of us," I said in an ominous tone as I walked passed her and back toward the building.

In a few short hours Brook and I were finally going to get everything out in the open. As my chest expanded in relief, I finally had hope. Hope that we were going to *get back to us*.

I was bloody well finished living without her. *Fucking done.*

Chapter 15
True Love Talks

Brooklyn

I WANTED TO believe him; so much I couldn't breathe. I still couldn't piece together why or how Wendy could be in his apartment, but Cade was so adamant he wasn't with her, that my heart needed to hope he was telling the truth.

When he'd said he loved me, the words were like a balm to my wounded soul, his arms around me like water in the desert. I needed to believe him so I could continue to exist. It was that simple.

I took a shower and threw on some old sweat pants and an oversized T-shirt, rolling up the sleeves a couple times and tying a knot in the hem. I didn't care how I looked. I was emotionally spent and exhausted from the scene on set. I'd left it all in back there, breaking down just watching him act out a scene that had a small resemblance to real life. I took a deep breath and ran a hand through my hair, that was still damp from the shower and hanging lose around my shoulders.

I decided to order pizza and beer rather than get a full-blown meal from room service. Cade liked Heinekens and pizza with everything on it. I wanted vegetables only, so I ordered half and half. I remembered how many times we'd done this while doing the first film. I smiled knowing he'd still want to help me eat some of the vegetable side.

I was unexpectedly calm, at ease. It was strange that I felt this way after all of the turmoil and even more unbelievable how badly I wanted this to work out with him. If I were honest, it wasn't that unbelievable. I needed Cade so much and wasn't sure I could lose him, even if that horrible night with Wendy was reality.

The truth was, I loved him and he must have been wasted off his ass because he seemed to need the details. I'd give them to him even though it would hurt doing so. I'd listen to him and then we'd see where we went from there. I didn't want a repeat of the scene in Japan, so I knew I had to tell him absolutely everything. Maybe by some miracle we'd get beyond this and be able to rebuild at least part of our relationship. I wanted to get everything back if we could. Whether he was or wasn't with her, it didn't matter enough to keep us apart.

I heard the knock on the door, and it was then that my stomach sank and the nerves kicked in. I went to answer it and Cade was there in black jeans and a T-shirt, the stubble on his face starting to be visible, his hair mussed like he'd run his hands through it a hundred times.

He was still so beautiful, his blue eyes searching my face intently. My heart thumped in my chest as he took me in his arms and hugged me close, kissing my temple. I felt his chest rise and fall in a deep breath. It was obvious he was pensive and nervous.

He smelled so good and felt so good. I'd missed him so much. I couldn't help myself; I let my head settle on his chest and my arms wind tightly around his waist. I took in his scent, a mixture of shampoo and musky cologne, I'd committed to memory.

"I ordered pizza, I hope that's okay," I said softly. I felt suddenly awkward, scared about the conversation that we were about to have.

"Sure. That's fine." He stepped back a little to look at me. His eyes were soft and hungry, even a little sad as his hand reached out to cup my face.

Oh God, this isn't going to be easy, but we need this, I thought.

I had music playing softly in the background, selections I knew he liked; most of which I had tried not to listen to in the past months because the reminder was too painful.

"Your reaction today on set was unexpected, Brook. You had everyone in tears." He paused and looked at the floor. "Especially me," he said softly.

My head bent and my hand went up to cover his hand as his thumb brushed back and forth on my cheekbone. I shook my head a little.

"I'm... " I struggled for what to say as I raised my eyes to his perfect features, drinking in the sight of him. It had been three weeks since I'd seen him and December in London since we'd made love. My heart stopped in my chest. "Sorry."

"It was real to me. It wasn't Ryan and Julia... that was us out there." He cleared his throat. "I mean, the situation echoed our own, but you have to know..." Cade trailed off.

I felt my voice tremble. "Even hearing you speak as Ryan about cheating on Julia; on me. Only Ryan couldn't ever cheat." My voice was soft, almost distant, yet there was a catch in my throat. Could Cade? "And the way you left in Tokyo was brutal."

"I know," he said the words so softly. "Except I'd never leave you, love. Not really, I was just so angry and hurt in Japan. I tried to tell you so many times since, but..." His voice was velvet and soft. "I didn't mean what I said when I told you I couldn't love you anymore."

I nodded. "Yeah, I know. I guess I just wasn't ready to listen."

I stepped back and his arms dropped to his sides. His brow crinkled and he looked pained. I knew that if I let him hold me and touch me, we'd never talk like we needed to.

"I've really missed you. Not being able to talk to you was..." his words dropped off as he stared at my face. "How have you been?"

I motioned for him to sit down. "Miserable, if I'm honest, Cade. I've been completely... devastated." My hand rose to cover my eyes. "Um," I swallowed the tight knot in my throat. "Do you want a beer?" I didn't wait for him to answer, but I went to the bar to get one. I felt vulnerable, and had to break the tension somehow.

"Thanks," he said softly as he took it from me. I could feel how fragile we both were.

I sat down on the opposite end of the bed from him. We sat in silence for a few minutes, neither one of us knowing where to start, but finally, I had to say something.

"I'm sorry, Cade. I shouldn't have disappeared the way I did. I should have talked to you the night you came to my room, but I just wasn't strong enough. I know I should have told you what was upsetting me. It was immature of me, but I guess, I just thought you already knew why."

"How would I know?" he asked, his tone still soft as he reached for my hand. His fingers were warm as they closed around mine.

"I've realized through all of this that I lost myself somewhere. I'm usually so tough and strong, but since last May when we wrapped and I came to London, I've just been a mess. I don't recognize myself. When I open my eyes—you're all I see."

His blue eyes, so beautiful as he looked at me, widened.

"Everywhere, every thought and memory is about you. The past, present, and future... you're all I can see in front of me. After that thing with Wendy...," Cade's brow crinkled and he opened his mouth to speak, but I pushed on, "it's all become convoluted and distorted, somehow." I got up to pace around the room.

"I've never been this emotionally raw or confused about anything before and it's shaken me up quite a bit. I feel so fucking helpless because so many things are out of my control, especially my feelings. I can't stop loving you even when it hurts so much, it's like I'm drowning and I... I can't save myself."

I could see that he wanted to speak, the panic showed plainly in his gorgeous face. "Cade, please let me finish or I'll never get it all out." I took a breath, and blinked at the tears that I felt pooling in my eyes.

"Oh, God." I ran a hand through my hair before continuing.

"When we were working you were a safe place for me. I loved being with you, I relied on you more than I realized and I loved you to a degree that was inconceivable to me. I... I let myself need someone for the first time in my life; let myself really feel and trust more than I ever had. Hmmph," I expelled my breath as I checked myself. "Let myself is the wrong way to put it. I have no choices where you're concerned. It's bigger than me, and it scared me." I let out a shaky laugh, my whole body trembling with emotion.

"See how weak I've become, and the worst part is that I know that my strength is what you found most attractive about me." My voice was shaking as I struggled to control my emotions.

I sat back down on the bed, and he took both of my hands in his.

"Brook; that's not the only reason I want you. Everything about you calls to me. You're so smart and loving, funny and sexy. You make me happier than I've ever been; you're so, so beautiful, and I love that you let yourself be weak with me. It shows that you trust me." He dropped his eyes to our hands. "I want to protect you from everything that hurts you."

He reached for me again and I pulled back to stop him. I didn't think I'd get through this if he touched me like that. His face contorted with pain as his hands fell back to his lap, so I moved toward him and put my hands on both sides of his face. I looked into his blue eyes and tried to explain.

"The point that I'm trying to make is that I still love you, too, so much, but it consumes me and clouds my judgment. I need us to be like we were before. It was so much less painful then."

It was Cade who pulled back then.

"No!" he exclaimed, his voice elevating. "It wasn't less painful for me. To be near you and want you so badly, but not be able to tell you or show you, to feel so close to you but not be sure you loved me, was living hell. I don't want that again." His face twisted and his voice was full of pain. "I love you, Brook. I want to marry you, not worship you from afar. I thought I'd made that perfectly clear." His tone was edged with anger mixed with sorrow.

"Yes, but things changed when Wendy..." my voice dropped off when I saw the anger overtake his perfect features. His mouth set, his jaw muscles working overtime, his brow dropping low over his eyes.

"Oh yes, here we go. Brilliant! Can you please tell me what the bloody hell you're trying to say?" His eyes flashed at me and his voice got louder.

"Cade, I don't want to fight like before, please? If you were anyone else, if what we had wasn't so mind-blowing, I'm sure this wouldn't be such a big deal, but with you, it just wrecked me. I know I should have told you all this last month, but I missed you and didn't want to start a fight." I felt the walls start to crumble around me as I struggled to keep control of my emotions. "I was trying to salvage something of us," I said wearily.

"But we did fight, didn't we? Because you were hiding something from me! And, I don't understand why. When was I supposedly with Wendy?" his voice was tight and his jaw clenched. "Just bloody tell me! I've been racking my fucking brain trying to figure it out and it's bloody impossible!"

I flinched. "Well, New Year's Eve." My voice shook, and I prayed I wouldn't cry.

He shook his head angrily.

"New Year's Eve, I went to a pub with Ethan, Dawson and Jennifer. Wendy showed up later, but I wasn't with her. I wasn't!" He turned and went to the window his back to me as he stood with a hand on his hip. "Ask Jennifer or any of them since you won't believe a goddamn word I say."

He was defeated, agitated, but then he turned to face me. "I'm hurt too, you know? I'm utterly destroyed by all of this. The fact that you would believe me capable of touching another woman after how it feels between us, is impossible for me to fucking comprehend! After all the time I waited for you, all that we've meant to each other—My God!"

Cade's hand went up to cover his eyes as he paused, and my heart stopped at the trembling in his voice. "It blows my mind that you doubt me, that you don't trust me!" His voice grew soft, thick with emotion as he looked at me again. "And now to hear you say that you've tried to stop loving me, you might as well bloody shoot me, because I'll be no less dead!"

My breath caught in my throat at his words and his eyes flashed as he took a deep, ragged breath.

"Jesus Brook! Don't you know how much I love you?" He ran his hand through his hair. "Ahhhhhhh!" he yelled, and I flinched again.

Then he sat down beside me and softened his tone, again. "Can't you see how destroyed I am? It hurts so much; I can't even breathe." He dropped his head and put his arms around it, his closed elbows hiding his features.

Tears started to fall, despite my valiant efforts to keep them at bay. "Please can we just lay it on the table so maybe we can move past this? My heart is breaking, Cade. Please." I wiped at my tears with both hands.

"Isn't that what I've been doing?" His voice was rough and deep. He moved closer to me and took both of my hands in his, the thumb of his right hand brushing over the ring finger on my left. "Where is my ring, Brook?" he asked brokenly.

"I have it with me. You can have it back if you want." My voice cracked on the last word.

"Hmmft..." He let out his breath. "Fuck no; I absolutely do not want it back. How can you even bloody say that, Brook? I want it on your finger where it belongs." He kissed my hand, his breath warm on my skin as he pressed his cheek against it. "I want this rubbish to go away. I can't take another minute of it."

I knew I just had to just tell him, so I took a shaky breath and plunged in. "I saw her there, Cade, okay?" His head snapped up to look in my face. "I saw it with my own eyes, so why are you denying it?" My shoulders were shaking with barely controlled emotion and my eyes were blurry with tears. "Please don't lie."

"What?" He looked stunned, his eyes wide, his brows raised. "You saw her?"

"I, um," I tried to clear my voice so I could continue. "Uhhhhmmm, I came back to L.A. so I could be with you." I watched his mouth gape and his eyes widen. The sobs were starting full force, tears rolling down my cheeks as I struggled to get the words out.

He was still as stone as he looked at me.

"I couldn't bear the hurt in your voice when I told you on the phone that I couldn't make it back, so I told Jeanne I had to go and hopped on the first available plane." I sniffed a little before I continued, "But the stupid plane was delayed and I couldn't make it back by Midnight."

"Oh, baby... you came back to me?"

I nodded. My chest was aching and the tightness had me gasping for breath

"I came to your place around 2 AM and Wendy answered the door. She was naked Cade, wrapped in the comforter from your bed, the one you had in your room in London." I dropped my head into my hands and cried hard. "I'll never forget how I felt in that moment. She was so cruel, smug; telling me that you were sleeping because you'd had a sex-a-thon, asking me what the hell I was doing there," my voice broke on the words.

He was frozen next to me so I turned toward him. "That's why, when I didn't return your calls the next day, I thought you'd figure out that I knew, and I wasn't strong enough to talk to you about it then. It was too soon."

"But..." I looked up into his face as confusion flooded his features. He was shaking his head, "that can't be." Cade was talking to himself. He rose from the bed and began walking back and forth and then sat down on the bed again. The look on his face was panicked.

"That can't be, Brook. I was so upset that we couldn't be together; I drank myself into oblivion that night. I barely talked to anyone. You were all I thought about. I didn't even remember how I got home."

He stopped as realization dawned on him. "I don't remember anything. Oh, God, I'll never forgive myself if..." His voice fell off and he was shaking as he looked at me, his eyes glassy with unshed tears. "If I let that happen."

"If you were that intoxicated, maybe you don't remember being with her." I rose from the bed and turned away from him, trying to push away my own pain as I made excuses for his behavior. "I'm sure you wouldn't do that under normal circumstances, but even knowing that you were drunk, it doesn't change that it happened, and it hurts so much." My voice breaking in barely a whisper, I told him the whole truth. "I hoped we could get back to how we used to be without reliving all of this, but I realized I had to tell you everything."

"That night, I couldn't breathe, I couldn't walk, I couldn't see through my tears—I could barely tell the cab driver to take me back to LAX." I tried to wipe the wetness from my face, but the tears wouldn't stop, and I was sobbing softly. "I turned right around and went back to New York. I got through the obligation, secured the film... . Then completely fell apart afterward."

He got up and came to me, one arm going around me, his other hand on my face, brushing my hair back.

"God, Brook, I'm so sorry you had to go through that, but you've got to believe that I wouldn't do that to you." His eyes were filling with tears. "I'd never hurt you like that, I'd never risk losing you. I never wanted her and you are my entire world. Jesus Christ, Brook, I need you to believe me." His blue eyes full of panic, his voice was rough with anguish. His forehead came to rest against mine, his warm breath on my face. "Please," he begged. "Just... *please*."

God help me, I couldn't stop my arms from flinging themselves around his neck as I sobbed into his shoulder and his arms tightened around my back, one hand sliding up to hold the back of my head. His face turned into the curve of my neck, as we clung to each other for dear life.

He was everything to me and all I wanted at that moment was to melt into him and forget any of this ever happened.

"Oh, Brook." He was crying too as he stroked the back of my head. "I love you so much; I'd rather die than see you so hurt."

I didn't think I had any tears left after the shoot earlier that day, but it was like a flood gate had opened and the sobs racked my body again. The stress of the entire thing made us both desperate and clinging to each other. I tried to talk through the hiccupping gasps.

"I hate myself for being so weak, but I can't stop loving you. Oh, God, help me stop aching, Cade," I cried and his face turned into my hair, pulling me even closer to his chest.

"Oh, babe, I'm so sorry. I can't lose you, please." He was raining kisses all over my face as he breathed my name over and over. "I'll get to the bottom of this, I promise. If I did anything so fucking reckless, I'll just kill myself."

We forgot the pizza, forgot everything and we just held each other for hours. Our bodies molded together on the bed, our hands stroking each other and Cade placing soft kisses on my face and then he took my mouth in a series of deep, searching kisses. We were soaking each other up, the months of separation and pain evaporating as the minutes passed. We quieted and just lay, totally entwined. My head over his heart and his arms wrapped tightly around me, we were content just to hold each other. I was so emotionally spent, my lids got heavy and I yawned.

"Go to sleep, love. I'm here and I'm not going anywhere," he said against my mouth before placing one last soft kiss on my lips. I took a deep breath as I snuggled against him and closed my eyes. "I'm so, so sorry, my love; so sorry. We'll sort through this whole thing tomorrow, I promise."

"I'm sorry too. It doesn't even matter, Cade. I just want you. I still love you as much as always, maybe even more. Being without you is not something I can do." I snuggled into him and our legs entwined. I felt him sigh and kiss the top of my head.

I had to trust him, to have faith in these feelings, to believe in what I saw in his eyes whenever he looked at me, and how it felt whenever he touched me. His words left me breathless, so all of it couldn't be a lie. My heart wouldn't let me believe anything else.

Caden

WITH BROOK ASLEEP next to me at least I knew we loved each other and that we both wanted to be back together, but still, I lay awake still trying to figure it all out. How could I have been so bloody stupid to let myself, drunk or not, get into such a fucking precarious situation? It could have cost me everything that mattered to me in this world.

Jesus Christ. Damn Wendy to hell!

My chest constricted at the pain I saw in Brook's face, her voice shaking as she told me about seeing Wendy at my apartment.

How could I let that happen? I racked my brain trying to figure it out. Brook seemed peaceful, sleeping in my arms, but my brain was blaring.

All I could remember was getting drunk at the bar with Dawson and Ethan. Jen was there making out with Dawson, and Wendy was annoying the hell out of both Ethan and me. She did try to paw all over me, but I pushed her off me and turned my back to her after screaming at her above the bar din "I love Brook, Wendy! Get the fuck off me!"

I'd made Ethan switch places with me so I could get away from her as I ordered more drinks for everyone. The next thing I remember was waking up in my apartment alone, with the worst hangover of my life, and Brook not taking my calls.

I was completely and utterly furious with myself. Could I have slept with her and not remember? For the love of God, I'd never forgive myself if that happened, and I'd beg Brook's forgiveness every day for the rest of my life.

I felt positive that I was in no state to perform that night, no matter who I was with, so could Wendy be lying? I sure as hell hoped so because she wasn't there when I woke up. If it didn't happen, what was she going to do? Try to convince me that I'd shagged her then blackmail me with it? Or, was her plan this entire time just to torment Brook? It was obvious she was green with jealousy or maybe she was helping that sod, David in some revenge ploy.

She'd practically stalked Brook during the first film, taking every advantage for publicity and to hang out with us. All of her insinuations and flirting with me were over the top, but I'd brushed her attempts aside. Obviously, I had to confront Wendy with Brook right beside me. It was the only way to get to the truth.

I thought I had handled this problem when I told Wendy I loved Brook after the photo shoot, but apparently that only made her more determined. Recognition dawned as I remembered how her words as she left that night felt like a threat. *"You'll regret this decision,"* she'd said.

Well, *she'd* bloody well regret it when I was done with her.

Brook stirred at my side and murmured my name, the arm across my chest creeping up to the back of my neck and curling into my hair. My heart swelled as my arms tightened around her. I loved her, and no way in hell was I letting that malicious little twit come between us. I shook my head at myself and sucked in a deep breath. How could I have been so careless?

I let my hand run up and down Brook's perfect little body, relishing in the feel of her as she snuggled more closely to my side. She thought I cheated, yet still loved me, still wanted me, and she trusted me enough to believe me when I told her I couldn't have been with Wendy, even though I couldn't remember the details.

I never wanted to see that kind of pain in her eyes again. I turned my face toward the top of her head and kissed it, breathing in her scent. I never wanted to let her go.

I tried to imagine how I'd have felt if I were the one to go to Brook's door and some naked man answered it. I closed my eyes at the tightness in my chest, and tried to swallow the lump in my throat.

It would kill me. I would have fucking broken the door down and beat the man to a bloody pulp. No question, I'd have jumped to the exact same conclusions Brook had.

I still couldn't believe she'd flown all the way back from New York to surprise me. She was amazing. Coming all the way back to L.A. so we could be together, only to be faced with that bloody nightmare. *Holy Hell.*

After all of this bullshit was cleared up, I was going to have it out with Pinnacle Studios, too. Enough was enough. We were going to be together and the rest of them, be damned. I didn't care about the contracts, the movies or my career, at this point. I'd schlep burgers before I'd let this carry on.

I wouldn't let them continue to put us in a position where the media, or anyone else, could do shit like this to destroy us. I was done, and I would protect Brook from this type of thing ever happening again. If the world knew we were together, there would be less speculation in the tabloids trying to hook one of us up with other people.

Resigned to what I needed to do, I relaxed and let myself enjoy the moments with her, to smell her hair, feel her warmth. It enveloped me like a warm bath as our limbs tangled together in the blankets.

My heart, mind and arms full of Brook, I felt sleep begin to overtake me. I was completely exhausted.

Tomorrow I'd talk to Ethan, and confront Wendy.

I'd either be able to take away all of Brook's fears, or if I *had* been stupid enough to shag Wendy and didn't remember it, I'd have to deal with the consequences and beg Brook to forgive me. She'd already told me she did... but would I be able to forgive myself for hurting her?

Dear God, please, please don't let me have been so fucking stupid.

Chapter 16
Freedom of Truth

Caden

I HEARD THE song I'd written for her playing and I realized it was Brook's phone alarm. I smiled to myself as my heart swelled. She wouldn't talk to me all this time, but she still had my voice as her alarm clock. She stirred at my side and I bent to nuzzle the side of her face.

"Ugh... no," she moaned. "I don't want to go." My arms tightened around her as she stretched and arched her back against me.

"Mmmmm. You feel so good. I've missed this." Her arms lay across mine in front of her and my hand went to cup one of her breasts, as I pulled her back against me. It was incredible to have her in my arms again.

"Cade..." She breathed as she turned in my arms to kiss my mouth, her arms going around my neck and into my hair on both sides of my head, pulling my mouth to hers. My mouth opened over hers and my tongue slid inside. She tasted so amazing, and I was fucking drowning in her.

We were starving for each other and we kissed wildly for a long time, sucking, teasing, licking, and our mouths moving in unison. She was so hot, her kisses like nectar that I couldn't get enough of.

"Make love to me." She arched her body against me, and I could feel the heat between her legs as she pushed against me. "I want you, Cade. Please," she whispered against my mouth as we came up for breath between our kisses.

The way she pressed her soft curves into me felt divine. I could feel my body, already hard, throb as more blood rushed through my veins. I wanted her badly as I pushed my pelvis to hers so she could feel how much. My hands worshiped her perfect breasts, down her ribs and waist, over the gentle swell of her glorious hips, as I kissed her again and again; hungry for her love.

"Mmmmmm. See what you do to me?" I teased her as my hips pressed my hardness into her warm center as I hitched her leg over my waist. My hand moved up her thigh and pulled her tight against me and I moved on her body.

"Mmm. That feels so good," she whispered near my ear before her mouth licked and kissed the side of my neck. "More," she moaned against my skin. "I want to feel you inside me, Cade. It's been so long."

Holy hell. "Jesus, babe, you make me so hot. Brook..."

My erection was screaming against her. I rolled her onto her back and kissed her deeply again, before placing a few soft kisses on her lips, drawing her lower lip into my mouth with suction.

I ground my lower body with hers and she moaned, arching up toward me, trying to recapture my lips, her hips undulating underneath me, the delicious friction causing me to groan.

"Oh God." I brushed her hair back and then my mouth hovered over hers. "There is nothing I want more than to make mad, passionate love to you, hear you moan my name, to feel your quivering flesh against me, on me, around me, to taste every inch of you and make you come all over me. I've dreamed of little else for months." I kissed her again, and her body surged against mine. "But not yet. We should wait, love. I can't believe I'm bloody saying that, but we should wait, Brook."

My body fought my mind. I wanted her so bloody bad; she was so beautiful and I had missed her beyond any comprehensive thought, but I shifted away just enough so I could look into her face. Her skin was flushed pink with desire, her lips swollen slightly from my kisses. My heart stopped. She was so beautiful, and she was mine.

"Why? Don't you want me?" Her eyes were questioning as her hand brushed my hair back and she raised her open mouth toward mine. I couldn't help it, I let my lips close around her lower one and pull on it, before repeating the action on the top one.

"Uhhh, are you serious? Of course I want you... more than *fucking air*," I whispered incredulously, as my tongue licked at her upper lip then I took it between both of mine in a kiss, my mouth softly brushed back and forth across hers as I struggled for control. "More than anything in the world. I just told you so."

"Then?" she paused.

"Honey, I want to clear everything up first. I need to get this bloody mess resolved, please?"

"I told you that I believe you." She touched my cheek, her blue eyes questioning as they burned into mine, her body continuing to grind into mine, and it was exquisite torture. She felt so fantastic against me. "Cade, none of it matters. All that matters is that you're still mine."

Resting on my elbows above her, our bodies pressed into each other, my thumbs brushed against both sides of her beautiful face.

"Making love has always been so special; so incredibly brilliant between us, I don't want any niggling doubt in your mind when we do this. I won't have you thinking about me with any other woman when we're together. I never want to put you through that, and I won't. No doubts when I touch you; *ever*."

She stared into my eyes for a minute and I saw the tears begin, her brow crinkled as she fought them. I kissed her open mouth softly, lovingly and nuzzled her nose with mine.

 "Don't cry, sweetheart. It's going to be all right. It's all going to be fine, my love. And then I'm going to make such sweet love to you, Brook. I'm bloody starving for you. Not just your body, but all of you." I knew the emotion was thick in my voice, so thick my throat was aching.

"Oh. Cade." Her words were breathy and her eyes closed as a single tear fell out the corner of each one onto the pillow. "Thank you for being so good to me. I believe you, babe."

Her head lifted toward me as her mouth reached for me to return to kissing hers. Her arms around me felt so safe as she brushed my mouth with hers and whispered. "I should've talked to you about it sooner. I 'm so sorry for wasting all this time, for putting you through this."

Finally, I gave her what she was seeking as my mouth took hers in another greedy kiss, my tongue plunging into her mouth and hers coming to meet it. She was so, so delicious.

"Don't cry my love, I understand. I would have bloody killed someone if the positions were reversed." I brushed her hair back off her face and my thumb traced the line of her jaw as I stared down into her blue eyes. "We're going to get through this, sweetheart, and nothing is going to separate us again, okay?" I kissed her deeply again and my hand slid up her thigh to pat her very luscious rump. "You've got to be on set soon, don't you?"

"Eew. Don't remind me." She hugged me and buried her face in my shoulder, kissing it with an open mouth and sucking a little. My lower body throbbed with need, and my heart pounded in my chest.

Her hands feathered down my back, sending goose bumps up my skin, until they reached my ass and her hands clamped down on the muscles and pushed me tighter into her center as she raised her hips into mine. Her eyes widened and she smiled as she did it. She was so fucking beautiful and I sucked in my breath.

"*Stop* torturing me, witch." I kissed her again, then rolled away from her and pushed her toward the edge of the bed. "You don't want to be late, but make sure Noah doesn't get any ideas. You're still Ryan's girl."

"I could never forget. Just don't *you* forget what you're going to do to me tonight. We have a lot of time to make up for." She smiled, her face shining with love and happiness as she went into the loo and turned on the shower.

"I won't forget, my love. Rather, I'll be plotting and planning all bloody day." I smirked as I got up from the bed. I was still in my clothes from last night. We had been so caught up in just being close to each other that I hadn't wanted to let go of her long enough to strip off my clothes before I fell asleep.

Hmmm. I decided to go take in the view even if I couldn't make love to her now. I went into the loo and leaned my shoulder on the wall. Watching her shampoo her hair, the lather running in waves down the gentle curves of her gorgeous body, my body ached and my mouth went dry.

"Ughhhh!" I groaned and she laughed at me.

I thought about my conversation with myself last night and I felt a new surge of determination. I wasn't going to allow anyone or anything to come between us again.

"NOW who's torturing you, Cade?" She laughed as she continued to wash her hair and skin.

"I know, but its exquisite torture; that." I nodded towards her naked body.

"I wish these hands on my body belonged to you." She ran her hands down over her breasts , stomach and hips, her eyes never leaving mine. She was so incredibly sexy, and she was teasing me.

"Mmmmm. Babe, we're going to confront Wendy, and bloody soon. I want to get this rubbish behind us as quickly as possible, okay? I can't take not touching you like this." I smiled and ran a hand through my hair. "My body's been aching almost as much as my heart has been." I was deadly serious.

"What if Wendy denies it in front of you?"

"How can she? You saw her."

"Yeah, but she can still insist the two of you got it on, and you just don't remember. I wouldn't put anything past her. I'm beginning to see her in a whole new light." Her voice held a trace of pain.

She was right, my mind was racing. *How was I going to get to the bottom of this?*

"The thing is, Brook; even if Wendy was attractive to me physically, her bloody personality turns my fucking stomach. I just can't imagine that I'd shag her even with *someone else's dick.*"

I smiled when she burst out laughing. At least we were laughing about it. "Um, Ethan took me home that night, so I'll ask him to join, if that's all right with you? He can attest to how bloody drunk I was, and not fit for anything other than sleep. Maybe he knows what happened."

I silently prayed that was the case, and that I hadn't slept with Wendy. The thought was so repulsive it made me shudder.

"Yeah, okay. He knows about us anyway, doesn't he?"

"I think he's known for months. Most of them have, but for sure since I screamed in Wendy's ear at the bar that night." I smirked.

"What?" Her head came up to look at me as she turned off the water.

"That wench wouldn't leave me alone, and I'd bloody well had had enough. I'm surprised it wasn't all over the tabloids the next day. Everyone heard it." I laughed at the memory. *Fucking, Wendy! That bitch.* I shook my head.

"Wendy has an in with the paparazzi, remember? They only print what she wants printed. I'm surprised there weren't pictures of the two of you at the bar that night. She would have gotten a lot of mileage out of being seen out with you."

She stepped out of the shower, her body glistening with the water droplets. I went to her with a towel and wrapped her in it as I bent to place a hot kiss on her shoulder.

"So um... What did you scream at her?"

She was curious and I could see the gleam in her eyes. She was enjoying this. I continued raining light kisses on her shoulders and neck sending shivers all down her body. She smelled so great, and her arms around me felt so wonderful.

"It's kind of fuzzy, but something along the lines of ; 'Get the hell off me because I'm in love with Brook.'" My arms slid around her back and she lifted her face to kiss me.

"I love you," she breathed against my mouth.

I looked at the heavens with a smile on my face and raised one hand toward the ceiling. "Thank God. I was dying *not knowing for sure.*" I teased with a crooked grin. She kissed my chest, and I ran a hand down her back.

"I'll convince you more, later," she promised. "I have to go. Noah is already calling me to see where the hell I am." She went to grab her phone as "I'm Too Sexy" played, but I stopped her by catching her in my arms.

I raised my eyebrow at the song and she shrugged. "What the fuck?" I asked at the ridiculous ring tone.

"I thought it appropriate considering." She giggled. "You know the model, thing."

"Well I don't like it," I growled and hauled her with me to fall on the bed. "He better bloody well keep his hairy paws to himself!"

She burst out giggling and my laughter joined hers. "Caden Carlisle! How am I supposed to answer this call with you doing this silly shit?"

"He can sod off!" I laughed, so happy to be here with her, she was still squealing with laughter. "You've already got a bloody man, haven't you?" I tickled her ribs.

"Stop, I'm going to pee my pants!" she giggled.

"But, you're not *wearing* any pants, my love." I grinned at her and ran my hand up under her towel to cup her luscious rump, and give it a little squeeze. "See?" I smiled. "I quite like that part."

She laughed again. It was truly amazing how different I felt now, than I did just twenty-four short hours ago. The laughter died out of our eyes as we lay together stroking each other. She was so beautiful and I was drowning in those eyes.

I sighed as I brushed her wet hair back. "Brook," my voice got serious, my eyes intent as I looked at her, the smile faded from her face at my expression. "I can't lose you. These last months..." I shook my head, "have been unbearable, like part of me was missing. I'm so sorry for not clearing this up sooner. As soon as possible, I want that ring on your finger for the whole damn world to see. Promise me you'll never leave me, please."

I kissed her then, softly, tenderly, my breath mingling with hers. Her arms tightened around my neck and she pulled me closer to her luscious body, as she returned my kiss with love and passion, I deepened the kiss, my tongue laving hers.

Jesus, she tasted so sweet. My heart leapt in my chest.

These arms, these lips, those gorgeous blue eyes, this body close to mine, her voice breathing my name, were my heaven, salvation, peace; all I needed in the world.

"I promise, Cade..." she whispered as my mouth descended once again to take hers.

My mouth was more urgent as my tongue moved into her mouth. Her mouth opened to mine and she gave me her tongue and I sucked it further into my mouth. She moaned as I opened the towel and my hand moved down her naked body. I'd told her I wouldn't make love to her right now, but my mouth and hands had a mind of their own. My hand ghosted down to hover over her breast, grazing the nipple with my fingers and she arched up into it. I let my palm cup it and I felt the nipple, hard against my skin, and my body surged in response.

I dragged my mouth down across her chin and neck. A series of open mouth kisses across her silky skin, led to my mouth closing and pulling on the pink nub. My body throbbed and she moaned.

"Oh Jesus, Brook. I want you. I've been dying." My breath was coming in short bursts as I raised my mouth from her body and pressed my forehead into her collarbone as I struggled to get control of myself. I felt her hands in my hair stroking and her mouth pressed against at my temple, her breathing as labored as mine.

"I want you, Cade." My arms closed around her body and I moved to bury my face in the curve of her neck, her wet hair all over my face.

Her phone piped up again, playing "I'm Too Sexy" and I groaned and rolled over onto my back pulling her with me. "Seriously?"

"Well," she said against my forehead, "Isn't it a better alternative than 'Beat it'?"

I burst out laughing. "Um, only just slightly." The look she gave me as she got up from the bed to gather her clothes admonished me, and I grimaced and then the corners of my lips lifted in a grin. "What? I'm jealous, so sue me. I don't like the thought of him getting all googly eyed at you." She knew I was teasing and shook her head at me as a small smile came to her lips.

I watched her dress and pulled out my phone to call Ethan. I prayed that tonight, everything would be resolved and I'd be making love to Brook all night long.

***

I ASKED ETHAN to meet me for lunch at this little place in Vancouver, called the Glowball Grill. Most of the cast had the day off and Brook was filming more of the photo shoot scenes with Noah. As much as I wanted to go over to the set to check on her, I knew I needed to get to the bottom of this thing with Wendy.

As I waited, several fans came up and asked for photos and autographs. I tried to be gracious, all the while hoping that they wouldn't hover throughout lunch. This was a very private conversation I'd be having with Ethan.

He was generally a goofball, but he was a great guy and I knew that I could depend on him to tell me the truth. He sauntered over and flopped down in the opposite side of the booth from me, after he gave an autograph to two girls.

"Hey, man. What's shakin?" He grinned.

"Thanks for meeting me. Would you like a beer?" I offered.

"Sounds good, Bro." He eyed me quizzically. "Soooo, this is heavy, huh?"

I was surprised at his intuitiveness. "What makes you say that?"

"Come on, dude. You're here for two weeks, and I haven't seen you with Brook outside of the set even *once*. Everyone knows you guys are tighter than a rattlesnake's ass." I grinned at his colorful American metaphor. "So if you're not hanging with her, *somethin's up*." He was matter of fact, but when I looked at him, he shrugged and his face broke into a huge ass grin. "So, what is it?"

The waiter came over and we ordered beer and our lunch. When he left, I sighed and began what I hoped would be an enlightening trade of information.

"Ethan, I need to talk about New Year's Eve."

"Man, you were drunk *off or your ass*! I've never seen you so hammered." He laughed as he took a drink from his beer. "Plus, that's how I got confirmation of you and little Miss Halloway." He raised his eyebrows at me several times. "Even though I had serious suspicions before that, we all did. At my party that night—fuck, you guys were *on fire!*"

I smiled and ran my hand through my hair. "So confirmation came when? When I yelled at Wendy?"

"Well yeah, that, and how you were mumbling Brook's name during the entire cab ride to your place. Jesus, dude, you got it bad." He continued to smirk as he shook his head at me.

"Hmmft." I grinned and let out my breath. "The fact is, I'm in love with her," I said quietly.

"*No shit*!! Really?" He smirked at me. "I couldn't tell from the way you've been mooning over her for the past freaking year, man." A slow grin slid across his face. "And she's sizzling, isn't she? She's got that innocent sex kitten thing going for her. I bet she's a tiger in the sack."

I felt myself tense and he could see I was getting prickly. "That's not bloody funny, Ethan." I couldn't help the strength in my tone, and I knew my brows fell over my eyes.

He put up his hands in front of him.

"Relax, Cade. A guy can't help but see what's in front of him. I do have a dick, after all."

"Yes, but don't get any ideas," I emphasized. "She's with me."

"Hey, relax, I know that, man, I was kidding. She's got it just as bad as you, anyway. She hardly ever takes her eyes off of you when you're around. I used to feel so sorry for that dumbass boyfriend when he was on set."

"*I* was the poor bastard! Seeing him hang on her all of the time literally drove me insane. She was loyal to him and I just had to watch. I'm sorry, Ethan. I shouldn't be so possessive, but she makes me feel very possessive." I shook my head, determined to get back on the subject I needed to broach. "I've never experienced anything like it. I feel like a cave man when it comes to her. It's crazy."

"No shit," he agreed. "It's no wonder, though. You had to see her with that douche for months."

"Um, yeah." I got to the point. "Last New Year's Eve, you know Brook was in New York?"

"Uh huh, that's why you drowned yourself in liquor. I remember," he said, taking a drink from his beer.

"Yes, about that. She came back to L.A. and went to my apartment. Apparently Wendy answered the door naked, but I don't remember anything about it. I'm hoping you can shed some light on what really happened." I felt my face tense up as I grabbed my beer and took a long pull.

"Oh shit, Cade. Um, I don't like the girl much, but she does have a sweet ass and nice pair of cans." He laughed as the waiter brought our lunch. He seemed to fidget a little in his chair, which made me a bit nervous.

I waited until the waiter left to continue. "She told Brook we shagged and what scares the bloody hell out of me, Ethan, is that I don't remember a damn thing about it. I'm praying that it isn't true, but...," I ran my hand through my hair and shrugged. "I was hoping you could help fill in the blanks. The pain it's caused Brook is really more than I can stand and it's the reason for the distance you've noticed. Did you see how she broke down on set yesterday?"

Recognition dawned on his features. "Yeah, I did and I was wondering why, but I get it now. That cheating talk in our scene."

"Yes. A by-product of this situation," I said softly as I nodded.

"Jesus, man." He looked at me seriously for a moment.

"Dawson and I had a bet going on how long it would be before the two of you got together during *The Future of Our Past;* we knew you guys had a thing for each other. For Christ's sake, it shows on your faces and the sexual tension, well..." He laughed again and his tone turned teasing. "Dude, it's really kind of pathetic." He punched me in the shoulder, trying to lighten the mood. "I expected more Hollywood star behavior. You can have any chick you want."

I was getting impatient waiting for his answer. "Ethan, you're killing me here. Can you just bloody tell me what happened on New Year's Eve?"

He rolled his eyes. "Sorry. Wendy left early after you wouldn't kiss her at midnight, remember?"

"I remember the yelling part, but not any kissing."

"Because there wasn't any kiss. I said she *tried*. You pushed her away and then she split. You drank nearly half the whiskey in Ireland that night, it's no wonder you don't remember anything. I had to carry you home around 3 AM. Wendy was there waiting for you in your bed, and yeah, she was buck ass naked." He shook his head. "Boy was she surprised to see *me*." He laughed heartily.

"Why didn't you tell me before this?" I asked.

"For what? I knew things on the set were gonna be tough enough with both Wendy and Brook here, and I didn't think you'd want Brook to know about it. Shit, *you* didn't even know. No harm, no foul, I thought. I'm sorry, Cade. I guess I should have realized then this thing with Brook might not have gotten so out of hand."

I felt as if the weight of the world lifted from my shoulders. "Yeah, well that's all in the past now. I appreciate that you're telling me now. What happened next? Did she stay after you left?"

"Would I let my *brother* get into a position like that with that bitch? No fucking way, Cade." He was laughing now. "You're lack of faith wounds me, man." He put his hand in his heart mockingly. He laughed as he shook his head. "Hell no, I told her that we weren't interested in any gang bangs and she should get her sorry ass dressed and hit the bricks. I waited for her to leave, put her in a cab in fact, and waved buh-bye as she drove off. Boy, was she pissed." He laughed again. "You were passed out cold, dude. You couldn't have even fucked a hole in the bed that night, Cade... you were so fucking gone. I made sure you were okay, and then I left."

"Thank God." I took a deep breath and ran both of my hands through my hair as I sat back in the booth. "I'm so glad I didn't do something stupid."

"In all seriousness, it's obvious how much you two dig each other. The fact that Brook's smoking hot is only a bonus, dude." He was smirking. "You struck the jackpot, you lucky bastard. I doubt you could screw anyone else even if you *were* wasted out of your mind."

"Yeah." I ran a hand through my hair. "She means everything to me."

Ethan lifted his hand in the air. "Waiter, could I get some Pepto Bismol? I think I'm gonna puke." He grinned again.

I laughed as relief washed over me. I hadn't betrayed my baby. *Thank you, God.*

"So when was Brook there? It had to be before three." He wanted to know more of the details.

"Yes, she said around two. Wendy was apparently very unpleasant to her."

"Unpleasant?" Ethan shook his head and smirked. "Cade. Why does that surprise you, man? That bitch doesn't have *anything* pleasant about her, other than her ass, that is. And after seeing her naked, that's only marginally so." He lifted his hand, fingers spread and shook it. "The cans are fake."

"Yeah. I think her bum is way too wide." We both burst out laughing.

"Yeah. Baby definitely got *back*," he laughed again and I leaned back in the booth grinning. "I mean *bum*," he mocked me.

"Thanks, Ethan. Man, you've just saved my bloody life."

"Do you need me to talk to Brook's *little ass*?" he asked, still smiling as he ate his lunch.

"Here's the amazing thing; she said she believes me and said she doesn't' need proof since we've talked through it. However, I don't want her to have any lingering doubts. My plan is to invite you, Dawson, Jennifer and Wendy to dinner with us and then we'd all have a little *chat*," I said and knew the anger was showing in my face and my voice.

"Cade, I didn't think you had it in you to be mean and nasty like that. However, I *do* have it in me, so hell yes! I'm in."

"I'm not going to be mean, but Wendy's going to know that she didn't get between Brook and me, and she never will. I tried telling her as much several times, but she wouldn't take me seriously. She is always taunting Brook about how she was going to shag me. She even asked Brook to bloody help her once and she throws David in my face continually."

Ethan's eyebrows arched. "Um, when *exactly* did Brook lose that little shit, anyway?" His mouth twitching in a grin.

"Shortly after we said goodbye after the first wrap party." I knew my expression softened at the memory.

"Yeah." He nodded in understanding. "We all saw how hard that was on both of you. Nice song you sang to her, too." I flushed at his accuracy. "So why don't you guys just come out with it already?"

"The studio thinks it will hurt the box office on the other films." I almost groaned aloud. "Our contracts forbid any involvement with co-stars. You have that same clause, in case you didn't know." I grinned at him.

"Well, shit. Then I guess you can't be *my bitch* either," he laughed. "Fucking suits!"

I took a bite of my lunch and could barely contain the smile on my face. I knew I looked like a git and I didn't care. I was happy as hell.

Chapter 17

Inner Bitch

Caden

"HEY," BROOK SAID into her phone. That voice was my favorite sound in the world.

"Hello, love. How is your day going? Are you finally on a break?"

"Yeah. They are checking the rushes and we're just waiting around. I'm bored stiff. I got the call sheets for next week, and we're doing some of the hospital scenes. At least most of it is with you."

"I miss you. It's been like six and a half hours since I've seen you." I closed my eyes. I was so thankful to be at the bottom of the whole Wendy mess. It was like my life could start again... and Brook was life.

"Only six and a half hours? It feels like days to me. Guess I miss you more than you miss me, huh?" I could hear the smile in her voice.

I chuckled softly. "That's hardly possible, my love. Why aren't you asking me about what happened with Ethan, hmmm?"

"Because I told you this morning that it didn't matter, Cade. I meant it," I heard her take a breath, "and I figure you'll tell me when you tell me."

"Have I told you how much I adore you today?" My heart swelled at her words. Even if this had worked out the other way, we would have been okay. I felt emotion flood through me.

"Not for six and a half hours." She laughed on the other end of the phone, the sound lighthearted and warm.

"Well, I'll make it up to you tonight."

She drew in her breath sharply, in indication of my words sinking in. "Does that mean you're gonna give in, and give me what I want this evening?" The lilt in her voice made me smile.

"No, I'm going to give you what *I want* this evening. It works out well that you want it too. Mmmmm, I'm hard just thinking about it. It's been too bloody long." I felt the grin split my face when I heard her gasp on the other end of the phone.

"Brook, I can finally breathe now. I'm so thankful that I wasn't so fucking stupid. I'm never going to drink like that again. It's a bloody miracle."

"I love you, Cade. I'm really anxious for tonight, too. So anxious."

I sighed into the phone and neither one of us spoke for a minute. I could hear her breathing through the phone. It got me so hot. I closed my eyes and ran a hand through my hair.

"Okay, I changed my mind. Tell me everything," she suddenly said softly.

"How long is your break, maybe I'll run down there. I could watch you when you're filming."

"I don't have that long, and um... "

"What is it, honey?" Maybe it was the length of time we'd been separated that made me uneasy at her hesitation, but I felt anxious.

"It's not a big deal, babe. It's just, it's that scene where Julia is in the sheet, so it might be weird. I think it would just be easier to get through it if you weren't here, I'm sorry. Noah is already irked at me because I told him I didn't feel like rehearsing tonight."

Jealousy infused my face with heat. "Like there are many more scenes to rehearse with him. He want's in your knickers."

Brook giggled softy. "That's cute." She teased. "Besides," she was teasing me now and I knew she was doing her best to make me feel better, "don't you have some plotting and planning to do?"

"Oh, yes, how could I have forgotten that?" I chuckled.

"Well, I don't have a clue because it's *all* I've been thinking about." Her voice took on a velvet quality, so sexy and I felt my body tighten. Amazing that just the sound of her voice could affect me like that.

"Oh, Brook. I want to lick your skin off, love. I want you so much," I said through clenched teeth.

She gasped at my words and I laughed that I could get a reaction from her as easily as she could from me.

Jesus, I felt so much better after my talk with Ethan; the difference between the world ending and not having a care in the world.

"I'm so glad we're 'us' again. I've really missed you." Her voice thickened and I knew the tears were welling in her eyes.

"Hey, don't cry, my love. I'm dying for tonight. I can't wait to get my arms around you. I'm going to call Ethan, Jen, Dawson, and Wendy and invite them to join us for dinner so we can get this bloody thing behind us, then I'm going to make love to that luscious body all night long. *All night*, Brook. I don't know if I'll be able to wait if I see you, so let's just meet at the bloody restaurant. What time are you finished?"

"Um, six, I think." She cleared her throat. "Okay, I *do* want to know what happened."

I smiled into the phone and ran my hand through my hair. "Ethan took me home, Wendy was there and naked, like you said. He put her in a cab, and I was passed out cold. That's really it. You must have been there before we got there, my love. I'm so sorry, Brook."

"Uhhhhh...," Brook let out a deep breath. "She must have come back."

Hmmm, she's more relieved than she let on.

"Yes. Are you okay? How do you want to do this, Brook?"

"Yeah, I'm good. I'm so relieved, Cade. I am glad this isn't hanging over us, but it wouldn't have made me leave you." Her voice turned serious.

"Nothing is going to come between us again. I'm committed to that, Brook." I could picture her nodding on the other end, since she didn't respond. I knew her so bloody well. "So, are you going to bitch-slap Wendy, or am I?"

She laughed out loud on the other end and the sound was so fucking beautiful. I smiled as I let my breath out.

"Mmmm... I think I should do it. If that's okay? My inner bitch is screaming."

"Yeah. I'm quite looking forward to it, actually. You'll be brilliant. I can just sit back and relax." I was so happy I thought she could *hear* my smile through the phone.

"Babe, I have to go. Martin is motioning for me. Text later with the time and place, okay?"

"Yes, I will. Love you."

"Love you, want you, need you," she whispered in the phone and once again my heart beat faster.

***

I'D CHOSEN A little Indian restaurant because I knew it was one of Brook's favorite cuisines, and I had Denise arrange for a private room where we wouldn't be disturbed for our little confrontation.

I'd asked Ethan, Jennifer and Dawson to come about twenty minutes earlier than I told Wendy to arrive. Brook was going to get there as soon as she could. I spent the afternoon working with Denise to get Brook a gift or two and she asked Jeanne to get a key to her room from the hotel. We put candles, fruit and champagne in her room along with the black negligee that I'd sent her out to get. She'd come back with five different ones so I could pick the one I wanted. My mouth lifted in a grin. She was a great manager, but better friend, and she shoved me in the shoulder when I asked her to make sure we had Twinkies and strawberries. The beautiful memories of San Diego were inspiring.

As I sat at the restaurant waiting, I was vibrating in anticipation for the coming evening. It had been too fucking long since Brook and I touched each other like that. I felt like I was starving and I couldn't wait to get this part of the bloody evening over with.

Dawson, Ethan and Jennifer all walked in together. They really were a good-looking group, and I was thankful for each and every one of them. Literally becoming like my brothers and sister over the course of these films; we had such a solid relationship that I was certain would follow into real life. Brook and I were lucky to be surrounded by such supportive friends.

Ethan was grinning from ear to ear because he already knew what was to come, and Jennifer and Dawson looked at me expectantly as they took their seats.

"Ethan told us this was big, but he wouldn't tell us what it was about. Can you let us in on it, Cade?" Jennifer asked.

I glanced at Ethan and he shrugged. "I thought it was your place to tell them, dude."

"Yeah, I appreciate it." They all took their places at the end of the table, leaving three seats at the other end, I took the one closest to Jennifer; Dawson was on the end and Ethan next to him. Leaving one chair on the end closest to me, and one directly across, open.

The restaurant was done in shades of gold and red; the lighting soft with candles on all of the tables. Soft Indian music played in the background. The waiter came and took our drink orders and I took the opportunity to speak to him and ask that he not interrupt us once we had our meal, then I turned back to Jen and Dawson.

"Um..." I cleared my throat as I began. "Brook and I have had some problems because Wendy lied to us both. She tried to convince Brook that I had sex with her on New Year's Eve, but that wasn't the case. Neither one of us knew the whole story, but with Ethan's help, we now know the truth."

Jennifer's eyes widened. "Oh, but she left the bar before us, didn't she?" She glanced at Ethan and he nodded. "Is that why Brook has been so sad? I thought it was for the film, but she's kept so much to herself. I wondered what was wrong."

"Yeah. It's been extremely painful and confusing, but thanks to Ethan, that's all behind us now. He took me home and knows that nothing happened. Wendy is a manipulative little bitch, and I feel that she needs to know we are on to her bullshit. I've asked you to join because I thought it would be the best way to keep her in line so she can't spread more lies about any of us. If she thinks we're all united, maybe she'll cease the bloody games. None of us can trust her, so I hope you don't feel we're putting you in the middle."

"No, Cade. We're glad to do it." Dawson put his hand on my shoulder before taking his seat next to Jennifer. "She's something else."

"That's one way of putting it." Ethan rolled his eyes and I nodded in agreement.

Brook walked in then, and stole my breath away. She was beautiful in a short blue dress, and black leather jacket. Her hair flowed down around her shoulders in cascading waves and her high-heeled shoes made her legs look like they went on for miles. Her make-up was more pronounced, her brilliant blue eyes glowed and her cheeks were flushed, the candlelight casting shadows on the planes of her face. I stood up to take her in my arms and kiss her temple. She smelled delicious and felt even better. I sensed the familiar quickening of my blood pressure at her nearness.

"You look gorgeous." Her arms tightened around me and splayed on my back.

"Thank you for the gift. I love it. I can't wait to wear it for you later," she whispered as she leaned up on tip toe. "Hey guys. I'm glad to see all of you. Ethan," Brook turned to him to give him a hug, "Thank you for helping us with this; all of you. I am so thankful you're my friends."

I pulled out her chair next to me and she took her seat at the same moment Wendy walked in. She was dressed more casually in jeans and a white T-shirt. She threw off her jacket as she approached and took the seat across from me.

"Hey, am I late?"

"Not at all, Wendy. Glad you're here." I was amazed at how calm Brook seemed in light of what was about to go down. She leaned back in her chair and crossed her legs.

"Brook, you're looking more dressed up than usual. What's the occasion?" Wendy raised her eyebrows at my girl.

"Oh, I just feel like celebrating tonight. Finally, the gang is back together." Her lips twitched in the start of a smile as she spoke.

Wendy gazed warily in my direction, and then her eyes went back to Brook as she tried to determine if we were going to confront her. It was obvious she was taking note of the way we were leaning toward one another and talking softly to each other. Her eyes hardened as she watched us.

That's right, bitch. She's with me. And we know what you did. Could she possibly think we'd let this slide?

Dinner progressed with casual set conversation. We talked about the premieres that we'd been to, and the scenes that were coming up for each of us. Finally the waiter cleared the plates, and brought a last round of drinks. I glanced at Brook and reached under the table to take her hand in mine. She squeezed my fingers.

"Um..." I hesitated, but only briefly; meeting Brook's eyes with mine. "Brook, are you ready to order dessert?" My mouth lifted into a smile as I watched her. Her eyebrows went up and she sat up a little straighter in her chair.

"Um, yeah." She smiled brightly at me and took my hand.

Ethan glanced at me and leaned back in his chair, he knew what was coming and he was fucking enjoying every second of it. Jennifer was leaning into Dawson and they were looking expectantly toward our end of the table but no one said anything. Wendy looked from one of us to the other, noting how everyone was watching her and no one was speaking. She had to feel fucking cornered.

"Wendy, we had another reason for inviting you to dinner tonight." Brook's voice was calm, methodical. "I wanted to clear the air about something."

Wendy shifted uncomfortably in her chair as she sat down her glass of vodka, and her eyes were hard as she stared at Brook and then glanced toward me. I'm sure she knew what Brook was getting at.

"The little stunt you pulled in January caused a lot of grief between Cade and I, and I'm not going to let that happen again. Someone I love deeply was hurt, and that fucking pisses me off."

"I don't know what you mean, Brook," she said with an air of aloofness.

Brook sighed and shook her head. "Cut the bullshit, Wendy. You're only embarrassing yourself even more. The fact is, I don't give a damn about you, what you think, or what you tell people. However, Cade wanted this conversation, so here we are."

"Cade and I are—well, let's just say he is not available for your little shenanigans and he really never was. Since you won't listen to him when he tells you he's in love with me, then I'm forced to step in. I'll admit, you hurt me in January when you answered his door to his apartment, but I know better than to believe anything you say or do ever again. We love each other, and you will never come between us. Never."

"But... I *was* with him that night, Brook. What? Did he tell you otherwise?" Wendy laughed softly as she tried to weasel her way out of the situation with more lies.

Brook's face hardened. "Are you really going there? *Really?* With Ethan sitting right here? Are you that stupid, Wendy?" she shook her head with a disgusted look on her face. "Now that I'm thinking clearly, I realize that if it did happen, you would've had pictures plastered on the front page of ten of the rag mags and all over the Internet. I can't believe I didn't think of that before, but I guess, indescribable fucking pain clouded my judgment."

Ethan leaned forward on the table, and made a gesture with his hand. "Wendy, just stop. You and I both know there is no truth to what you say. You'd be better off to just apologize, and move on."

Wendy's face flushed a bright red.

"Where the *fuck* do you get off, Brook?" Her voice elevated in volume and pitch. "For months you've been denying any relationship with Cade, other than that he is your best friend. You tortured and abused him with your little hard-to-get routine, throwing David in his face, constantly. Fuck! You hurt them *both*. And now you sit here and think you can just say you love him and it erases all of that? You're a liar, and you have the nerve to accuse me?"

I watched Brook' face. She smirked; her voice remained calm as her fingers entwined with mine on top of the table this time. "I don't trust you, Wendy, and deep down I never did. Of course, I wasn't going to tell you the fucking truth! Cade absolutely knows everything. He's the important variable here, not you. He's known for quite some time how much I love him, and *for how long*."

Wendy's eyes widened and her chin snapped up as she glanced at me. I nodded to confirm Brook's words.

"Hmmmpht." Brook let her breath out in a snort "And, where do I *get off*?"

She looked over at me and I let go of her hand, leaned over and pulled her chair close to mine, then my hand went to her leg to grasp around her bare thigh. She brought her hand up to my hair, stroked down the back of my head and kept stroking the hair at the back of my neck. Her touch sent goose bumps down through my whole body.

"Um, *this*... " Her hold on me tightened, "*this is where I get off. With whom*," Her eyes bore into mine and I felt my dick twitch at the look in her eyes. She tore her gaze away to look at Wendy. *"And how."*

Fuck me. She did NOT just bloody say that! My heart swelled in my chest at the same time as I wanted to laugh out loud. I was so fucking proud of her.

I couldn't help the huge grin that split across my face, but Brook's face was deadly serious. My eyes glanced around the table at the others, and they all were doing their best not to laugh. Ethan's shoulders were visibly shaking as he burst out laughing, and fuck if I could help running my hand through my hair again.

Brook leaned her head against my shoulder, and the scent of her perfume assaulted my senses, my hand continued to rub her thigh.

"You were right about one thing. He *is* all you imagined, and so much *more*. Beyond your wildest... fucking... fantasy. But he's *my* reality. I'm sorry I couldn't share that with you before but we wanted to keep our private life, private. Everyone else sitting here knew, but we knew we couldn't trust you."

Wendy just stared at her with her mouth hanging open. Brook's focus was on me, even though she was talking to Wendy and I could see the desire flood her features when she looked at me. This was something she was doing for me, for us; and she was going to hammer home her point.

"Here is my problem; Cade won't make love to me until we had this little chat with you. He wanted to make sure I knew he'd never fucking touched you before he'd agree to give me what I want."

The others were staring at Brook and my eyebrows were raised and I was smiling, almost laughing aloud at Wendy's stunned expression, but still in shock at Brook's words. My free hand ran through my hair several times. I was surprised Wendy didn't get up and run out. Brook was brutal, and she was stunned into silence.

Bloody hell, this was fucking hilarious.

I turned toward Brook and brought her hand to my mouth to place a kiss on the inside of her wrist. I could feel her pulse under my lips as I raised my eyes to hers.

"It's what I want, too, baby," I said softly against her skin, but loud enough for Wendy to hear me.

"Then I think we're about finished here, hmmm?" She looked at me, and I nodded and brushed the back of my knuckles against her cheekbone. Her eyes never left mine as she spoke to Wendy. We were sending an indelible message.

"Mmmmm... Cade promised me this morning that he was going to make me come all over him tonight, and I am so beyond ready for him to keep that promise. And he's so good at keeping his promises, Wendy. Incredibly good."

Ethan let out a long whistle with a huge ass grin on his face, and Jennifer gasped out a laugh. I almost choked on my beer as I felt my body throb at her words.

She was so bloody beautiful, and she was all mine. I was so turned on a stiff breeze would make me come.

Determination, combined with the desire on Brook's features as the candle light from around the room, flickered in her eyes.

Dawson and Wendy were stunned, neither one of them moved.

"Are you *beyond ready*, too, Cade?" She smiled at me sweetly but her voice was full of sex.

She was such a sexy little devil. *Jesus Christ!*

I swallowed hard. "Jesus, Brook. You have no idea love," was all I could say.

She leaned over and pulled on my neck to bring my face closer to hers. "Give me a taste, Cade. I miss you so much." She licked my top lip with her luscious little tongue and her hand came up to my face her thumb dragging across my lower lip as she leaned in and spoke.

I didn't need a second invitation, the private room making it okay to do as I wanted. My mouth swooped in to cover hers and she instantly opened to me and we kissed deeply, our mouths moving together until she finally pulled away, and our lips clung together as we separated. She tasted so delicious; I forgot we had an audience. I wanted more.

"MMMM… yummy. I'll be keeping a few promises of my own, baby." She brought her hand up and wiped at her mouth with the back of her hand, as she turned to look at Wendy. Her eyes were intent on Wendy's face, her message loud and clear. No one spoke, everyone stunned into silence.

She leaned in to whisper something in my ear, but then stopped and turned back to Wendy. She leaned into the table toward her. "Oh, I forgot you don't like it when Cade and I have private jokes or little secrets, so I'll let you in on this one." Her hand came over to grab my leg and she leaned into me.

"Baby… ?" She brought her eyes to mine and licked her lips.

"Yes, my love?" I played along with her, a smile tugging at my lips as I looked into those emerald eyes.

"I'm not wearing any panties." I gasped and she kissed my lips softly, and brushed my jaw with her other hand. "Just give me just a few minutes, honey? Just a *few*…"

I smiled as something secret passed between us, and she smiled back. I nodded and leaned in to kiss her once more.

Holy fuck! I doubt I'll be in any condition to walk out of here for several minutes.

Jennifer gasped again and the guys both chuckled.

"Ethan, Jennifer, Dawson, thank you so much for being here with us tonight. You're all such good friends. I love you all. Wendy, you'll find it harder to play your little games since we all know what you're capable of now. I feel sad that you've reduced yourself to this."

She got up and bent to place a soft, wet kiss on my mouth and she pulled on my lower lip with her teeth as she drew back.

"See you in a bit," she said the words against my mouth and then turned to leave. I stared after her intently and imagined her commando under her short dress, and what I was going to be doing with her in less than 30 minutes time.

I knew my eyes were smoldering after her as my hand came up to my mouth. I'm sure that was part of the effect she wanted to give Wendy. A fucking exclamation point on just how intimate our relationship was.

Ethan dropped his head into his hands and burst out laughing. "Holy shit! That girl has balls. I wouldn't have missed this for the *fucking world!*"

Jennifer brought a hand to her mouth to stifle a laugh and Dawson shook his head with a grin. "You're one lucky bastard, Cade." I laughed and nodded.

"Hey!" Jennifer nudged him.

"Don't worry, sweetie. I'm an even luckier bastard." Dawson smiled at her and she leaned in to kiss him.

Wendy gathered her things and rose to leave. Clearly humiliated, her face flushed bright red. She turned back to me; her eyes glassy.

"You all think this is so fucking funny, don't you? Cade, are you that pathetic, to be led around by your dick? I cared about you when she didn't give a fuck about you..." she began.

I put up my hand to stop her.

"Wendy, first of all, if I'm being led around, it's by my heart, not my dick. I've been telling you for months that I'm in love with Brook. She felt you needed to see it to get the point, and we both know you don't give a whit about me. You only care about publicity, and what you can get off of each and every one of us. You hurt the one person I love most in this world with your bloody lies."

My voice was hard as I continued. "We are all aware of your paparazzi tipping ways and if any of this gets out, Brook and I will deny it, and all of these wonderful people around me will deny it as well. You'll be made to look like a scorned woman with an ax to grind, with absolutely nothing to back it up. The world will see you only as some pathetic woman that I didn't want anything to do with. It won't help your image or your career. It's certainly not the type of publicity you want, so I'd seriously consider your next move carefully. And um... on the off chance you haven't gotten the point already, Brook and I, are a united front. Pinnacle won't bloody fuck with us because they need us on these films now. If you try to damage us again, we *will fuck with you*. I'll make sure you never get another acting job again. Is that clear?"

She just turned and stalked out.

I stood up and shook the guys' hands and gave Jennifer a hug as I started to walk out. "Um... I've got somewhere I *absolutely* need to be. I'll take care of the bill on my way out. Thank you for being here for Brook and me. If you'll all excuse me?"

"You *are* one lucky bastard, Cade. Do it justice and make me proud, man," Ethan called after me with a laugh.

I laughed and put my hand in the air in acknowledgement as I left the room. I had every intention of making love to her until I brought her body to quivering fulfillment over and over again. My mouth went dry and my body tightened again. I was throbbing with want, need and so much love. I couldn't bloody wait to get back to Brook's hotel.

I took a deep breath as I got in the waiting car, smiling from ear-to-ear.

Yes, my girl certainly has balls. She was fucking brilliant! I loved this side of her.

My phone vibrated in my pocket.

I love and I want you so much right now.
Cade, please hurry.

I sighed and leaned my head back on the seat, my mind flooding with images of Brook waiting in the black lace and silk nightgown I'd bought for her. My heart started to race until I felt it would fly from my chest.

Chapter 18

I'm Yours

Brooklyn

I LEFT THE safety latch on the door flipped out to prop the door open so Cade could get in if I were still getting ready in the bathroom. No doubt, he'd be upset I took a chance like that, but I couldn't risk him being trapped out in the hall; especially since this wasn't his hotel and he already had to sneak in and get up the fourteen floors without anyone seeing him.

He was so beautiful tonight, and our little exchange in front of Wendy and our friends was so fucking hot. He was staring right into my soul and despite my mission at the time; I was totally lost in those blue eyes. And the kiss he gave me at the end of it was so amazing I'd never wanted it to stop. It curled my toes and started the burning throbbing between my legs that was still a nagging ache.

Three months.

Three *damn* months.

Even if I could forgive Wendy lusting after my beautiful man, I'd never forgive her for costing me three months of touching him, loving him and making me feel like I wanted to die without him. I took a deep breath as I reminded myself that it was over now, and he was going to be holding me, loving me in a matter of minutes. My heart was already pumping the blood around my body at increased speed.

I'd pulled my hair up on top of my head in a messy heap of curls with tendrils falling on both sides of my face. The black lace and silk chiffon gown he'd left for me was drifting lightly over my body, brushing my curves and my erect nipples, only to float around my hips to the top of my thighs.

It was beautiful. It made me *feel* beautiful, sensual... and totally sexy. The lace covered portions of my body in diagonal appliqués across my breasts and over my sex, strategically placed as they wrapped like ribbons in the sheer material of the rest of the gown. Showing just enough, but leaving plenty to the imagination to wet Cade's appetite.

My hands ghosted down my body in the candlelight. I raised my eyes to look at myself in the mirror and tried to see what Cade would see. My cheeks were flushed and my eyes glowed with desire for him. I'd put on my bracelet and my engagement ring and the beautiful gems glistened in the soft flickering light. I'd placed some light pink gloss on my mouth that added little color, but gave a wet quality to my lips. I bit my lower lip as I heard him in the other room.

"Brook..." I heard him call my name as I cracked the door to the bathroom. "Why isn't the door bolted?"

I smiled as he fulfilled my prediction, but didn't answer. The candle I'd placed in the other room illuminated him as he tore his black T-shirt from his body and began to unbutton the closure of his jeans. The music from my iPod dock played softly in the background.

His muscled chest and arms were so perfect, his hair so sexy as he ran his hand through it. God, I adored how he did that. His face was so incredibly breathtaking; the strength in his jaw and the line of his brow, the straight nose, all so perfect. My heart thumped painfully in my chest.

How did God make someone that beautiful? The world would never be the same. At least, mine never would.

He kicked off his shoes and opened his jeans the rest of the way as he turned toward me. He was so uncommonly sexy, the muscles on his chest and stomach getting more and more defined, and the trail of hair disappearing into the top of his boxer briefs visible in the opening of his jeans. It made my heart race and my body quicken, just looking at him.

Cade's features softened the second he saw me. My body was shaking, I loved him so much and I wanted him. I was starving, dying for his touch.

He didn't say a word, but sucked in his breath and closed the five steps that separated us, his hands reached up to cup both sides of my face, as his mouth gently took mine.

Oh God.

My heart was bursting as his tongue slid into my mouth and my arms slid up around his neck to fist in his hair as the kiss deepened. He groaned into my mouth as he devoured me, and neither one of us could get close enough. His arms slid around my body and he lifted me off of the ground as he brought my mouth level with his and continued to kiss me over and over again. I pulled his mouth closer, deeper into mine and sucked on his tongue.

Kiss after kiss, we couldn't get enough, my feet still dangling off of the floor and our breathing becoming more and more labored. When he finally dragged his mouth from mine to burn a trail across my cheek and into the curve of my neck, I found my voice.

"Oh Cade. God, I've missed you. I've missed you so much," I whispered into his shoulder, my voice breaking on the words.

His arms dropped slightly down over my ass as he lifted me up and I wrapped my legs around his waist.

"Brook, Oh my God... I love you. You're so beautiful." The overwhelming emotions flooded through us both. The loss we'd felt, the desperation, the longing, lust and so much love. It was all more than either of us could bear as he brought his mouth back to mine and I opened my mouth for him as I kissed him back with everything I had. My body was clinging to his, wrapped all around him.

He walked with me to the bed as he pulled his mouth away and put his forehead to mine. "I'm sorry, honey. I wanted to take this slow, but I just fucking... *can't!* I can't wait one more second to have you. It's been too bloody long. I'm sorry."

"Later, there's time for going slow later. I want you, baby." I panted against his mouth as my hands pulled his head down so his mouth would resume the sweet torture as he lowered me to the bed. My heart squeezed in my chest and I knew I'd never make it through this without tears falling. God, it was amazing how much I loved him, so much it physically hurt and left me gasping for breath.

Cade's eyes were locked with mine as he laid me down on the pillows and brushed my hair back off of my face. He bent his head and sucked my lower lip into his mouth, never breaking my gaze. He moved away to remove his jeans, his eyes a physical caress as they roamed over my body in the black chemise he'd given me.

"You're so amazing Brook; so bloody beautiful. If I could only look at you for the rest of my life, I swear it would be enough." His eyes were smoldering into mine, and his love for me was never more apparent than what I read in his face at that moment.

I enfolded him in my arms as he settled down into me, his elbows resting beside my head; we finally slowed down as his mouth returned to shower mine with dozens of open mouth, wet, sucking kisses. He slowly tasted me, and I couldn't get enough of him. I felt his erection pressing against my pubic bone and I couldn't help arching up, seeking to feel him closer, still. The friction of our bodies increased and brought panting breaths and groans out of both of us.

I wasn't wearing panties and as Cade moved on me, the friction of steel hardness on slick flesh incited and teased. He felt so good sliding against me, and he was teasing me, knowing how much it increased the want. Holding him close, his heart beating over mine, was something I needed, all those months of missing him still an ache.

Finally, he slid into my body, filling and stretching me. My heart swelled as my hands traced down his back as he started to move within my body.

"Oh my love. Brook... I can't do this again. I can't be without you like this again. You feel so amazing. You're mine. Tell me." He nuzzled my nose and placed soft kisses on my face as he waited for my words. "I need to hear it. Dear God, I need to hear it, Brook."

All I wanted was for him to move inside me and for his mouth to be on mine. "I'm yours, Cade. Only yours, forever."

After that he dove back into my mouth and his body moved with greater urgency with mine. Each thrust more delicious than the last, his tongue coming into my mouth to slide against and with mine, our mouths sucking, licking and coming back for more again and again. I brought my knees up to bring him in deeper as I clenched around him and he groaned against my mouth.

I didn't know how long we made slow love like that; I was so lost in the sensations, savoring every touch of his hands, his mouth on mine and his body so exquisite I thought my heart was breaking. My body began to tremble as our hips ground and undulated with each other. His breathing was heavier too, so I could tell he was getting close.

"Oh Cade, you're so amazing. I'm so close... uh, uh, ummmm..." He had me panting with each delicious thrust.

He kissed my neck and moved up to my ear. "Babe, I'm coming for you, too. I never want to be without you again," he said as I felt myself go over the edge and my back arched and my muscles began to spasm around his delicious length.

"Oh yeah, that's it, Brook. Oh, babe; Brook, Brook—Uhhhh... I love you." He arched and thrust into me one last time. His muscles tensed as I felt him twitch as he spilled deep within me, groaning out my name one last time.

I clenched and milked around him, I wanted every drop of him inside of me, my body still pulsing with the pleasure he brought from me. Both of us shuddered and trembled as we lay panting, coming down from the climax. My heart was beating fast, so full of my love for him. The tears I'd been fighting finally spilled from my eyes as I wrapped my arms around him and kissed his shoulder and then the side of his face.

"I love you, Cade. I love you, okay?" I started to sob a little bit, I couldn't help myself and he rolled with me onto his side so he could look in my face.

His hands were gentle as he pushed my hair off my face and kissed my mouth.

His thumbs wiped at my tears. "Okay." His mouth raised slightly in a soft smile as he looked at me. "Okay, Brook." He placed a soft, slow kiss on my trembling mouth.

The piano intro of *Breathe Me* came on the iPod dock as we lay there and it caused more tears to fall from my eyes. "This song... " I couldn't continue right away.

Cade just lay there gazing at my face, wiping my tears and softly brushing my body with his fingers, constantly stroking my skin.

"This song, says everything I needed to tell you. I only ended up hurting myself more by leaving you and it was my fault because I didn't try to talk to you. I needed you to save me... I was dying without you." He reached out to me as the chorus played and folded me in his arms as I cried. "I was so lost without you. It was so hard."

"Me too, love. I holed up with your diary for weeks. I wouldn't have survived without that lifeline to you. Seeing concrete proof that you loved me is what saved me. I was dying too." His blue eyes were liquid as he looked at me.

"I'm sorry," I said softly. I wasn't sobbing, but the tears wouldn't stop raining from my eyes.

"Shhhh, Brook. Hush. It's over. We're together now and I'll never leave you. It's going to be okay, my love." He kissed the tears from my face, his voice barely a whisper.

"I'm sorry I cry so much, I just... " I brought my eyes up to his and couldn't look away. I reached to brush my hand against his strong jaw. I needed to touch that beautiful face, so soft with love in his eyes.

He shook his head. "Brook, it's okay. I love you, so much. It's okay."

"That's why I cry." More tears silently fell on the pillow.

"What? You cry because I love you?" His fingers ghosted over the trail of tears on my face as we lay on the pillows together.

"No, it's because I love you. It's like my whole heart and every cell of my body... is *so full of you*, that there isn't any place for all that love to go, and there's more and more of it all the time. More than I can even *deal with*, so it just... spills over." My voice cracked on a sob. "It spills over... "

He gathered me close and buried his face in the curve of my neck. "I fucking love you more than I ever thought it possible to love anybody, Brook. I'm going to tell you a million times in the next eight hours, and a million times throughout my life. I love you. I love you so much."

"I know. That's the beautiful part. But, this much love; it hurts, doesn't it? I wouldn't trade it, I *want* it, but it hurts, and it will hurt more. That is the price for such unspeakable ecstasy, isn't it? This unspeakable agony? But, it's *so* worth it to me."

"I'll never let anything hurt you, my love."

"You can't stop it, Cade. One day one of us will lose the other."

He looked at me as his brow crinkled slightly and he brought his hand back to my cheek.

"Do you mean when we get old and die, because that is the only bloody way that will happen, Brook."

I nodded. "Yes." I smiled through my tears. "Even in seventy years, I don't want to lose you."

"Oh, honey. You're so precious." He took my left hand and ran his finger over the ring on my third finger. "Thank you for this," he kissed the ring and then the top of my hand. "And thank you for tonight in the restaurant. You were brilliant, my love. It made me want you so bloody much. I wanted to take you right there in front of everyone."

I smiled at his crooked grin. "I know. That was so fun. I never knew I could be such a bitch."

He shook his head at me. "You weren't a bitch. You were just making sure she knew to keep her mitts off what was yours. It was bloody brilliant."

His hands were roaming all over my body, down my thigh and up again. As his hand moved upward the hem of the gown came with it and he brought it further up, his hand moving up over my ribs to my breast.

"Mmmmmm...," he whispered as his fingers found the nipple and I felt it harden in his hand. He propped up on one elbow so he could look down on me and let his other hand continue its exploration of my body. His hand moved up to the side of my neck and his thumb brushed my jaw as he bent to take my mouth with his.

My hand moved down his chest until it closed around his manhood and he groaned in my mouth. He was hard again and I wanted to give him pleasure. I was on my back and I turned toward him, my free hand running up his chest and into the back of his hair as I pulled him closer during the kiss.

"Sweetheart, that feels so good," he breathed out the words, and I felt his delicious breath fan over my face. His hands moved down my body, until he was parting the flesh between my legs, seeking, searching...

"Uhhhh...," I sighed. "Cade." I was just as breathless as he was, both of us touching the other. My hands were moving up and down on him and when I got to the head my fingers tightened and pulled slightly, and I could feel the drops of pre-cum start. I knew he was excited and I loved that I could bring him to this, at the same time that he gave me so much pleasure.

His fingers continued to tease, and finally, he slid two of them inside me.

"Uhhh... God... Brook. You're so wet for me, but so tight. I have to be inside you." He groaned against my mouth as his tongue slipped between my lips. I slipped my tongue toward his, my mouth opening and pulling on his. This kiss got deeper and wilder as he moved over me, and began his slow, tortuous play with my body.

The slippery sensations it caused were so incredible. Again and again he teased, until we were both moaning.

"God, Cade... please," I begged as I dragged my mouth across his chin and down his neck, sucking on the skin. "Please."

He slid deep inside me in one full thrust, and I wrapped my legs tightly around his waist.

"My God." He had me gasping.

"Hold on to me, Brook." I did as he asked and wrapped my arms around his shoulders as he lifted me with the arm that was tight around my waist. Our bodies never separated as he moved back to his knees and both of his arms slid beneath my hips and ass to move me up and down on his body.

My head fell back at the amazing sensation and Cade began to run kisses down my neck and across my shoulders. Our breathing sped up and I raised my head to look into his blue eyes. His lips were parted, his hair wild from my hands raking through it, and his cheeks were flushed with desire.

"It feels so fantastic. I love the way you fill me up. I can't get close enough to you."

My hands fisted in his hair because I wanted more and more of his kisses. I licked at his lips with my tongue and pulled the top one in to lightly suck on it.

"I know. It will never be close enough, Brook. You were made for me; your body fits mine like a glove. I want to be inside you for the rest of my bloody life," he said just before his mouth smashed into mine, to hungrily devour my mouth.

Again, my heart rushed. We moved in perfect unison, the muscles in his arms taking my weight effortlessly and my arms and legs wrapped around this man I loved so much.

His arms wrapped around my hips to anchor me as he moved within me and he rested his forehead on my collar bone, I felt his hot breath coming in hectic bursts on my skin as his muscles tightened underneath my hands and both of us started to tremble. Again and again he thrust into me, by body tightening around him; I felt my orgasm building within me as I clung to him.

"Brook," he hissed out my name. "I can't hold off anymore. I need to come. Ahhhh! Oh, babe."

"I want you to—I want you to... " I couldn't breathe as my body started to spasm around his. I was amazed our lovemaking was always so satisfying. It had never been like that with David and I was sure it was because the emotions with Cade were so intense.

Cade's greedy mouth came back to mine as he tensed and held on to me even tighter. His body flexed and stilled against mine, but his mouth continued its sucking and teasing of mine. The kisses growing softer, but still deep, as his arms slid up around my back to the back of my head. He held on to my hair and kissed me again and again. He continued to make love to me with his mouth, his tongue tangling deliciously with mine.

I couldn't get enough. "I could kiss you forever," I whispered against his mouth as I drew back and he pulled on my lower lip with both of his. I dropped my head to his shoulder as we both struggled to regain control of our breathing. My arms were wrapped around his shoulders and my hands played with the hair at the back of his neck and his hands moved up and down my back to my hips.

They settled on my ass and he looked into my face and nuzzled my nose with his. "My God! That was incredible."

I felt a soft smile come to my lips as I nodded. His eyes were languid and there was a soft sheen of perspiration on his skin. I could taste the salt on my tongue when I kissed his neck. I turned my face toward him, as I nestled into him and he lowered both of us back to lie down on the bed.

"Are you tired, my love?" His hands played lovingly in my hair.

"Not at all. I have a surprise for you." I smiled happily.

"Strawberry Twinkies?" His mouth broke into a grin. Okay, so he was telling me he was hungry. I rolled my eyes. Typical of Cade to be starving after sex.

I laughed. "No, although, I'll be happy to get them for you, babe."

I moved from him reluctantly and pulled the nightgown down as I went to the basket of snacks that Stephanie had ordered for us. "Should we open the champagne? It sounds good with the strawberries, doesn't it?"

His eyes followed me around the room but he didn't say anything, so I looked at him pointedly. "Cade? Do you want the champagne? Hmmm?" I held up the bottle and pointed to it with raised eyebrows.

"Oh, sure, love. I'll open it. Give it here."

I walked over to him with the ice bucket and the bottle and went back to grab the glasses, strawberries and his God-forsaken Twinkies. "Where did you go there?"

"Nowhere. You're just so beautiful. Sorry if I was staring."

My face flushed in pleasure and I couldn't help the pleased smile that spread across my face.

Jesus. You are the beautiful one, I thought.

"Okay, so what's my surprise?" he asked as the champagne cork flew across the room and the bottle overflowed on the floor. "Shit. I should have gotten a towel first."

I sat on the bed in front of him, my legs curling under me. "I'm not on the production schedule tomorrow." I raised my eyes to his as I ripped open the cakes.

His face split in a big grin. "Really?

"Uh huh." He reached for the back of my neck and leaned in to kiss me.

"That's just brilliant. It means I really can make love to you all night." He grinned at me as he poured the champagne into the two flutes. "How'd you manage that?"

"I just told Martin I had a heart ache and needed the day off. After I lost it the other night, he understood."

Cade's face softened as he remembered that night, a small frown knitting his brow.

I reached out and took the glass from him and set it on the bedside table. "Hey, no frowns. It's working out to our benefit, isn't it?"

"Brook..." I leaned in and kissed his mouth before he could say anything.

"No being sad. The feelings between us just made these movies that much better. There is a ton of pain in this one and now I have something to harness. Think of it like that, okay? I know you love me, Cade. You leave me in no doubt."

He smiled softly. "Okay." He reached out to take my hand in his.

"What have you been up to? Any new projects on the horizon?" I realized how long it had been and how much had gone on that we didn't know about each other.

"Um, I read for a new movie that would schedule between the second and third movies. It's in New York, so at least I won't be half way around the world.”

“What kind of movie is the new one? What’s it called?” I was genuinely interested.

“*Only Us*. It’s about people who have horrible family lives and the romantic connection between them that basically saves them both.”

I involuntarily stiffened. “That sounds deep. It was bound to happen. Everyone wants to see you panting and kissing. I should know.” I smiled slightly despite the discomfort I was feeling over it.

“I know what you’re thinking, Brook. Just stop.” He ran his hand down my arm to take my hand.

“Oh? What am I thinking?” *He thinks he knows me so well.*

“That my method acting will make me fall in love with this new co-star. It won’t happen.”

I didn’t say anything but just squeezed his hand.

“Anyway, that isn’t what happened with you, Brook. I loved you before we were even born, okay?” He leaned in to place a soft kiss on my mouth as his fingers traced my cheekbone.

“I know. I’ll live through it, *I guess*.” I joked. I knew in my heart he loved me and I had to trust it. “Just remember that when it’s *me* smooching some other dude on the big screen, got it?”

He nodded and kissed me again. *Mmmm, he tasted so good.*

“Will you do something for me while I stuff strawberries up these Twinkies asses?” I giggled at him. He burst out laughing as I began pulling the hulls from the fruit. Good, that’s what I hoped to accomplish.

“Anything. What do you want?” He was still laughing as I held out the first strawberry filled Twinkie for him. Cade grabbed it and took a big bite.

“Well, I haven’t heard you play in months, so will you play

something on my guitar for me?"

"Mmmm, these are so great. Sure, what do you want to hear?"

"It doesn't matter. You pick," I said as I took a bite of his dessert. It really did taste like strawberry shortcake. Yummy.

"Well, when I was in the studio in December I heard a new song from an American band. They were there recording after I finished doing a demo for a producer. It isn't released yet, but I really loved the acoustic guitar and the piano, so I've been learning it."

"Are you telling me you only heard it once and you remember the entire thing?" I shook my head. He was so fucking amazing and he didn't even see it.

"Yeah, I guess." He shrugged as he picked up the guitar. I took a sip from the champagne and it was so sour after the sweetness of the Twinkie that my face wrinkled. Cade openly laughed at me.

"Ugh! Something has to be done about that." I took a large strawberry and squeezed it over my glass, letting the juice from the fruit mix with the champagne. I dropped the mushy mess into my glass and licked my fingers.

"Wait," he said as he pulled my hand toward him and sucked the juice of each of my fingers. His tongue swirled around and my heart thumped in my chest. "Mmmmm. You make that strawberry taste so delicious." He grinned at me.

"Okay, Cade. I know how talented your tongue is, but right now I want to hear the talent in your fingers."

He went to pick up the guitar as I went to wash the stickiness from my fingers in the bathroom.

"Are you sure you don't want to *feel* my talented fingers, instead?" I stopped and shook my head. I could hear the smile in his voice.

"Um... that is tempting, but why can't I have it all?" I flirted with him outrageously and knew he loved it.

"You know I'll give you anything you want." His eyes bore into mine as he settled back down on the bed with the guitar. Naked Cade and my guitar. Could it get any better than that? I bit my lip as I watched him begin to strum and pluck at the guitar.

"What's this song called? I love the melody."

"*Call your name...* I used to think about you a lot when I was in London this last time, during all that happened. I'd play this song over and over. I missed you so much and this song sort of spoke to me through my confusion."

"I'm so sorry."

He shook his head and looked at me with serious eyes, as he started to sing.

The words were perfect and the lyrics so spot on to our situation. I felt my chest constrict and the tears start to well in my eyes as I watched him. He was so beautiful, so talented and amazing. The pain behind his eyes was vivid as he sang. I figured he'd been singing this song to me every time he played it over the past three months, and I couldn't believe I caused him so much pain. All because I was afraid to talk to him; to confront the possibility that he might not want me. I should have known that was completely and utterly impossible. I dropped my head and first one then another tear fell. Stupid me.

When he finished the song, Cade's eyes were glassy as he set the guitar down and moved toward me. He gathered me close and his hand came up to the back of my head as I buried myself into him. My arms slipped around his back and I breathed him in.

"I'm sorry. I'm so sorry," I said sadly. "I never meant to hurt you like that, Cade. Forgive me."

His arms tightened around me and I felt his lips at my temple.

"I'm sorry too. We both made mistakes but we're not going to make those mistakes again. I love you, so much. We have forever to be together. All of this bullshit just made me love you more, Brook, okay? Every time you touch my heart, whether it's pain or joy; I'll always love you more and more."

I gasped as a sob escaped my chest. I nodded and pulled back to look at him. His blue eyes were filled with tears too. I closed my eyes and the tears squeezed from my eyes and I felt my heart would explode. "Me too, see? I'm spilling over again. I'm fucking overflowing."

It was too much, so much emotion. Cade took me back in his arms and pulled me across the bed, his mouth latching onto mine. He made love to me again and again all night long, and it was more than I could ever dream of. Crying, laughing, loving, touching, devouring; we couldn't get enough of each other. By some miracle, I knew we never would.

It was always going to be this beautiful between us.

Chapter 19

Copycat

Brooklyn

THE KNOCK ON my hotel room door startled me because I wasn't expecting anyone. As I dragged myself out of bed and made my way to the door I glanced at the alarm clock on the nightstand. It was only 11 AM and I didn't have to be on set until evening, so I'd been looking forward to sleeping in.

Crap.

Cade was with me until the early morning hours and we'd spent the night in each other's arms, doing little sleeping. It was so beautiful, but our insatiable appetite for each other was taking a toll on us. Even when we weren't making love, we were talking about anything and everything.

My poor baby. He barely slept and would be dragging today, but I couldn't tell him last night. He didn't want to hear that he needed to sleep when he wanted to make love again and again. Since our reconciliation, one or the other of us snuck into each other's hotels just about every night, but I wasn't complaining. We spent every second we could together and still it wasn't enough.

Sarah and Gavin were in town now and we were shooting some of the hospital room scenes, and Cade and I had a solo scene tomorrow.

I couldn't imagine who would be on the other side of my door, since Noah was done filming and no rehearsals were scheduled with any of the others.

Cade had a scene with a newly cast actor and I wouldn't see him at least until close to dinnertime.

I looked through the peephole in the door and I couldn't believe my eyes. *Jesus, what was he doing here?* I opened the door.

"David? What are you doing here?" I put my arm on the door jam, hoping he'd understand that I wouldn't be inviting him in.

"Wow, what a greeting. I'm glad to see you too, Brook. I thought we were still friends, at least." He stood with his arms folded as he looked me up and down. I was thankful I was fully clothed in old sweats and a T-shirt. He looked different, like he was trying to be more masculine, more like... I shut my mind off abruptly. I didn't want to make the comparison, but I couldn't help it as my eyes roamed over him.

"We are, but I still don't get why you're here," I said hesitantly. There was no real explanation for him being in Vancouver. I ran my hands through my hair.

"Aren't you going to invite me in?" He had on a stocking cap, a blue flannel shirt over a white T-shirt and black jeans. His hair was longer and he had about three days' worth of beard growth on his face.

"No. No, I'm not."

Shit.

I couldn't ask him in. Cade would fucking lose it if he found out

David was alone with me in my room. Not that I was worried that anything would happen, but still; Cade would flip considering what happened in Rome. I wasn't prepared to risk it.

"Why? I thought I proved that I could be your friend during these past months, Brook. Haven't I?"

He was right. He had been a good friend to me during the months when I'd been separated from Cade. I hadn't told him much about what happened except that Cade and I weren't together anymore. Despite his feelings; he hadn't gloated or said 'I told you so'. I had to give him credit for that.

"Yeah, sure, David, but... just why are you here?"

"Brook I'm doing my job, *and* being your friend, too."

"Your job?" I raised my brows and shook my head. I was unaware of any *boyfriend* appearances on the schedule for this week and if there were, *I sure as hell* would have spoken to Cade ahead of time.

"Yeah. I'm supposed to come up here a few times and hang with you, get a few pictures snapped for the parasites, etcetera. I thought we could go to lunch and hang out. I miss you. So are you gonna make me hang out in the hall all day?"

"Yeah... maybe. I wasn't told about your visit, David. How did you know I wouldn't be filming today?"

"Wendy called me. She also told me you and she had a big fight over Mr. Wonderful. She's really upset and she wants to talk to you, *without* your Brit. We've all been friends a long time and so she figured if I came up here, it would make it easier for you and her to mend the fences."

I felt myself stiffen in protest.

It was only two weeks since the confrontation and I'd been avoiding her ever since. When I was forced to face fans with Wendy, I acted as normally as possible; like she was still my friend. She'd asked me to talk and she'd even tried to apologize, but I was too nervous about trusting her again so I made excuses constantly. Obviously, I had to get through these movies with her around, so I tried to keep the interaction to a minimum and keep our relationship on a professional level. It was uncomfortable, to say the least.

"Brook, for God's sake. I'm standing in the damn hall. Please?" David pleaded.

"Well..." I hesitated. "I can't ask you in, David. I need to call Jeanne and see who the hell arranged this without telling me. Can you wait for me in the lobby? I'll call you when I'm finished talking to her, okay?"

"Brook..." He was chagrined; his face clearly showing his annoyance.

"Look, David, that's the best I can do right now." I let the door close without waiting for a response.

This was just what I needed.

I grabbed my blackberry and dialed Jeanne.

"Hello, Brook. How are things up in Van City?"

"Well, that depends. What the *fuck* is David doing showing up on my doorstep? Not only is he here uninvited, it's like he's trying to *be* Cade. Shit, I mean, he's wearing clothes that are indicative of Cade, same brand of sunglasses, hat, unshaven! I mean, Jesus, Jeanne!"

"He *what*?" she asked incredulously.

"Yeah. He just showed up; mini Cade!" I was pacing around the room. "Whose idea was this anyway?"

Jeanne burst out laughing. "I don't know why he's there dressed up like Cade, but I do know that the studio wants a few appearances from him during the film. We talked about this Brook. Are you serious? Mini-Cade?" She was still chuckling.

"He's trying to look like Cade, and yeah, we talked about it and I knew we'd have to do this a couple of times, but I thought I'd have some notice. Someone should have let me know. Can you please tell me what is so damn funny?"

"What's funny is David trying to dress up like Cade, and your reaction. You're hilarious, Brook," Jeanne was still chuckling.

"No, I'm not!" I huffed. "I'm really upset, Jeanne. So he's here, and I'm sure there have been paps already trailing him, so now I have no choice but to hang out with him today. This is just *fucking great!*"

"I'll try to find out who set this up, but we knew we'd have some of this to contend with to secure the contracts, so what is the big deal?"

"The big deal is that I didn't know about it, and Cade doesn't know. He's working, so I won't be able to let him know in time. I don't like the idea of parading David around Vancouver behind his back. I need to talk to him, but David is already downstairs. Crap!" I sighed and ran my hand through my hair again. "Look, I'll deal with it, but please find out who is behind this and make sure it doesn't happen like this again."

"Okay, Brook. I'm sorry. I understand that the studio should have told you and I'll see what I can find out. Keep me posted on what's happening."

"What's happening is that I'm going to try to get in touch with Cade, and then I'll walk around a little in public with David and then he leaves. End of story."

"Cade will be okay, Brook. Do you want me to try to get in touch with him?"

"I'll keep trying. Just because I'm out with David, doesn't mean I can't call Cade."

After I ended the call, I threw on some clothes and pulled my hair back. I called Cade, but he didn't answer so I was forced to leave a message.

"Hey babe, I've got a problem. The studio sent David up here for a boyfriend appearance. The paps have already had him at the airport and followed him to the hotel, so I have to spend some time with him today and let the leeches take some snaps. I'm really upset, but don't know what else to do since he's already been spotted. I wasn't told in advance, obviously. I'm sorry. Please don't be mad. It's only because of our contracts. Call me when you get a break. Love you."

I changed out of my sweats and into some jeans, shoved my phone in my back pocket, grabbed my bag and ran down to the lobby to find David sitting in the foyer with Wendy. I stopped dead in my tracks for a minute.

Wendy? I couldn't get a break.

My steps slowed as I approached. The hotel was good about keeping the photographers outside, but they were sure to pounce once we left.

"Hey," I said as they both looked up from the conversation they had been having. "Hi, Wendy."

"Hi, Brook. Thanks for letting me tag along." Her eyes were wary and I couldn't tell if she was sincere or not, but my gut was screaming that I shouldn't trust her, and I didn't realize that I was *letting her* do anything. "We thought we'd get some sushi and then walk around downtown Vancouver a little, would that be okay?"

Tag along? This was fucking great, but what could I say? "Yeah, that's fine. To be honest, I just want to get this over with. No offense to either of you, but this is part of my job, and that's it."

David rolled his eyes. "Brook. We always had fun when we hung out, didn't we? Can't we just get back to that?"

We walked out into the sunshine, and the fans were screaming and asking for autographs. Wendy and I posed for a few photos before the three of us were able to get into the cab David hailed and head downtown. It was a pretty day and I just concentrated on the city rushing by the cab. I'd been surprised by the architecture in Vancouver. All of the balconies running completely around most of the skyscrapers reminded me of some sixty's movie rerun I'd seen when I was younger.

Sitting in the cab; Wendy and David made small talk about the filming and the different places in Vancouver we should check out and I just stared straight ahead. They had me in between them so not much else I could do.

"Imagine Dragons are coming here next month. I'd like you to come with me to the concert, Brook. We can ask Cade to join if you want."

I felt myself tense and my fists clench. Of course, she'd want Cade along. "Wendy, so much has happened; I don't know."

She looked exasperated. "I'm sorry about what happened, okay? But to be fair, you have to admit that you didn't tell me that you were with Cade. I didn't know, so your reaction wasn't really fair."

David didn't say anything at all; he just watched the two of us, so that told me that Wendy had shared the whole sordid mess with him.

"Hmmmph." It was true I hadn't told her Cade and I were together, but he'd told her he loved me, and that didn't change what she did or how she let me believe that she'd slept with him. "Why did you even go there? You knew how he felt."

"Brook, come on. You knew I wanted to be with Cade. I'm sorry, but he's hot, everyone wants to do him." I stiffened at her words, and even David was getting uncomfortable with the conversation, by the way he was bristling in his seat. "But, I wouldn't have tried if you would have told me the truth."

Yeah, right. My mind protested.

"If that's true, why did you let me think you two had sex? You saw how upset I was."

"Because, I felt ridiculous that you'd found me there with my clothes off. I thought that it was Cade at the door and you took me by surprise, and then I was unsure what to do. Upset is the last reaction I expected from you, Brook. I was wrong, and I'm sorry. I think you more than retaliated, didn't you?"

My arms were folded in front of me as I looked at her through hooded eyes. She was right. I did annihilate her in front of most our friends.

"I was just so pissed. I missed out on three months with Cade, and what I can't forgive is how much it hurt *him*. Wasn't it a little presumptuous of you to think he'd sleep with you? I mean, he'd been telling you over and over that he loved me, hadn't he?"

She reached out to put her arm around me. "Yes, but as far as I knew, you didn't want him." She shrugged. "Be reasonable, Brook. I admit it, I wasn't thinking straight. I hoped that if he'd had a little too much to drink, I could convince him to be with me, and then after—well, that he'd want to be with me again."

Jesus. Did I have to hear this?

"I adore you, Brook, and I want to work this out, even if it's in baby steps. This is a start, isn't it? I thought if I came along today, Cade wouldn't be as upset since you wouldn't be alone with David."

Wendy leaned her head against mine and squeezed my shoulders. It was a little too much fake-love for me at this point, and I pulled away from her.

"Gee, thanks, Wendy. Thanks a hell of a lot."

She shrugged at him as she moved away from me finally.

My phone vibrated in my pocket and I pulled it out. Of course, it was from Cade.

Are you with him now?

I typed out my response.

**Yeah. Wendy is here, too. I'll explain later.
Will I see you for dinner?**

"Wendy, I think it's Cade who deserves the apology and I'm sorry, but I still can't trust you. You'll have to prove that you're sincere before I'll ever be able to do that." My voice was quiet and I was still extremely skeptical, however it would make doing *Don't Forget to Remember Me* easier if there wasn't constant tension on set.

"Sure, if that's what it takes, I'll apologize to him too. I do feel bad, and now everyone hates me. My life hasn't been all sunshine and roses these past two weeks either."

We pulled up at the restaurant and the minute the cab door opened the cameras started firing.

Hmmm... funny they knew where we were going.

"Did Pinnacle tell the press where we'd be or did you, Wendy?" I sounded snarky, but fuck, that would be so par for the course!

David grabbed my hand and smiled at me as he put his sunglasses down over his eyes. Damn if those weren't practically identical to

Cade's. *What the hell was he trying to do?*

"I did, Brook. It's part of it. We have to get pictures, or I don't get paid. Understand?"

David certainly was in a good mood as the three of us walked into the restaurant, and Wendy was all smiles for the cameras as well. She wasn't hurt by our argument, in the slightest. She was so painfully obvious.

I, on the other hand, wanted to be anywhere but with the two of them and I was annoyed. I didn't care at all. Maybe we had to get a few pictures, but I'd be damned if I was going to look like I was enjoying myself.

After lunch, Wendy wanted to go check out some of the shops in downtown Vancouver, and it really didn't matter to me what we did. I was obligated to a couple of hours and that was going to be the end of it.

As we walked down the street, David kept pulling my hand into his and I'd find any excuse to pull away. I knew I'd get a tongue lashing from the suits, but hell, I couldn't help it. All I could think about was how this was going to make Cade feel, and since he hadn't returned my text yet, I started to worry. I knew we were solid, but this was still going to be hard for him.

I couldn't resist, I finally had to ask David about his clothes.

"Um, what's up with your little CC make-over? Seriously dude, it's sort of pathetic. The press is gonna eat you alive." I rolled my eyes at him, and then regretted my words.

I could see that he was hurt and embarrassed; the skin of his face was getting redder by the second. It didn't help when Wendy laughed and covered her mouth with her hand.

"Do you have to try to hurt me all the time, Brook? Jesus, isn't what I've been through for you enough already? Don't you care about me at all?"

Yes, I cared about him. You don't spend years of your life with someone and then just wake up one day and forget everything they'd meant to your life. He was a good person, a good friend. I lowered my eyes as I struggled for what to say.

"David, I'm not trying to hurt you, but you shouldn't try to copy Cade. You should just be yourself." I put my hand on his arm in the form of an apology. "You have a lot of great qualities of your own."

"I'm not *copying* him. I just thought this was the type of look that you were attracted to now."

I sighed. "I wasn't attracted to a particular 'look', David. I don't want to hurt you more, but it's just Cade. It doesn't matter what he wears, how long his hair is, or whether he shaves or not. That isn't it. I'm sorry you've been hurt. How many times can I tell you that?"

"It doesn't hurt that Cade's so drop-dead beautiful, does it, Brook?" Wendy was looking at some shoes but she still put in her two cents.

Will the real Wendy Reed please stand up? I felt sure this one was it. She was so blatantly insensitive to other people's feelings.

I shook my head in barely veiled disgust, and moved off to the other side of the store away from both of them and checked my watch. This was more than enough time to be out with them and so I decided that the afternoon was over. Finally, my phone went off in my pocket.

Hey, love. Some of the film got exposed and we have to reshoot at least half of what I've done today. So, I won't be able to make dinner. Sorry, sweetheart. Can you let me know when you're away from David?

*
I love you, more.*

I sighed in regret.

"I need to get back. I have to take a nap before my scenes tonight."

I typed out a text response to Cade.

Going back to the hotel now. I miss you.

***

It was nearly 10 PM and I was exhausted. Sarah, Gavin, Jennifer and I had shot and re-shot one of the hospital scenes twenty times and I was sick of it. My eyes searched for Cade all night, but I hadn't seen him. I hadn't heard from him either, so hopefully he was getting some much-needed sleep, but I decided to go to the sound stage where he was scheduled just to check.

Martin was having the crew reset the scene because he wanted to get one more take of the lead-in, when I finally saw Cade across the set.

His arms were folded across his chest with one hand up to his mouth as he talked to the production manager. I made my way toward him as if pulled by gravity. I was praying that I had some time to talk to him before my scene resumed.

When Cade saw me moving toward him, he excused himself from his conversation so he could meet me halfway.

"Hey, you." His voice was low, so no one else could hear. My eyes were drinking him in, the eighteen hours since we'd seen each other seemed like forever. My hands ached to reach out and touch him. "I wish I could kiss you. I've missed you today," he sighed.

I nodded and bit my lip. "Missed you, too. Are you almost done?"

"Just a couple of shots. They need me against this background so they can match it up with what we lost today. What a bloody nightmare that was. I think someone lost their job over it."

"That's harsh." His eyes were searching mine and I could see the questions behind them.

"Well, it was an expensive mistake. It puts the whole thing behind schedule." He paused and took a deep breath. "I saw the pics of you and the idiot today. PopSugar and eOnline have them up." He looked around the set to make sure no one was listening.

"Already? Those assholes sure work fast." I couldn't help myself; I reached out and touched the front of his shirt.

"Yeah. Did David work fast today, too?" His brow dropped and his lips pursed as he looked at the ground.

"Hey. If you saw them, you had to see how pissed and bored I was. I thought about you all day. I was worried about how you were going to take it."

"Yeah. My head knows, Brook, but I still bloody hate it. He didn't try anything did he?" I could see the memory of Rome flash across his features. "I will fucking kill him."

"No. Wendy came along because she said she was trying to make it up to us; that she thought that you'd feel better about it if I wasn't alone with David." I looked away from his face to smile at a production assistant who was passing by us.

We couldn't have the crew speculating about our relationship. Any one of them could make significant money by leaking information about Cade and me.

"Well, in a way, the logic is good. I wish I could kiss you right now." His hand reached out to mine for an instant before he let it drop to his side. The electricity I felt at his touch always amazed me.

"You look so tired. I think you need to sleep tonight, baby." My voice was quiet as I searched his face.

"I am tired, but I want to be with you. Can I sleep with you in your room?" He was so beautiful with his brows raised over his sparkling eyes and that boyish grin playing about his mouth.

I felt my own lips curve in a bright smile. "As if I'd let you do anything else. But we both need to *sleep*, Cade, okay?" I poked his stomach again and he grunted good-naturedly.

"Brook, places!" Martin called to me from forty yards away.

"Meet you in your room later, then, honey, yeah?" Cade said, as I turned to leave.

I love you. I hoped he could read it in my eyes.

***

I LAY NAKED in my bed waiting for Cade. I told him we needed to sleep, and so I probably should have had something on, but I knew he loved being completely naked with me in bed. My skin on his; he said it was his favorite thing to wear.

It made my heart beat faster just thinking about it. He was so romantic, so amazing. Perfect in everything he said to me, how he touched me, and how much he loved me. I wanted to melt right into him.

Our call in the morning was at 9 AM, so he'd need to get right to sleep. I felt my eyes getting heavy as I let thoughts of him flood my mind and heart. I hugged a pillow as I lay on my side and fought the sleep that tried to overtake me. I wanted to wait for Cade and had music playing to keep me awake.

I wasn't sure how much longer he'd be, but this had been one long fucking day for him. 4 AM to 1 AM. Finally, I heard the key card in the door. My body jazzed, and my heart raced.

Jesus. Okay, Brook, play sleeping or you know what Cade will do, and he needs to rest.

I tried to keep my breathing deep and even as I listened to him take off his clothes. He went into the bathroom and left the door open slightly and I heard the water running as he washed up and brushed his teeth. Soon, very soon, he would be wrapped all around me. Mmmm... .

I felt the covers lift behind me and he came in next to me. One arm slid under my pillow as his body folded up against mine, and his other arm came around me. I should pretend to be asleep, but I couldn't help my arm coming up over his to pull him closer. He scooted near me and the warmth of his skin flooded down my body from my shoulders to the back of my calves. One of his legs came forward to slide between mine.

Cade's arm tightened and his breath fanned out on my neck as he bent to place his open mouth on my skin. Oh God... "Mmmm," I moaned softly. His hand cupped my breast and I felt my body respond as he rubbed his thumb in circles around the nipple and I pressed back against him. He was already hard as he surged forward against me.

I turned my head over my shoulder toward him. "Baby, stop. You need sleep," I whispered, "You're going to get ill."

"I need *you*, Brook. I missed you so much today, and knowing you were with that little shit, just drove me crazy. Just one time. You feel so good." His mouth continued its tingling assault on the skin of my neck and shoulders as both of his arms wrapped around my body to roam over my skin.

I knew damn well I wouldn't be able to resist or deny him. He owned me as much as I owned him.

"Cade," I whispered as I took the hand closest to my face and sucked his fingers into my mouth.

"Oh God, Brook." His forehead dropped to the back of my head and his breath rushed hot over my shoulder and back.

His free hand went lower on my body between my legs and he let his breath out as his body reacted to the feel of me beneath his hands. His touch set me on fire as I arched against him and the sounds he made left me in no doubt how it was affecting him too.

"Uhhh... ..," My mouth parted and my head fell back against his shoulder as his hands continued to explore and excite me. He knew my body so well, knew exactly how to touch me to bring my body to the brink easily. His fingers moved in little circles and then pushed lower into my body to bring the slick wetness up and around as he continued to torture me.

I surged back against him silently begging for him to enter me as I sucked on his fingers like I'd suck on his body. "I love that I can make you feel like this. Jesus, Brook, I'm so turned on."

He groaned and then pulled his fingers from my mouth to move his hand to my breasts so he could tug and rub the nipples between his fingers. I couldn't take much more. I gasped as my hips surged forward.

The hand inside my body withdrew as he lifted my leg up to rest my foot on his calf, giving him the access he needed. He guided his dick to my opening and slid inside from behind. "Uhhhhh... " A soft moan tore from my lips as he brought his hand back around to resume touching my clit, moving down until he could feel where our bodies joined and back up again.

"Oh, yes, Brook. I've thought of nothing else all day. God, I want to lose myself inside you."

My body arched and moved with his as we thrust against each other, surging and grinding. I clenched around him each time he thrust into me and he groaned and kissed the side of my neck as our movements became more frantic.

As if I wasn't flooded with sensation from Cade's touches, goose bumps flooded my skin as his breath fanned over the wetness he'd just left on my skin. Again and again, he kissed my neck and shoulders, and it felt so tantalizing it had me tingling all over.

His breathing sped up as we made love to each other and my hand reached around to grab the back of his thighs as he continued to thrust into me. His hands were working their magic on my body as I felt myself start to tighten and the undeniable sensations building so strong within me.

"Oh, babe..." He gasped against my shoulder and his fingers of one hand tugged at my nipples, while the other had me on the brink of falling over into orgasm. My body was clutching around him, trembling against him and I pulled his hand back to my mouth and took his middle finger deep into my mouth and licked and sucked up and down on it.

"Uhhhhhhhhhhhhh." His breath left him in low groan.

"Cade, I'm close baby." Thirty seconds later, he had me. "Mmmmmmm... Uhhhh... " I pushed back against him as he moaned out my name at the same time as he tensed behind me. I felt him tremble and shake as he his orgasm overtook him. Making love with him only brought us closer and I never wanted it to end.

His arms were still wrapped around me and his fingers lightly teased my body until he was sure he'd gotten every last shudder out of me.

I lay entwined in his arms, his hand coming up to take mine and pull me closer as he kissed my shoulder.

"Christ, Brook. I can't live without touching you like this." That velvet voice, so thick with love and passion was the last sound I'd ever need to hear on this earth. I closed my eyes and surged back against his body, still inside my own, as I kissed his hand. "Love you."

"In case you can't tell; I love you just as much." His arm tightened around me and he let out his breath and nuzzled into the back of my head.

When our breathing returned to normal, I hoped he would just fall asleep. He needed it so much and I was worried about him. After a few minutes he spoke.

"Was everything okay today? David didn't touch you, did he? I'll bloody kill him."

I turned around in his arms so that I could touch his face and look into his eyes. The pain of the months of my being with David still held a scar for him. "No one touches me but you." When he didn't answer, I pressed. "Okay?"

His blue eyes were almost black in the darkness as his mouth dipped to take mine in a deep, soul-searching kiss. His tongue met mine and I couldn't help pressing my mouth closer into his as he groaned in my mouth. When he pulled back, his teeth were nipping at first my upper lip and then the lower one. It was so damn sexy as he brushed the hair off of my face.

"Okay. No one touches you but me," he agreed, his chest rising as he drew in a huge sigh as his arms drew me closer. I snuggled into his shoulder and kissed his neck, my arm sliding across his stomach and my leg coming up over his.

I let my fingers rub soft circles in the little bit of hair on his chest as his breathing became more even and my eyes got heavy.

We were both exhausted as we drifted off to sleep completely wrapped around each other, heart, body and soul.

Chapter 20

Deluge

Brooklyn

WE WERE BETWEEN takes when I saw her. What was she doing here? It wasn't like Jeanne to visit on set, or even come to location at all. She'd made the one exception when she came with me at the start of filming, but that was because of the broken situation between Cade and I. This was totally uncharacteristic of her, and it immediately worried me.

I walked over to the director to check if I had time for a short break in order to find out what Jeanne needed. We still had two months of filming yet, so maybe a short delay now wouldn't matter.

"Martin, my manager is here. Do I have a few minutes to talk to her?"

We were trying to get all of the scenes that included Gavin, Wendy and Sarah finished the same two weeks as the parking lot scenes and the hospital stuff, and today it was one of the office scenes.

"Yeah. Is fifteen minutes enough?" He smiled. He was growing on me. During the first film, he'd been more uptight, but now he seemed relaxed.

"Yep. I'll make sure of it."

I walked toward Jeanne, my eyes searching for Cade as I went. His scenes were finished for the day, but he would've let me know if he'd left set. He had to be around somewhere.

I approached Jeanne and had to admit I didn't like her expression. She looked strained, and tense; like she wasn't looking forward to this conversation.

"Hey." I greeted her casually. "Not that I'm not glad to see you, but what are you doing here? Did you find out who authorized David's uninvited appearance last week?" I ran my hands through my hair and instantly one of the hair and make-up people appeared, as if by magic, to fix the mess I'd just made of my Julia hair.

"Yes." She glanced at the woman working on my hair. "Excuse me, but I really need to speak with Miss Halloway alone. Will you be very long?"

"No Ma'am. Just a minute more." She fluffed my hair, and then dusted my face with powder, and a touch more blush.

"Thank you, Nancy." I smiled at her as she moved away, then turned back to Jeanne.

"What's up?" I asked anxiously. "You look like your dog just died."

"The studio sent David up here. They expect two or three such appearances at least, Brook. I had Joel call them and he read them the riot act about not giving you notice, but that's the best news I have. It seems there's too much scuttlebutt about you and Cade. Some of the major gossip columnists are blogging about you almost daily."

"Yeah, I know. We read a lot of it." I laughed. "It's sort of funny."

"*No*, it isn't, Brook." Her face was stoic. "The suits at Pinnacle feel it is detrimental to box office success if you and Cade are proven to be a couple. You've got to be more careful or there'll be hell to pay." She saw me stiffen as my mouth tightened into a fine line.

"It's dumb. You'd think it would help, not hurt, ticket sales." I was frustrated and pissy.

"I don't agree with their bullshit rules Brook, but we're bound to honor these contracts."

"But... we *aren't* going out in public alone. The only time we even go out to eat together is with several of the others along. Most of the time, it's with the entire group!" I felt my face flush; the heat burning my cheeks like fire. "He doesn't touch me or kiss me; hell, we barely talk on set!"

"Apparently, someone saw Cade sneaking into your hotel through the back entrance two nights ago."

My eyes widened as I sucked in a breath. "Were there pictures?" I asked.

"No, but someone wrote about it on a blog. Jesus, Brook, there are thousands of fan sites that we have to be careful about. This shit spreads like wildfire." She pulled her cigarettes out of her purse, and put one to her lips. She looked at me over the top of it as she lit it and took a long puff.

"So, what? What do they expect us to do?" I looked at the floor and bit my lip. "It isn't like I'm the only one staying in that hotel. Who says he was coming to see me?"

She looked at me sternly and shook her head. Clearly she didn't think anyone would swallow any other possibility.

Fuck. Okay, so I am the only one he'd be coming to see. Is it my fault the world knows it?

"Well, the San Francisco Music Festival is this weekend and they are planning on sending Cade down for that, and David is on the schedule to come up here and occupy you…" She took a drag from her cigarette.

I felt the anger rise within me. "We're supposed to go to L.A. for the Kid's Choice Awards this weekend," I said tightly.

She shook her head. "Not anymore. They're sending Noah instead. The excuse is that they want to give him some more exposure, and they absolutely do not want you and Cade traveling together right now."

My blood pressure rose, and I turned to walk a few steps away before turning back to her. I could see Martin behind her readying to begin shooting, so I'd have to get back soon.

"I have to hang out with David all weekend? Do you know what that is going to do to Cade? I'm so sick of this bullshit, Jeanne!"

"Brook, lower your voice. *Now*," Jeanne ordered. "I might be able to figure something out for you to spend a little time with Cade, but for the most part, yes, you'll need to spend the weekend with David." Her face softened as she saw the angry tears well in my eyes. I quickly blinked them away.

"I can't share a room with David, Jeanne, okay?"

"Of course not, Brook. I'll make sure that he has a room on the same floor as you, so you can both come and go together without actually staying together." She closed the distance between us and put her arms around me. I was stiff, so pissed I was shaking, and I pulled away from her.

"Jesus. This is just too much, Jeanne. I know this isn't your fault, but I hate that we 're prisoners of these fucking contracts! I don't even care if we finish the film if this is how it's going to be." I felt completely defeated and Jeanne's eyes widened and something like fright flashed across her features.

"Brook, I won't let you throw your career, or Cade's, away just because you find this inconvenient." She took on a motherly tone.

"It's not about inconvenience; you know that. It's about how Cade *feels* when he has to see me with David. Now you're sending him off to events without me, and then what? He has to flirt with fans? The next thing you'll tell me is that the studio is going to make him hang out with Wendy or something," I spat out in disgust. I ran a hand through my hair in frustration.

"This has to be done, so just do it and stop complaining, and yeah, they've mentioned having Cade be seen out with Wendy—"

My head snapped up and I glared at her.

Jeanne lifted both of her hands, fingers spread in front of her. "— *Just* to take the speculation off of the two of you."

"No." I shook my head adamantly. "Just... *No!*"

"Apparently a broken relationship between the two of them wouldn't have the same devastating effect; they can't have the two leads in a romance breaking up in the middle of the filming, or premieres. We've talked about this, Brook."

"*We're not going to break up*! I have to watch Cade with that bitch? She's been trying to bang him for a year, and he has to endure me in the company of a man who has openly admitted that he wants me back?"

"Brook, we're ready to start. Places, please," Martin called me back to set.

"Ugh! When?" I asked.

"Tomorrow through Sunday. And neither one of you can be seen coming and going from the other's hotels, not even *once*. Is that clear, Brook? I'm sorry, but that's the way it is."

"This isn't just about being able to sleep with Cade, Jeanne! Jesus!" I spat at her. Martin was motioning me back with his hands. "I have to go. I'll talk to Cade tonight, but we need to make a plan to make this as painless as possible."

"Okay. I agree. I'll do what I can to help."

Oh my God! Could this situation get any worse? My mind railed.

I let out my breath and my head dropped back as I walked back to my mark. Cade was sitting offside to watch the scene and I was sure he could tell by my face that something was wrong. I watched his gaze moved to where I just came from. He saw Jeanne standing there, then looked at me one more time, questioningly. I shook my head.

When he got up and strode over to Jeanne, I knew she'd be having the same conversation with him and he was going to be upset. Upset was a damn understatement, and it would be three hours, at least, until I could talk to him about it.

I couldn't think about it now. I had to get my head into the scene.

***

I STOOD WITH my hands braced on the counter in the bathroom as I waited for David to come get me. Cade left for the Music Festival the night before, while I holed up in my room, alone. He'd texted me all night long, which was how we maintained our sanity. He was furious after he'd spoken to Jeanne, and I could do little to make him feel better. It was one thing to have to stay away from each other for five days, and quite another to have to hang out with Wendy and David. My stomach clenched painfully.

I wasn't sure what was worse; thinking of Cade with Wendy, or having to deal with David. Okay, I *was* sure which was worse.

Jeanne arranged for David and me to "double date" with Wendy and Cade and just the thought of it made me sick to my stomach. I sure as hell didn't want to sit across from the two of them all night, not being able to touch him, and then have David hanging all over me. I wanted to stay in and forget the whole damn thing.

The sound of the key card opening the door made my heart thump in my chest. I quickly turned from the bathroom and entered the sitting room of the suite just as Cade came walked in. He looked incredible, dressed in all black; jeans, button down shirt, leather jacket and stocking cap. His eyes met mine, and then he swept me up in his arms, his hand coming up to the back of my head and his face turning into my neck. He took a deep breath as he held me tight.

"Bloody hell. I don't want to do this." My arms were around his waist and back as I pressed into his chest. "Fucking Pinnacle."

"You aren't supposed to be here," I whispered, even as my arms wound around his middle tightly, "but you feel so good. I missed you last night."

"I don't give a fuck if I'm *supposed* to be here or not. I belong with you."

I nodded and splayed my hands out on his back to press him closer. He kissed the top of my head and rubbed circles on my back before bending to take my mouth with his.

Jesus, you taste so good, I thought as his tongue teased my lips apart and slid against mine again and again. There was another knock at the door, which forced us to separate, but our mouths wanted to cling to each other.

"Damn it!" His mouth ghosted mine as he spoke. "How in the hell am I going to live through tonight?"

"You will. We both will. It sucks, but it's not real. Just remember it's *not real*, Cade." I rose up on tiptoe to press another open mouth kiss on his delicious lips as the knocking resumed. I hoped I could take my own advice.

I moved out of his arms and began toward the door, but he stopped me. His warm fingers closed around my forearm and pulled me back into his embrace. Strong arms enfolded me and lifted me off the floor. My arms slid around his neck and my hands went into his hair. He looked deeply into my eyes and I could see fear, longing, love and a hundred other emotions flicker in the blue depths before they closed, and he placed a deep, soulful kiss on my mouth.

"Let them wait. I love you, Brook." He pressed his forehead to mine as his hot breath rushed over my face. "Please don't let him touch you. I can't bear to watch it. Please."

"I know. I won't, babe. I love you, too," I whispered against his mouth. The knocking came again.

"Brook, for Christ's sake. Let me in," David called impatiently from the other side of the door.

Cade stiffened and set me on my feet, then brushed his fingers across my cheekbone.

"How do you want to do this? Should I just meet you at the restaurant?" he asked softly.

"Yeah. That would be easier, wouldn't it? Less torture." I touched his cheek and then went to grab my jacket and purse. "I'm coming, David!"

Turning one last time to look back at Cade as he moved into the other room, my heart stopped at the look in his eyes. I opened the door and stepped into the hall. David stared after me silently as I walked past him toward the elevator.

Caden

I TEXTED WENDY and told her to meet me out in front of the hotel. This was going to be the worst night of my life. Watching that little prick fawn all over Brook and pretending to be on a date with that twit, Wendy, was going to be hell.

And, then what? I was supposed to stay away from Brook all night, take Wendy out to a club after dinner to make it more *official* and make sure we were seen.

Fuck, I thought. *I hope Wendy won't mind being ignored once we get there.*

In the cab on the way, I felt weird; like I was suffocating in the closed space next to her. She glanced at me, looking me up and down, before she finally broke the silence.

"Look, Cade. I wanted to apologize for before. I should have listened to you when you told me you weren't interested in me, but honestly, I couldn't see any reason why you wouldn't like me." She dropped her head, and looked out the window. "I guess it bruised my ego and I made it a mission to prove you wrong." She paused and contemplated what to say next. "But, I'm trying to help, now. Brook's been a good friend for a lot of years, and I really didn't think she was interested in you. She was good at hiding it, I guess. I'm sorry that I hurt you guys."

I sighed. I wasn't sure if I believed her, but she made the words sound sincere. "Okay, Wendy. I accept your apology. I hope you believe me now when I tell you that Brook is the most important person in my world," I said softly so the cab driver wouldn't hear our conversation.

She smiled softly. "Listen, I get it. I do. And, to prove it to you, I need to tell you something… " The look on her face was pensive.

"What is it?"

"Well, David is my friend too, and he talks to me. I'm probably betraying his confidence, but I know he wants Brook back. He's going to try to get her back, Cade."

I turned quickly to look into her face. It wasn't anything I didn't already know, but hearing someone else say it aloud, somehow made it more real.

I nodded. "Yeah. Actually, I've known for a while. He'd be a fool not to try. She's an amazing person."

Her lids dropped over her eyes and she bit her lip. Obviously, my words caused her pain and that wasn't my intention.

"I appreciate that you told me. I hope we can work past all that's happened. I'm sorry if you've been hurt as well."

"Oh, hey." Wendy shrugged. "I just wanted to have a little fun. I'm fine. Really. Don't worry about me." She reached out and took my hand as the cab stopped by the curb. I'd chosen an obscure little restaurant that wasn't well known because I wanted to get through this evening as painlessly as possible. What a bloody oxymoron.

Despite my efforts, there were at least a hundred fans and paparazzi outside waiting for us when we arrived at the restaurant. I could only hope Brook and David were already inside.

The screams increased and several girls were rushing toward me, restrained only by the bodyguards. My personal bodyguard, John, stood between me and the biggest share of the screaming women. I hated this part of my work. Bloody hated it, but it was part of the job.

"I'll sign. It's okay," I told him, and went through the routine. Cameras flashed like crazy as paparazzi took pictures of me with

Wendy and I placed a hand at the back of her waist to guide her in, and we made our way through the double doors. The studio execs would be ecstatic and the fans would eat it up, but my heart sank. It was a role: just another role, but one that had the potential to ruin my relationship with Brook.

Can I leave now that the evidence of my 'date' is solid? I wondered.

Wendy preceded me in, and I found myself searching the room for Brook as we walked into the building.

She and David were sitting at a table in the corner. Thank God Jeanne had asked the manager to put us somewhere semi-private so we could avoid as much traffic and attention as possible.

"Hi David, Brook," Wendy was congenial and calm. I wished I felt as at ease. My stomach tightened at the closeness David's chair was sitting to Brook's; his arm draped casually over the back of it.

Wendy slid into the seat next to David and I took the one opposite him but next to Brook. Her chair was pulled closer to his than mine, and it didn't go unnoticed by me. I ran my hand through my hair, my fingers itching to pull her closer to me instead.

"Good evening, David." My eyes slid to Brook's face. I could see how difficult the situation was for her as David responded.

"Cade. How have you been?"

So, I guess this was going to be an evening of small talk.

"Absolutely brilliant up until now, I suppose." I took a deep breath as the waiter came to take our drink orders. David's eyes hardened as he looked at me, then softened as he turned back to Brook. He was sending me a message.

"But not as *brilliant* as the evening I'm about to have, hmmm?"

The little wanker was taunting me.

Don't even fucking think about her like that, you bloody bastard;

I wanted to yell at him.

I lowered my voice. "I don't know what ideas you have floating around in your head, David, but this doesn't change the fact that Brook is with me. It will be *me* holding her naked body next to mine, and *my name* she'll be moaning into the darkness... My mouth on hers as I take her tonight." My eyes were hard on his face, and my voice had a deadly edge. I glanced at Brook, worried that she'd be pissed at me for saying it out loud, but right now, all I cared about was making sure he knew she was mine.

"We'll see. You know; I had her *first*," he replied with a smirk.

Brook gasped and put a hand over her eyes.

"Fuck, boys! All this male bonding makes me horny," Wendy scoffed with a smirk. "If you drip any more testosterone, I'm afraid I'll grow a dick; so cool it."

I ignored her, my eyes continuing to bore into David's. "I think I just saw *your life* flash before my eyes," I growled and hoped to hell he got the message.

"David, Cade; please. Can we just get through this?" Brook shook her head at both of us as her face flushed bright red.

David shrugged slightly before bringing his eyes back to mine. He grabbed her hand that was resting on top of the table and pulled it to his mouth. He was daring me, challenging me, and fuck if I didn't want to beat that smug expression off of his face.

I felt so jealous and possessive. *Stop fucking touching her!* I wanted to jump across the table and pull her hand from his.

Throughout the evening, my eyes were constantly on Brook and David, save for the few times that Wendy managed to draw me into conversation; asking me about my new projects. She wasn't trying to be overly flirtatious, just enough to make the illusion of the "date" real when the waiters came around or the other patrons watched us.

Brook's eyes followed Wendy as much as mine were on David. Talk about fucking uncomfortable for all of us. I bloody hated that little bastard and vowed that I would not let the studio force me into this type of situation again. It was beyond unbearable.

I watched David push her hair back and touch her face over and over and it was all I could do not to fly across the table and rip his bloody head off. I didn't want to bloody see it. It did nothing but remind me of the many times I'd suffered through his visits up to Portland during production of the first film. Brook's eyes found mine and I knew she was silently willing him to stop, her hand slightly pushed him away several times.

My blood pressure was rising and I was drinking way too much, yet barely touching my dinner. The food tasted like cardboard in my mouth and I had to remind myself that drinking around Wendy wasn't a good idea. I still couldn't trust her. This whole situation was a huge mess and I was reaching the end of my rope with Pinnacle Films. I was going to call a meeting, and soon. I didn't give a flying fuck if they ever signed me again.

"Brook, you aren't eating. Are you okay, luh,-" I stopped myself before I said the word. I let out a deep, frustrated sigh. I wanted to reach out and touch her, but couldn't.

She smiled weakly at me. "As well as you are," she said softly as her hand reached out to touch mine. It froze in mid-air as she suddenly pulled it back.

Wendy finally put her hand on my arm, "Cade, let's go to the bar at the hotel for while. We'd ask you two to join, but Brook can't yet, right?"

Brook's face hardened angrily. Pointing out Brook's underage status was the first slightly bitchy thing Wendy had said all night.

Okay, so if they couldn't go out, what would they do? Stay in? Fuck that!

I felt like my skin was falling off, crawling all over me, I couldn't breathe. It had to be as bad or worse for her. She knew my charade for the evening wasn't over.

We all stood up to walk outside; David led Brook out ahead of Wendy and I. His arm was wrapped around her waist and his head dipped to whisper in her ear. It looked very intimate, and I wanted to throw him across the bloody street.

On the curb, we stood and stared at each other for an uncomfortable moment. I could read the worry and anxiousness in Brook's expression as her eyes searched mine. Wendy and David forgotten, we couldn't tear our gazes away from each other. It was as if gravity pulled me to her, and I wanted to give in.

"Okay, so thanks for coming out. Cade, Wendy," David nodded to both of us as he hailed a cab. The cameras were flashing so I could not even hug Brook goodbye. Her eyes were glassing over as he pushed her toward the cab and she climbed in.

I felt my chest tighten as I watched him drive off with my girl. Wendy hooked her arm through mine and turned me away to walk down the block in the opposite direction their cab was headed.

As we walked, I pulled my arm from hers. "I was just trying to make it look real, Cade. I'm sorry," she said hesitantly.

"No, I understand. Um, thanks. I'm sorry, too. I'm a little preoccupied. I won't be great company tonight."

"That's fine. There's a band so maybe we'll have fun. You might, if you try." I shoved my hands into the pockets of my jackets and grimaced.

We had a fairly large band of fans and press trailing us down the street and we started to walk faster. We finally reached our destination and headed straight into the bar area, with the photographers flashing and the fans following us in.

I took my phone out and text Brook immediately.

That was so hard. Glad it's over. Please let me know when you're alone so I can call you. I love you, beautiful girl.

"Cade, come on. Let's get a drink and talk. Just talk, okay?" Wendy persisted.

As if I'd let anything else happen, I thought.

As the night wore on and I had no message from Brook, I became more and more agitated. What the bloody hell was going on? Wendy found some of the fans more interesting conversationalists than I turned out to be, milling around the bar laughing and talking to everyone. I moved to a dark corner and kept checking my phone. I wanted to disappear into the background.

I was sick to my stomach, scared and fighting the urge to run right over to Brook's hotel. It was getting harder, by the moment, to stand there when it felt like I wanted to jump out of my bloody skin. I trusted her. I knew she loved me, but logic fought with the anxiety attack I was having.

I checked my phone again, and let my head drop back as I looked at the ceiling. No message; no call.

"Cade, will you look over here, please?"

A middle-aged fan wanted to take my picture, and while I was usually very gracious in my attempts to accommodate them, I wasn't in the mood and knew that my misery showed plainly on my face.

I put up my hand. "Please no pictures… just… not tonight. Please." I could see the disappointment rush across the woman's face, but she nodded and moved away. I turned back to the bar and texted Brook again.

Where in bloody hell are you, Brook? I'm worried now!

An hour later there was still no response, so I made my way over to Wendy.

"I've got to get out of here. Stay if you'd like. I'll send the driver back for you."

She shook her head. "No, I'll come with you now."

More paparazzi looking for photo ops hounded us as we left the bar and piled in the car and again at the hotel as we went inside. Wendy and I didn't touch as we went into the hotel and then the elevators. No hand holding, no arm and arm, nothing staged for the pictures. I had up an invisible wall, and finally, she was starting to respect it.

"Thanks, Wendy. I'll see you on set." The elevator stopped on her floor and she turned to speak to me after she stepped out, her hand holding open the door.

"Cade, I really do care about you and didn't mean to hurt you. I hope you know that."

"Yeah. Let's just all try to be friends. Thanks." My voice was flat, dismissive, and emotionless as I reached out to punch my floor button again, hoping she'd get the hint. "Goodnight."

She moved back and the door shut. My eyes closed as I contemplated what I wanted to do.

What I wanted to do was run straight to Brook's room. It was what I absolutely *needed* to do. I had to, or I'd go insane.

Decision made, I dialed my driver and asked him to meet me in the garage by the stairwell. Screw the studio and their rules about no visits to each other's hotels. I'd played a puppet enough for one evening.

***

I PUT THE key in the slot and waited for the click and green flash before slowly turning the handle so I could ease the door open. Truthfully, I knew I wouldn't find Brook with David, but maybe she wouldn't be here yet, or she could be sleeping. I hoped it was the latter. After all we'd been through, neither one of us should be worried about this evening, but it was still difficult to see her with him. The pain we both dealt with in January and February was still fresh, and emotions were still a bit raw.

The light in the sitting room was casting a low, golden glow showing the open door to the bedroom. A trail of clothes scattered the floor from the bathroom to where Brook's suitcase was open on the luggage stand. My heart relaxed. At least she was here, and she was safe.

Tentatively, I made my way to the bedroom and peeked around the door. The window curtain was open slightly and the moonlight from outside cast a bluish sheen on the bed. Brook was lying in the center of it dressed in shorts and my white T-shirt.

The covers were messed up like she'd been tossing and turning, bunched up around her shapely legs. She was on her back with her head turned away; both of her hands up by her face on the pillow, but she was clearly asleep as her chest rose and fell in even rhythm.

I tangibly relaxed and took a deep breath. I hadn't realized how uptight I was all night. As my muscles unwound, my legs began to shake. I took a seat in the chair in the corner by the window to take off my shoes. I let my head fall back for a moment before my gaze was drawn back to watch the sleeping girl in the bed. I pulled my hat off and ran my hands through my hair. It was sweaty and messy.

Minutes passed, maybe hours. I didn't know how long I sat there watching her beautiful face; listening to her breathe and her soft moans as she changed position. Her lips parted and she said my name. My heart leapt inside my chest. I ached to wake her and make love to her for hours. She was so incredibly gorgeous, even in sleep. So soft and inviting, her body called to mine like a siren's song.

A few moments later, something changed. Brook's breathing came faster and she began to tremble; her chest heaving, back arching and hands fisting in the blankets. Then, she started to cry in her sleep. I was frozen in place for a few seconds until she sat straight up; her arms came to rest on her bent knees and her head fell into her hands. She sucked in a ragged breath

"No! No more!" Her voice cried out as her body continued to shake. "No more... I just... " Her voice softened as she woke up and realized it was a bad dream. "I can't do this anymore." Her low sobs filled the room as she cried into her folded arms.

I wanted to rush to her, but didn't want to startle her. I moved quietly to her side, knelt down beside her and reached out to caress the back of her head.

Her head snapped up out of her arms and she raised her tear-streaked face to look at me.

"Cade. Oh God, you're here," she breathed as I gathered her closer. I moved to sit on the bed and pull her onto my lap. Her arms slid around me, too, as she curled her body into mine. She was so incredibly loving and so, so trusting. Protectiveness and love for her flooded through every cell in my body, my heart expanding until I thought it would burst. I wanted to give her everything I had, and more.

In that moment, I knew with Brook is where I needed to be; always. With her, around her, inside her... she was where I was home. She clung to me, still crying softly and as my arms tightened, I knew I'd never be able to let go of her. Not ever.

"Cade... I can't hide how I feel anymore. It's too hard. Jesus, it's too hard... isn't it?"

I turned my face into the curve of her neck as I breathed her in.

"Yes, my love. It's too bloody hard. Completely fucking impossible." I drew back and pushed her hair away from her tear-dampened face so I could kiss her mouth. "I hated every second of tonight." I kissed her again, my tongue gently sliding and slipping against hers as she opened her mouth to me and moved her lips with mine.

"I was worried when you didn't answer your phone. Why didn't you?"

"I lost the stupid thing. I was so upset. I knew you'd be wondering and imagining all sorts of unspeakable things." Her eyes widened as I wiped the tears from her face with the pads of my thumbs. "You were, weren't you?" Her eyes, though still teary, narrowed in mock accusation and the corner of her mouth lifted in a small smirk.

I smiled softly at her. Brook knew me so well. "Only a little." I shrugged slightly. "I know he wants you back, and he'll be resourceful in convincing you, that's all."

She laughed softly through her tears. "He could be freaking Houdini, and he'll never take me away from you." Her lips were ghosting over mine, teasing as she spoke. "Never," she placed a kiss on my mouth, "never," she said again before another soft kiss, "never."

That was all the torture I could take as my mouth closed over hers and I pressed her back on the bed, as I began to fulfill the promise I'd made to David at dinner. To have her body naked against mine, hear my name on her lips would ease the hurt we'd both been exposed to over the course of the evening, soothe the ache in my heart.

 Our mouths were seeking each other's out in frantic play, and our hands worshiped every inch of the other as we tore the clothes away.

I was torn between my desperation to merge our bodies and my desire to savor every touch and kiss, her skin like sweltering silk beneath my fingers, I wanted to touch and taste every inch of her. I raised her arms to slide her shirt up and off her luscious little form and my mouth moved to the curve of her neck and my hands closed on her hips to push her back and down on the bed.

Her legs parted for me and her arms around my back pulled me down between them. It felt delicious as her little hands worked their way under my shirt and she pushed it up and off of my body. I still had on my jeans, but only her white lace panties stood between me, and my glorious prize. My hand found the moist heat between her legs.

"Uhhhh..." Her hips bucked up to my hand and I could feel the blood surge to swell my own body even more. I was aching, straining until I was grinding against her.

"Oh, Brook, babe you feel so good. I needed this, honey." Her hands tried to free me from my pants as our mouths clung to each other and then her hot little mouth was dragging across my jaw and down my neck as she kissed and sucked my skin into her mouth. "Tonight was torture." I groaned, and then gasped, as her hands closed around my dick and she pressed and pulled with firm pressure.

I rolled over so I was on the bottom and her mouth continued to drive me insane, her hot little tongue licking its way down to my nipple where she flicked and teased in time with the movements of her hand on my cock. I felt her breath on my abdomen moving lower, licking down the trail of hair that led her lower. My head fell back and my hands were seeking to touch her flesh but it was getting further and further out of my reach.

"Brook, I need to touch you," I murmured softly.

Her head came up as her blue eyes burned into mine, and her hands moved to my jeans. I lifted my hips as she peeled them away from my body. Seeing her bare breasts heaving, her nipples erect and that sexy little piece of white lace wrapped around her gorgeous hips combined with what I knew she wanted to do almost made me explode. Her forehead came to rest on my stomach below my navel as her hot breath rushed over my skin. I felt my dick twitch in response. "Just lay back. I want to taste you. I want you to come in my mouth."

"You don't have to do that to prove you love me. Uhhhhh..." My breath left my body in a huge rush and my hands reached above me to grab onto the headboard as I watched her mouth close over the head of my dick. My eyes rolled back in my head while her tongue teased around the rim and she grasped the base with her hand. Her other hand raked down my chest, over my hips and thigh, her nails causing goose bumps to rise on my skin as my hips thrust forward. She took me in until I could feel the back of her throat; it was almost more than I could bear. Jesus, it was absolutely amazing; Heaven on earth.

"Brook... Brook... Brook... Oh, God, Brook... " She had me panting her name aloud as I felt my balls tighten. She sucked with her mouth and moved her hand up and down in unison as the other closed gently around my sack to pull it from my body slightly and when she put pressure on the skin below it, it was like nothing I'd ever felt. My body tensed at the immense building and I knew it was going to take me down like I'd never been before.

My heart felt as if it would fly from my body as she took me over the edge and I burst in her mouth. "Brook. I... fucking love you... so much." My words broke as my body shook with spasm after spasm as I continued to spurt in her mouth. She took it all, swallowing and sucking until my muscles stopped jerking and I fell back completely spent.

The second her mouth began kissing up my body, I sat up and pulled her to me. My hands going into her hair, I kissed her mouth and tasted myself on her tongue. My mouth was wild on hers, sucking her tongue deep into my mouth. I'd just come hard and yet it would never be enough. I wanted more. More than anything, I wanted to give to her what she'd just given me.

"Shit, that was incredible. Why are you so good to me?" I whispered on her mouth, that glorious, beautiful mouth.

"Its simple. You mean more to me than anything. You're everything." I rested my forehead against hers while I regained my breath and her hands went lovingly into my hair, stroking as she kissed along my jaw. "And, I want to be everything to you, too."

My arms closed around her as I hugged her close and once again emotion overwhelmed me. My throat got thick and a steel band wound around my chest. How could this delicate woman bring me to such earthshaking ecstasy, mind blowing physical release and flood me with so much love that I felt I could drown in it?

I drew back to look into her beautiful eyes, eyes that could drown me and at the same time burn me alive. I pushed her hair back from her face. It was so soft as I continued to stroke it and my other hand cupped her face.

"You *are* everything, Brook. I was dying tonight. Even knowing that we'd be together like this; I hated him touching you at all. I can't stand it. God help me, I find myself wishing no one had ever touched before me." Her eyes softened and welled with tears and her arms slid up around my neck and she brushed her nose against mine as she spoke. Her voice was like wine and sugar, so sweet it left me drunk in the way it melted around me.

"Cade." My name came out like an ache. "No one ever has *ever* touched me like you have. You make me feel like I've never felt, and I love you more than anyone has ever loved anyone, ever. I'll remember every touch for the rest of my life will be from you. Your hands, your mouth, your body are all that exist for me. There was no one before us. Not like this."

Tears fell from my eyes as I brought my mouth back to hers like a starving man, and she responded to me in every way I needed her to. Every time I was sure that I couldn't love her more, she brought more out of me. I knew what she meant about her love spilling over in her tears, because I was right there with her.

"Brook," I gasped as I buried my face into her neck and kissed her over and over. "I can't let go... I'll never be able to let go."

I silently thanked God for her as my hands moved over her body and brought her to life underneath me. Giving and taking our mouths sucked more and more love from each other, and it was so amazing.

"I'll die if you do," she cried against my mouth. "Cade, I'll die."

We made love until the sun came up, and fell into an exhausted sleep wrapped in each other's arms stated, satisfied and enveloped in the deluge of what we felt for each other. My heart was so full of her I couldn't take anymore, and I felt safe in her love.

Chapter 21
Everything

Brooklyn

"YES, I KNOW my dad and brother are coming."

I was beginning to sound exasperated, but this whole bullshit situation was wearing thin. I understood David's frustration, and I felt bad about it, but it didn't change anything.

"Brook, you'll make me look like a moron if I'm not with you for your birthday. Is that what you're trying to do?"

"No. That's not it, but things are different now and you were just up here last weekend. No one is going to think anything of it if you're not here tonight."

"So, that's it, then. Things are different and so you throw me out with the trash." It was more of a statement than a question and my heart felt heavy. I cared about David, but he'd become like a good friend or older brother. "All the years don't matter?" The pain in his voice was intense. "I get it. So, how will I get your present to you?"

I sighed, trying to figure out what to say. I couldn't accept a gift from David under the circumstances. It just seemed wrong.

"Please don't get me anything. The whole situation is messed up, David. I'll always love you as a good friend and I hate that you're hurting, but my life is different now. It's been months and I was hoping that it was getting easier for you by now. You've certainly led me to believe you're doing well." I was desperate to make him understand without hurting him further. "I mean, why don't you go out with friends? Go to a club or something. Wouldn't that be more fun than dragging your ass all the way to Vancouver just for a dinner?"

"Oh, I see," he let out a huge push of air into the phone. "I'm supposed to just find someone else to amuse myself with? Is that all I was to you?"

My heart dropped. "No, I don't think you see at all. I can't help what happened. I didn't choose it. I'd never choose to hurt anyone, especially not you, David. *Jesus.*" I ran a hand through my hair in frustration.

"Wendy called. She said she wasn't invited either. Are you going to let a guy come between you and your friends? I mean, I understand that I have no value, but you've been friends with her a long time," he said in sarcastic disgust.

"Did she tell you *why*? Didn't you see the story all over the place?" I was finally getting pissed. "After the little façade last weekend, she made it look like she'd spent the night with Cade again. She blew off her flight when she was expected in L.A. after they were photographed together the night before. She's a fame-whoring bitch. We've just had enough of the bullshit!" I sounded harsh, even to myself.

"Oh, you've had enough? How do you think I feel? You know I still love you and yet I have to come up there and watch you with him," his voice was increasing in volume and I knew the tone well.

"No. You absolutely do *not*. You don't see me with Cade; it's him who has to see me with you. Stop trying to act so injured. You're getting paid to do this. You didn't have to agree." I looked at the clock and realized I was going to be late to the set. I didn't want to have this conversation with David on the way down to the car, so I had to get this over with.

"Well, maybe I don't want to do it anymore!" He was yelling through the phone and it startled me.

"Then don't, David! *Don't.* I don't want you to anyway. I'm tired of everyone getting hurt and Cade is so done with it. We just want to be together. That's all." My eyebrows rose in exasperation as I smashed my feet into my Chuck's and grabbed my leather jacket.

"Thanks a lot, Brook."

Ugh! I groaned silently.

"I'm very sorry! How many damn times do I have to say it? It's my birthday and I'd like to spend it without unnecessary tension. I can't do that if you and Cade are both there, and I need him to be with me. I had to finally choose, David. I had to follow my heart."

The phone went dead as he hung up abruptly.

Oh well.

I was sad someone I cared about was hurt because of me, but I knew who I couldn't live without.

***

AFTER I WENT to the set, the day passed in a happy blur. Cade and I had some scenes with Ethan, Jennifer and Dawson, and Wendy. Despite Wendy's presence, the mood was pretty lighthearted. It was my birthday and I wasn't going to let her screw it up. I glanced at

Cade, who was a few yards away talking with Martin. It was hard to believe we'd known each other for eighteen months and this was the second birthday I'd spent with him.

The cast and crew threw a little mini-party for me over the lunch break and it was fun to have them all celebrating with me. One of the production assistants gave me a bouquet of roses. He'd been nice and very helpful during filming, and it was evident he had a slight crush. Martin shook his head with a knowing smile and Cade winked at me. I bit my lip to stifle the grin that wanted to spread across my face.

"Thank you, Mark. You're very sweet," I hugged the young man; careful not to crush the flowers.

Cade faded back, but I always felt his eyes on me, always watching. During lunch, Mark came to sit next to me and at that point, so did Cade.

Uh oh. I smiled to myself. This was flattering and I was anxious to be near Cade and wondered how he would react to the other guy's attentiveness.

Mark made small talk during lunch and Cade just sat across from me smirking as he ate. He didn't say a damn thing.

"Brook, do you have big plans tonight? It must be hard to go out without being mobbed."

"Um... I am going out. My brother and father will be here, and we're going out. Some of the cast will tag along as well," my eyes ricocheted off of Cade's before returning to Mark's face. I offered a gentle smile, knowing he was hoping for an invitation.

"Oh. That sounds like fun."

"Yes, it will be," Cade finally interjected. I shot him a look but he only grinned wider and forked in a mouth full of food.

The poor kid got so flushed he excused himself only seconds later.

He must have been intimidated as hell. The blue eyes across the table never wavered from mine as Mark said goodbye and left.

"What?" I asked as Cade continued to stare.

"You weren't just flirting with that poor unsuspecting lad, were you?" I knew he was teasing by the glint in his eyes and the smile on his lips.

"Yeah, I guess I was." I wanted to reach out and touch him so much but I had to be satisfied with a smile.

"Yes, you definitely were. Are you going to break his heart?" He laughed and I shook my head, but I was trying not to smile. It delighted me that even though he wasn't angry, he was the tiniest bit jealous of the young production assistant.

"You're very happy today, Brook. I like the way it looks on you." His velvet voice washed over me like a caress. That voice was my undoing and I felt my face flush. As intimate as the two of us had become, he could still make me blush.

We were alone. The others who joined us for lunch had filtered away, allowing me to say what I wanted. "I am. Very. I'm looking forward to tonight when Nate and Dad come in. I haven't seen my dad in several weeks, and I do have the most beautiful boyfriend in the world to make love with me all night."

"Hmmph," Cade let out his breath and ran his fingers through his hair. "All night? I think I'll need a nap first," he laughed out loud.

"You're gonna get in trouble for messing your hair up. Sally will have your ass."

Cade rolled his eyes. "I'll take my chances. What does your dad usually do for your birthday?"

"He always gives me cash, but this year maybe I should be giving him some instead." I giggled at the absurdity of it, but it was true. The first film had done well and we'd be given a better salary on the second installment. "Denise and Jeanne were right to negotiate our contracts together. They did an amazing job, didn't they?"

"Yes, but what will I do with more money? Who needs it?" He shrugged carelessly. He was hugely famous and he didn't care or act the part. He was real and down-to-earth, and it was one of the things I loved most about him. .

"I know. But think of it this way, the more they get for us, the more they get and it's fun, isn't it? I don't care about stuff either, but it's the principal. Maybe we can buy an island or something so we can sneak off by ourselves."

I reached across the table and took his hand in mine. His warm fingers closed around mine and he rubbed the top of my hand with his thumb. "Speaking of stuff," I began, "I hope you didn't get me anything for my birthday. I don't need anything but you."

"What are you saying, *Julia*? I shouldn't send you roses or get you gifts?" His American accent easily fell over his voice as he took on his role as Ryan.

I raised my eyebrow and shook my head gently. "I only need you."

He smiled softly at me and pulled my hand across the table and up to his lips. We weren't supposed to have any PDA's, but the touch of his lips on my wrist made my pulse speed up.

"Besides, Cade; material stuff doesn't mean anything. I already have my bracelet, the guitar, and the ring," my free hand went to my shirt to cover the chain that held my engagement ring under my sweater, "and, I do have you. That's something every woman in the world between the ages of twelve and sixty-five will gladly kill me for." I waggled my eyebrows playfully causing Cade to roll his eyes.

"Whatever," he dismissed in amusement.

Martin called places and we made our way back to the set. Cade released my hand, and walked behind me. I was acutely aware of the absence of his hand in mine, my skin still burning in memory of his touch.

"Happy birthday, honey. I love you." He leaned down and whispered in my ear, his hot breath washing over the skin of my cheek and neck. My heart stopped.

"See? That's perfect. All I need," I said with a smile.

***

THAT EVENING, AFTER we left the restaurant, Cade and Dawson planned on getting together for one of our jam sessions in my hotel room. Nathan and Dad were staying in the same hotel, and Daniel Mayfield, Cade's good friend, who was also in Vancouver, joined us for dinner as well.

I'd had a great time after I could stop staring at Dawson's hair. He had a pound of hair gel spiking it up, which looked odd considering his hair was pretty long. When I'd joked with him about it he said he was trying to take some of the press off of Cade and me. Either way, it looked hilarious. I'd never seen anything like it, and I never expected Dawson to do something so weird with his style.

Cade left the restaurant with Daniel and Nate after he'd signed a bunch of autographs outside on the street. Dawson took me, and my dad, with him. Cameras flashed as I walked out with his hand in mine and he threw me a wink. I answered by squeezing his hand.

"Big mistake, Dawson. First thing in the morning the gossip rags will say we're hooking up."

"Probably before the evening ends," he agreed, with a nod.

"Well, they should know I could never sleep with you tonight. Your hair would poke my eye out!" I teased him as he hunched down in the cab so his hair wouldn't crack on the ceiling.

He just laughed out loud.

Jennifer had a commitment in L.A. so she was unable to join us and Ethan had fallen ill with what we thought was food poisoning and was in his room recuperating.

Cade told Wendy she wasn't allowed to show her face at my birthday party. He was still pissed about the "overnight" innuendo of the previous weekend. Of course, she'd said she just overslept and missed her plane. I tried to give her the benefit of the doubt, but Cade was less forgiving and didn't want to deal with her at all.

He ordered wine with dinner. The drinking age in Canada was only eighteen and I could join him in a glass. I felt mellow and relaxed but not intoxicated from the effects. His eyes oozed over me all evening and heat flushed my skin with his every glance. No, I didn't want to be drunk tonight because the look in his eyes said the celebrations were only just beginning; later when we were alone would be very special. He was so beautiful and I was on fire for him. I was looking forward to the time when everyone left, but I wasn't going to deny that the time we spent playing music was always a blast.

When we all flooded into my suite, I removed my jacket and called room service to order some snacks and dessert. Cade played bartender; taking everyone's drink order acting the gracious host. I wandered over to him and leaned on the bar.

"Hey sexy," I said in a quiet voice only he could hear. He looked up from what he was doing and smiled.

"Have you had a good birthday so far, my love?" The dimples in his cheeks appeared and his eyes glowed, echoing the small smile that played on his lips.

"Mmmm... So good. I've been able to look at my sexy man all night, and he is gorgeous. What else could a girl ask?"

"I can think of a few things. It's only going to get better, babe. Is your dad going to stay long?" Cade asked suggestively. I couldn't help but smile as heat rushed through me and my body quickened at his unspoken promise.

"As long as the others, I suppose. Actually, I'm hoping he'll leave earlier so you don't have to pretend to go back to your hotel." He handed me a glass of white wine, and my fingers brushed against his as I took the glass. "What are you going to sing for me?"

"It's a surprise." Cade leaned unperceptively toward me, but I could feel every breath of space that separated us. "I want to kiss you so badly it hurts." He leaned on his folded arms; his eyes dropping to my mouth. He bit his lower lip and my heart pounded wildly and heat built between my legs. He reached out and delicately brushed his fingers along my cheekbone. Electricity shot through me at his slightest touch.

"Okay, are you going to torture me all night? Is this what you're giving me for my birthday?" I couldn't help staring hungrily at his mouth, my eyes silently begging for him to kiss me.

"Hey, you two! Let's get the party started." Dawson came over to get a beer and interrupted our private conversation. "Come on, birthday girl." He put his arm around me and led me over to the couches. I handed Nate the beer I'd brought for him, and Cade walked over to hand my dad a glass of Crown Royal.

"Dawson; I'm sorry man, I just have to ask. What the fuck were you thinking in regard to your hair tonight? I mean, if we point you into a stiff wind, you'll bloody take off!" His blue eyes sparkled with laughter.

Dawson shoved Cade's shoulder in retort. "I didn't have time to shower before dinner and so just put some water through it. Big mistake with all that glop in it." He grinned. "You're just jealous because you don't have the guts to do it."

"Right." Cade shook his head then he strapped on his guitar and took a seat across from me, and my dad.

Throughout the course of the evening they played some of Dawson's songs from his band as well as a couple Daniel and Cade were working on.

Cade wanted me to sing something too, but I was tired and I was enjoying just watching him.

He was just so flipping amazing. I would've been happy to watch him all night, and the three of them together were spectacular. I'd spent a good part of the evening sitting beside my dad and snuggling into him. I could smell the cinnamon candies and tobacco emanating from him as I rested my head on his shoulder. My eyes were starting to get heavy from the wine I'd drunk and I was on the verge of falling asleep.

"I think I'm going to head back to my room, honey. I have some calls to return and it looks like you need to go to bed."

"Huh?" I raised my head from his shoulder. "Okay, Daddy. Will you and Nate join me for breakfast before you go back to L.A. tomorrow?"

I stood up to walk him and Nathan to the door and hugged both of them goodnight.

"Sure, sugar. We'll call you in the morning. Thanks for your hospitality tonight, Cade," he said as he reached out to shake the younger man's hand.

"It was my pleasure, sir. Anytime. I'm glad you were able to join us."

"You're a very talented musician, son," he said as he patted Cade on the shoulder.

I wasn't sure if the pleasure on Cade's face was from the compliment or because my father had called him 'son'. Either way, I felt proud. My heart swelled at the realization my father was beginning to love him, too.

It felt natural to say goodnight to my family with Cade by my side.

"Happy Birthday, sis." Nathan slugged me in the shoulder lightly then ruffled my hair.

"Thanks. I'm glad you came up with Dad, Nate. I love you, *I guess,*" I teased.

After they left, Cade wrapped his arms around me and led me back to the couches where Dan and Dawson were waiting.

"Honey, I know you're tired, but we have one more song to do tonight, and then we'll call it a night, yeah?"

I put my hand around his bicep just above his elbow and rested my head on his shoulder as we sat together on the couch.

"Okay. Is this my present?" I beamed at him.

"Yes. Daniel and Dawson have graciously offered their extraordinary talent to make it as special as possible. The song is called, *Everything.*"

Everything. *How apropos,* I thought.

I'd just told him last weekend that I wanted to be everything to him, and here he was singing me a song about it. It was impossible to believe that someone so wonderful and thoughtful could really exist.

My eyes welled up, but I smiled and snuggled closer in behind him on the couch as they started to play; the three guitars blending, each one playing a different strain of the music, all of them composing the delicate strains.

Cade started to sing to me, his voice strong and clear. I listened to the lyrics that were so perfect, my hand tracing lightly up and down his back.

When the song ended, Cade put down his guitar and pulled me forward across his lap.

"That was just beautiful, thank you. I love you so much." I lifted my hand to the side of his face and stroked his jaw as his mouth descended softly on mine, tasting my lips so gently. I felt his hand at the back of my neck under the curtain of my hair as he kissed me.

"Not as much as I love you." His deep voice was low.

Dawson and Daniel were putting their guitars away and discretely getting ready to leave when Cade pulled away when we finally registered what they were doing. He stood, lifting me with him and setting me on my feet, so we could walk them to the door.

"Thank you so much for coming tonight, and for the song. It was amazing. I love you both."

Daniel hugged me and kissed my cheek. "Thanks for making my mate so happy, love," he whispered in my ear.

"He makes me happy. He's a gift." Cade's friend smiled and hugged me again.

"Hey mate, no putting the moves on my girl." Cade gave Daniel's shoulder a squeeze while I was kissing Dawson on the cheek.

"You're a good friend, even if your hair is off-the-charts bonkers." I nudged Dawson's shoulder as he passed me on his way out the door of my suite.

Dawson laughed as he went out the door with Daniel.

The minute the door closed Cade was putting one arm around my waist and the other under my knees as he lifted me and carried me to the bedroom. I snuggled into him and placed several kisses on his jaw and neck on the way.

"Baby, do you want a bath or just sleep?" I ran my hand down the back of his head and pressed my mouth to his.

"Neither. I want you."

"Honey, you're dead on your feet. We have all the nights in the world to make love, Brook. Let me just hold you tonight, hmmm?" He laid me on the bed and sat down beside me.

I ran my hands up his chest enjoying the feel of the solid muscles beneath his shirt, as he leaned over to turn on the lamp next to the bed.

Cade took both of my hands and kissed first one wrist, then the other, before getting up and peeling off his T-shirt and coming back to me.

I was tired, but I tried to fight it. The wine made me so sleepy, but I wanted to be with him so much it hurt. He quietly undressed me as I watched his face, softly kissing my shoulders, neck, and stomach as he exposed each portion of my body.

Soon, I was left with only my blue silk bikini panties on, and he pulled me up to put the shirt he'd just taken off, over my head. I smiled up at him.

"You're so sweet to me all the time. How do you do that?" I ran my hand up his bare arm and over his shoulder to the back of his neck. I pulled his mouth to mine and he gave in and slid his tongue into my mouth and kissed me hard. We hadn't really kissed like this since that morning, and he tasted amazing.

"I missed you a lot today. Even though we were together, not being able to touch you and kiss you like this... I miss it."

Cade groaned against my mouth, our breaths mingling. He sucked my lower lip into his mouth as he pulled it from mine. I felt myself moving forward to try to reclaim his mouth.

He kissed my temple, and then pulled the covers back.

"You've got an early call tomorrow and I don't want you tired, baby. You need sleep, but I do have one more surprise for you," he whispered against my mouth and then nudged my top lip with the tip of his tongue.

"Cade, if you're refusing to make love tonight, you shouldn't kiss me like that. It's mean." I put a teasing pout on my face.

"Hmmmph!" He snorted. He reached out and cupped the side of my face and then kissed the side of my mouth.

I heard the bedside drawer slide out and he was placing a small flat box wrapped in sliver paper and a burgundy ribbon in my hands.

My eyes widened as I looked at him. "But I thought you weren't getting me a gift."

"Well, I did. Open it, my love. I've been dying to give it to you for the last two weeks."

I sat up a little in bed and took his hand in mine as I looked into his eyes. They were aquamarine pools that darkened as he watched me. I could see the pleasure in his face as he waited for me to open the box.

The ribbon gave way and I peeled back the silver paper to reveal a white jeweler's box. My hand hovered over the top.

"Cade, what did you do?"

"Just open it already, Brook."

I flipped open the top of the box and nestled inside was a beautiful braided chain bracelet. The chain was very delicate in platinum or white gold and sparkled just slightly. In the center, opposite the clasp was an infinity symbol in the same metal. The sideways figure eight was filled with two pear shaped gems. A diamond on one side and an emerald on the other, one my birthstone and the other, his.

"How are you always so perfect?" My fingers ghosted over the bracelet. It was so beautiful and meant so much. I raised my eyes to his, and once again, he'd brought me to tears with his incredible love.

"Do you know what it means?" Cade asked. His hand came out to cup my face.

I nodded as a tear fell on my cheek. "It means you love me forever; that we are forever."

He took the bracelet from the box as he fastened it around my left wrist. It fit perfectly and it was gorgeous as it glistened on my skin.

"Yes. *We* are forever, Brook." He kissed the bracelet on my wrist and then removed his jeans, turned off the light and got into bed next to me. "I know you have the other one, but that's Ryan and Julia's. This is you and me."

I curled into him and his arms enfolded my body.

"I know. Thank you. You're a miracle," I whispered against his chest. "I love you so much."

His thumb was rubbing over the symbol on my wrist. I turned my face into his neck as my arm slid around him, to snuggle in close. His hand moved to my hair and I felt his breathing increase.

"Are you sure you don't want to make love tonight?" I whispered, dragging my mouth up to his.

He flipped me over instantly, his hand moving my hair off my face as his mouth hovered over mine.

"No. I'm not sure at all."

In the next second, his mouth smashed down hotly on mine and we were wildly devouring each other, his body pressing into mine and mine surging up to meet his.

No more words were spoken for the rest of the night. Both of us gave everything of ourselves to the other; endless, searching kisses, gentle caresses, breathless gasps, and passionate climaxes.

At the end of it, our hands were twined together, our breaths mingled as our mouths clung together, and our bodies were left trembling. My heart was bursting at the worshiping way he breathed my name.

"Brook. I love you. I love you."

He was everything. I was everything. We were everything.

Just—*everything*.

Chapter 22
Never Enough

Brooklyn

I WAS SO tired. The time on set was flying by and I was acutely aware. Cade and I spent every minute together that we could, and there were appearances or events that the studio arranged that included us with one or more of the others almost every night we weren't filming. I cringed. Last night it was a concert with Wendy and just her. It was an ordeal and Cade had been on the phone ripping into Denise the minute we realized it. We were used to the routine of not touching and keeping our relationship quiet, but last night was brutal. I tried to be civil and maintain the illusion of our friendship, while Cade, on the other hand; ignored her completely.

I'd just left Cade sleeping in my bed, and was on my way to meet Noah in the lobby to take us to set. We had a few retakes to do today. I wondered if the lack of sleep would affect my ability to work today.

After the late night, Cade didn't try to make love to me and we snuggled all night. My body reacted automatically to his nearness and my mind was racing about his desire to confront the studio about their policies, so my mind wouldn't let me sleep. I probably didn't fall asleep until 3:30, and I had to be up at 5:15. I blinked my eyes. They were dry and burned.

Noah was waiting in the seating area of the lobby looking totally spry and wide- eyed, dressed in jeans and a brown T-shirt.

"Hey, Brook. Are you feeling all right? You look..." He shrugged and frowned.

"Extremely tired. Cade and I went to a concert last night with Wendy and I didn't get enough sleep. Stupid me, I should have stayed in and gone to bed early."

"But the studio is the studio," Noah began and his mouth twisted wryly. "Bastards."

I rolled my eyes and nodded. "Yeah," I agreed, lowering my head as we passed through the hotel doors out of habit.

We walked out to the cars, and due to the early hour, the fans lingering were few. We signed a few autographs, posed for photos briefly, and soon were on our way to the set of Mike's photo studio.

"Brook, do you think you and I can get some rehearsal time for the office scene? Maybe tonight? That scene shoots in two days."

I glanced at him and smiled. "Sure. If we get finished early enough today, I'd like a nap first, if that's okay? What part do you want to rehearse?"

"The whole thing. It's just you and I, and we haven't spent as much time together as I think we should. Also, we have a lot in the next movie, so we should hang out more. You spent so much time with Cade *on* the first film getting into character, I thought you'd want to do the same with me." He shrugged. "This is new to me and I worry I'll crash and burn."

"Don't worry, Noah. I feel very comfortable with you." I slugged his shoulder.

"Yeah, I know we're friends, Brook, but we have to be deeper than friends for some of the scenes, and I need to get in the zone. I'm sort of worried you won't let it happen, because of...," he suddenly stopped and looked out the window, like he was embarrassed.

"Because of?" I asked hesitantly. I wracked my brain to recall a scene where Mike Turner and Julia Abbott were more than friends and came up blank.

"Well, I've known that you and Cade had a thing going, and I assume he's not going to like you getting close with me or anyone, for that matter."

"He knows it's for the job." My brow furrowed. "If that sort of thing is necessary," I pointed out. "Cade and I will both have other films where we'll have to do close or romantic scenes with others, and well, yeah, it's uncomfortable, but we'll deal." I put my hand on his shoulder, "What are you worried about?"

"I care about both of you guys and I knew there was something strained between you when we first got to set. I didn't want to ask what was up, but it occurred to me that it might be because the last two movies have so much more interactions between you and I, that he is upset."

I sighed and shook my head. "Nah, that wasn't about you or the movie. We've got it all worked out now. Don't worry. It's all good." I leaned in and nudged him with my shoulder.

"Well, I noticed that you were so happy in Tokyo when we got there and then on the flight home you were so closed off. Did something happen there?"

Noah noticed my hesitation and so continued... "If you don't want to tell me, I'll understand."

We were just getting to the set, but I turned toward him and shook my head. He was right; we did need to be closer to film these scenes and so I decided it was okay to let him into some of my personal stuff.

"Um, it didn't happen there, but we had a fight about it during that trip. It was about something Wendy did last January. She led me to believe..."

Noah's warm brown eyes widened, "Ah. Cade didn't mess with her, did he? She's fun to hang out with, but I never know what's real and what isn't with her."

Exactly. Wendy was a consummate actress in real life as well as on film. "No, but for three months I thought he had and we weren't communicating. It was really difficult, but we're even closer now because of it."

"Well, don't go giving her any credit. I saw the gossip about her supposedly staying with him the night that David was in town, and was sort of confused by all of that. I mean, if you and Cade are together, then why has David been around?"

"Pinnacle orchestrated it. They want the illusion that I'm still with David because they're worried it will ruin box office pull if the truth gets out. Also, for another film Cade has on the docket. About Wendy spending the night with Cade—he wasn't with her that night. He was with me." I ran my hand through the long strands of my hair and managed a grin. "It's all this elaborate illusion."

We climbed out of the Navigator and walked toward the make-up trailer. The sun was just starting to turn the sky subtle shades of orange and red as it rose on the horizon. My blackberry vibrated in my pocket. I had a text from Cade. My heart swelled in my chest and I smiled.

"Cade?" Noah asked.

"Yep," I answered as I opened the message.

"Okay, see you later, then."

 I nodded as I read the message.

Lonely in this bed without you, love.
I'll be thinking about you today.
Should I come to the set later?

Since I'd committed to spending the evening with Noah, I'd need a chance to talk to Cade during the day. I sent a text right back.

You better. Or I'll punish you.

Thirty seconds later it vibrated again.

Mmmmm, that sounds kind of delicious.
Maybe I WANT to be punished?

I laughed and started typing as I sat down in the make-up chair.

I'll always give you anything you want.

"Brook, you have to keep your head up please," Sally, the make-up artist said. "Can't David talk to you later?"

I blushed and inwardly groaned. The bullshit lie was firmly in place for the crew, too.

"Sorry."

I pulled my head up and looked in the mirror as she worked. When the vibrating of my phone alerted me to Cade's response, I was itching to look at it. I had to wait ten minutes until she finished styling my hair and Mickey, her assistant, came in to finish my make-up. He was only a little older than me, well put together and very stylish, with a great sense of humor. I looked forward to seeing him again.

"Sally is so blind. David? Pffft! Yeah, right. So, Brook, do you have something to tell me today, doll? You're looking awfully tired this morning. Get a lot of exercise last night, did you?"

I rolled my eyes and shook my head. Mickey was hilarious. "It's not what you think. It's all work, work, work. Well, and a concert at the Metropole."

He shook his head as his eyes met mine in the mirror and his brows went up in consternation. "Girl, you are wasting an opportunity of a lifetime if you aren't pouncing on that luscious piece of man candy! And, it's obvious he adores you. If you don't do something about that soon I'm gonna have to seduce him *myself*." Being openly gay, he'd tried his hand at flirting with Cade on occasion, which made Cade bristle.

Mickey had me laughing and I decided to spill. Cade's intentions with Pinnacle would mean everyone would know soon, as Mickey already suspected, so fuck it.

I waved my phone in the air. "Speak of the devil. I need to return his message. Will you give me a few minutes?"

"Sure girlfriend. We bitches have to stick together," Mickey said flamboyantly with a snap of his fingers.

I chuckled as I pulled out my phone; opening Cade's latest text.

Tonight? What time will you be done?

> *I hope early, but promised Noah*
> *I would rehearse with him.*
> *Maybe around 10?*

Mickey began stuffing napkins around my collar so he wouldn't get my costume splattered while he worked on me.

After I sent my response, Mickey interjected again.

"Is he even more glorious naked? Oh my God! You have to tell me! I swear I have wild fantasies about that boy! He makes my little heart flutter and my, well... you know... grow! "

"Oh, Mickey!" I laughed. "You know I can't kiss and tell." I smiled and bit my lip as I looked at Cade's latest message.

> *Seriously 10? Can't you shelve him until tomorrow?*

> *Be nice. I already promised. I'll try to*
> *get a nap so I'll be rested for after.*
> *You up for that?*

"Listen, you lucky bitch, are you gonna let me work, or what?" Mickey complained as another one came in. "You've obviously got him all worked up. I'm so jealous!!"

> *Baby... I'm always UP for you, and I'm starving.*

"Okay, Mickey. Last one." I raised my eyebrows at him and grinned.

"Well, who am I to stand in the way of true *lust*? At least someone's getting to sample that luscious ass. Good thing I love you, honey, or I'd have to scratch your eyes out," Mickey laughed. "Are you at least getting him down here so I can ogle his beautiful ass?"

I laughed out loud and nodded, pressing send on the phone.

Mmmm... me, too. SO hungry. See you on set?

"Nope. I'm getting him down here so *I* can ogle his beautiful ass... but feel free to join in. I'm okay with sharing the view... just not the package." We were both giggling as he went to work on my face.

Mickey gasped at me, "Bitch."

I fell into a fit of giggles.

***

IT WAS LUNCH and there was still no sign of Cade, so I took out my phone to call his mother about his birthday. There was a message from Wendy waiting on the screen.

Going back to L.A. today (at Cade's request) to give you guys some space. Hoping this will show I really do want to be friends again. Call me sometime. ~Wendy

At Cade's request? I wondered what prompted that and why he hadn't mentioned it.

She must've finally realized he and I were the real deal. Still, I had some resentment that I needed to work through, but maybe in time I could forgive her and try to get some of our former friendship back. Cade and I had talked about it, so I knew he wasn't as willing to forgive her so easily. I hadn't seen much of his temper, but when I had, most of the time Wendy was involved.

After we'd been back in Vancouver, she'd started texting and calling him almost daily and that fact made me question her motives. Cade was right; we couldn't trust her. The only way to make sure she wouldn't interfere was to tell each other absolutely everything she said or did, no matter how insignificant. Communication was key. I'd learned that lesson the hard way.

I dialed Lillian in London and waited for her to answer. After a few rings, the call went to voice mail.

"Hi Lillian, it's Brook. I wanted to surprise Cade for his birthday and wondered if you and Carter could get away and come to Vancouver? Layla and Oliver are invited as well if they can make it. My treat. Please call me back so we can talk a little. I want everything to be perfect. I can't wait to talk to you. Love you."

I hung up the phone and a velvet voice spoke behind me.

"Want to tell me who it is you're in love with that isn't me?"

Shit.

I turned around quickly to find Cade only three feet away and I was wondering how much of that conversation he'd over heard.

I laughed nervously and his brows went up.

"Oh, um... that was just my mother. I haven't talked to her all week so I called... she didn't answer."

His lips pursed and I knew the wheels were cranking in his head.

"I guess you didn't hear the whole message or you wouldn't have that dumbass look on your face." I laughed and shoved him with my shoulder as I started walking back toward the set.

He laughed softly at my side.

"Besides, I know someone who, if not exactly in love with you, sure has a huge boner for you, you lucky, lucky boy!" I giggled and increased my pace.

He followed me and caught my arm. "What the fuck are you talking about, Brook?" The corners of his mouth lifted in an adorable grin and I drank in his features as the touch of his hand on my arm burned through my coat.

"Can't tell. I'm sworn to secrecy for life." But I nodded toward the make-up trailer so he'd know I was talking about Mickey.

"Bloody hell. Not *that* again. It isn't bad enough to have all the screaming girls, I have to put up with blokes as well?" We were both laughing hysterically. "Fuck me."

"Don't say that too loud, or they'll be forming a line to your left."

"Mmmm..." he teased. "Will you be at the front of the queue?"

I nodded and licked my top lip. Playing sexy games with him like this was fun.

Cade's eyes darkened and he reached a hand toward me but then dropped it as I shook my head almost imperceptibly. We both knew we had to wait until after the meeting with Pinnacle to be completely open on set. His face dropped a little so I continued to tease him.

"It must be hell to be so sexy that everyone wants you. Poor you. Mickey wants you in a bad way. He said he loves ogling your beautiful ass..." I raised my eyebrows a couple of times to put an exclamation point on it.

"I see. Have this conversation this morning, did you?"

I nodded and bit my lip coyly, "Yes, during our text fest."

"And? What did you say?" His eyes were sparkling, and he wanted to hear that I had laid my claim.

"Well, I told him he could look all he wanted, but I owned that beautiful ass... of course. What else would you expect me to do?"

"Ah, that's my girl. I'm dying to plant a huge kiss on that gorgeous mouth."

"Yeah, don't I wish?"

My phone rang and it was Lillian so I couldn't answer it. Damn. Cade was going to wonder why, but just then Mark came to get me and I'd never been happier to see him.

Saved by the production assistant.

"Brook, Martin asked me to find you. They're ready to start. Do you need anything right now?"

His face was flushed and he looked at me expectantly.

"No, thank you, Mark. I'll be right there. Cade and I just need a couple more minutes, okay?"

"Uh, yeah." His disappointment was obvious that he wouldn't get to walk me back to set, but he turned away and I turned back to Cade. He was gorgeous and my eyes looked at him adoringly.

"Much as I'd like to stay here and *ogle you* myself, honey, I've gotta go. We should only have this one scene left, but I don't know how many takes it will be."

"Looks like we both have little boys trailing after us," he nodded toward Mark's retreating figure. "You mentioned a nap. Will you get time?" He grinned at me and I knew what he was thinking.

"Well, that depends on this certain man I adore. Is he going to *let* me sleep?" I asked sheepishly.

"Of course. I'm meeting Ethan and Dawson at the gym this afternoon, just for that reason. It's so much easier to resist you when I'm not in the same room." He smiled wide as he watched me. He sobered before he continued. "I wish you hadn't agreed to play with Noah all night."

I rolled my eyes. "You're terrible. I have to sometimes; for the development of the characters. You know that. Are you seriously jealous? I know you like Noah."

"Yeah, he's a nice kid and I'm not jealous of him, but of the time, yeah, and..." He stopped and took my hand lightly in his.

"And, what?"

"It's just that rehearsing in your room all night was our thing, so I guess it bugs me a bit."

I felt my features soften and I wanted desperately to wrap my arms around him.

Yes, it was our thing; so many nights during filming, almost every night.

"I know. I think about that a lot, too. Do you want me to come to your room when I'm finished? If I invite Noah to dinner, maybe I'll be done sooner."

"Yeah, the sooner the better. I'll hang with the guys for dinner, then."

"Brook!" Martin was calling me.

"I love you," I said softly. Cade walked the rest of the way back with me, Noah was already waiting as places were called, and Mickey was there to retouch my make-up with a big-ass smile on his face.

"You delivered, girlfriend. I could just kiss you."

"Well, as you said, we bitches have to stick together," I said dryly.

"I swear if I could, I'd grow a vagina just for him," Mickey said breathlessly. "I've never wanted to be a sister so much in my entire fucking life! Why does he have to be straight, anyway?"

I burst out laughing and Cade glanced my way, his face flushed. He knew that we were talking about him and it made him visibly uncomfortable. He ran his hand through his hair and looked away.

"Jesus, Mickey. I'm going to ruin all of my make-up!" I was

laughing so hard I had tears running down my face.

***

"I'M TIRED, NOAH. We've rehearsed this enough, don't you think?" We'd worked on the photography scene for the past hour and besides, I was sensing that he was getting a little too into it.

"Um, do you think we've got it down?" He sat down slowly on my bed.

"Uh, yeah. We've got the lines nailed and I really have to get over to Cade's. I've barely seen him all day."

Noah was watching me put on my shoes and grab my jacket but he didn't make a move toward the door.

I slid my arms into the jacket and stood in front of him. "Noah?"

"I can see why Cade fell for you, Brook. You're so great. I really enjoy working with you. It's effortless."

"Noah, yeah, you're great to work with too." I felt my stomach clench; I knew where this was headed.

"It's more than that. It feels—"

"Look, please don't go there." I shook my head after I cut him off. "I think you're a terrific guy, a good friend, but that's all it is. Don't fall into the fantasy of the script. It's not real." I crossed my arms in front of me.

"I know it isn't real and I respect Cade a lot, but it doesn't change the fact that I'm feeling..."

I cut him off, "You feel hormones at getting close to a woman. It's normal, but that's it. Got it?"

He stood up and put a hand to his head as his face flushed, he was horribly embarrassed.

"I'm sorry, Brook, but isn't that how it started with Cade? I mean..."

I was at the door; I opened it and waited for Noah to precede me out.

"No, Noah. It was different with Cade. I mean, yeah, we spent a ton of time together working on the script, but we had an instant connection. I can't really explain it. It just happened."

He nodded and looked at the floor as we left the room.

"We have those scenes with Cade coming up; will he want to rehearse all three of us? I think we should. I promise I'll be completely professional."

I ran a nervous hand through my hair as we walked into the hall. "Um, I'll ask him." I averted my eyes because I just couldn't look him in the face. The last thing I wanted was this type of complication. Hopefully, Noah would see it was just the result of working so closely together. I didn't want something like this to interfere in our friendship.

"I hope you won't tell Cade about this. I don't really... Well, I don't want my stupidity to interfere with the movie. He'll be upset, won't he?"

"I don't keep secrets from him, Noah. We have so much against us that we've promised to tell each other everything, but um, I don't think he'll be upset. I think he'll understand."

Noah looked uneasy and I could see his brow drop over his eyes. He reached out and touched my arm. "How are you getting over there? I'm taking a cab, should I have it pull around in the garage to get you?"

"That's sweet, but Peter is waiting for me in the garage. We can't have someone not on the payroll doing it. Do you want to ride with me?"

"Would Cade mind?" he asked hesitantly.

"'It's just a ride, Noah. He won't mind. Come on." I reached out and pushed the button for the third floor and when the door opened, looked both ways in the hallway. Noah quickly followed me to the stairwell to the basement. I stopped at the door between the stairs and the garage to peer through the window.

A man and woman were making their way to the elevators, and the limo was waiting off to one side.

"The limo is here, but we have to wait just a minute."

After the two disappeared in the elevator I pushed open the door and ran to the limo and Noah followed me inside.

"Hey, Peter." I greeted the driver. "Noah needs a ride back to the hotel as well. You can let him out in front after you drop me in the garage, okay?" His appearance out front might actually help divert attention from my trip up to Cade's room.

"Yes, miss," Peter replied, as he pulled out of the garage. It was only a few blocks to Cade's hotel and I bolted out of the limo up the stairs to Cade's room.

I knocked softly and within seconds the door opened and I was enfolded in a pair of strong arms as I was lifted right off of the floor. My arms slid up around his neck and into his hair as his mouth took mine in a deep kiss. I gasped as his tongue parted my lips but I opened my mouth to move in unison with his.

"God, Brook, you taste so good. What took you so bloody long?"

"Shut up and kiss me," I moaned into his mouth as we continued our onslaught of each other. My hands continued to stroke through his hair as our kisses softened and he brought a hand up under the curtain of my hair to hold my head. His thumb stroked back and forth on the sensitive skin under my ear.

His arms around me felt so good, and his scent floated all around me. As he turned his face into my neck, took a deep breath, and then ghosted his lips across my cheekbone back toward my mouth. "I smell him on you," he murmured.

I froze and drew back.

"Seriously?"

His mouth placed a soft kiss on my mouth, sucking the top lip into his mouth and then moved to bite at the lower one.

"Yes. I have you memorized, Brook. I'm sorry, but I can smell him." His hand slid down the back of my head to grasp around my hair.

"Ugh, Cade. I don't want that." I pulled back and started to peel off my shirt and went into the bathroom. "I'm gonna take a shower."

"Babe, it isn't gross or anything like that, it's only that I can smell his cologne on your clothes. It's really nothing."

"Hell, yes it is. That is not what I want you to be thinking about when you're kissing me Cade. Just let me take a quick shower." I stripped off my jeans and underwear and stepped under the hot spray.

Cade was leaning against the counter of the vanity watching me, his eyes appreciative and intense.

"I need to tell you something anyway."

"Okay, as long as I can keep watching you," he said as the steam accumulated on the clear glass doors. I couldn't see his face, but I could hear the smile in his voice. "What is it, love?"

"No big deal, but we did say we'd tell each other everything from now on, so..."

"Brook. Just bloody say it."

"Well, I think Noah is developing a little crush on me. I chalk it up to raging hormones and spending time together."

Silence. He didn't say anything.

"Cade?" My stomach sank. "Did you leave?" I squeezed some shampoo out of the bottle and ran it through my hair.

"No, I'm here, honey," he answered quietly.

"What are you thinking?"

"Just that it was inevitable, I suppose. You're a beautiful girl. What happened?"

"We were doing a scene and we'd read it several times, and he just said he could see how you'd fall for me during all of our work together on *The Future of Our Past*."

"Yeah, and?"

"And, I feel like he's my little brother and I told him so. Seriously, Cade, he was totally embarrassed and more worried about how it would mess up his relationship with you if I told you, than how I would take it." I rinsed the conditioner out of my hair. "I told him you'd be cool, but that I had to tell you. So... are you cool?"

"I understand how he'd be smitten with you. I was. He's a good kid."

Relief washed over me and I smiled. "I did tell him that from the moment we met, we were hooked, and it wasn't because of the work. The work just gave us an excuse to be together."

I started when the door swung open and Cade in all his naked glory stepped into the shower with me. As always, the sight caused stirrings deep within my body and my head fell back to look into his eyes. The color was a slightly darker, smoky blue and heavily laden with desire.

"Sorry if I startled you, my love."

Cade's arms slid around me and mine automatically went around his slim waist and I kissed his chest, as the water poured over his hair and skin.

"It's okay; you can make it up to me..." I whispered against his skin and then my mouth closed around his left nipple. His fingers traced down my back and up again.

I took the soap and lathered up his skin, my hands going over his chest, back and tight abdominals. His eyes were heavy as he watched me and then his lips bent to my neck. He gasped as my lathered hands moved lower to grasp around his erection. It swelled and pulsed in my hand. He was so beautiful, rock hard, yet the skin was soft and velvety in my hands.

"Jesus, Brook. God that feels good." His hands closed around my wet hair to pull by head back so he could ravage my mouth with his. I sucked on his tongue like I was starving, and I was. I was always starving for him. No matter how much I kissed him and no matter how often his body was inside mine, it was never enough.

My hands moved up and down on his length and his moans echoed in the shower. It completely turned me on that I could bring him to this much pleasure.

"Fuck, baby. I can't... I want..." His hands came up my body under my arms until he held me around my ribs and he lifted me up against the side of the shower. My arms went around his shoulders and my legs wrapped around him. He filled me completely and he felt so huge as he stretched me around him.

"God, Cade. You feel so incredible." He pushed open the shower door as I wound around his body and walked into the bedroom and to the bed. The lights were low and his eyes intent on my face as he lowered us both to the bed.

His arms came down on both sides of my head as his pelvis began moving into mine, each thrust long and deep. His nose nuzzled into mine and his hot breath rushed over my cheek as he placed several open mouthed kisses along my cheekbone. It was so sweet and soft, so tender and my heart felt like it would burst.

"Oh, Brook. I could make love to you forever."

"That works for me," I whispered against his mouth before our tongues mated, thrusting into each other's mouths like his body was thrusting into mine. Our kisses deepened and slowed and the movements of our hips did the same as the sensations started to build, slowly, but I could tell the slow build would bring a strong and amazing release.

I didn't want him to stop kissing me. I didn't want him to stop moving within my body as I fought the orgasm I knew was inevitable. "Cade, I want this to last... I don't want to stop... oh God," I breathed against the skin of his neck, and then sucked his skin into my mouth as I felt my body begin to quiver and tremble around him. "Uhhhh, Cade, I can't..." My arms tightened around him and my hands tugged his hair to bring his mouth toward mine.

"Let it go, baby. Let it go. Brook..." He brought those beautiful, perfect lips back to mine as he sucked and teased my mouth into a matching response, our tongues sliding back and forth with each other's. I was gasping against his mouth as I came and he tensed and groaned as he exploded inside me. "Oh, baby. I love you." He was panting, his breath coming in uneven gasps.

Maybe two minutes passed and then his mouth was moving down my neck as he slid out of me and moved down my body. His mouth closed over one of my nipples to suck and tease while his fingers moved down between my legs to part the flesh that was still throbbing from the effects of his lovemaking.

"Cade... baby, you don't have to..." I gasped as his fingers softly nudged the sensitive bundle of nerves at the core of my very being.

"Uhhh... ummm."

"Let me show you how much I love you. You said you didn't want it to stop and it's not going to; not until I've worshiped you until you can't take anymore. Not until you beg me to stop, not until I'm sure you know just how much I love you. Because I do... I do, Brook."

My head fell back and my body trembled beneath his hands and mouth. Once again he amazed me in the unselfishness of his love.

Amazing, incredible, beautiful, sexy, wonderful... he was all these things and so much more, and I was overwhelmed... *again.*

Chapter 23
Absence Makes the Heart Grow Frantic

Brooklyn

I LAY ON the bed in my hotel room staring at the ceiling for the past two hours since Cade left. This was it... he was on his way to L.A. to read with the actresses up for the female lead in his next film, *Only Us*. I fucking hated the title because it told the story of what the film would require of Cade.

"Hmmph," I let out my breath as I twirled my hair around my finger. I knew he'd have to kiss them and I kept hearing his voice in my head... "It's only my job." I knew it was his job, but shit, it still made my stomach clench.

If that wasn't bad enough, the meeting with Pinnacle was scheduled for this morning and I'd be biting my fingernails to the bone until Cade called me later tonight to tell me how it went. I had the damn weekend off and was stuck up here alone. I'd thought about calling Nathan to ask him to fly up and keep me company, but Noah was here and Cade would be back Monday morning.

Two days.

Surely I could keep myself occupied for two days. I could re-read *A Love Like This* if nothing else. The weather was chilly, but nice. If those damn paparazzi would lay-off, I could go walking or shopping. Jennifer was still here because there was a cast party and some of the new actors would be on set next week. It didn't make sense for her to leave either. Maybe she and I could go out and do something.

My phone rang on the bedside table and I grabbed it. It was Lillian.

"Hey Lillian! Did you talk to Carter, Layla, and Olivier about Cade's birthday?"

"Hi honey. Yes, Carter and I would be delighted to come, but Layla is going to Switzerland with a friend and Oliver has to work. It's so nice of you to invite us, Brook."

"Oh, not at all. I know it would mean the world to Cade to have you here. He's so difficult to buy gifts for. I have such a hard time figuring it out, and this will be perfect." I was smiling, even though Lillian couldn't see me face.

"Brook, the Christmas gift, the diary, is so precious to him. He takes it with him everywhere in his guitar case. Did you know that?"

My voice got quiet. "Yes. I catch him reading it sometimes when he thinks I'm not watching."

"During those six weeks when he came back to London at the first of the year, he was so despondent, he'd barely talked to any of us. Layla mentioned he always held it in his hands when she went to visit him at his flat."

"Yes... he told me. About that, Lillian; I'm very sorry that happened. I'm not sure how much Cade's told you..."

"Not that much dear. Just that you weren't talking to him and that he didn't know why. He was very hurt, we barely saw him. He wouldn't come over or go out with his mates. Layla was the only one who saw him, more than once or twice, during those weeks." She paused for a couple of seconds. "Brook, it's none of our business and we trust Cade to work out his own life, but we're glad you've gotten back together. He loves you very much. Sometimes, I think more than he should."

I felt my throat tighten and tears well in my eyes. I struggled to speak, so I cleared my throat.

"Uhhhhhggghh. Um, it was difficult for me as well, but I hope you know I love him more than anything in the world. I'd never intentionally hurt him. The stuff we deal with is crazy. It's brutal, but we're doing a better job of communicating and keeping perspective now, so I don't think we'll have a misunderstanding like that again. I don't want to have secrets from Cade or from you, Lillian. I went to his apartment to surprise him when I was supposed to be in New York for an audition, and another woman answered the door without any clothes on."

"Oh my God!" Lillian gasped.

I didn't want her to get the wrong impression so I rushed on.

"Yes, that's how I took it too, but the fact was, Cade wasn't even there. I was so hurt that I just closed down without talking to him. That was a mistake, and I should have listened to him. It's all been straightened out now."

"He didn't stray did he? I can't imagine he'd risk—" Her voice was questioning.

"No." I shook my head. "And if I weren't such an idiot, I'd have realized. I was just too scared to know for sure; if that makes any sense? My heart was broken, and I was afraid knowing details would make the pain worse."

"You poor dear. I'm sorry, Brook. Surely, I'd have thought the same thing."

"Well, I appreciate your understanding and that you can forgive me for causing Cade that kind of pain. At the time, I just couldn't get beyond my own."

Lillian sighed on the other end of the phone. "Well, talking to him now, he's very happy and the entire family loves you. We're delighted for you both."

"Lillian, honestly, I'd love him regardless if he slept with someone else. I'd already decided I couldn't be without him, either way."

"Well, don't say that, dear. We women shouldn't give men permission to cheat just because they know we won't leave them," she said sardonically. "Even my son."

I laughed at her expression. "You're right, but I know he won't do that. I'm positive of it now."

"Darling, I'm very proud of you both. You're so mature for your years. Now, about the birthday; Caden doesn't know we're coming, does he?"

"No. I thought it would be fun if we walked into the restaurant and you were there. I've asked another of our friends to plan the party because we have to keep my involvement a secret from the public."

"Oh? Is it a friend of Cade's?"

"Yeah, Ethan Ranfeld. He's already back in L.A., but he agreed to make the arrangements. Most of the actors will be off set by then, but he's a great to help me, even though he won't be able to attend."

"Will the party be a large one?"

"No, only us, a couple of the actors, and a few of the crew members that Cade is good friends with. Probably our director, and Cade's production assistant will be there, too. Will you be able to stay for a few days? Maybe you can come to set and watch us work one day?

Cade would like that."

"I'd love that dear. I'm sure my husband would as well, and I'll plan on it. I was going to make our plane reservations today."

The phone in the room started to ring. "My other phone is ringing, Lillian, so email me the details of your trip and I'll arrange for the boys to pick you up and get you a room in Cade's hotel. I'm really looking forward to seeing you!! I have to run. Tell the others I said hello. I love you!"

"Love you too, darling. Take care of yourself."

I scrambled to grab the other phone.

"Hello?"

"Hey good looking, wanna come out and play?"

"Uh...," I recognized the voice and was taken off guard again. I felt my face flush red hot.

"Brook? Are you there? It's a beautiful day! Let's go out," David said. I'd be damned if he wasn't too happy about it.

Okay, so they didn't just do this to me again!

"Where are you?" I was afraid of the answer.

"In the lobby," he paused at my gasp. "No big deal, this is more because I miss you than it is for Pinnacle. I came to make peace. Let's just hang as friends, if it makes you feel better. They've got Noah out canoodling with some other actress from a new movie he signed with. It's all publicity for the suits, but I really did want to see you."

"Uh, well...," I sank down on the bed. "You've got to let me know in advance, David! This causes a shit storm for me when you just show up unannounced. I thought we talked about this!"

"Look, I know Mr. Wonderful is MIA today, so I thought it would be less uncomfortable and we could just have fun like we've done a million times, okay?"

I looked at my watch. It was 10:30 and Cade would be in his meeting with the studio executives.

Fuck! Fuck! Fuck!

"David! How many people have seen you? Have you been photographed?"

"Who cares?" My heart dropped like a stone to my stomach at his words. "Let's just have some fun. We can go to lunch and walk around downtown, maybe go for a bike ride or something?"

My brain was racing. Maybe if I went along with him, it would be the last of David's obligations to the studio and I'd be free and clear. The timing was good because Cade was having it out with the producers at this very moment.

I was uncertain but due to circumstances I couldn't get in touch with Cade. It was impossible to call Jeanne or Joel because they were in the same damn meeting! Maybe Joel would read a text...

"It seems pretty convenient that you show up right when Cade leaves. You must have passed each other in the air. You're idea or the studio's?" My eyebrows rose and I sighed loudly.

David hesitated. "Um, I think they must have planned it that way, but does it really matter? What's he doing down there anyway?"

I was confused because David seemed unconcerned and really laid back.

Was it only a few weeks ago that he was confronting Cade over dinner?

Exasperation tightened my chest and my lips thinned in annoyance. "Do you really give a rat's ass what he's doing down there?"

"Nope," David answered in amusement. "Just making conversation. So meet me down here in twenty minutes. Does that give you enough time?"

"David... I don't know," I replied hesitantly.

How would Cade take it? Even if I didn't hate it myself, I wasn't looking forward to his reaction.

"Brook, come on. Do you want to be my fucking friend or *not*?"

"Ugh! Okay, but if you screw me on this, David, I'll never forgive you."

Caden

I HAD MY first series of read-throughs for my next film later in the afternoon and again the next morning, but this meeting with Pinnacle was the most important reason for this trip. Maybe, just maybe, this would be the end of the bloody bullshit.

Jeanne, Denise and Joel were waiting in the lobby of the Pinnacle headquarters when the limousine delivered me directly from the airport. They all looked extremely polished; all business, with brief cases in hand, and I was grateful to have such an eloquent and professional team behind me.

I hugged Jeanne and Denise, then shook Joel's hand firmly.

"Thank you all for being here."

Joel smoothed down the front of his shirt and tie. "Cade, I'm here to advise you that the contracts are still binding and the studio can retaliate with the repayment of fees and keeping you off future projects. Please be aware of the consequences before going in there. Brook only has one other movie on her docket and she is more vulnerable than you. Remember that," he warned.

"I know." Maybe this wouldn't be as cut and dried as I thought, but something had to change. "I'm not that worried at this point," I said, with more confidence than I felt. I didn't care about my career, but hers was just getting started. "We're mid-series, and their hands are as tied as ours."

He shook his head and Jeanne spoke up.

"Joel, I don't think they'll fire Cade or Brook on any of their new projects because the production staff has already been compiled, and pre-production has started. They'll lose a lot of cash if they try to recast at this point."

"*And*, as Cade said, they absolutely need the two of them for the rest of the series," Denise said as she laced her arm through mine. "Let's not forget that little point. I agree; we have more clout than they give us credit for. They're hoping we don't realize it, but they're in for a surprise. Let's go kick some ass, shall we?" She smiled up at me as we walked into the elevator.

When we arrived on the floor that housed the main office suite, we waited for the pretty young receptionist to show us into the conference room. "Can I get you any refreshments while you're waiting?" she asked.

"I'd love some coffee with cream," I replied, my early morning was catching up to me, and I wanted to be as alert as possible.

Jeanne and Denise also requested coffee, but Joel shook his head. "Nothing for me, thank you." His tone was all business.

The Pinnacle team entered the conference room a few minutes after us: two women and three men. Three of them were probably lawyers, with the marketing manager and one of the three producers of the *Remembrance* series. I only recognized Todd, the producer, and Nancy, the marketing manager. I'd met Todd a couple of times, but I only knew Nancy from a picture that was included in some media materials I'd received post production for a press tour.

After the introductions were made, one of their lawyers pulled out a chair and motioned for all of us to sit down. After we were seated, they starred at us blandly. Finally, Nancy spoke.

"Cade, this is your meeting. You called it, so what's it about? Also, why are Joel and Jeanne here? Are you changing management? We only expected Denise."

I glanced at Jeanne, and she nodded for me to continue.

"Yes, I called it, but it is for *both* Brook and me. Jeanne and Joel are here to represent her interests."

Nancy's face tightened.

Yes, it's heavier than you anticipated, I thought. I could see them start to fidget and it calmed my nerves.

"So?" Todd started. "Negotiations are closed on the money. You two have gotten a nice fee, plus a percentage of the take, so that's it for us."

I huffed. *Idiot.*

"We aren't here about money; it's something entirely different. I'm sure you're aware that Brook and I are involved. Our relationship is the focus of this meeting, and I expect to get it over with quickly," I said, and watched them all stiffen, especially Todd and Nancy.

Nancy was a pretty woman; late thirties, blonde hair and thin. "Yes, well you're in violation of your contracts and you've already done enough damage as it is. Don't you know what kind of effect this could have on the film's box office receipts?" she railed at me. "That affects you as well. You're each getting five percent of the take."

"Yes, I know, but box office is your problem, not mine. We're aware of your concerns and they are duly noted. Our managers and attorneys have clarified your reasoning and while we understand, we feel the contracts are in violation of our personal rights," I put up my hand to stop Todd when he opened his mouth to speak.

"We have no intention of going public with the relationship yet, but we don't want to sneak around between hotels anymore," I continued. "If you feel it necessary to waste money by getting each of us our own room, then so be it, but they will be at the same property going forward. We want to be together and we're sick of the hassle."

"During the promotion of the movies we need you on lock-down. Sorry Cade, but the focus needs to be on the movies, not you and Brook. It's my job to build box office and that's what I will damn well do!" Nancy paced back and forth across the room while she spoke.

I ran my hand through my hair impatiently as I looked across the table, and then up at her. No doubt she was paid on results. I felt Jeanne move in closer and lean forward slightly. She folded her hands on top of the table and smiled at them coldly. Nancy's returning smile was stiff.

"Maybe we can come up with a compromise. Surely you remember what it's like to be young and in love? Brook and Cade are professionals and will deliver the goods, but they deserve the right to be together without all of this corporate bullshit, don't you agree?" Jeanne asked.

"Cade, I get it. Brook is a hot little number," Todd put in. Anger flashed and heat began to rise in my face.

"Just bloody stop right there! This is *not* about shagging her, and I'm insulted that you would imply it is. We are *in love* with each other, and while we understand the logic behind the promotional rules and Pinnacle being worried a break up will ruin box office, we want to be together. I can promise you, we won't break up. But," I started to raise my voice, "*if* that were to happen, Brook and I would be the model of professionalism and we would complete our obligations without interruption. You have my word."

"We can take your fee, cancel your upcoming films. You could be ruined. Don't fuck with us, young man," Todd retorted.

I just looked at him and laughed. "Really? You'll ruin *us*? You need us far more than we need you and that's a bloody fact. Yes, you could cancel the two movies we've signed with you, but we could walk on the rest of this series*!* Everyone sitting at this table bloody well knows that the series is the cash cow pulling the rest of your little projects along. If you want to grow so you can finally compete with the big production houses, you can't dick around with current success."

My face was strained and I could feel the muscles working in my jaw, but my voice was resolute. I might be young, but I'd been working in the business for years and I knew how shit worked.

"Cade," Denise cautioned and placed a hand on my arm; I was so bloody pissed by this point, I didn't give a damn.

"Do you think the fans will come see the films if you tried to recast Ryan and Julia? Do you think the author of the books will agree?" I crossed my arms over my chest, leaned back in my chair and waited for them to answer. They all bristled in their seats so I continued with a shake of my head. "No. We all know the answer is clear. So, I think you've got it backwards. Don't *fuck* with *us*."

Silence. No one spoke for a good minute and a half. I took a deep breath and continued.

"The solution is simple," I stopped when my phone vibrated in my pocket. I pulled it out and opened Brook's message. "Excuse me."

Pinnacle sent David up here, and it's the same song and
dance as before. The press already had him,
so I have to go out for a bit.
Sorry, I didn't know until my phone rang at 10:30 this AM.
Counting on you to give those fuckers what for. Love you.

I sighed again, disgusted with the people sitting across the table from me.

Bloody hell! This wasn't happening anymore, either. I felt my blood pressure rise.

"Either you help us be together quietly or we'll be together *loudly*. You do have a choice, but those are your only options. I guarantee we will both walk off of these films without a backward glance. We're talented enough to make a living without the backing of Pinnacle or the *Remembrance* franchise, and frankly, we don't give a flying fuck about money or fame. We only want each other. We've had too much grief as it is, and we're bloody done."

Nancy was less forceful when she answered. "Cade, you're being unreasonable. Think of the risks you're taking. The entire world believes that Brook is with David, so she'll be painted as a two-timing whore who steps out on her boyfriend; and the press will position her as falling for every new co-star she is cast with going forward. You must think of her."

"Oh, I *am* thinking of her. This bullshit has cost us a great deal and we're tired. It's none of your business so I'm not going into it in detail, but I'm in love with this girl and she is the only thing that matters. You're making more money off of me than I'm making off of you. Remember that." They all stared at me with their mouths open and if I wasn't so angry, the situation might have been funny.

Joel pulled out his phone to check his messages, and I watched as his mouth tightened.

"My client just informed me that you forced David Landis on her again this weekend. I thought we'd already had these discussions? This is absolutely the last time he will show his face in Vancouver unless she expressly invites him, is that clear?"

Todd stood up and went to the side bar to refill his coffee. "We're under contract with him, and if we have to pay him then he's going to fulfill the contract."

"Whatever your contract is with David, it doesn't confine my client. She is under no obligation to acquiesce. I'm prepared to take this to court if need be. It's a violation of her civil rights."

Jeanne stepped in. "So what, Joel? David is up in Vancouver? Now?" I could see it in her face how pissed she was. Joel just nodded and threw his phone down on the table.

I never realized how jealous and possessive I was until I was faced with that little wanker so bloody often.

"I want him gone for good, or I'm done. No more negotiation," I growled through clenched teeth. Jeanne shot me a glance before she sat back and addressed the Pinnacle team.

"In the best interest of my client's reputation, we'll dance your little dance a little while longer..." I started to sit up, and she put a hand on my arm, "that is *publically*, because we'll need time to feasibly solidify a break-up before Cade and Brook can be a couple out in the open. Keep in mind that this charade is necessary only because of the one Pinnacle has already created. It's very unfair to these two young people. Brook has been apart from David for months, yet she is forced into uncomfortable situations and she's been a good sport, but enough is enough."

She tented her hands in front of her on the table, "You will make it easier for Caden and Brook to see each other in private. No more separate hotels and an increase in security to ensure their privacy. Do what you want as far as promoting the films as long as it doesn't malign either of their characters or hurt future opportunities. And no more fake boyfriend visits."

"But for *Don't Forget To Remember Me* we have to foster other relationships!"

"You're delusional. Do you think that the fans want to see 'Julia' appearing with other men in the cast? Get real. No, they're going to that film to see if Julia remembers Ryan. Did you even read the story that you're trying so hard to promote?" Denise rolled her eyes and took a drink from her cup. "Jesus, you people amaze me."

"Okay," I interrupted, "Bottom line is; we'll compromise. We'll help you promote the subsequent films, as you ask, but no more appearances from Landis, no more Wendy being shoved down my throat. No more separate hotels, and we will be going out in public together on occasion. Most of all, I want some freedom with Brook when we go to the Italian Film Festival. She hasn't been to Italy and I want to take her to some of my favorite places." The festival was just after the end of filming the second movie, and Brook and I would be separated for months afterward while we worked on other projects.

"We won't tolerate public appearances, Cade," Todd stood and walked around the table, "at least, not ones we don't arrange and script."

"Todd, didn't you hear me? You're not in a position to tell us what to do. We'll be discreet, but we won't be prisoners any longer. We've got two bloody years left on this series, and we aren't going to be caged up in our hotels the entire time," I challenged, meeting his eyes without flinching.

Fucking weasel.

"We can still walk off these films if that is what we have to do."

Nancy sighed heavily. "You're scheduled for Cannes in May, before Italy. Can we compromise so the whole thing isn't screwed?" she asked as she turned to her cohorts. The men didn't look happy, but they nodded at Nancy before she looked back toward the four of us.

"I'll authorize Brook to move into your hotel the weekend you are away in France; you still do your appearances there without her, and we keep the relationship as private as possible until *A Love Like This* is released?"

"What about Italy? I'm leaving for New York right after that, and we need time together there."

"Yeah, we'll put you in the same hotel there too, but no public PDA's. No holding hands, kissing, or even walking arm in arm. Not yet."

"I have one other concern regarding the promotion of future films that do not include Brook," I said as my eyes narrowed.

"Here we go! You've already got us hanging by the balls!" Todd was exasperated and I laughed at his expression. "You realize that you'll need to promote with whoever is cast as your romantic lead, so we *will* expect you to go out in public with her." My next film began pre-production in a couple of months and as of yet, the actress hadn't been cast.

I shook my head at the ridiculousness of the situation. "Do you realize how absurd you sound? I can't be seen in public with Brook because she's my co-star, but I *must* be seen in public with this yet-to-be-named co-star? Ridiculous." I'd had enough and rose from my chair. "I'm going to be late for my bloody readings... Um, that is, if I'm still employed on these films?"

I could see them all clenching and stiffening. I waited until Todd nodded and I felt my lips quirk in a grin.

What were they going to do? Take away my bloody birthday? I felt like laughing out loud.

Jeanne spoke up. "Brook may not be comfortable with outings

with the co-star. If Cade has to be seen in public with her on occasion, I want someone else with them. Another person who it's known is only his friend. Denise, who do we know that lives in New York?"

"Sarah does, but I'll see who else I know. That's a good idea, Jeanne," Denise added.

"Oh, for God's sake! Is she really that insecure?" Nancy spouted off. "I thought she was a professional with a growing reputation for being tough. That's what you guys are always shoving down my damn throat."

I turned on my way out of the office. "Oh, it's not for her, she's tough as nails. It's for me. I don't like other women pawing on me, even if it is for publicity. Moreover, I'm sick of the rags lying about my actions. This is my goddamned *life*! To comply, I will not openly admit to being with Brook; I'll avoid answering questions, but if any lies emerge that need direct dispute, I will not hesitate to do so. If you do your job and concentrate on promoting the films the right way instead of through vicious gossip, you'll have no worries. Better get busy then, hadn't you?"

Nancy and the others looked at us without speaking, their expressions full of anger and frustration, but they knew they were wrong and that they needed us.

Joel stood and began to gather his things.

"Gentlemen, ladies. Thank you for the meeting." He put his papers back inside his briefcase as he spoke. "I'll have the clause with all of the provisions we've discussed drawn up and on your desk by the end of the week. These contract amendments are non-negotiable and we will expect them signed and back to me no later than the wrap of *Don't Forget to Remember Me*. If they are not, my clients will *not* be returning to the set of *A Love Like This* mid-August. Have a wonderful day." He grinned broadly.

They all followed me out and I took a deep breath when I stepped inside the elevator. I felt better, except for David tagging after Brook all bloody day. I took out my phone to send my girl a message.

The meeting went pretty well. We still have to be discrete, but they'll put us in the same hotel. How bloody long is that weasel scheduled in Vancouver?
He's history after this. Love you back.

Brooklyn

THE AFTERNOON WITH David had been surprisingly relaxing. We played around downtown Vancouver like the friends I felt we were. I was relieved the pressure seemed to be off and he didn't badmouth Cade or try to talk about getting back together. After Cade's text, I felt better knowing there wouldn't be another one of these unexpected visits and happy *this* David, the one with me today, was the one I remembered, and missed.

Finally.

"Thanks. This has been fun. Like old times." I offered a genuine smile. "I'm glad we can finally get to this place. I really missed this between us."

David nodded as he took a lick off his ice cream cone. "Yeah, me too."

The paparazzi had been around a little, but not too much, which was adding to my relaxed mood, as well as Cade's easy attitude when I'd told him about David's visit. He was on his way to his reading, and he'd told me about the meeting. Not perfect yet, but at least we were moving in the right direction.

"This isn't quite like old times, though," David said softly, as he dotted my nose with his ice cream.

I wiped it off, warily. This could go either way. "What do you mean?"

"Well, we used to give each other piggy back rides, but I bet you're too weak now," he laughed.

I laughed and flexed my bicep muscle at him. "What do you mean? I'm a tough bitch, remember?"

"Yeah, you used to be, but you seem more frail now." I felt his eyes on me and wanted to break the tension.

"Huh? You probably can't lift me either, marshmallow boy." I poked him hard in the stomach.

"What? That's low Brook?" He was smiling, so he guessed I was teasing.

"Maybe, but true, anyway, see?" I ran and hopped on his back, but his hands clamped around my thighs, keeping me there.

"Yeah, you were saying?" His hands squeezed around my knees. It tickled, so I laughed.

"David, stop! No fair."

Click, click, click...

I heard the faint sound of the cameras in the distance, and instantly jumped off David's back trying to quickly move to his side.

Shit! Shit! Shit! Stupid move on my part. Those damn paps were always around at the worst possible time.

"Thanks for being my friend again, David, really. It will make Nate and my parents happy. They miss you."

"Yeah, it feels good. So, since you're free this evening, will you have dinner with me? Maybe we can watch movies, order pizza and just hang out? Then we won't have to worry about the press."

His face seemed sincere and he was more and more like the David I knew, but he was careful not to mention Cade.

"Um...," I hesitated. Cade, and his reaction, was first in my mind. He was expecting photos, but not to hear I'd been with David all evening alone in a hotel room. Pizza and company did sound better than spending the night alone, and Cade was seeing Ethan and Dawson in L.A., so we wouldn't be available to talk much. Maybe he'd be too busy to even call at all.

"Come on. Just friends, I promise," David coaxed. "

"Okay, but not too late. I want to be in by ten or eleven." I cocked my head to the side as I tried to read his face. I wish I could be certain he was sincere about being friends.

"Sure. Where do you want to do it? My hotel is sort of secluded. I didn't see any press when I checked in."

"No fair again. You told me on the phone that you'd been seen." My expression twisted wryly.

"Yeah, but I didn't say it was at my hotel, did I?"

I shrugged. "No, I guess not. Don't take this wrong, David, but I can't go to your hotel with you..." Even though I'd decided to relax and treat him like the friend he'd always been, I knew that would be tempting fate and definitely set Cade off.

"Brook, is this how it's always gonna be? You have to ask Carlisle's permission for everything you do? What happened to *you*? Doesn't he trust you?"

Wow. Direct hit.

My face flushed with heat and I shoved my sunglasses back down over my eyes. We got into the waiting black SUV that the studio provided to pick us up.

"Yes, but you've taunted him recently, within the month, David. He's only human and he had a lot to deal with last year. Don't be unreasonable. I'm not willing to do something that I know will upset him. I'm sorry."

Obviously my answer wasn't what David wanted to hear, but it was the truth.

"I'm trying to turn over a new leaf, but you won't invite me to your room, so where else can we go? Do you want to go out?" David was beginning to get exasperated. "The press are like vultures."

I bit my lip in uncertainty. Going out would be worse and more confirmation of my relationship with David would not be what Cade would want.

So far, David hadn't done anything to lead me to believe he'd act out of line, but I knew deep down that he still cared more for me, and that was the problem. I didn't want to go back to my empty hotel room with little prospect of talking with Cade, so what choices did I have?

Maybe it was wrong, but right at this moment Cade was reading with, and probably kissing, multiple women to audition them for his new movie. Hanging out with David kept me from thinking about it.

I'd been more than clear with David that I was in love with Cade, and since we'd have the two-month separation coming up soon, Cade and I needed to learn how to trust each other. I battled internally. It irritated me that David pointed out that I was asking Cade's permission... *Is that what I'm doing?*

"David, why don't we order a pizza and drinks and just have the driver take us around Vancouver? That way, we have dinner, but we don't go back to either of our hotels. It sort of solves the problem, doesn't it?" Even to my own ears it sounded totally weird, but it was either that or be alone all night.

He shook his head at the suggestion, and his mouth quirked sardonically. "Seriously? You want to eat in the back of the Suburban?"

I shrugged. "I appreciate how great you've been, but I just can't go back to either of the hotels with you. Please understand." My eyes were apologetic, and his softened as he looked at me.

"Brook..." David reached out and took my hand, and I withdrew it a little more quickly than I intended.

"I'm trying to be your friend, but this hurt me a lot." His eyes glazed over with tears.

David was someone I cared about for a long time. It hurt to see his pain and know I caused it, yet I stiffened because I wondered if the entire day had been a lie. Was it all an act?

"David. We've been through this so much and I just can't keep doing this. I hope you believe I never wanted to hurt you. The whole thing was confusing and overwhelming for me. I fought it for a long time, but all I did was end up hurting all of us in the end."

"Please don't tell me how hurt Cade has been, Brook. He won, after all." David dropped his gaze to our hands and shrugged.

"Cade has always been very respectful, David. He was never anything but a gentleman, we just..." I felt emotion rise in my chest, love for Cade and hurt for David.

"Stop talking about him," he begged. "I'm trying to be your friend, Brook. I want to be, but I can't help wanting more."

He reached into his pocket and fumbled around. "I realize that it's my fault because I didn't give you what you needed, but I'm ready to do that now."

He pulled out a ring box and opened it.

I was so stunned, all I could do was gasp; completely frozen as I stared at him.

This couldn't be happening.

"I didn't want to do this here. I have this beautiful hotel suite with an ocean view, and I wanted to take you there, have dinner and..." his words fell off and he waited a few seconds before he continued, "but since you won't go, you leave me no choice. I love you, Brook. Will you marry me?"

I watched the pain in his face as he waited for my answer and any anger I felt slipped away. My heart broke for him, but I didn't love him; not the way he wanted me to.

I felt claustrophobic and scared, like a caged animal that was running from a hunter with no escape in sight. My heart sped up and my mind raced as I ran my hand through my hair nervously.

How in the hell did I let this happen? Why did I let myself get sucked in again? I let my guard down and that was a mistake; my punishment was to be in this same damned situation again.

"David, don't. I should never put you through trying to be my friend. I love you, but it's just not romantic love. It hasn't been that way between us for a long time. You deserve more." I began, but he cut me off.

"Please don't patronize me by telling me what you think I deserve." His eyes were wild, tears falling onto his cheeks as his voice rose in volume. "What I *fucking deserve* is not to have my life destroyed because of a damn movie, a slick talking asshole, and a weak girlfriend. Did he seduce you the moment you met?" David's voice softened again, "How could you let him come between us?"

My heart hardened slightly as instinct to defend Cade grew. "Cade *never* took advantage of the situation, or of me, David. I know you know that. We were never involved until after you and I split up."

"Not involved? I saw the way his eyes followed you and the way you always hesitated to let me touch you whenever he was around. Of course you were fucking involved! From *day one!*"

I felt sorry for his pain as his face crumpled and fell. I put my arms around him, and for a short moment he let himself fall into me and hug me back as he cried into my shoulder. "Please Brook. Please marry me; say you're mine again."

My heart seized inside my chest. "David, I can't. *I can't.* I'm sorry. If I could take your pain away, I would. Please try to move on. I want you to be happy and spending time around me only hurts you, so we can't do that anymore. At least, not for now."

I pulled back from him and touched his face with my hand for a moment then sat back in the seat.

"Driver will you please take me back to my hotel?"

David grabbed my hand, "No, Brook, I'm sorry. Let's get that pizza now."

"David, I can't. It's not a good idea. We've both handled this badly, so can we just part hoping that someday we can be friends again? Please? I don't want to hurt you, but I will never leave Cade. He is my heart, and I can't be without him."

I was going to say 'I can't live without him' but there was no reason to make David feel worse. I knew I never wanted to have this conversation again; we'd had it too many times, and this time David was broken. Not something I wanted for him, but I knew in my heart that as harsh as this was, it would finally be the end.

We pulled up in front of my hotel and I detangled myself from David's arms.

"I wish you everything wonderful in your life and hope someday you can forgive me. If you can't, I'll understand." I touched his face one more time, then turned and quickly exited the car.

Incredibly, there were no photographers or fans hanging out at the entrance, so I flew through the doors and into the waiting elevator. Finally a chapter in my life had closed and it was sad, but it was time to embrace the future; a future I knew lay with Cade, but I was sad for David and that I'd lost his friendship.

Hot tears ran down my cheeks as I grieved the loss. I ached for the only person who could comfort me; whose strong arms kept me safe, and whose heart loved me beyond all others.

I opened the door and threw myself down on the bed, staring out the window at the moon.

Cade, I need you.

Caden

I DIDN'T CALL Brook last night. After the first round of readings, I'd gone back to my hotel, fired up the laptop and searched for the new pictures of her with David. What I saw didn't sit well. She looked so happy and maybe it was selfish, but I was angry and jealous. I didn't give a shit if it was for show.

Okay, I was pissed off. Pissed off enough not to call her. She'd texted once and I didn't respond. I knew in my gut she'd realize that I was upset and maybe that's what I wanted. I was down in L.A. fighting for our right to be together, and she was up piggy backing it around Vancouver with that little fucker. I was supposed to stay in L.A. until tomorrow, but I wasn't having it after those pictures. I rushed to the airport after the second round of readings this morning.

Bloody hell. I hated the sick feeling I still got at the thought of the two of them together.

Top that all off with another round of screaming fans chasing me, and my bodyguards, through LAX; it'd been a rough couple of days. I ran my hand through my hair as I sat down in first class after stowing my guitar case in the overhead compartment.

I leaned my head back on the seat and closed my eyes behind my sunglasses. Maybe I could sleep during the flight. I sure as hell didn't sleep much during the night, even though I'd gone out drinking with Ethan and Dawson. I took a deep breath to help me relax, but my lungs resisted.

How was I going to survive being in New York for two and a half months while Brook was in L.A. with David? Fuck!

I tried to shake off the jealousy, telling myself that this was all a Pinnacle set-up, and it would be the last of them. But then, I'd seen those damn photos...

The flight attendant came by and asked if I wanted breakfast.

"Just some orange juice, thank you," I answered as I took off my glasses and glanced around the cabin. Screw sleeping. It wasn't happening.

The first class cabin was relatively empty, but I did notice a young actress who'd played a small role in one of my movies last year. She was sitting across from me and when I caught her gaze, she smiled. After a moment of trying to remember, I recalled her name was Susan Westmore.

"I really loved *The Future of Our Past*. You were great in it." She leaned toward me so I could hear her. "I saw it five times."

"Oh, thank you." I wasn't really aware of much she had done, other than some girly series on one of the cable networks that I didn't watch. I felt awkward. What should I say?

"Can I come over to talk to you?" Her eyes fell to the empty seat next to me. I always had Denise book two seats so I could maintain some degree of privacy when flying commercial airlines.

I nodded, "Oh, sure."

We chatted about basic Hollywood bullshit during the flight, about upcoming films and such. Mostly, she was interested in the series and where it was going, what it was like working with Martin and Brook. Thankfully, she didn't flirt and seemed genuine.

"I know you're probably sick of everyone asking about your chemistry with her, right? Everyone seems so interested in that," she said absently, as she munched on some fruit.

"Oh, yeah. All the time, but um... well, it's right on the screen for all to see." I shrugged. "I'm not sure why they keep after it like they do."

"You're kidding, right? I've seen some of the interviews and photos. You two look like you're really into each other. I bet that's hard for her boyfriend to watch."

I bristled in my seat. "I suppose."

"Well, I just read online this morning that he proposed to her this weekend when he went up to see her. Maybe now, he'll feel less threatened."

What the fuck? I almost choked on my orange juice as my heart exploded. *What did she just say?* I swallowed and tried to hide my reaction.

"Brook is a close friend, but I'd no idea that they were talking about marriage. Where did you read it?" I tried to keep my demeanor calm and my voice level even though my heart was pumping in my chest. It was probably just the rag mags spouting off again, but my body reacted none-the-less.

"Well, I don't remember the site, but he got some fancy hotel on the ocean and supposedly they spent the night there and he proposed. I guess you can just ask her when you see her on set. It's exciting for her."

I swallowed the pain in my throat, and tried to speak, "Were there pictures of them at the hotel?"

"I didn't see any pictures from the hotel, but there were some of them out together. They were so cute. She looked so happy."

I put my sunglasses back on so that Susan wouldn't be able to read my eyes. I struggled to control my emotions and told myself it was nothing. My stomach hurt and my skin was on fire.

Wouldn't she have called or texted me about it if it were nothing? Did his proposal make her feel things for him again? Fuck, I was driving myself insane.

"Listen, I'm going to be in Vancouver for a couple of days. Maybe we can all get together. What's your number? I'd love to meet Brook and the rest of the cast, and maybe you can tell me the good clubs in the city?"

"Huh? Oh, sure." I proceeded to give her my number and program hers into my phone, for appearances. The last thing on my mind was socializing.

When the plane landed I couldn't get through the bloody airport fast enough. Would Brook be at her hotel, or his? I decided not to call her, but instead go straight to her hotel. Susan followed behind me in the airport and the paparazzi snapped several pictures.

"I'll have my driver give you a lift if you don't mind waiting for photos and autographs. It's constant, and sometimes it's a bother, but I try to be nice about it."

"Sure, thanks." Susan smiled as she tried to keep up with me.

Her shorter legs and high heels made it difficult, but it didn't slow me down.

Once inside the limo, I told Peter to drop Susan off first. I didn't want any witnesses to my sneaking into Brook's hotel from the garage, but I was going to get to the bloody bottom of things and fast.

When we finally arrived at Brook's hotel, my heart was pumping madly inside my chest and I couldn't catch my breath. When Peter pulled in and I bolted up the stairs two at a time.

Chapter 24

I Know Who I Can't Live Without

Brooklyn

WHEN CADE DIDN'T answer my text the previous night, and I still hadn't heard from him yet today, it meant he was upset. While I was anxious about him, I was also pissed.

So what? He just wasn't going to talk to me now?

He knew David was in town and that there would be photos. I made sure to text him the minute I knew, so what the hell?

I wasn't going to call or text him again, damn it! In fact, I was going to ask Jennifer to go shopping later. Cade wasn't scheduled to be back until tonight, and I wasn't going to sit my ass in this hotel room waiting for him to throw me a communication crumb all day long. In fact, maybe I'd be the one avoiding the calls when he finally came to his senses.

I'd spent the evening last night reading *A Love Like This*, feeling sorry for David, and also getting more and more uptight about Cade not returning my messages. Frankly, it sucked ass. I felt bad about

David; sorry to lose a close friend and sad to say goodbye to such a big part of my life.

Yesterday with him had been nice, relaxing and even comforting; until he pulled out the ring. Jesus, I didn't see that one coming. Our relationship was always so carefree and casual. I mean, he'd never even been jealous before Cade; not once. Come to think of it, I wasn't either. Not of David.

That should've been a clue, but I was too young to realize. He was the first guy who paid me any sort of attention and he was two years older. In the five years since I'd met him, he'd been my friend more than anything else, and I'd miss him.

Maybe that would be hard for Cade to accept, but I had a life before him. Just because he became everything the day we met, didn't mean everything before him was erased.

I threw the book down on the bed, giving up on the morning's attempt as well. I just couldn't get into it, and I didn't like that there was even the hint that Ryan would cave to that bitch, Jane. I felt like Julia; indignant that he would fail me.

I'd read it several times and I always found myself left with this feeling of emptiness and sadness when Julia took off for France. Each time, I found myself wishing for an alternate plot line; like if I read it enough I could somehow will it to be different.

Couldn't Ryan see how Jane manipulated him through guilt? And not just once; but several times? After everything Julia sacrifices for him, too. Ughhhh! My chest tightened just thinking about it. No wonder Julia leaves.

If I'd have written the series, my Ryan would have been different; no momentary lapses toward Jane, no sticking up for her or making excuses for her behavior when it was so freaking obvious that she was trying to take him from Julia. There would be no question in Ryan's mind… ever. Thank God Ryan redeems himself at the end of the series.

Sure, in Kahlen Aymes' version, he knew who he couldn't live without, but was it a *choice* she made? I shook my head.

Men! My mind screamed. *Men are so stupid sometimes!*

It should have been impossible to put his focus on anyone else, no matter how guilty he felt. Ryan finally sees what Jane is doing, but only after Julia does something drastic; shouldn't he have always known how she felt? Weren't they *that connected*? Ryan should have seen she missed his friendship, not just his physical love.

They were soul mates, weren't they? They were everything to each other, right? So how could he not see her pain? Love isn't a choice, it just *is*.

I wanted Ryan to know Julia's heart without words. My heart wanted it to be that way in the story, because that's how I really felt. About Cade. He was my Ryan.

There were no questions in my mind, no momentary lapses, no matter what happened, no matter how much pain we had to endure… he could make me walk through hell, yet I would never waver in my love for him.

It would always be Cade for me. But it wasn't a choice. It was undeniable and completely out of my control. I had to be with him and I knew it; even if he was being a stubborn jackass who wouldn't answer my texts or calls. Even if he was acting like a baby about a couple of stupid photos, when he'd just been making out with a bunch of different women this weekend! And even if we were going to have a huge fight tonight because I was completely pissed… We'd still be together.

Okay, so how was I going to handle him tonight? Should I

show him I was mad as hell or should I treat him with kid gloves? I understood his angst over David, but how long would it be before he realized that I was his forever?

Goddammit!

I promised myself that after the Wendy fiasco, I wouldn't let myself believe any bullshit and completely trust him. Did it bug the shit out of me that he was making out with those actresses yesterday? *Hell yes*, but I was certain he loved me, so why the fuck wasn't he just as secure that I loved him? Maybe I'd learned something from Ryan and Julia that he still had to figure out.

I pressed my lips together, feeling decidedly bitchy.

I lay back on the bed but was startled when I heard the door click as a card key passed over the electronic lock on the outside. Cade was back early.

He pushed the door open and walked quickly into the suite, looking around as he moved toward the bedroom, and throwing the keycard across the room. He was angry; it was written all over his expression and the forceful way he moved. What was he looking for? His face was flushed and he was breathing hard as he moved toward me then stopped a few feet away. Cade glared down at me, but didn't say anything.

"Hey, you're back early." I sat up and stumbled for something to say to lighten his mood. He was guarded as I rose from the bed and took a couple steps toward him. He looked tired and he hadn't shaved, and he was furious as hell.

"Sorry if you're disappointed." His voice was flat and a muscle in his jaw twitched as he clenched his teeth. His blue eyes were full of fire.

I frowned and my hands clenched at my sides as my own anger

swelled.

"Fuck you. What's your problem?"

"Hmmph!" Cade huffed; his mouth quirked but his eyes remained hard and unchanged. He stood still as stone. "Fuck *me*? Are you sure it's *me* that you're fucking?"

I couldn't believe my ears and my skin turned to liquid fire.

Did she really just say that to me?

"Well, maybe it won't be, you asshole. I know you're probably pissed about the pictures, but I don't deserve this abuse from you, Cade."

"Oh, yeah. I'm upset about the woman who said she loves me more than life draped all over another guy for all the bloody world to see, and looking happy as hell while she does it," he said as he walked into the bathroom and splashed water on his face and the back of his neck. "Fucking hell! Why would I be upset about that, Brook?"

I sighed wearily and shook my head, the anger draining out of me. "Cade, are we really doing this? Are we fighting over some stupid pictures? Are you even interested in talking to me, or do you just want to have a tantrum?" I asked in a softer tone.

"Fuck *you*, Brook! I was down in L.A. fighting for *us*, and you were parading around Vancouver flaunting that little bastard in my face. Haven't I dealt with that long enough?" The tone in his voice was hard and the volume increasing. "But no! That's not *all*, right? You went to his hotel and he proposed! Is that how it went? How much more do I have to endure? When's the bloody wedding?"

My lips thinned into a tight line. *What the fuck?*

I hoped I wouldn't even have to tell him for the simple fact that he would flip and blow it all out of proportion, exactly like he was doing.

"Did you let him touch you? Did he kiss you?" I could see the pain behind his eyes, but I was mad at him for thinking that was even a remote possibility. I didn't want to be around him when he had no faith in me.

"Why don't you just leave? You don't know what the hell you're saying and it's obvious you aren't interested in anything I say anyway. Just get the fuck out!"

"No! Not until I hear you say you're mine! That you belong to me and no one else!"

Don't you know that by now? The thought exploded in my brain. I just stared at him, my body shaking with emotion.

He rushed forward, his arms sliding around me as he crushed me to his body. He was breathing hard, and still furious as his eyes bore into mine. Furious, scared, and insecure; and, desperate.

How could someone so amazing, so beautiful, and talented, feel insecure for even one second?

His scent washed over my senses and I could feel the heat of his breath on my face, and despite the anger flaring between us, my heart beat faster at his nearness. My lips parted as his eyes dropped to my mouth.

Cade's hand came up to the back of my head while he crushed his mouth to mine. I was too stunned to move as he dragged his mouth across my cheek, down my chin, and onto my neck as his free hand closed over my breast. I knew that the best way to calm him down was to respond even though he was rough in his touches. I knew he loved me and wouldn't hurt me.

As angry as I was, I loved him even more. My heart ached that he would doubt me, but I knew his heart was hurting, and he needed reassurance from me. He was as vulnerable as I was; his heart just as fragile.

My hands slid up his chest, and around his shoulders; finally into his hair. Cade groaned against my skin and pulled back to look into my face. His hand slid to the side of my face and his thumb rubbed against my lower lip, dragging back and forth before he brought his mouth back to mine. I kissed him back, sucking on his mouth like I couldn't get enough. The kiss got wild and deeper, his hand on the side of my face pulled me closer, and I pulled the hair at the back of his head in a desperate attempt to bring our mouths closer.

He pushed me up against the wall and pressed into me. I felt his hardness on my stomach and my body reacted of its own accord. I wanted him, but I couldn't let it happen like this, in anger.

My hand slid down his body to his ass, and I squeezed the firm muscles and pulled him tighter into my pelvis; lifting my leg around him.

"Brook... Tell me that you're mine. Only mine."

I could hear the anguish in his voice and tears filled my eyes as his right hand laced with my left and he pressed his forehead to mine. His sweet breath, coming out in hot pants from exertion and heartbreak, washed over my face. As his fingers closed around mine, he felt the ring on my left and he froze in place. Suddenly, he pulled back to jerk my hand up so he could see the ring on my hand.

Did he think he'd find David's ring there?

His features softened as his eyes fell on the engagement ring that he'd given me. His eyes came back to my face as the tears fell from my eyes, and tumbled down my cheeks. His mouth was only inches from mine; hovering over my lips, waiting.

"I shouldn't have to say it!" I said brokenly, my tone urgent. "What the hell were you expecting to see? You should know by now that it could only ever be you. It kills me that you'd think any other ring would be on my finger." My right hand came up to his shoulder to push him off of me as I ripped my left from his grasp. He stumbled back from me as his eyes came back to my face. His chest was heaving, and I was crying.

"Yes, David proposed, but after everything I've said to you, how I've told you that you're my entire *fucking world*, you should have no doubt where my heart is! What is it you said to me in Tokyo? Oh yeah, do you *feel me* like I feel you? This is *us*? Well is it? *Is this us*, Cade? If it is, what the fuck *is this*? I thought we were beyond any doubt by now."

I wiped at my tears, but they wouldn't stop raining from my eyes. A sob rose in my chest, as Cade took a step back toward me.

So many emotions flashed across his features; regret, hurt, lust, desperation. Gentle now, he put a hand to my face but I turned away before he could touch me. I longed to fall into his arms, but I just couldn't.

"Brook... I was just so...," he began, but I interrupted him.

"I need you to leave. I can't deal with this right now," I said quietly as I went into the bathroom and shut the door behind me. I leaned trembling against it as I turned the lock.

I felt lost and alone, like part of me was missing. I slid to the floor, wrapping my arms around my bent knees as I fell apart.

He didn't argue or plead with me. I heard the outer door to the suite close behind him.

***

FOUR HOURS LATER, Cade had called six times and texted four times, but I didn't answer any of them.

> *I'm sorry.*
> *Forgive me. Please.*
> *The thought of him touching you makes me crazy.*
> *I feel like I'm falling apart, but I love you.*
> *Please, Brook. Talk to me. I can't breathe.*

I'd decided I didn't want to talk to him on the phone or on text. We needed to connect in person.

I understood how he felt, even if it was completely unfounded. He'd told me he was a possessive boyfriend, and sometimes I even liked it, but it hurt when he didn't trust me. Being jealous when someone flirted with me wasn't the same as thinking I would betray him or go back to David. We needed to talk and get this all out before the separation at the beginning of June or we'd be in trouble.

My heart thumped heavily in my chest. It would be difficult enough without all of this doubt surrounding us. We had to be completely solid in our trust of each other.

Cade was under a lot of pressure; the meeting with Pinnacle; the auditions, and of course always the mobs of fans chasing him were bound make him crazy. When the one thing in his life he was sure of became clouded in lies and innuendos, it was not unusual for him to have a volatile reaction and close down.

He did the same thing I'd done when I'd seen Wendy at his apartment. The only difference was he *did* come to talk to me, but I didn't go to him in January. I wouldn't make that mistake again.

I called the limo service and asked if Peter could come pick me up in the garage of my hotel. I wore a dark green blouse and jeans, and put some smoky and silver shadow on my eyes, some cream blush and light gloss on my lips. I curled my hair in to a fluffy style, and wore the two bracelet's Cade had given me. I'd just need to be careful to keep my hand in my pocket or under the table, but Cade needed to see I belonged to him, even if the world couldn't... and the jewelry was a symbol of that.

"Good evening, Peter. I hope you're well tonight." Cade's British formality was wearing off on me, as much as my Americanisms were becoming second nature to him.

"Yes, Miss Brook, thank you," he said pleasantly and smiled at me into the rear view mirror, "Will you be joining Mr. Caden tonight?"

"Yes, please. Did he go out for dinner or is he back at the hotel?"

"No, miss. He went out. He met Miss Westmore and her friends. They met on the plane today and she asked him to show her some of the hot spots in town."

I sat back in my seat, contemplating whether Cade would want me to crash his party or not. Either way, we couldn't talk with a bunch of people around. I wondered who was 'Miss Westmore'.

"Oh, well... maybe you should take me back to my hotel then."

"No, miss. Mr. Caden said I should bring you to him if you called for a ride. Is that acceptable?"

Thump. My heart bounced around my chest. He knew I'd come to him.

No choices, out of my control, and *his*.

"Yes, Peter. Thank you."

I walked into the club and saw him right away. He was sitting at a table close to the door, with several other people. Fans were hovering around devouring him with their eyes, but they didn't approach. Hmmm... not the usual way they behaved.

He was beautiful, but he looked tired. I watched him slam a shot as two girls came up to me and asked for my autograph. I signed for them, and they threw their arms around me and took selfies of us with their phones. I smiled and engaged with them, thinking if they'd take photos of Cade, soon the whole world would know we were in the same bar.

"Thank you, Brook. We love you. You're so great. Can't wait for *Don't Forget to Remember Me!*"

I smiled again. Cade's head snapped up at the sound of my name, his eyes soft and apologetic as they met mine.

I smiled at the rest of the table as he introduced me and pulled up a chair next to his. So, Miss Westmore was Susan Westmore. She was nice and sincerely interested in talking to me, asking many of the same questions the interviewers had about the film and my career.

Cade was pensive. I could tell he was still unsure of my state of mind and I needed to find a way to communicate with him that I was okay. As I made small talk with the others, my left hand reached for his under that table. His warm fingers laced through mine immediately, his thumb rubbing over the top of my hand and I squeezed his slightly.

He sucked in a deep breath, glancing at me; the corners of his mouth lifting in a small, sad smile.

"So Brook, I hear congratulations are in order. I saw online earlier today that you've gotten engaged to your boyfriend," Susan smiled warmly at me. Ah, so she was the culprit who planted the misunderstanding in Cade's mind.

The music was loud and so I leaned into her. "No. David did propose, but I said 'no'... in fact, we broke up."

Her face fell, "Oh, I'm so sorry."

I shrugged and shook my head, "No, don't be sorry. We were more like friends anyway. I'm just sorry that I hurt him."

Susan's eyes flashed knowingly between Cade and me. .

"The music is really great, isn't it?" Cade saved us by distracting her.

"Oh yes! Wanna dance, Cade?"

"No thanks, Susan. I'm not really in the mood; plus I'd be mobbed on the dance floor. I'm quite enjoying the solitude tonight. It's a miracle that no one is intruding."

A little while later while the others were out dancing, he leaned in to me, his voice softly laced with sadness. "Thanks for coming to find me, sweetheart. I'm very sorry, my love. I can't explain how crazy I get when it comes to you. It does something to my insides. I love you, so much."

"I know." I looked down, nodding, as my heart tightened. I tried to swallow the emotion rising in my throat. "Me, too. Can we talk about this later when we're alone? It's enough to know we're okay now. *Are* we okay?"

His blue eyes blazed into mine even though they were soft as he looked at me. His mouth curved in a small smile. "Always."

"Good." My chest expanded with a deep breath, "So then, can you give me a brief run-down of the meeting today?"

"Yes. I told them we'd walk off of the series if they didn't make it easier for us to be together. I said we'd be discreet and not announce our relationship yet. We have to put some time between your public break-up with David and our becoming official or it might hurt your image."

"And yours," I put in.

Cade's left shoulder lifted in a half-shrug. "Whatever. Not exactly optimal, but I'll live with it. Joel told them we wouldn't show up to *A Love Like This* if they didn't agree. No more visits from David, either."

His hand tightened on mine again and his eyes searched my face. "It's been almost a year since I broke up with him. It sucks that we have to wait, but at least there's a light at the end of the tunnel. As long as we can be together and David won't be an issue, anymore, I'm good with it. He won't want to see me now, regardless."

Cade's brow dropped over his eyes and his lips pursed. "Are you all right, love? It's obviously bothering you."

"Cade, stop. I'm sorry he's hurt and that I'm losing a friend, but I'm not sorry about us. That's the truth."

He nodded slightly.

"We'll push Pinnacle a little and go out together on occasion, even though they don't like it. The sooner we start dropping hints, the sooner we can be open. In fact, Daniel is having a concert in Vancouver next week. Will you go to that with me? Hang out backstage? It can be our *first date.*"

Cade grinned at the absurdity of the façade and I couldn't hold back a big smile. "It's ridiculous! My mouth has touched every inch of your skin, but we've yet to have our first date."

I nodded and nudged him with my shoulder. "I think I'm going to go back to the hotel. Looks like we still can't go together?"

"Probably not, but I'll come to you if you still want me." I could hear the regret in his voice because he doubted me.

"You know I want you. We can talk back in my room, okay?"

"Yeah. I love you," he said, his voice low as he leaned his head toward me.

I pulled back from him when I noticed a couple of women eyeing us with speculation.

I cleared my throat. "Um, yeah. Ditto. Tell the others it was nice meeting them and goodnight for me, please?"

I wanted to kiss those sweet lips but turned and walked out of the bar to the waiting limo.

Caden

THE SUITE WAS dark except for some flickering candlelight coming from the other room. I was filled with relief as I followed the soft sounds of music into the bedroom. Thank God I'd been wrong. Brook was lying on her stomach with her head turned away from me, both arms bare and golden on the pillow around her head.

I kicked off my black dress shoes, threw off my jacket, and unbuttoned my shirt before sliding onto the bed beside her. She smelled of soap, perfume and Brook. I cradled my head in one folded arm then reached out to her with the other.

I almost fucked up big time today, but here she was; warm and with me.

Totally mine. Still.

I bent my head to breathe in her familiar scent and place my open mouth on her shoulder in a seductive kiss. I wanted to make the pain of the last twenty-four hours up to her in the most reverent and clear way. My mouth lifted just enough to ghost over her skin as my hand ran down her back, sliding below the sheet. Her skin felt like warm silk, and was completely bare under my hands as I explored her gentle curves.

Brook's head lifted and turned, allowing her to look into my face. Her blue eyes were languid and glistening in the candlelight. No words were needed as she lifted a hand to my face and ran her fingers along my jaw and then closed them over my chin. I couldn't resist the pull to press my mouth to her beautiful lips. The kiss was wet and open, soft and deep, so delicious. I groaned, my tongue entering her mouth and my arm around her waist pulled her body closer to mine.

My heart swelled as love for her washed over me in waves. She was so good, so beautiful... how could I doubt that she loved me? I was a stupid fool. "Brook..."

"Shhhh... Just feel me, Cade," she whispered as her hand slid around to the back of my head and her nose nuzzled into my neck. Goose bumps broke out on my skin as her other hand ran down my chest, over my abs then retraced their path.

I slid my hands down her arms and around her, closed over the soft cheeks of her bum, never breaking the kiss. Suddenly, I wanted to rid her of the sheet that separated us. I pushed it away impatiently, which finally allowed her breasts to press against my bare chest deliciously. We were both equally aroused and it was pure heaven. My dick throbbed as I felt her nipples harden against my chest.

"Oh, baby... I want you."

"Yes," she breathed softly against my skin and I rolled with her so that I was leaning over her so I could kiss her. "Yes, Cade. Make love to me. I'm all for you."

Her words fell around me in a whisper, and filled up every fiber of my being with wonder. I brushed back the hair from her face as I took her mouth again, softly drawing her lips into my mouth one by one and then hovering above her. Brook's breath was warm as it fell on my face; so sweet. As my mouth lifted from another delicious kiss, I leaned my forehead against hers and closed my eyes.

Oh my God.

Emotions overwhelmed me. I'd come so close to losing this, losing the love of my life so many times. She was precious; my entire world revolved around her touch, her words, her very existence. My chest tightened and my arms gathered her close. I wanted her closer and to never let go.

"Brook... I..."

She pulled my mouth down to hers again and licked at my lips. "Shhh. Shhhh... I love you, make love with me now... and just shhh. This is us."

Those words were an echo of the script that brought us together, but they were more than a mirror. They were my whole life.

I stared into her bright blue eyes and they were clear and deep as if she was looking straight into my soul. I opened my mouth to speak and she shook her head as she tilted her chin up, begging me to kiss her, love her, and wipe away all of my insecurities. I gave into our need and want. My hand roamed lovingly over her naked curves and her leg lifted up around my hips as I pressed my body into hers, kissing her again and again; each more passionate than the last. It didn't matter that I was still dressed. It felt amazing but I just want to please her. My heart exploded with my need to show her how much I loved her.

Her little hands roamed up my shoulders and pushed my shirt down my back and off of my arms. I shifted to help her, and when my weight leaned to one side, she used the leverage to gently push me down on my back as she moved over me. My eyes feasted on her creamy skin and her delicate bone structure, down her face and neck to the gracefulness of her arms and her firm, perfectly round breasts with the perky pink nipples. My mouth went dry as I longed to bring my lips to her flesh.

She stared into my eyes as her hands went to the waistband of my jeans. She popped the button and slid down the zipper before her hand slid inside to close around me, grasping, tugging and teasing my dick as it swelled even tighter in her hand. I thought I would burst with pleasure. "Uhhhh... Brook..." I gasped out her name.

I wanted to be free of the material between us so my hands moved to my jeans and my hips came off the bed and the movement achieved two things. I was able to push the material down my hips to a degree, but I ground into her softness even more. I glorified in watching her lips part and her head fell back as she put more weight on her legs to help me remove my jeans.

She fell over me, her hair raining all around my face and hers as she stared into my eyes before bringing her face closer and finally teasing my mouth with hers. I couldn't take any more; my arms circled her waist and raked up her back and down again. When I reached for her hips, my fingers closed around her hipbones and pulled her wetness tight against my length.

"Oh, God...," she moaned as her hips moved and ground up and down, over me, exciting both of us even more. My breathing came in quick gasps and my hands reached for her breasts as she sat up and her hand reached between us, lifting me as she started to sink over and around me, her knees curled around my hips.

"You feel so incredible, and perfect. You're so beautiful, so warm and wet around me."

I had to touch her. I wanted my mouth on her so I bolted upright, still buried deep inside her and one arm curled around her hips to pull her closer as we established the slow, deep rhythm we both needed. I brought the other up and cupped her breast so I could close my lips around the nipple and draw it into my mouth to suck on it. It was obvious she liked what I was doing because of the little mewling sounds she made deep in her throat.

Those sounds, her heavy breathing and the way my name left her lips... If I could only hear one word for the rest of my life, it had to be my name on her mouth when we made love like this.

She was trembling, clenching around me and drawing me closer to the edge. "Jesus, love... I 'm... so..."

I wanted to kiss her again and again and I dragged my mouth from her breast and up her neck to her chin. Her head had fallen back in a gasp and I couldn't reach her lips, so I flipped her over onto her back. Her arms went around my neck and into my hair and it was Brook demanding that I kiss her, always in tune with me; she wanted the closeness, too. She bought her knees up and her legs wound around my waist. I sank even deeper into her body as my mouth devoured hers. My tongue slid into her mouth and she opened to me and matched me kiss for kiss.

"I'm so in love with you, I can't live without you, Brook."

"Cade... I know. Me too. Uhhhh..." I felt her teeth sink into my shoulder as her body convulsed and clenched around my dick and she clawed at my back with her hands.

"Oh, babe..." Both of my hands closed around her head as she arched against me. I lost it, then. I couldn't help thrusting as deep as I could as I exploded within her warm body. She was so soft, so smooth, and so amazing. We continued to kiss each other and grind our hips together as we both jerked and trembled with the waves of pleasure that washed over us.

"Oh, God, Brook... I never want to be without you. Never."

Her arms wrapped around me as she kissed my shoulder and then the side of my face.

We were both breathing hard as I nuzzled into her nose and kissed her mouth several times. "You taste so sweet, honey."

At my words her hands moved to my hair and pulled my mouth closer as she sucked my tongue into her mouth and kissed me deeply.

"So delicious... you're my favorite thing in the world, Cade. The most important thing in my life." I heard the tears in her voice and brushed her hair back and looked into her eyes. My heart swelled in my chest because I realized how much she meant those words. I swallowed the rising lump in my throat.

"I'm so sorry, sweetheart. I should have known that you wouldn't go back to David." I pulled out of her and tugged her with me until she lay on my chest and I could wrap my arms around her. "I'm a bloody fool."

Brook's hot tears dripped onto the skin of my chest. One of my hands traced gently down the arm she lay across my stomach and the other stroked her long, luxurious hair. I leaned down and kissed her forehead.

"Don't cry, Brook. I'm sorry. I was wrong."

"I'm scared, Cade. So scared."

I turned my face into the top of her head and breathed her in as my arms both tightened around her. I didn't have to ask what she meant. I knew, and I was fucking terrified too.

"We'll be okay, Brook. I don't know how because it will be bloody hell... but we will make it through it and still be us." My heart constricted like I had a steel band around my chest, preventing me from breathing.

She turned her face into my chest and held me tighter. I could feel her body shake with the silent sobs that were flooding through her. "Will we? We can't even survive two days."

She pulled herself up a little so she could tilt her face up to mine and look at me. I kept stroking her body and her hair as I looked into the wet blue depths. I couldn't speak, my throat closed and no sound would come out. I never hated my fame as much as I did right now.

"You just have to know that I'd never want anyone else, and you have no cause to worry. You should feel secure anyway. I mean, every woman in the free world wants you. I'm the one who should be afraid of losing you, but you shouldn't be jealous at all. I could never be with anyone else," she said softly before her words dropped off.

I turned toward her so that we were facing each other and I could look into her eyes as I finally found my voice.

"Brook. I can't even put into words how bloody bonkers I am over you. I get so insane, so fucked up, when I think about you with anyone else. Not even making love to you, but that you could care about someone else, or that I could lose you. I feel like my insides are falling out and I'm out of control. It's wrong, but I can't help that I feel that way. It's just *ridiculous* how much you mean to me."

Brook smiled softly at me through her tears. "I think it's kinda perfect," she whispered as she reached out to trace her fingers along my jaw. "I never want to stop touching you, feeling you, or loving you. Even if I wanted to, I can't. Don't you know that yet?"

I felt my eyes well, and my throat ached. "Yes, I do. I feel the same way."

She nodded. "Yes. I was reading *A Love Like This* today for the tenth time, and I find I don't like parts of it. I want it to be different. Like it is between us."

I frowned, trying to read her meaning in her eyes.

"Ryan should have known. Julia should have, too. I just..." her eyes rose to mine as she spoke, "don't like that they ever doubted each other. Her heart should be so full of him that she couldn't have left. They should have always been together, no questions, no doubts... no choice. "

Understanding dawned on me and I felt my heart thump in my chest. She was so incredible. I couldn't believe how perfect she was as I bent to kiss her luscious mouth. "He needed a bloody lesson, for sure. But, we doubted, too. I'm just happy it's over. I don't bloody deserve you."

"It doesn't matter if you do or not... it's not my *choice*. Even if you can be a blind, stubborn ass who should *know* I adore you, you're still perfect in my eyes."

My heart pounded in my chest as I gathered her close and buried my face into her neck as I spoke, her arms twined around my body felt like heaven.

"Are you sure you made the right choice, Julia?" I teased her in Ryan's American accent.

"Hmmmph." She smiled and touched my lips with the fingertips of her left hand. The candlelight glinted off of the diamond ring that I had placed there.

"Ryan, I know who I can't live without." I returned her smile as she said Julia's line. It should have stopped there, but she continued, "In this reality, there is no question, never the possibility of anyone else for me, Cade." She breathed my name, and it was music to my ears. "You're burned on my soul, always and forever."

Chapter 25

I Could Not Ask For More

Caden

IT WAS CRAMPED and loud in the backstage area of the small venue that hosted Daniel's concert, but it was fantastic to be out with Brook, and *just* Brook. This was the first time we'd been out together without other cast members along to keep the media dogs off our scent. Most of the cast already left Vancouver and wouldn't be back until a cast party which would serve as a wrap on the second film, and also, to introduce the new actors, added who would join the third and final film, to the rest of the cast. Brook and I were living this script, and I was more than apprehensive about the actress they were choosing to play Jane.

In only a month I'd be heading to New York to begin shooting my next film, *Only Us*. I was leaving the day after the MTV awards where *The Future of Our Past* was up for several awards. Saddened by the thought of the impending separation from Brook, I realized it was going to be harder than I'd thought. The only other time we were apart that long was during the Wendy episode, and the weeks between the promotional tours, but never for this long. I was already anxious, and wondered how in bloody hell I'd make it through.

I was also concerned about the inevitable drama the press would cook up about my new co-star and me, and how Brook would handle it. It was always the same shit, so I fully expected it. Two films back-to-back would elicit drama seeds regardless if they were through the same studio or two different ones. One studio would essentially kill two birds with one promotional stone, and two competing studios would try to keep the focus on their film. Either way, I was screwed.

I'd gotten word last week that they cast a woman named Leah St. Clare opposite me for *Only Us*. Honestly, I couldn't remember much about her other than she was blonde, ordinary looking and was a regular on an America network TV. She was a good actress, no question, but she certainly hadn't affected me like Brook had during her audition. No one could ever be like Brook. The memory was comforting but my heart already felt the loss of not working with Brook everyday. Flashback to the end of *The Future of Our Past* and this pain was equally intense. We weren't together then, and I didn't have the right to want her and miss her. Now, she was mine and I'd grown used to having her with me every night. No question this would be an adjustment, but one we'd have to deal with if our relationship were to survive long-term.

I was anxious to find out my production schedule so that I could compare it to Brook's for her new dystopian flick. My brain was already clamoring to work out when we'd be able to see each other. Denise warned there wouldn't be many times during the twelve weeks of my shooting schedule when we'd have the same days off. Brook would even have less than I would, due to her fitness training.

Damn Pinnacle! They probably planned it that way to keep their blasted illusion alive. There was more than one way to confine our relationship, and those fuckers would use any means they could come up with.

Brook was dancing around with Daniel's girlfriend and some overly attentive male fans about twenty feet in front of me. I took a pull of my beer, leaned against the wall, content to watch. Most of the people in the backstage area were friends of Daniel's and although some of the fans could see us behind the curtain from the front of the stage, I was beyond caring.

I'd worn a hoodie to help hide, but I acknowledged it was probably completely pointless. Being incognito was something I couldn't get away with anymore and it was even more difficult when Brook was with me. Twitter really fucked us. We couldn't go anywhere for more than twenty minutes without being mobbed. I found it maddening. Surprisingly, the female fans were less touchy and demanding when Brook was around. She was always nice to them; more than gracious, but something about "Julia" being with "Ryan", just made them back off. I grinned at the thought.

Thank you, Kahlen Aymes. You made my entire life the day you sat down to write The Remembrance Trilogy *because it brought Brook to me.*

I glanced at the object of my musings. Brook was dressed casually too. This togetherness in public was still new to us, so we'd been reining it in all night. I wanted to touch her, hold her, act like her boyfriend, but instead, I was in the background watching other blokes flirt with her.

I nursed my beer and chilled, watching her dance and perch on the edge of the stage. The only obvious thing about my actions was that I couldn't take my eyes off of her. The looks she shot at me were completely mesmerizing and the little secret of our relationship was overtly sexy. Those poor bastards dancing with her could dream, anyway. My lips turned up in another grin.

I'd never get used to the feeling of my heart filling up my chest whenever I looked at her, how my fingers itched to touch her, or my mouth longed to taste her. The love was unbelievable. After nearly a year of being together, it was as exciting as it was when we first met, but now we had a depth that came from knowing everything about each other.

I met Brook's eyes and made a head motion indicating she should come back to my side. The guy who was talking to her leaned in and put an arm around her shoulders as he said something in her ear. She shook her head and then moved away from him toward where I stood in the back room.

I was leaning nonchalantly against the wall, and she came to stand in front of me, pressing her back flat against it. Her position allowed her to talk to me, yet still see the stage.

"You're looking very happy! Daniel's great. Are you having a good time?" She flashed a gorgeous smile; her face was flushed due to the heat in the bar, the cramped quarters, and the two hundred people stuffed into the small space.

I leaned down to speak to her and her perfume assaulted my senses. "Yeah. I'm glad we did this, but it would be so much better if I could wrap you in my arms as I'd like," I said, as I handed her the drink I was watching for her. "You looked like you were having a good time dancing with those guys."

Brook's eyebrows raised and she bit the corner of her lower lip. "Oh, yeah. Sure I did, but they weren't the dance partner I really *wanted.*" She nudged into me and her free hand slid around the back of my waist to drop to my ass. When her hand closed around one of the cheeks and squeezed, her eyes flashed flirtatiously.

My face split into a smile and Brook laughed out loud. "You're playing with fire, little girl."

"Is that right?" she asked as she licked her lips, glancing up at me through hooded eyes. She was so bloody sexy, I couldn't stand it. It was all I could do not to pull her into my arms and kiss her full on the mouth for the entire bar to see. "Well, that's good, cause' I like things *hot.*"

"Mmmmm." I know you do." I grabbed her hand, turned and pulled her back into the throng of people behind us.

"Excuse me. Pardon us," I said to the women standing behind me as I worked my way through twenty or so people to take Brook into the backstage area behind the curtain behind the band. We received inquisitive glances as we pushed our way through them, but I was beyond caring. "Excuse us, thank you."

"Cade... are you sure this is such a good idea?" Brook asked.

I wanted space and a lull in the din of the music. I wanted her against my body and my mouth on hers. *Now.*

Daniel's band began playing a softer song as I pushed her up against one of the walls behind a curtain and pressed my body into hers. Her breath left her chest and rushed warmly over the skin on my neck. Her eyes fell to my mouth. I bent, and licked her upper lip with my tongue as my hand rested on the wall beside her head. I leaned in toward her so I could ghost her mouth with mine.

"Yes... I think it's an excellent idea," I whispered against her mouth, before parting her lips and sliding my tongue into the warm depth of her delicious mouth. She moaned into me as her mouth worked with mine, and her tongue moved inside my mouth.

Oh God. She tasted so good, and it must have been, what? Hours, since I'd kissed her like this?

Her hands slid around my waist and under my sweatshirt and shirt. My skin was damp with perspiration but I wasn't sure if it was due to the heat of the bar or the desire that was washing over me. Her cool little hands curled into my skin, the nails making me shiver despite the heat.

I cupped her cheek gently, and then the back of her head as our kisses deepened and became more urgent. I loved the feel of her response. She pressed into me as her breath came in faster gasps matching my own. I felt my dick thicken and swell against her softness. It felt so good; almost to the point of pain.

Somewhere in the back of my mind, I heard people milling around, but it didn't really register. I was so caught up in the moment, her kisses so exquisite I was lost completely to everything else but Brook. I pulled her hips closer to mine and she moaned. Minute after minute passed as we made out under the curtain, and I never wanted to stop kissing her.

"Cade... uhhhh... you don't play fair. I was trying so hard to be good," she said against my mouth before sucking my lower lip into her mouth then pulling her mouth from mine.

I pressed my forehead to hers and took a deep breath. "Trust me, love, you're very, very *good*. So good, it's bloody insane," I said suggestively. "I *don't* want to play fair."

"Yeah, I *want* as well, and I don't care how you play, as long as you play." She giggled softly, and brought her hand up to my jaw and then her thumb moved over my lower lip. I kissed it and sucked it into my mouth as her eyes met mine and I could see the desire smoldering in the blue depths. "You're so beautiful."

"Hmmph!" The corners of my mouth twitched in the start of a sardonic smile. "That baby we're gonna have in ten years is going to be amazing, yes? Because I think you're the most beautiful thing I've ever laid eyes on."

Brook gasped at my words. Truly, I couldn't wait for that day.

I brushed the hair back from her face and kissed her softly one more time before I moved back from her. It wasn't easy to control the desire I felt surging in my veins. Her eyes were molten fire as she looked at me and I didn't want to tear my gaze away, but I realized we should get back to watching the concert. We were playing with fire.

Someone would see us if we weren't careful; and there was still the worry that, at least as far as the world knew, she'd only split with David a week ago.

My fingers threaded through hers as I turned to go back to our perch nearer the stage when I noticed a waitress was looking at us with interest.

Fuck.

"Crap," Brook said in a rush as she noticed her presence too. "We're screwed."

"No. Wait." I pulled her with me toward the girl.

"Hi. Can I talk to you for a minute?"

"Do you need something from the bar?" she asked hesitantly.

"Yes, in a moment. Do you know who we are?"

"Sure. Everyone does," she said nervously.

"Yes, well, you know we're in town shooting our next movie, right?"

"Uh huh."

"Are you a fan of the series?"

"Um, not really. I don't know much about it other than the chatter I hear around town. Everyone is always trying to get a look at you both, but that's all."

I smiled and ran a hand through my hair. I was going to invite her to the set to watch us work in order to get her to keep quiet about the kiss she'd obviously witnessed, but if she wasn't a fan, that wouldn't help. Brook's hand squeezed mine as she shifted back and forth beside me.

"We will need a vodka cranberry and a Heineken when you have a moment, and um, we'd really appreciate it if you could keep quiet about, um..."

"No problem. I didn't take any pictures. Don't worry, it's cool."

"Yeah, thanks," Brook inserted, "See, we were uh... rehearsing this big scene. A very important scene." She chewed her lower lip, knowing full well the waitress knew what was really going on. She started laughing playfully and the waitress nodded knowingly and winked.

"Uh, right. I'll be back with those drinks." She smiled wryly as she walked away.

"We're rehearsing a scene? Is that what we were doing?" I teased.

"What? She knew I was being a smart ass," Brook protested but she was still smiling. "Obviously we wouldn't rehearse here."

When the waitress brought the drinks, I put three one hundred dollar notes on her tray. "Keep it, and thanks," I said, and her eyes got wide.

"You don't need to do that," she objected.

"No, it's my pleasure. We don't get this kind of help often, and I really appreciate it. Privacy is a scarce commodity to us these days." I smiled and the waitress nodded.

"Thank you," she said as she moved off.

"Jesus. Dazzle her much? Poor thing didn't stand a chance."

I leaned into Brook and smirked at her. "If I didn't know better, you sound jealous, love."

"Hmmph! In your dreams, Carlisle," she scoffed as she took a sip from her drink.

"Good. I hate jealous women!" I said playfully and took a drink of my beer.

Her eyes burned me alive as she bit her lower lip and shook her head ever so slightly. As much as I'd wanted to take her out tonight, I found myself longing to be alone with her between the sheets.

"Mmmm." Brook acknowledged. "Well, what kind *do* you like?"

My mouth opened and I smiled as the air rushed out... "Um, the beautiful, strong and sexy type with a sarcastic wit. Blonde with deep blue eyes, perfect little body and, uh, she has to love me unconditionally."

"Oh, is that all? Had any luck with that?" she asked with mock sarcasm.

"Yeah. I think I'm the luckiest wanker on Earth," I said softly as my hand ran up her back under her hair to caress her neck. She shivered and it did strange things to my insides that I could affect her that way with the slightest touch.

"Well, I'm even luckier, because my list is even longer than yours."

Pleasure shot through me at her words. "Do tell," I urged.

This would be good. I licked my lips and leaned down to hear her above the music. She looked up at me through half closed lids and cocked her head to one side.

"Well... very introspective, thoughtful and responsive. He's sensitive, not afraid to show his feelings, he knows me better than anyone in the world. Um, he's *incredibly* good looking with dark blue eyes that can look greenish when he's confused or worried. He has the most beautiful, strong features and amazing sex hair that I love to pull and tug on when he makes love to me. I love the way it gets him all worked up."

I raised my eyebrows at her. *Did she know that?*

She nodded as if she'd heard the question in my mind. "He's tender, very passionate, and talented. He has the most gorgeous mouth and the things he can do with it? Wow. He can bring me to my knees. He makes love to me with his words, his beautiful voice so full of velvet and sex; just the sound of it can make my panties damp."

My heart was thumping in my chest and my dick was completely paining me again. Her eyes and words were serious as she continued.

"And he has a huge di.."

I put my fingers to her mouth. "Okay, I get the picture..." I couldn't stop smiling even if I'd wanted to, the fact that she loved me that much left me breathless and completely aroused. "Let's not give these people the same picture, hmmm?"

A throaty laugh burst from her and I loved it.

"Oh, well...," she said dryly, raising her brows at me as she crossed her arms in front of her, "I'd bet money of them already have that same picture taped up on their bedroom walls, on their computer screens, and in their dreams. In fact, I'm sure of it."

"Irrelevant, anyway. I'm sure he only has eyes for you," I said as I drew little circles on her back with the fingers of one hand. "Doesn't this mystery man need to be in love with you or is that of no consequence?"

She chewed on her lower lip as her face sobered and her eyes met mine, "I know he is. I feel him all around me. He's in my heart, on my skin, in my mind, inside my body. Even when he's not with me, I feel him as if he were standing right next to me."

I curled my arm around her waist and drew her closer to me.

"I feel you too. So much, Brook." My throat thickened as I spoke, "Please remember that when I'm gone."

She swallowed hard and her eyes glassed over momentarily, as she gave me a little nod. "You mean, *don't forget to remember you?*"

My heart dropped. One thought; one split second, and we went from laughing, to sadness.

"Yes. Exactly. Want to get out of here? I'm suddenly feeling the urge to *rehearse* a whole lot more," I said as my hand moved up and down her back.

"Won't Daniel be disappointed if you leave now?"

"I did promise we'd get together for a little while after he's finished, but right now I don't care. I just want to be alone with you, love."

"We can be, but I don't want you to blow off your friends because of me. Let's just hang for a while. I don't have to be onset until late afternoon tomorrow."

I nodded reluctantly. I almost felt guilty on this film. She had a lot more retakes with Noah because they were both new actors. Retakes marked the end of production in Vancouver. One more reminder that this was winding down, and so soon, I'd be leaving my beautiful girl for New York.

My hand lifted to the back of Brook's head and my hand wrapped around her hair. She read my mind once again, and her arm tightened around my waist. She rested her head on my chest for a brief second as she blinked back the tears.

Oh, baby. I'm going to miss you so damn much.

Brooklyn

IT WAS STILL dark and utterly quiet as my hands searched for Cade next to me in the big bed. But only his scent lingered in the empty space. The sheets were cool which meant he'd been gone for a while. I pushed into a sitting position and ran my hands through my hair as my eyes adjusted to the darkness.

I was in Cade's suite, in his bed; but where was he? The bedroom door was closed but there was a small beam of light streaming in beneath it. The light was faint, but I decided to follow it and I searched for something to cover my nakedness. Cade's grey T-shirt lay discarded on the floor and I picked it up, bringing it to my nose to inhale his scent. A mixture of cologne, salt and distinctly Cade flooded around me as I pulled it over my head and shoved my arms in the sleeves. My ears picked up some soft strains of his guitar coming from the other room.

We'd stayed until the end of the concert and invited the band back to Cade's hotel room. Daniel and his girlfriend, Sarah, were the last to leave in the early morning hours, and afterward, Cade picked me up and carried me to the bedroom without a word. His lovemaking was clinging and desperate, and the passionate way his hands held me, and his deep kisses echoed some unspoken pain. Unspoken; but not unknown.

We still had a month together and while I was trying so hard not to think about it, and to concentrate on finishing *Don't Forget to Remember Me* and our upcoming trip to Italy, the two and a half months we'd be apart was already hanging over us like a hurricane threatening to drown us. If we weren't careful, it could ruin what remaining time we had left to be together. I'd become so used to his presence; how would I get through it?

My fingers rolled up the sleeves on Cade's T-shirt as I reminded myself that the month remaining also included a five day separation right before Italy when Pinnacle would send Cade off to Cannes to pimp his upcoming film, *Only Us.*

Joy. I could hardly wait.

I opened the bedroom door and followed the music and soft light into the sitting room of the suite. Cade moved one of the upholstered chairs over to the sliding glass doors off the balcony so he could look out over the city lights as he strummed and plucked his guitar. Only the light over the bar cast him in shadows, his features unreadable as he faced the windows.

He wore flannel pajama bottoms and a white T-shirt; his feet were bare. His hair was a sexy mess and his jaw clenched and worked as a bevy of emotions crossed his features. He didn't hear me approach as I walked up behind him softly and went to my knees. He was slightly startled when my arms slid around his neck and my chin settled on his shoulder. I turned my face into the side of his neck and kissed it softly four or five times.

"I love you," I whispered against his skin. "I love you, Cade."

He'd stopped playing and one hand came up to cover mine on his chest. He lifted it to his mouth and brushed his warm lips across my knuckles. "I know. I love you, too," he said softly, obviously still lost in his thoughts.

"Are you okay? Do you want to talk?" My heart constricted and I closed my eyes.

He shrugged.

"What are you playing?"

His thumb moved back and forth on my hand that he still held to his lips. He spoke and the hot breath rushed over my skin. "You know me. I choose songs that echo my emotions in the moment."

I trembled as the heaviness of his words settled on me. Obviously, he was feeling our impending separation as heavily as I was. "Do you want to share with me? I'd love to hear it."

He sighed, "I'm just feeling…"

I turned my face into his neck again. "I know," I breathed into his ear, "me too."

"I'm sorry."

"Don't be. This is real. Your feelings are why I love you. Don't try to hide them."

Cade sighed deeply and kissed my hand again. "Why are you so amazing? I still don't know where you came from." The sound of his breath rushing out of his lungs accompanied its warmth on my skin. "Humph."

I moved around to the front of his chair and settled down on the floor beside him, leaning up against his leg. My hand slid into the opening at the bottom of one leg in his pajamas as I rubbed his calf. "Play it for me?"

"It might make you cry…"

"So? If that happens it only means I understand what you're trying to say… as always, okay?" I felt my throat tighten even before he started to play. "You know I love listening to you."

"Yes," he said as his fingers began to strum the guitar, "I'm so thankful for you, Brook. You're like a balm to my soul."

I squeezed my eyes shut as I recognized the introduction strains of *I Could Not Ask For More*. It was perfect. His voice was soft and soulful as he began to sing. I could hear my emotions flooding through the notes and his voice.

Tears already stung at the back of my eyes as I moved so I could look up into Cade's face while he sang to me. He was so sad and beautiful. My heart ached, breaking in my chest, at the pain that echoed through his voice. His eyes were liquid and his throat muscles worked as he sang, the song made more beautiful because he was the one singing it. My arms hugged my knees in front of me and I rested my chin on my hands to stop it from trembling. It took all the strength I could muster not to burst into tears as I listened to the lyrics until he finished.

He set down the guitar and I immediately scrambled up onto his lap, curling into him like a little child. My hands slid around his neck at the same time Cade's strong arms closed around me and held me tight. He turned his face into my shoulder as we both held each other tight and tried not to cry.

"That was so beautiful." I could hardly get the words out.

"Brook, leaving you—" He paused and I slammed my eyes shut. "It just hurts so bloody much."

"I know, I feel like I'm dying. But if we didn't love each other so much, it wouldn't hurt like this. So I'll take it, Cade, okay? I'll take all the pain that comes with loving you like this. It means so much."

"You're everything. All I want in the world is to be with you. I don't want to go."

I looked up and brought my hand to his face before placing a soft kiss on his trembling mouth.

"Let's try to be happy these last weeks. I can't bare to waste one second being sad." Even as I said the words, I knew it would be impossible not to think about it, but I would concentrate on making him happy and putting a smile on his face as long as I could. I was filled with love and resolve as my mind and heart mirrored the words of the song he'd just sung.

It's impossible to love me more than I love you, Cade. If you loved me only half as much... I couldn't ask for more.

Please join Cade & Brooklyn
when their story continues in...

Beyond
FAMOUS
Famous Novel – Three

Late Fall 2015

Kahlen Aymes is a USA Today best selling author who writes steamy romance novels that cross genre lines between New Adult, Adult Contemporary and Erotica.

Kahlen has been on several bestseller lists including Barnes & Noble, Amazon, Smashwords, Publisher's Weekly, iBooks and USA Today! She began her writing career writing Twilight Fan Fiction and won multiple awards in the genre, including BEST Author, BEST Robsten, Best All-Human that Knocks You Off Your Feet and several others!

Her interests include reading, as well as writing, theater arts, cooking, roller skating and going for long walks. She is the proud mom to one teenage daughter and two golden retrievers.

She LOVES writing more than most anything else, and you can count on her to deliver strong, relatable characters, deep and detailed plots, and emotion overflow!

Facebook: https://www.facebook.com/kahlen.aymes.author?fref=ts
Goodreads: https://www.goodreads.com/search?utf8=
Twitter: @Kahlen_Aymes
Pinterest: https://www.pinterest.com/kahlenaymes/
Booktropolis Social https://booktropoloussocial.com/index.php?do=/

Visit Kahlen's website for merchandise, signed books, Julia's recipes, missing scenes, events, Kahlen's Blog, and series playlists: KahlenAymes.com

News/Giveaways & Eclusive Ecerpts/ Book Disscussion

Sign Up:Kahlen's Newsletter: http://eepurl.com/RuW4X
Join: Kahlen's Book Babes on
FB: https://www.facebook.com/groups/252301134873105/

Request an eBook autograph at: http://www.authorgraph.com/authors/
Kahlen_Aymes

Literary representation and rights information: McIntosh & Otis Literary, Inc.
353 Lexington Avenue • New York, NY 10016
Tel: 1-212-687-7400 • Fax: 1-212-687-6894 • Email: info@mcintoshandotis.com